The DIVIDED STATES of

HYSTERIA

BY HOWARD CHAYKIN

WRITER & ARTIST
HOWARD CHAYKIN

COLORISTS
JESUS ABURTOV
& WIL QUINTANA

LETTERER
KEN BRUZENAK

EDITOR
THOMAS K.

PRODUCTION
KEN BRUZENAK

WITH THANKS TO RAMON TORRES,
CALVIN NYE & DON CAMERON

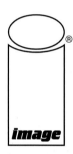

IMAGE COMICS, INC.

Robert Kirkman — Chief Operating Officer
Erik Larsen — Chief Financial Officer
Todd McFarlane — President
Marc Silvestri — Chief Executive Officer
Jim Valentino — Vice President
Eric Stephenson — Publisher
Corey Hart — Director of Sales
Jeff Boison — Director of Publishing Planning
& Book Trade Sales
Chris Ross — Director of Digital Sales
Jeff Stang — Director of Specialty Sales
Kat Salazar — Director of PR & Marketing
Drew Gill — Art Director
Heather Doornink — Production Director
Branwyn Bigglestone — Controller

IMAGE COMICS.COM

THE DIVIDED STATES OF HYSTERIA TP.
First printing. January 2018.
Published by Image Comics, Inc. Office of publication:
2701 NW Vaughn St., Suite 780, Portland, OR 97210.
Copyright © 2018 Howard Chaykin, Inc. All rights reserved.
Contains material originally published in single magazine form as
THE DIVIDED STATES OF HYSTERIA #1-6.
"The Divided States of Hysteria," its logos, and the likenesses
of all characters herein are trademarks of Howard Chaykin, Inc.,
unless otherwise noted. "Image" and the Image Comics logos are
registered trademarks of Image Comics, Inc. No part of this
publication may be reproduced or transmitted,
in any form or by any means (except for short excerpts
for journalistic or review purposes), without the express
written permission of Howard Chaykin, Inc., or Image Comics, Inc.
All names, characters, events, and locales in this publication are
entirely fictional. Any resemblance to actual persons (living or dead),
events, or places, without satiric intent, is coincidental.
Printed in the USA.
For information regarding the CPSIA on this printed material
call: 203-595-3636 and provide reference #RICH–772934.
Representation: Law Offices of Harris M. Miller II, P.C.
(rightsinquiries@gmail.com). ISBN: 978-1-5343-0383-6.

Part One

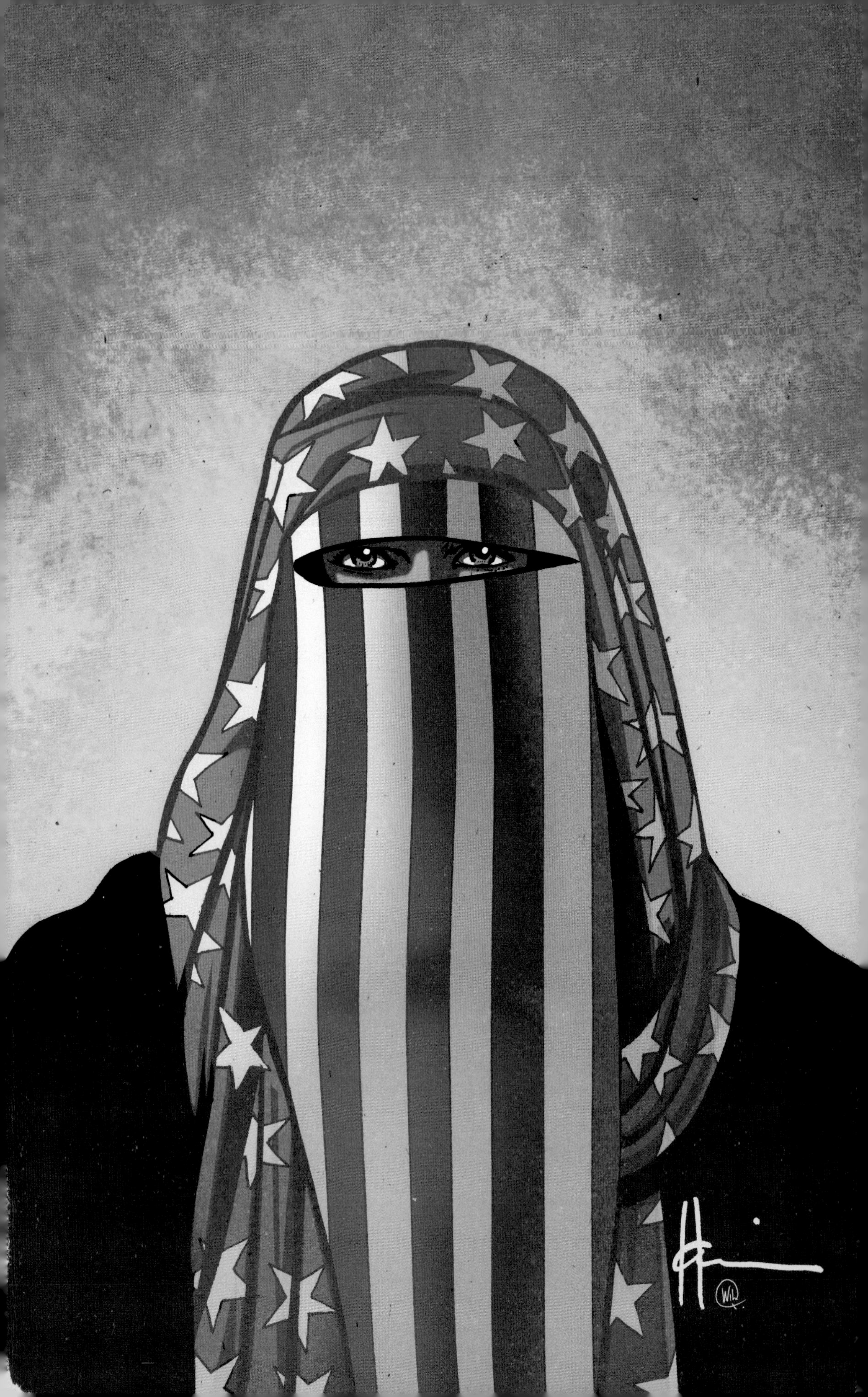

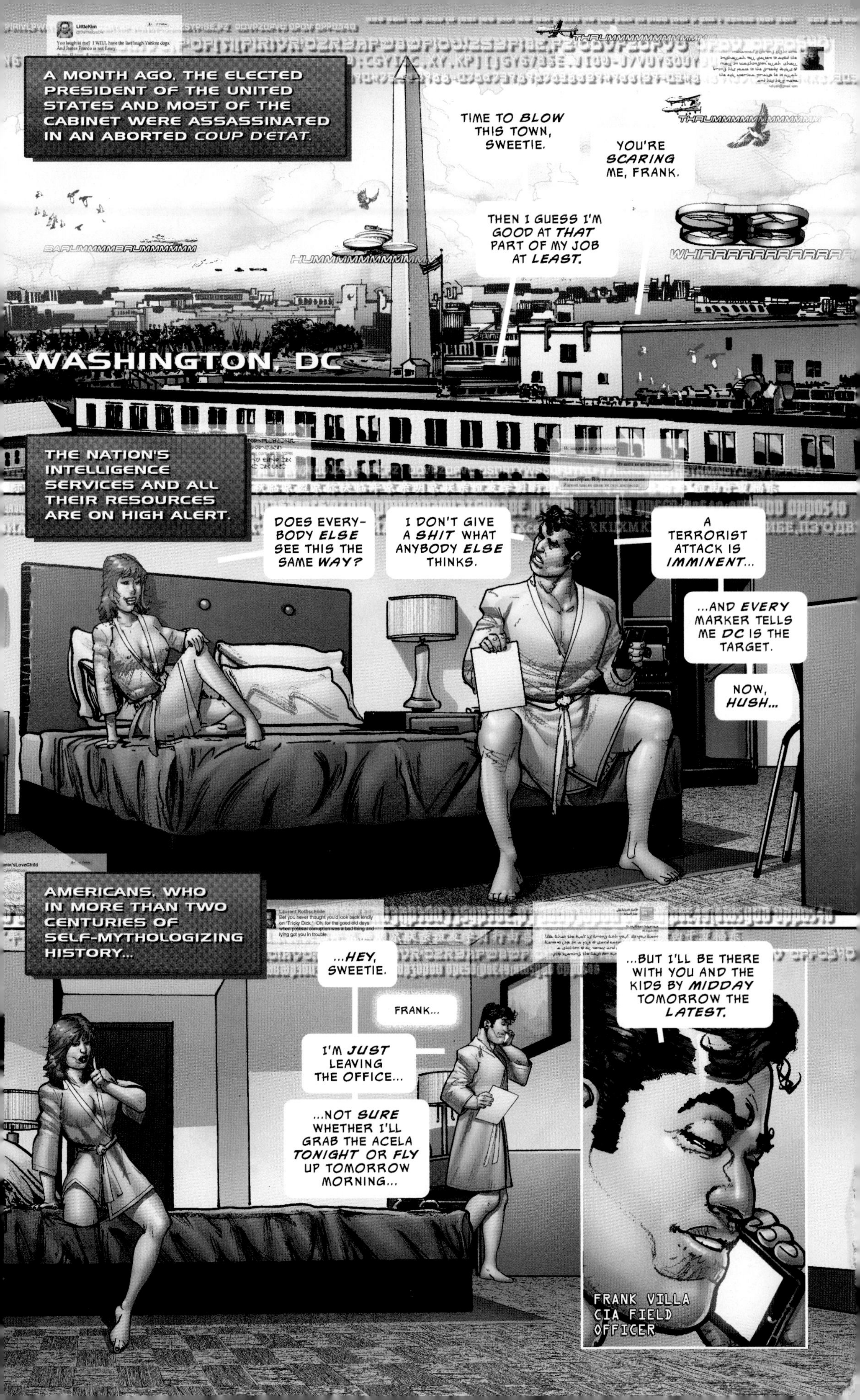
A MONTH AGO, THE ELECTED PRESIDENT OF THE UNITED STATES AND MOST OF THE CABINET WERE ASSASSINATED IN AN ABORTED COUP D'ETAT.
TIME TO BLOW THIS TOWN, SWEETIE.
YOU'RE SCARING ME, FRANK.
THEN I GUESS I'M GOOD AT THAT PART OF MY JOB AT LEAST.
WASHINGTON, DC
THE NATION'S INTELLIGENCE SERVICES AND ALL THEIR RESOURCES ARE ON HIGH ALERT.
DOES EVERYBODY ELSE SEE THIS THE SAME WAY?
I DON'T GIVE A SHIT WHAT ANYBODY ELSE THINKS.
A TERRORIST ATTACK IS IMMINENT...
...AND EVERY MARKER TELLS ME DC IS THE TARGET.
NOW, HUSH...
AMERICANS, WHO IN MORE THAN TWO CENTURIES OF SELF-MYTHOLOGIZING HISTORY...
...HEY, SWEETIE.
FRANK...
I'M JUST LEAVING THE OFFICE...
...NOT SURE WHETHER I'LL GRAB THE ACELA TONIGHT OR FLY UP TOMORROW MORNING...
...BUT I'LL BE THERE WITH YOU AND THE KIDS BY MIDDAY TOMORROW THE LATEST.
FRANK VILLA
CIA FIELD OFFICER

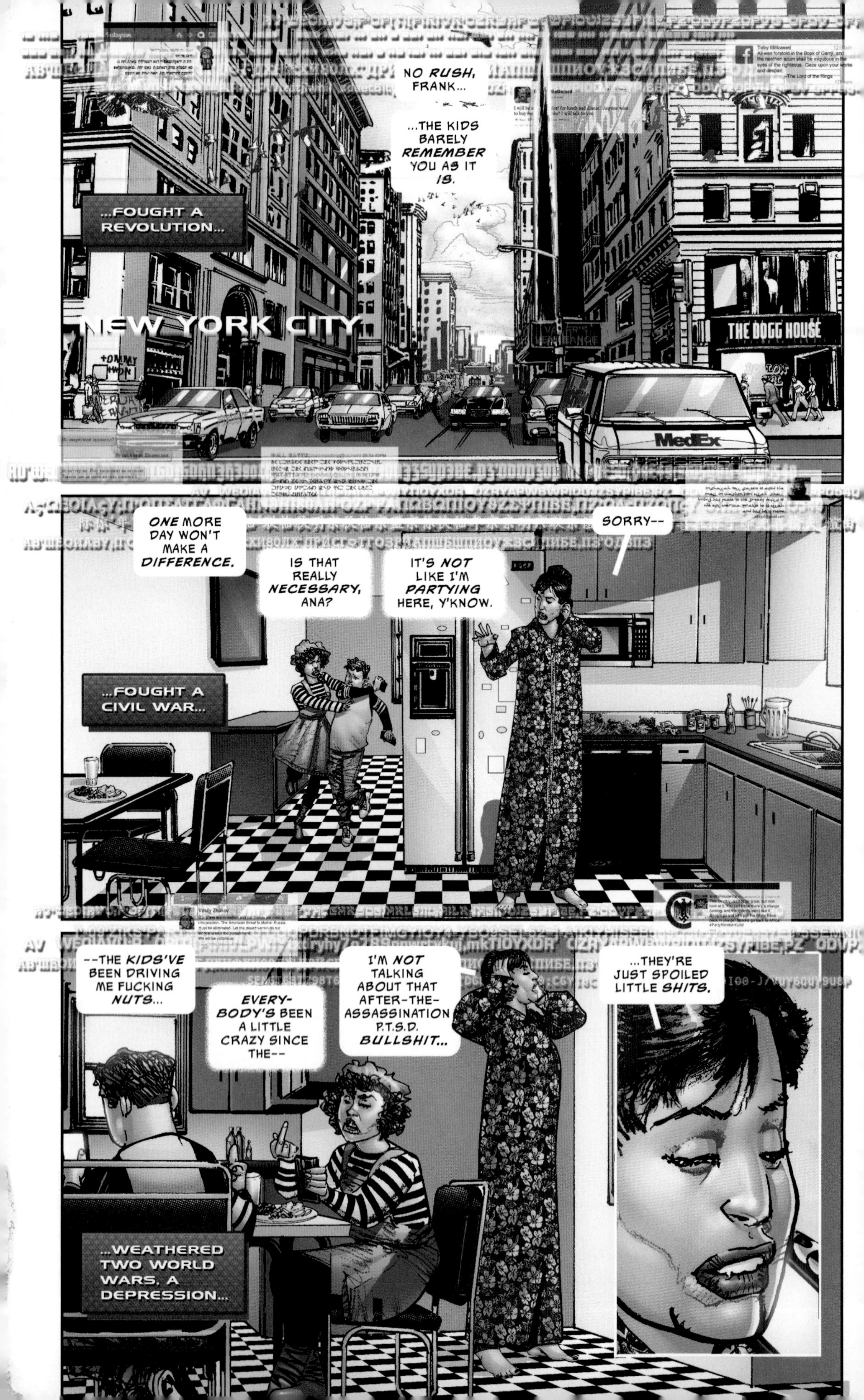

...FOUGHT A REVOLUTION...
NEW YORK CITY
NO *RUSH,* FRANK...
...THE KIDS BARELY *REMEMBER* YOU AS IT *IS.*
THE DOGG HOUSE
MedEx
...FOUGHT A CIVIL WAR...
ONE MORE DAY WON'T MAKE A *DIFFERENCE.*
IS THAT REALLY *NECESSARY,* ANA?
IT'S *NOT* LIKE I'M *PARTYING* HERE, Y'KNOW.
SORRY--
...WEATHERED TWO WORLD WARS, A DEPRESSION...
--THE *KIDS'VE* BEEN DRIVING ME FUCKING *NUTS...*
EVERY-BODY'S BEEN A LITTLE CRAZY SINCE THE--
I'M *NOT* TALKING ABOUT THAT AFTER-THE-ASSASSINATION P.T.S.D. *BULLSHIT...*
...THEY'RE JUST SPOILED LITTLE *SHITS.*

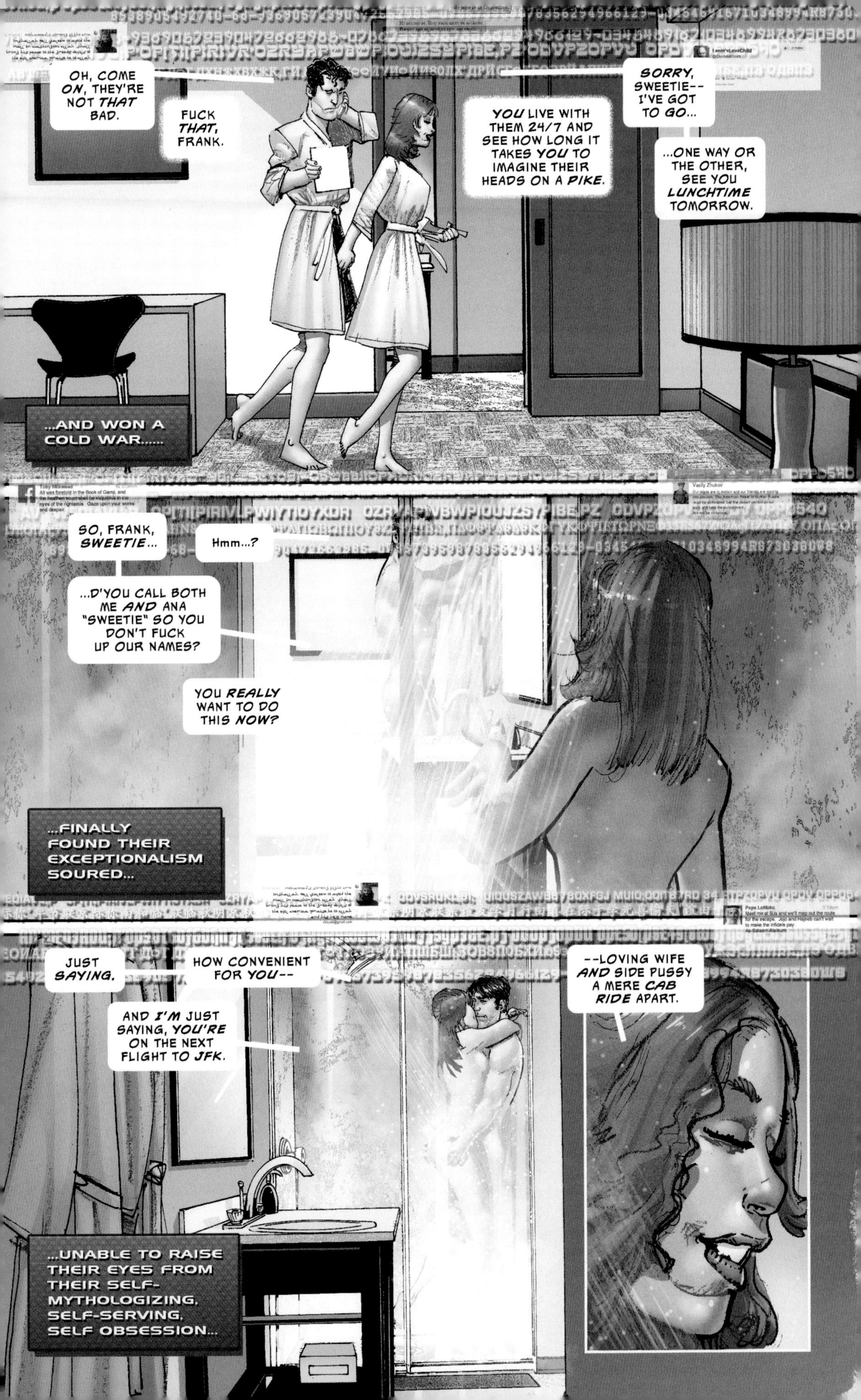
OH, COME ON, THEY'RE NOT THAT BAD.
FUCK THAT, FRANK.
YOU LIVE WITH THEM 24/7 AND SEE HOW LONG IT TAKES YOU TO IMAGINE THEIR HEADS ON A PIKE.
SORRY, SWEETIE-- I'VE GOT TO GO...
...ONE WAY OR THE OTHER, SEE YOU LUNCHTIME TOMORROW.
...AND WON A COLD WAR......
SO, FRANK, SWEETIE...
Hmm...?
...D'YOU CALL BOTH ME AND ANA "SWEETIE" SO YOU DON'T FUCK UP OUR NAMES?
YOU REALLY WANT TO DO THIS NOW?
...FINALLY FOUND THEIR EXCEPTIONALISM SOURED...
JUST SAYING.
HOW CONVENIENT FOR YOU--
AND I'M JUST SAYING, YOU'RE ON THE NEXT FLIGHT TO JFK.
--LOVING WIFE AND SIDE PUSSY A MERE CAB RIDE APART.
...UNABLE TO RAISE THEIR EYES FROM THEIR SELF-MYTHOLOGIZING, SELF-SERVING, SELF OBSESSION...

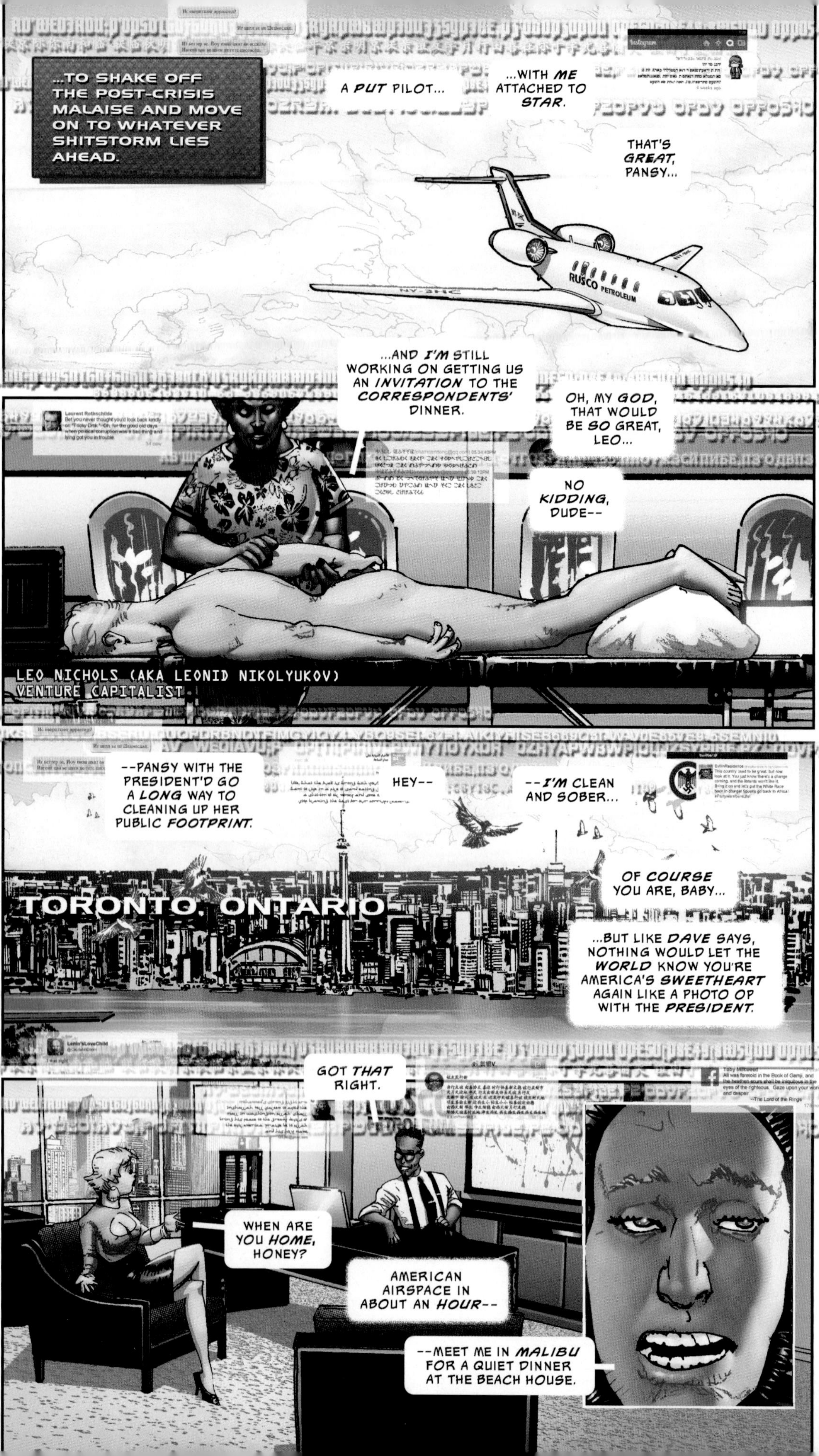
...TO SHAKE OFF THE POST-CRISIS MALAISE AND MOVE ON TO WHATEVER SHITSTORM LIES AHEAD.
A PUT PILOT...
...WITH ME ATTACHED TO STAR.
THAT'S GREAT, PANSY...
RUSCO PETROLEUM
...AND I'M STILL WORKING ON GETTING US AN INVITATION TO THE CORRESPONDENTS' DINNER.
OH, MY GOD, THAT WOULD BE SO GREAT, LEO...
NO KIDDING, DUDE--
LEO NICHOLS (AKA LEONID NIKOLYUKOV)
VENTURE CAPITALIST
--PANSY WITH THE PRESIDENT'D GO A LONG WAY TO CLEANING UP HER PUBLIC FOOTPRINT.
HEY--
--I'M CLEAN AND SOBER...
TORONTO, ONTARIO
OF COURSE YOU ARE, BABY...
...BUT LIKE DAVE SAYS, NOTHING WOULD LET THE WORLD KNOW YOU'RE AMERICA'S SWEETHEART AGAIN LIKE A PHOTO OP WITH THE PRESIDENT.
GOT THAT RIGHT.
WHEN ARE YOU HOME, HONEY?
AMERICAN AIRSPACE IN ABOUT AN HOUR--
--MEET ME IN MALIBU FOR A QUIET DINNER AT THE BEACH HOUSE.

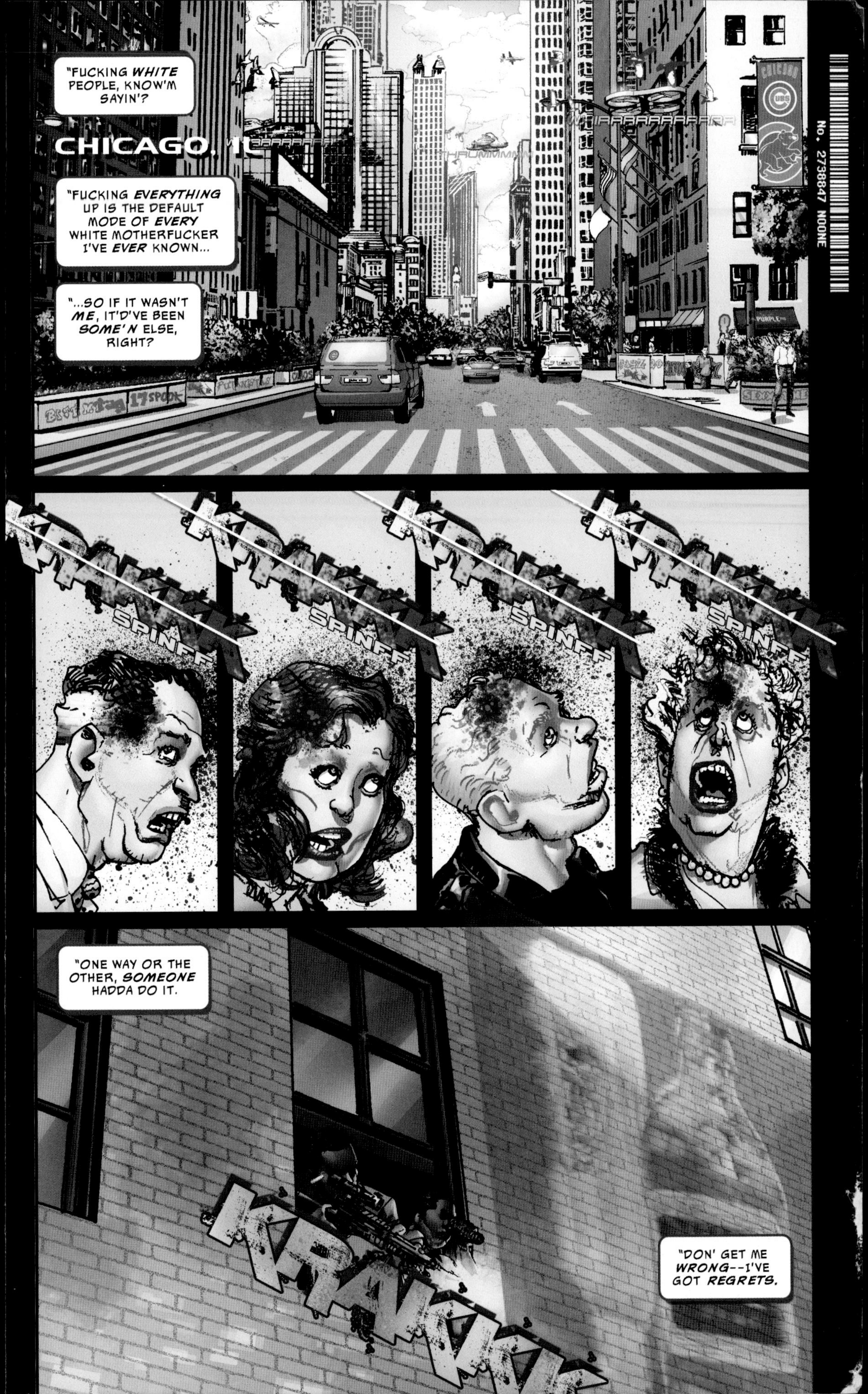
"FUCKING WHITE PEOPLE, KNOW'M SAYIN'?
CHICAGO, IL
"FUCKING EVERYTHING UP IS THE DEFAULT MODE OF EVERY WHITE MOTHERFUCKER I'VE EVER KNOWN...
"...SO IF IT WASN'T ME, IT'D'VE BEEN SOME'N ELSE, RIGHT?
No. 2738847 NOONE
SPINFF
SPINFF
SPINFF
SPINFF
"ONE WAY OR THE OTHER, SOMEONE HADDA DO IT.
"DON' GET ME WRONG--I'VE GOT REGRETS.

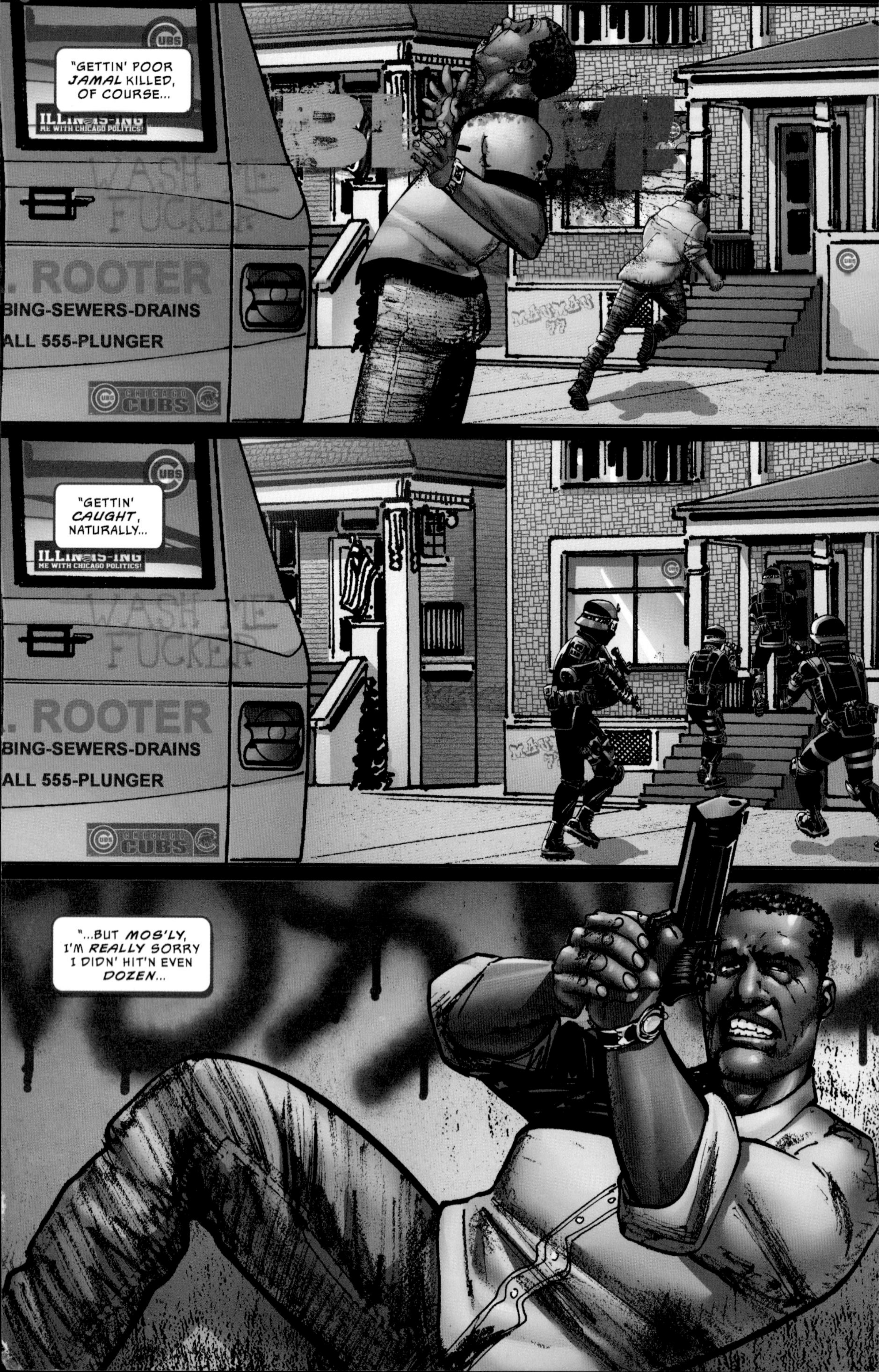
"GETTIN' POOR JAMAL KILLED, OF COURSE...
ME WITH CHICAGO POLITICS!
. ROOTER
BING-SEWERS-DRAINS
ALL 555-PLUNGER
CHICAGO CUBS
"GETTIN' CAUGHT, NATURALLY...
ME WITH CHICAGO POLITICS!
. ROOTER
BING-SEWERS-DRAINS
ALL 555-PLUNGER
CHICAGO CUBS
"...BUT MOS'LY, I'M REALLY SORRY I DIDN' HIT'N EVEN DOZEN...

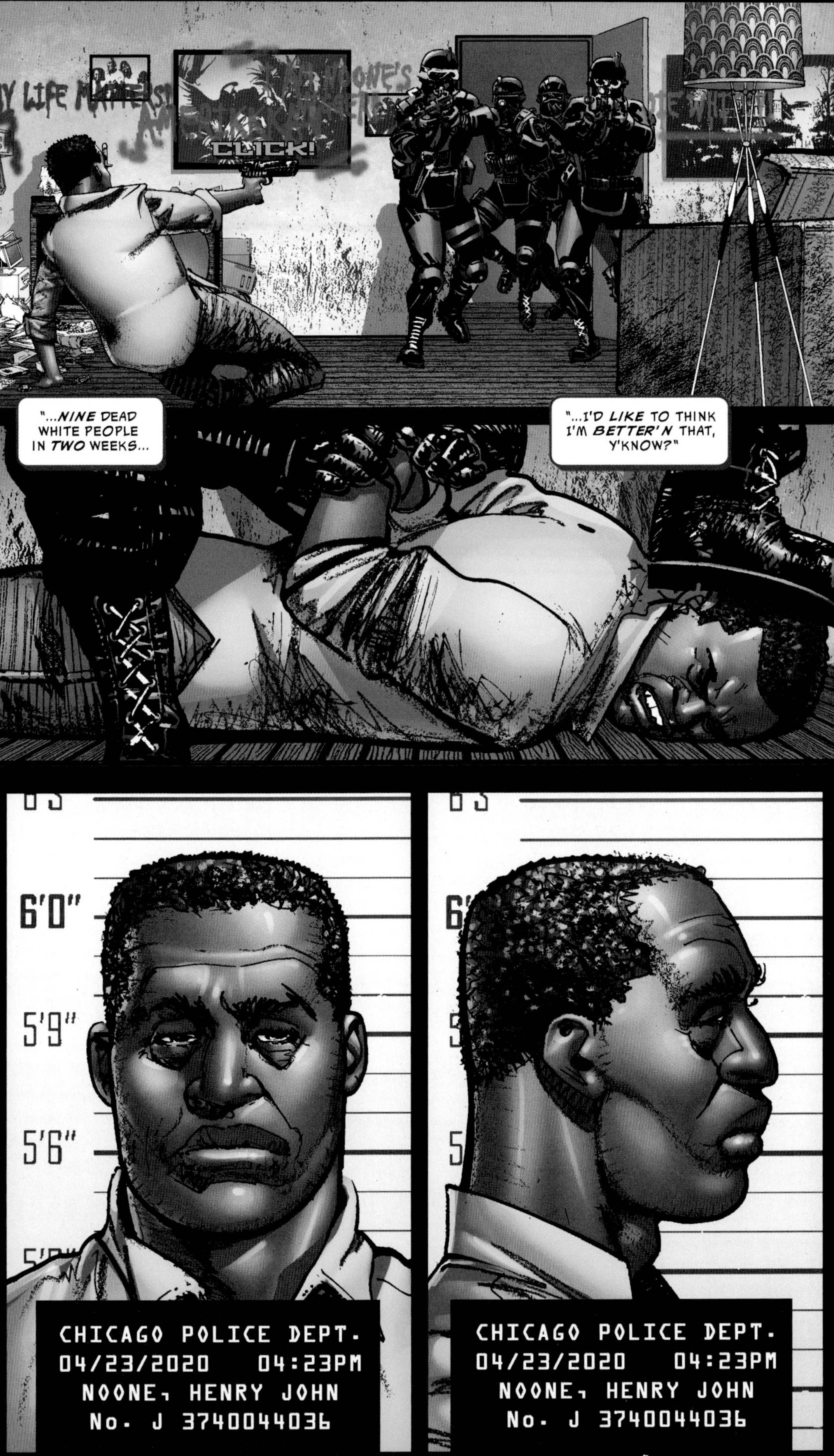
CLICK!
"...NINE DEAD WHITE PEOPLE IN TWO WEEKS...
"...I'D LIKE TO THINK I'M BETTER'N THAT, Y'KNOW?"
6'0"
5'9"
5'6"
CHICAGO POLICE DEPT.
04/23/2020 04:23PM
NOONE, HENRY JOHN
No. J 3740044036
CHICAGO POLICE DEPT.
04/23/2020 04:23PM
NOONE, HENRY JOHN
No. J 3740044036

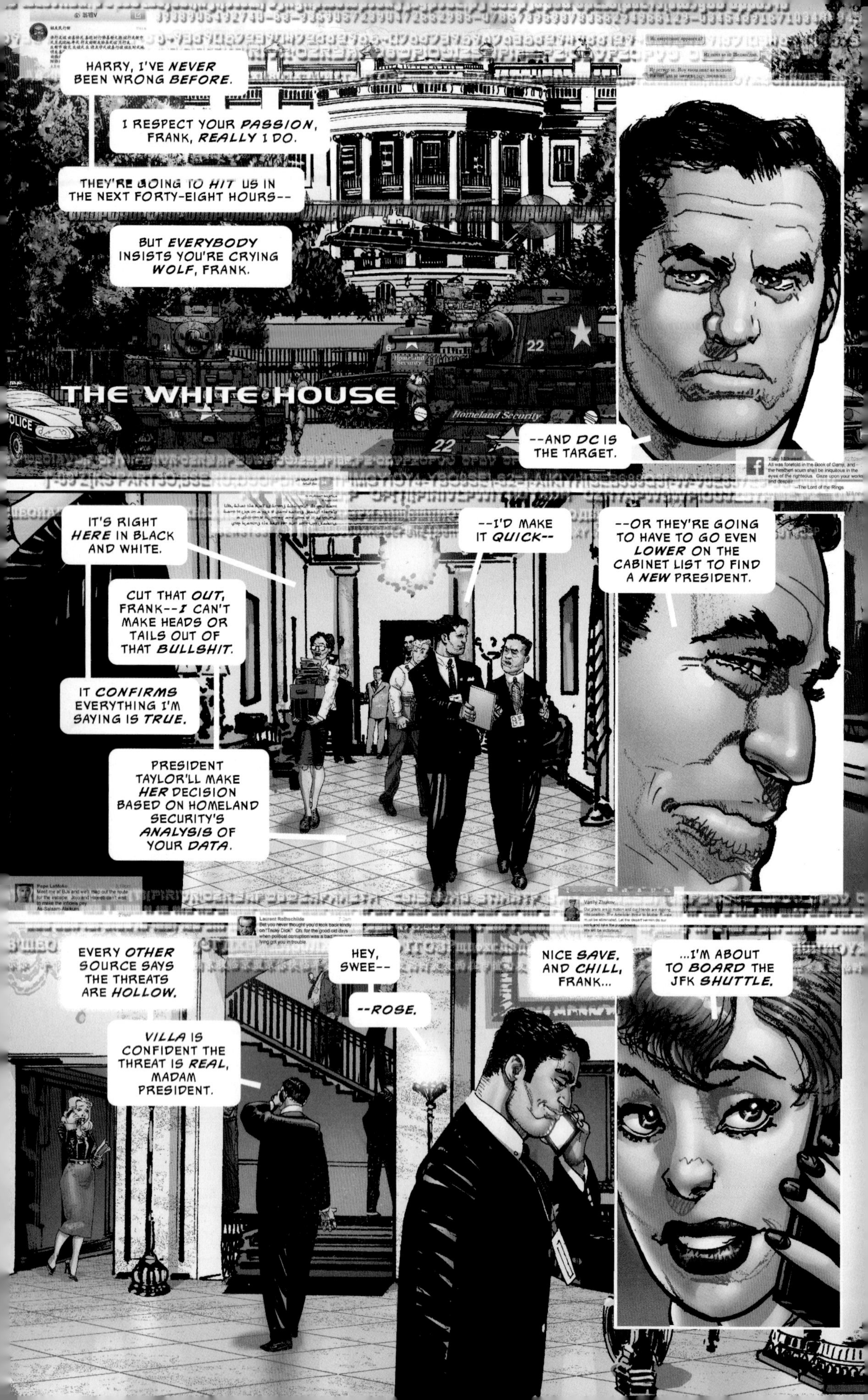
HARRY, I'VE NEVER BEEN WRONG BEFORE.
I RESPECT YOUR PASSION, FRANK, REALLY I DO.
THEY'RE GOING TO HIT US IN THE NEXT FORTY-EIGHT HOURS--
BUT EVERYBODY INSISTS YOU'RE CRYING WOLF, FRANK.
THE WHITE HOUSE
POLICE
Homeland Security
--AND DC IS THE TARGET.
IT'S RIGHT HERE IN BLACK AND WHITE.
CUT THAT OUT, FRANK--I CAN'T MAKE HEADS OR TAILS OUT OF THAT BULLSHIT.
IT CONFIRMS EVERYTHING I'M SAYING IS TRUE.
PRESIDENT TAYLOR'LL MAKE HER DECISION BASED ON HOMELAND SECURITY'S ANALYSIS OF YOUR DATA.
--I'D MAKE IT QUICK--
--OR THEY'RE GOING TO HAVE TO GO EVEN LOWER ON THE CABINET LIST TO FIND A NEW PRESIDENT.
EVERY OTHER SOURCE SAYS THE THREATS ARE HOLLOW.
VILLA IS CONFIDENT THE THREAT IS REAL, MADAM PRESIDENT.
HEY, SWEE--
--ROSE.
NICE SAVE. AND CHILL, FRANK...
...I'M ABOUT TO BOARD THE JFK SHUTTLE.

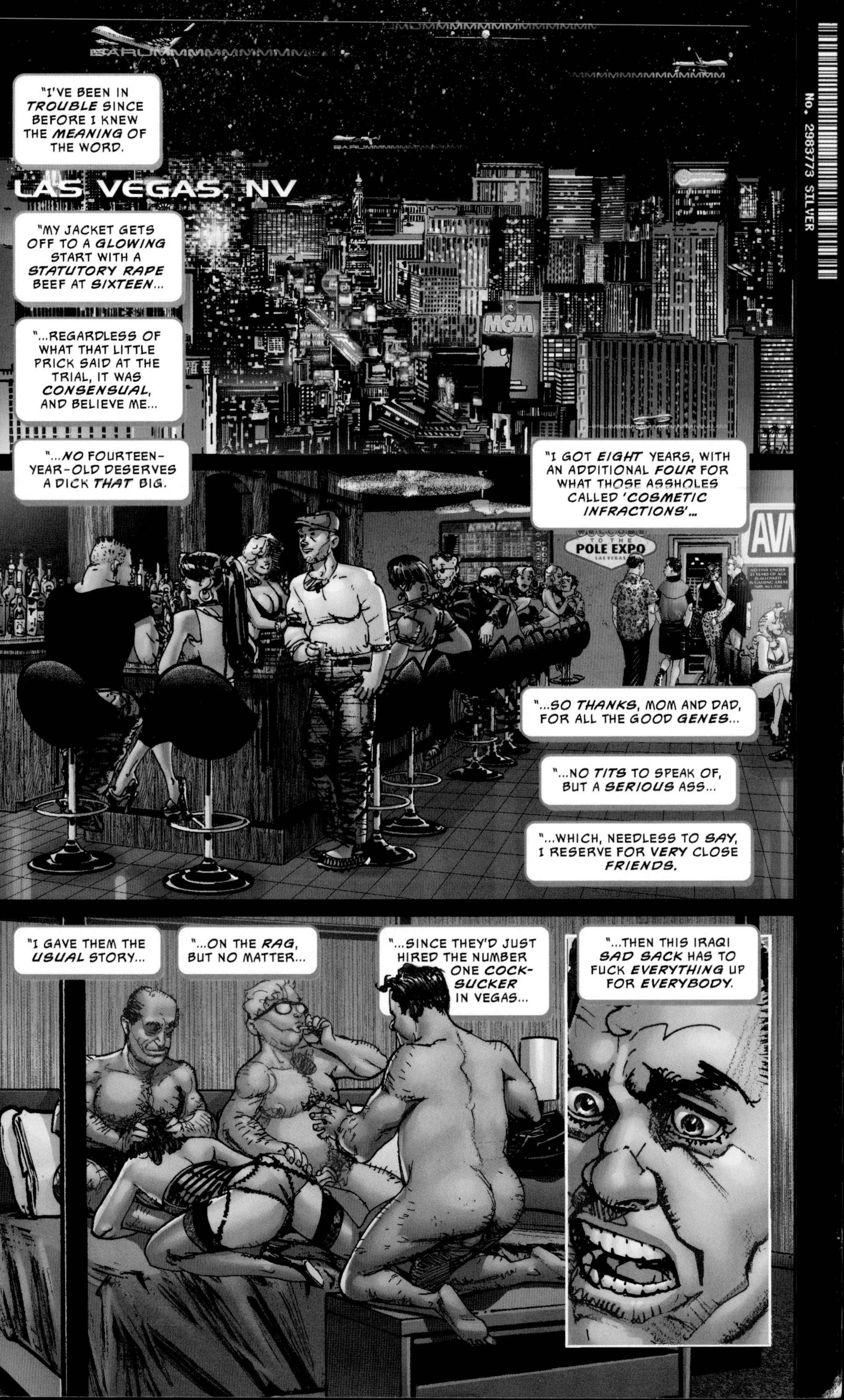
"I'VE BEEN IN TROUBLE SINCE BEFORE I KNEW THE MEANING OF THE WORD.
LAS VEGAS, NV
"MY JACKET GETS OFF TO A GLOWING START WITH A STATUTORY RAPE BEEF AT SIXTEEN...
"...REGARDLESS OF WHAT THAT LITTLE PRICK SAID AT THE TRIAL, IT WAS CONSENSUAL, AND BELIEVE ME...
"...NO FOURTEEN-YEAR-OLD DESERVES A DICK THAT BIG.
MGM
"I GOT EIGHT YEARS, WITH AN ADDITIONAL FOUR FOR WHAT THOSE ASSHOLES CALLED 'COSMETIC INFRACTIONS'...
POLE EXPO
"...SO THANKS, MOM AND DAD, FOR ALL THE GOOD GENES...
"...NO TITS TO SPEAK OF, BUT A SERIOUS ASS...
"...WHICH, NEEDLESS TO SAY, I RESERVE FOR VERY CLOSE FRIENDS.
"I GAVE THEM THE USUAL STORY...
"...ON THE RAG, BUT NO MATTER...
"...SINCE THEY'D JUST HIRED THE NUMBER ONE COCK-SUCKER IN VEGAS...
"...THEN THIS IRAQI SAD SACK HAS TO FUCK EVERYTHING UP FOR EVERYBODY.
No. 2983773 SILVER

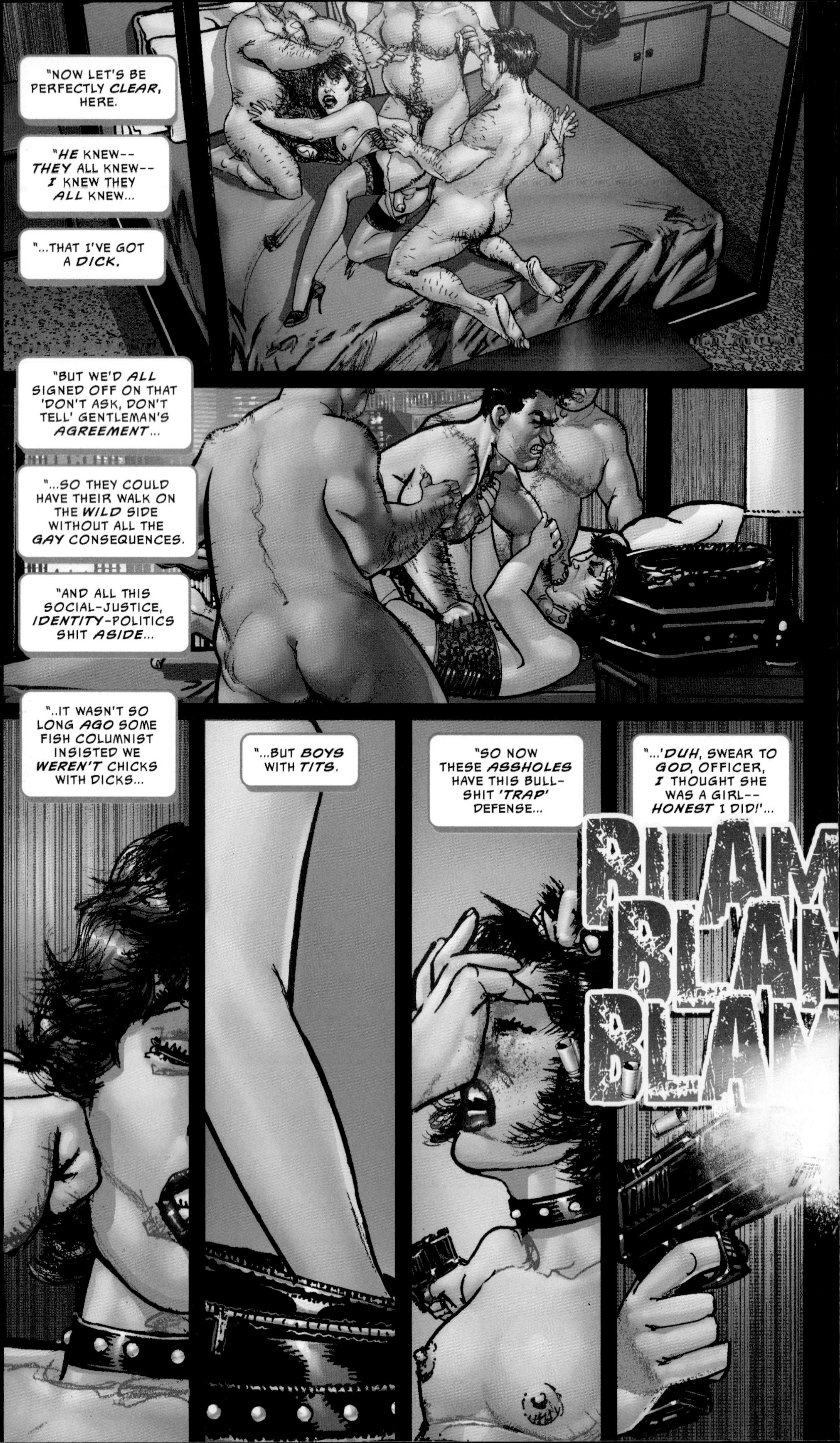
"NOW LET'S BE PERFECTLY CLEAR, HERE.
"HE KNEW-- THEY ALL KNEW-- I KNEW THEY ALL KNEW...
"...THAT I'VE GOT A DICK.
"BUT WE'D ALL SIGNED OFF ON THAT 'DON'T ASK, DON'T TELL' GENTLEMAN'S AGREEMENT...
"...SO THEY COULD HAVE THEIR WALK ON THE WILD SIDE WITHOUT ALL THE GAY CONSEQUENCES.
"AND ALL THIS SOCIAL-JUSTICE, IDENTITY-POLITICS SHIT ASIDE...
"..IT WASN'T SO LONG AGO SOME FISH COLUMNIST INSISTED WE WEREN'T CHICKS WITH DICKS...
"...BUT BOYS WITH TITS.
"SO NOW THESE ASSHOLES HAVE THIS BULL-SHIT 'TRAP' DEFENSE...
"...'DUH, SWEAR TO GOD, OFFICER, I THOUGHT SHE WAS A GIRL--HONEST I DID!'...
BLAM

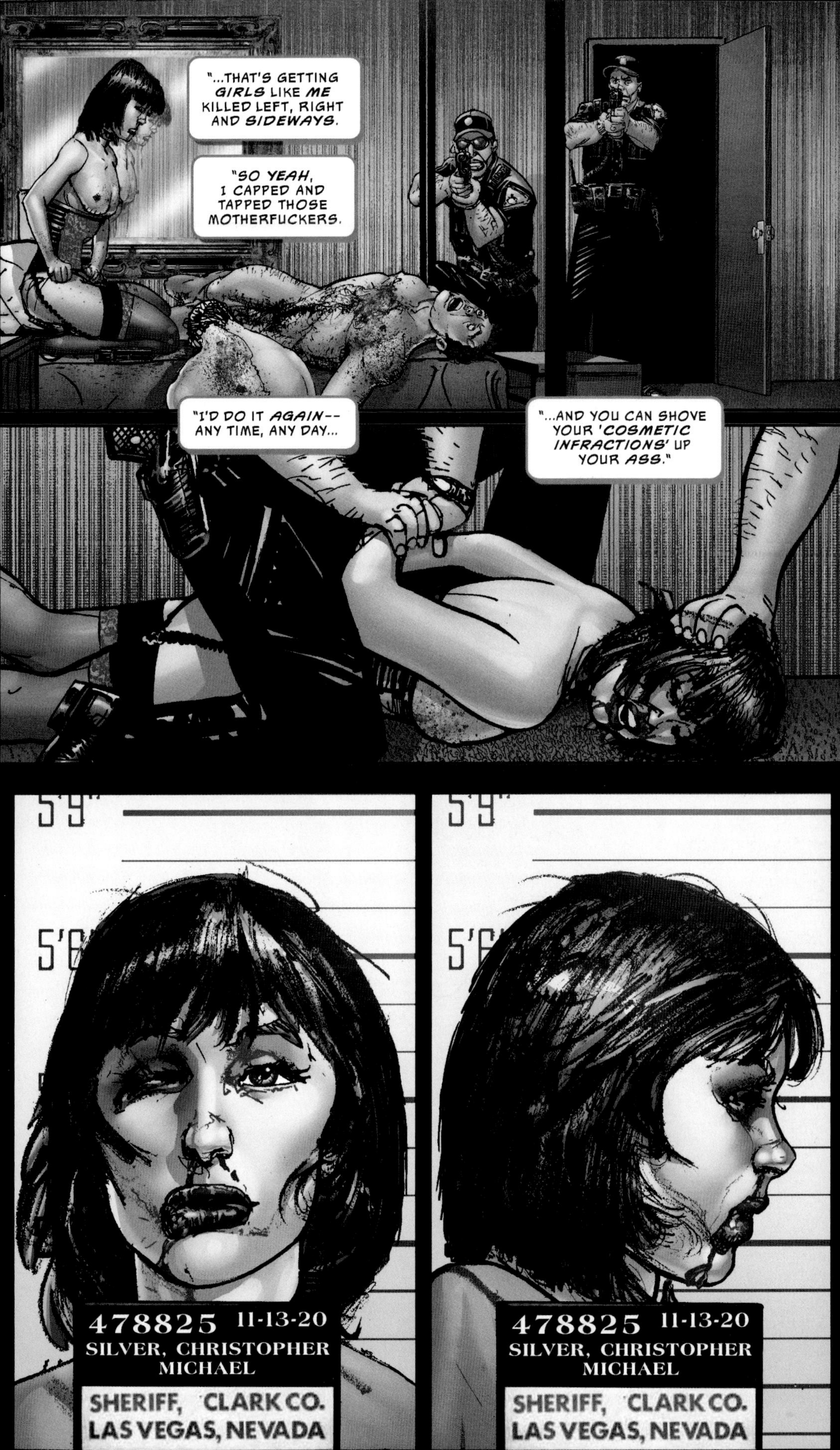
"...THAT'S GETTING GIRLS LIKE ME KILLED LEFT, RIGHT AND SIDEWAYS.
"SO YEAH, I CAPPED AND TAPPED THOSE MOTHERFUCKERS.
"I'D DO IT AGAIN-- ANY TIME, ANY DAY...
"...AND YOU CAN SHOVE YOUR 'COSMETIC INFRACTIONS' UP YOUR ASS."
5'9"
5'6"
478825 11-13-20
SILVER, CHRISTOPHER MICHAEL
SHERIFF, CLARK CO.
LAS VEGAS, NEVADA
5'9"
5'6"
478825 11-13-20
SILVER, CHRISTOPHER MICHAEL
SHERIFF, CLARK CO.
LAS VEGAS, NEVADA

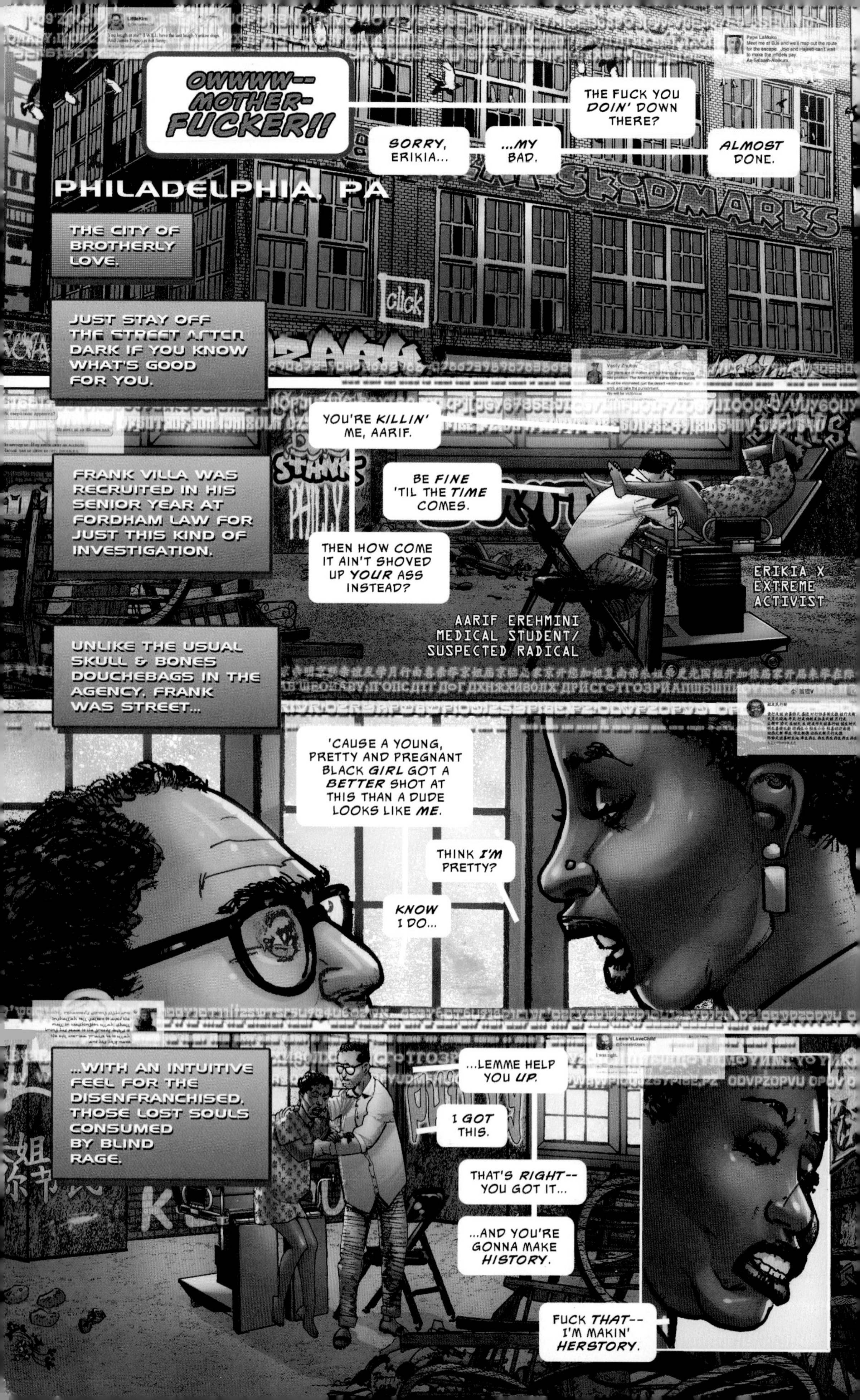

OWWWW-- MOTHER-FUCKER!!
THE FUCK YOU DOIN' DOWN THERE?
SORRY, ERIKIA...
...MY BAD.
ALMOST DONE.
PHILADELPHIA, PA
THE CITY OF BROTHERLY LOVE.
click
JUST STAY OFF THE STREET AFTER DARK IF YOU KNOW WHAT'S GOOD FOR YOU.
YOU'RE KILLIN' ME, AARIF.
BE FINE 'TIL THE TIME COMES.
FRANK VILLA WAS RECRUITED IN HIS SENIOR YEAR AT FORDHAM LAW FOR JUST THIS KIND OF INVESTIGATION.
THEN HOW COME IT AIN'T SHOVED UP YOUR ASS INSTEAD?
ERIKIA X
EXTREME ACTIVIST
AARIF EREHMINI
MEDICAL STUDENT/ SUSPECTED RADICAL
UNLIKE THE USUAL SKULL & BONES DOUCHEBAGS IN THE AGENCY, FRANK WAS STREET...
'CAUSE A YOUNG, PRETTY AND PREGNANT BLACK GIRL GOT A BETTER SHOT AT THIS THAN A DUDE LOOKS LIKE ME.
THINK I'M PRETTY?
KNOW I DO...
...WITH AN INTUITIVE FEEL FOR THE DISENFRANCHISED, THOSE LOST SOULS CONSUMED BY BLIND RAGE.
...LEMME HELP YOU UP.
I GOT THIS.
THAT'S RIGHT-- YOU GOT IT...
...AND YOU'RE GONNA MAKE HISTORY.
FUCK THAT-- I'M MAKIN' HERSTORY.

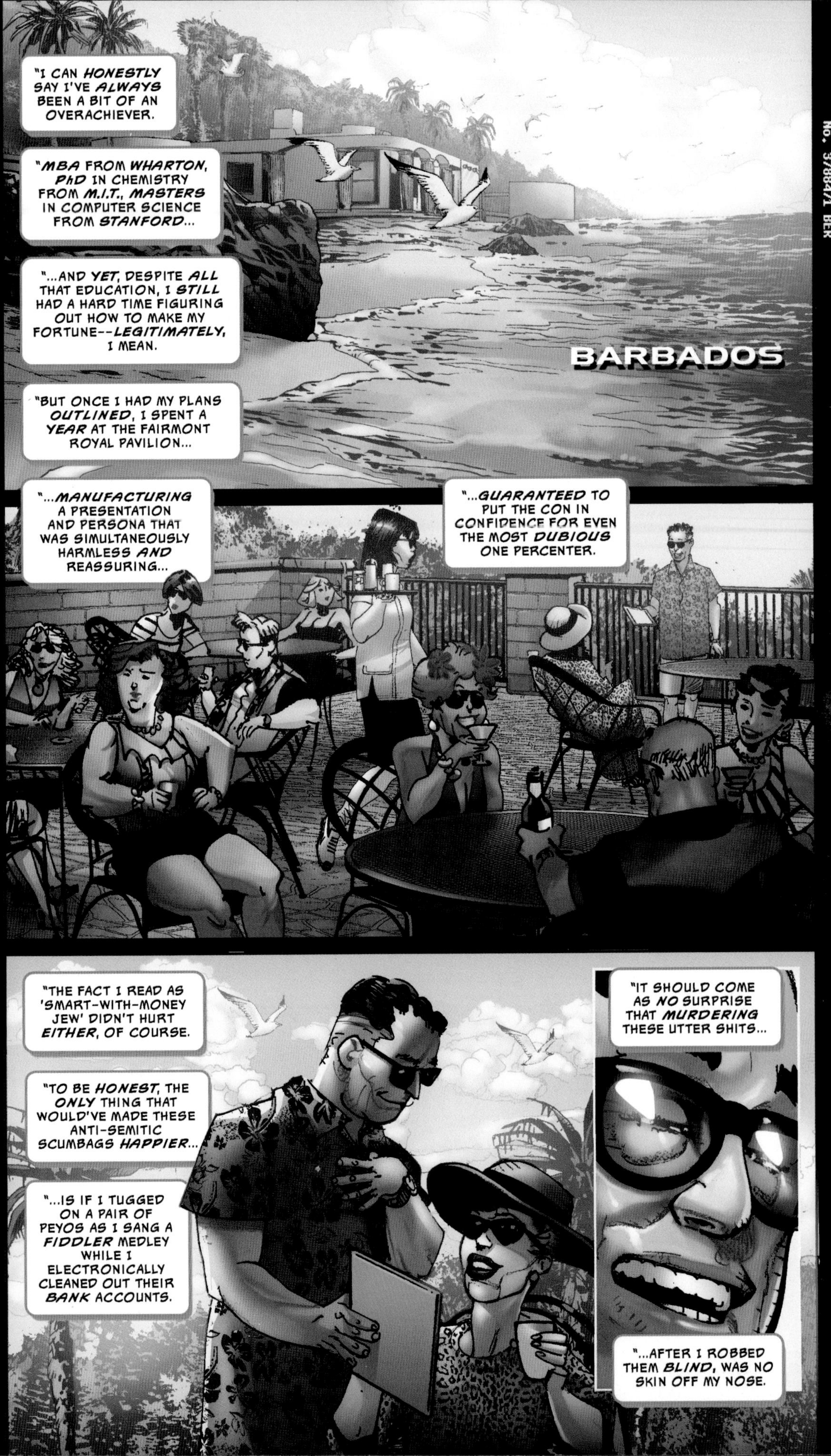
"I CAN HONESTLY SAY I'VE ALWAYS BEEN A BIT OF AN OVERACHIEVER.
"MBA FROM WHARTON, PhD IN CHEMISTRY FROM M.I.T., MASTERS IN COMPUTER SCIENCE FROM STANFORD...
"...AND YET, DESPITE ALL THAT EDUCATION, I STILL HAD A HARD TIME FIGURING OUT HOW TO MAKE MY FORTUNE--LEGITIMATELY, I MEAN.
BARBADOS
"BUT ONCE I HAD MY PLANS OUTLINED, I SPENT A YEAR AT THE FAIRMONT ROYAL PAVILION...
"...MANUFACTURING A PRESENTATION AND PERSONA THAT WAS SIMULTANEOUSLY HARMLESS AND REASSURING...
"...GUARANTEED TO PUT THE CON IN CONFIDENCE FOR EVEN THE MOST DUBIOUS ONE PERCENTER.
"THE FACT I READ AS 'SMART-WITH-MONEY JEW' DIDN'T HURT EITHER, OF COURSE.
"TO BE HONEST, THE ONLY THING THAT WOULD'VE MADE THESE ANTI-SEMITIC SCUMBAGS HAPPIER...
"...IS IF I TUGGED ON A PAIR OF PEYOS AS I SANG A FIDDLER MEDLEY WHILE I ELECTRONICALLY CLEANED OUT THEIR BANK ACCOUNTS.
"IT SHOULD COME AS NO SURPRISE THAT MURDERING THESE UTTER SHITS...
"...AFTER I ROBBED THEM BLIND, WAS NO SKIN OFF MY NOSE.

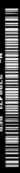

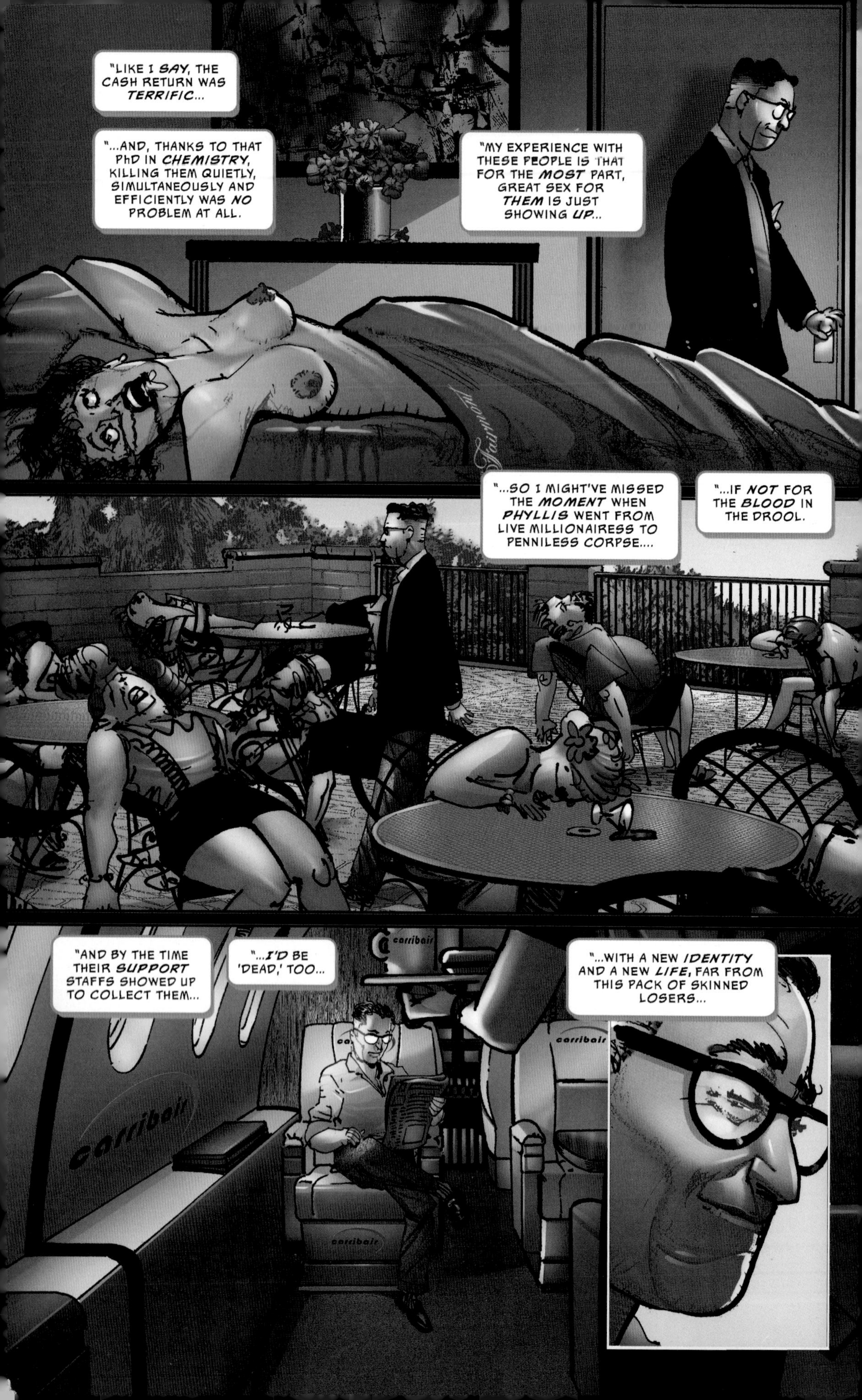
"LIKE I SAY, THE CASH RETURN WAS TERRIFIC...
"...AND, THANKS TO THAT PhD IN CHEMISTRY, KILLING THEM QUIETLY, SIMULTANEOUSLY AND EFFICIENTLY WAS NO PROBLEM AT ALL.
"MY EXPERIENCE WITH THESE PEOPLE IS THAT FOR THE MOST PART, GREAT SEX FOR THEM IS JUST SHOWING UP...
"...SO I MIGHT'VE MISSED THE MOMENT WHEN PHYLLIS WENT FROM LIVE MILLIONAIRESS TO PENNILESS CORPSE....
"...IF NOT FOR THE BLOOD IN THE DROOL.
"AND BY THE TIME THEIR SUPPORT STAFFS SHOWED UP TO COLLECT THEM...
"...I'D BE 'DEAD,' TOO...
"...WITH A NEW IDENTITY AND A NEW LIFE, FAR FROM THIS PACK OF SKINNED LOSERS...
carribair

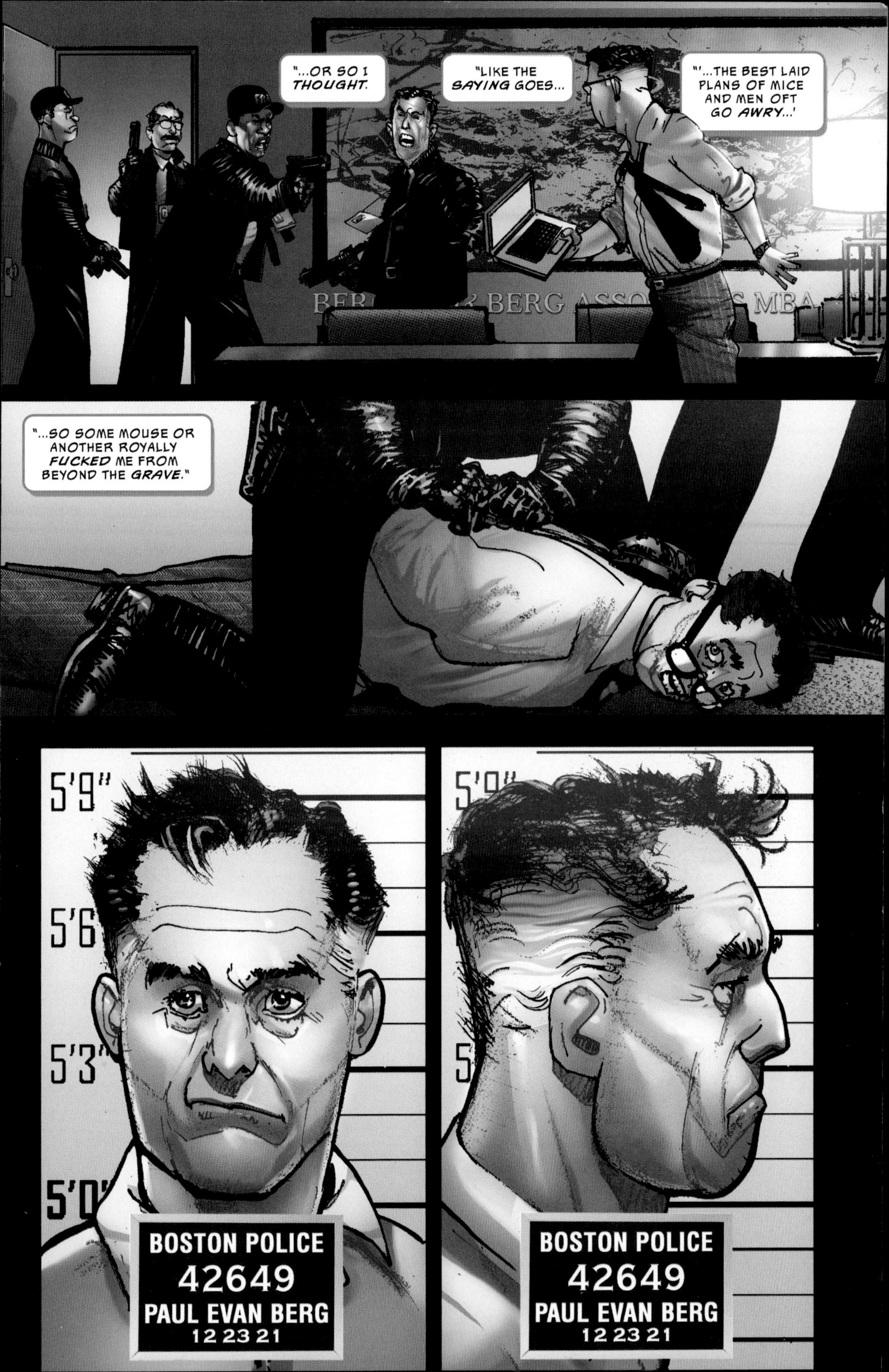
"...OR SO I THOUGHT.
"LIKE THE SAYING GOES...
"'...THE BEST LAID PLANS OF MICE AND MEN OFT GO AWRY...'
"...SO SOME MOUSE OR ANOTHER ROYALLY FUCKED ME FROM BEYOND THE GRAVE."
5'9"
5'6"
5'3"
BOSTON POLICE
42649
PAUL EVAN BERG
12 23 21
BOSTON POLICE
42649
PAUL EVAN BERG
12 23 21

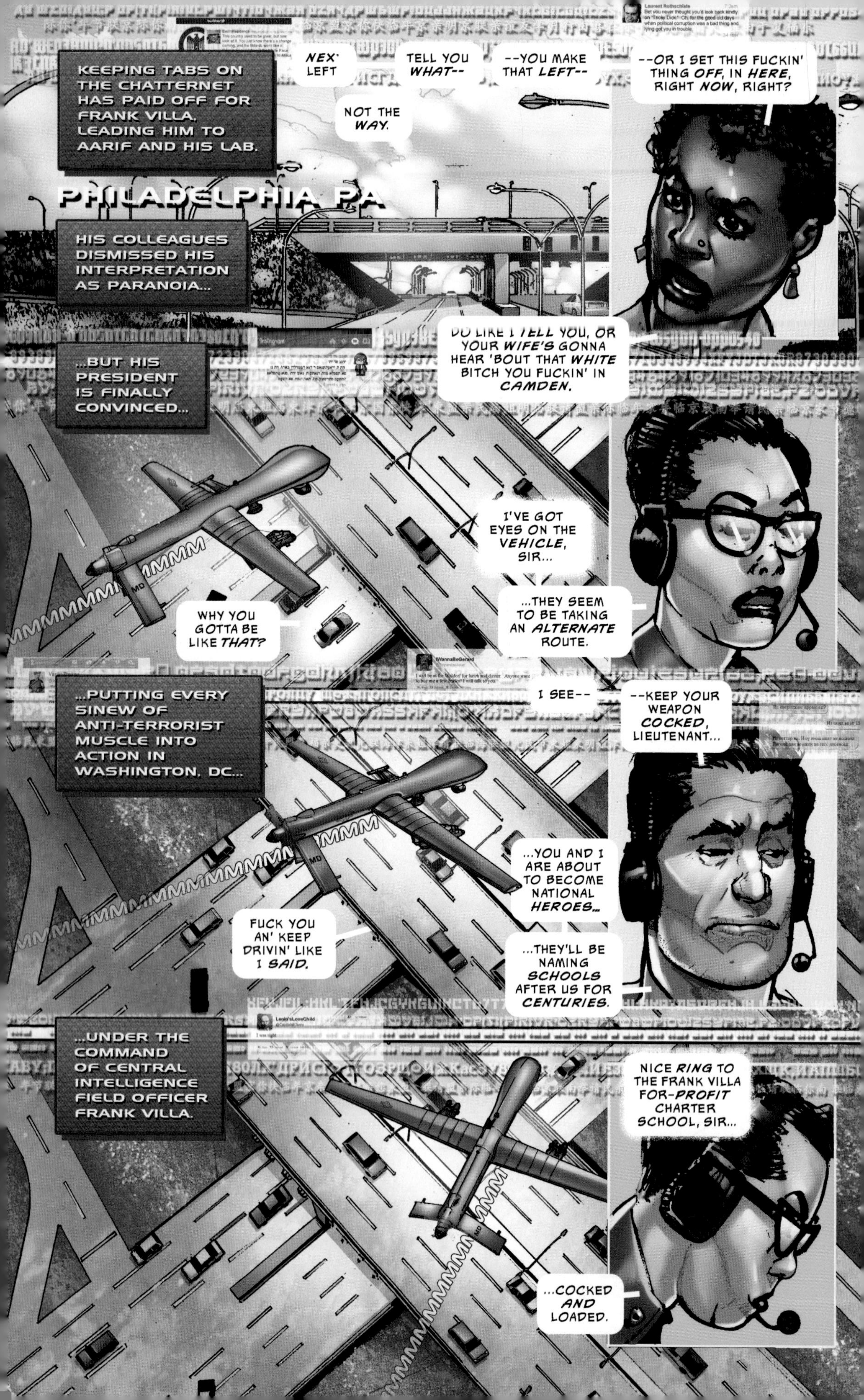

KEEPING TABS ON THE CHATTERNET HAS PAID OFF FOR FRANK VILLA, LEADING HIM TO AARIF AND HIS LAB.
NEX' LEFT
NOT THE WAY.
TELL YOU WHAT--
--YOU MAKE THAT LEFT--
--OR I SET THIS FUCKIN' THING OFF, IN HERE, RIGHT NOW, RIGHT?
PHILADELPHIA PA
HIS COLLEAGUES DISMISSED HIS INTERPRETATION AS PARANOIA...
DO LIKE I TELL YOU, OR YOUR WIFE'S GONNA HEAR 'BOUT THAT WHITE BITCH YOU FUCKIN' IN CAMDEN.
...BUT HIS PRESIDENT IS FINALLY CONVINCED...
I'VE GOT EYES ON THE VEHICLE, SIR...
...THEY SEEM TO BE TAKING AN ALTERNATE ROUTE.
WHY YOU GOTTA BE LIKE THAT?
...PUTTING EVERY SINEW OF ANTI-TERRORIST MUSCLE INTO ACTION IN WASHINGTON, DC...
I SEE--
--KEEP YOUR WEAPON COCKED, LIEUTENANT...
...YOU AND I ARE ABOUT TO BECOME NATIONAL HEROES...
...THEY'LL BE NAMING SCHOOLS AFTER US FOR CENTURIES.
FUCK YOU AN' KEEP DRIVIN' LIKE I SAID.
...UNDER THE COMMAND OF CENTRAL INTELLIGENCE FIELD OFFICER FRANK VILLA.
NICE RING TO THE FRANK VILLA FOR-PROFIT CHARTER SCHOOL, SIR...
...COCKED AND LOADED.

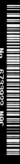

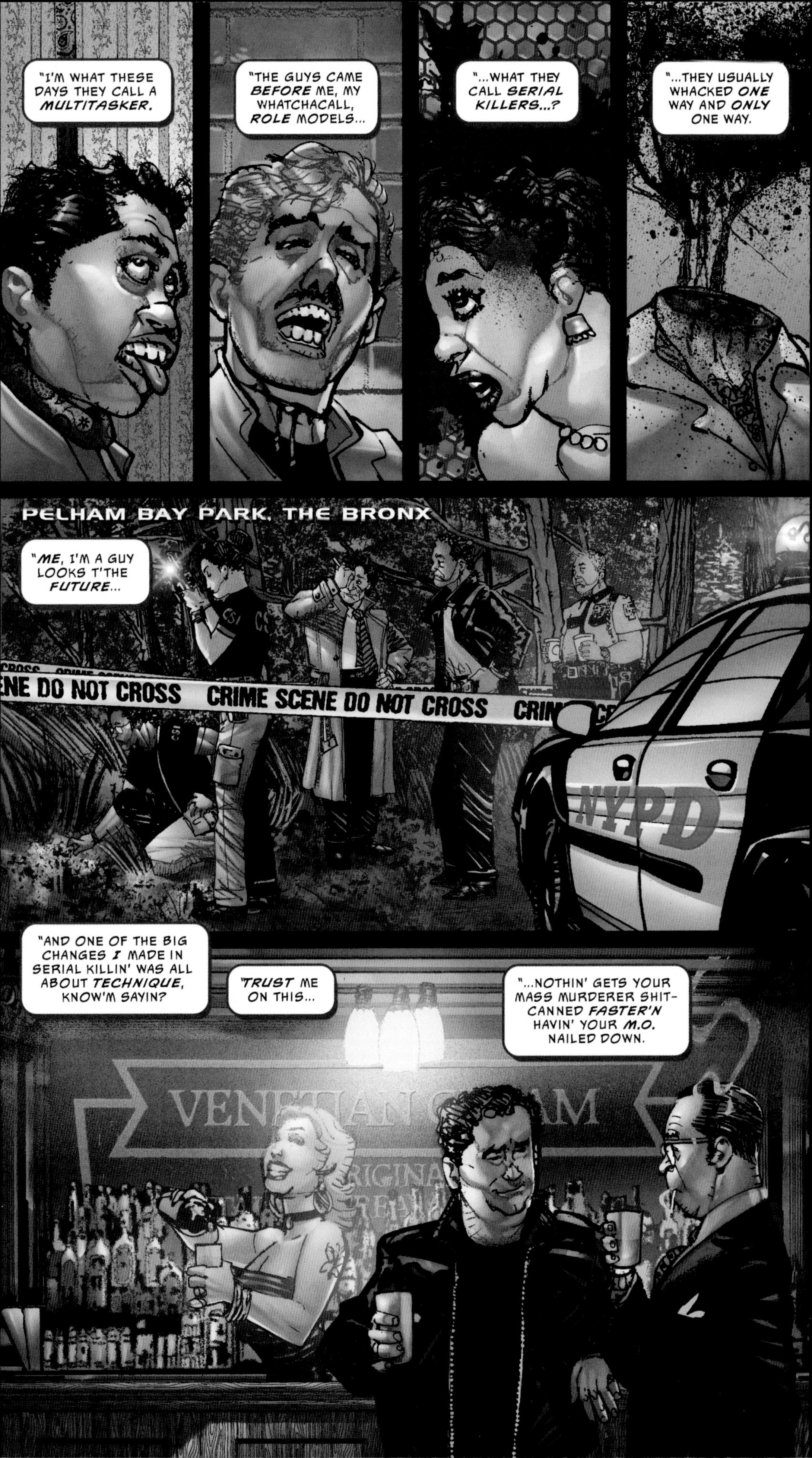
"I'M WHAT THESE DAYS THEY CALL A MULTITASKER.
"THE GUYS CAME BEFORE ME, MY WHATCHACALL, ROLE MODELS...
"...WHAT THEY CALL SERIAL KILLERS...?
"...THEY USUALLY WHACKED ONE WAY AND ONLY ONE WAY.
PELHAM BAY PARK, THE BRONX
"ME, I'M A GUY LOOKS T'THE FUTURE...
CRIME SCENE DO NOT CROSS
NYPD
"AND ONE OF THE BIG CHANGES I MADE IN SERIAL KILLIN' WAS ALL ABOUT TECHNIQUE, KNOW'M SAYIN?
'TRUST ME ON THIS...
"...NOTHIN' GETS YOUR MASS MURDERER SHIT-CANNED FASTER'N HAVIN' YOUR M.O. NAILED DOWN.

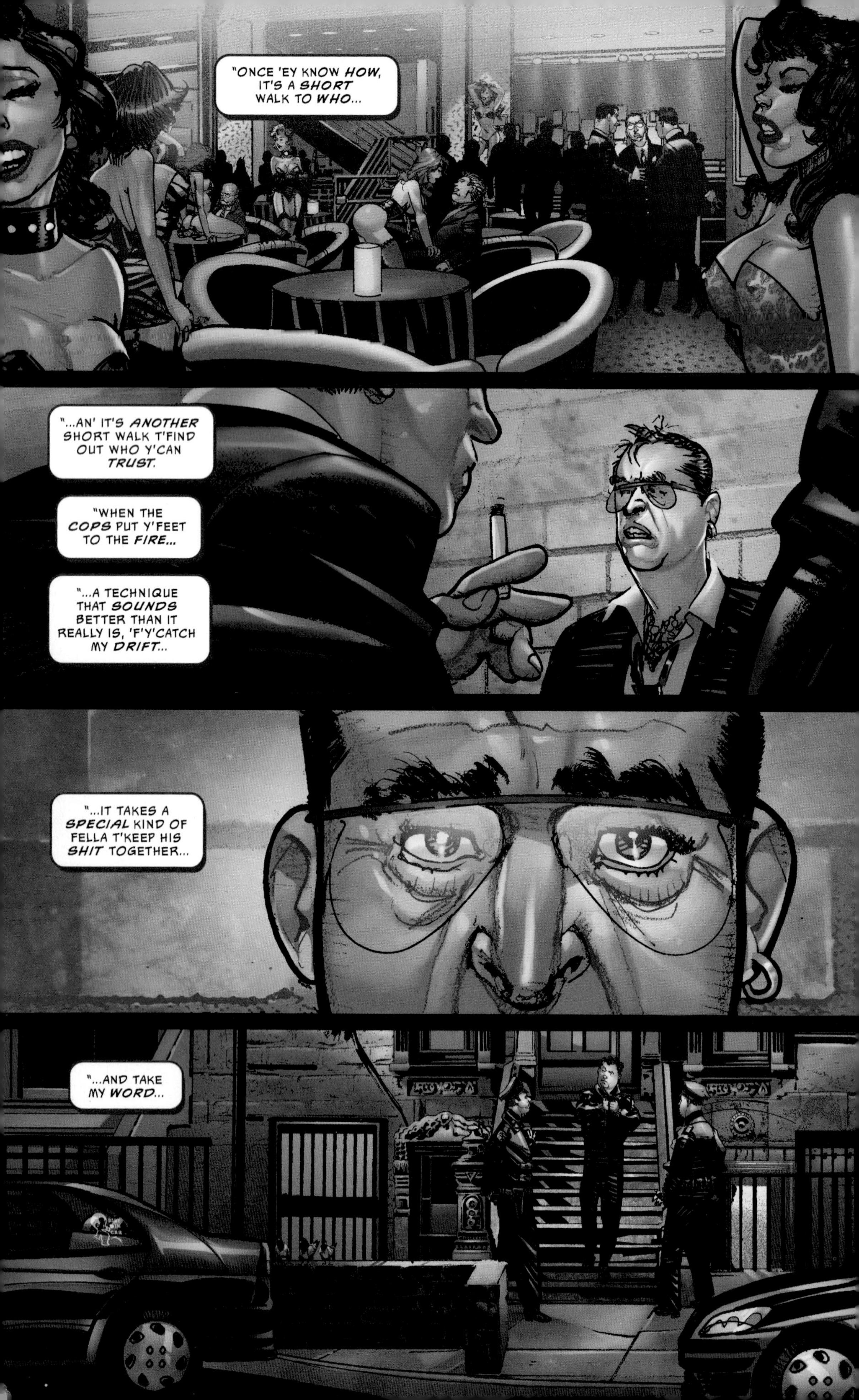
"ONCE 'EY KNOW *HOW*, IT'S A *SHORT* WALK TO *WHO*...
"...AN' IT'S *ANOTHER* SHORT WALK T'FIND OUT WHO Y'CAN *TRUST*.
"WHEN THE *COPS* PUT Y'FEET TO THE *FIRE*...
"...A TECHNIQUE THAT *SOUNDS* BETTER THAN IT REALLY IS, 'F'Y'CATCH MY *DRIFT*...
"...IT TAKES A *SPECIAL* KIND OF FELLA T'KEEP HIS *SHIT* TOGETHER...
"...AND TAKE MY *WORD*...

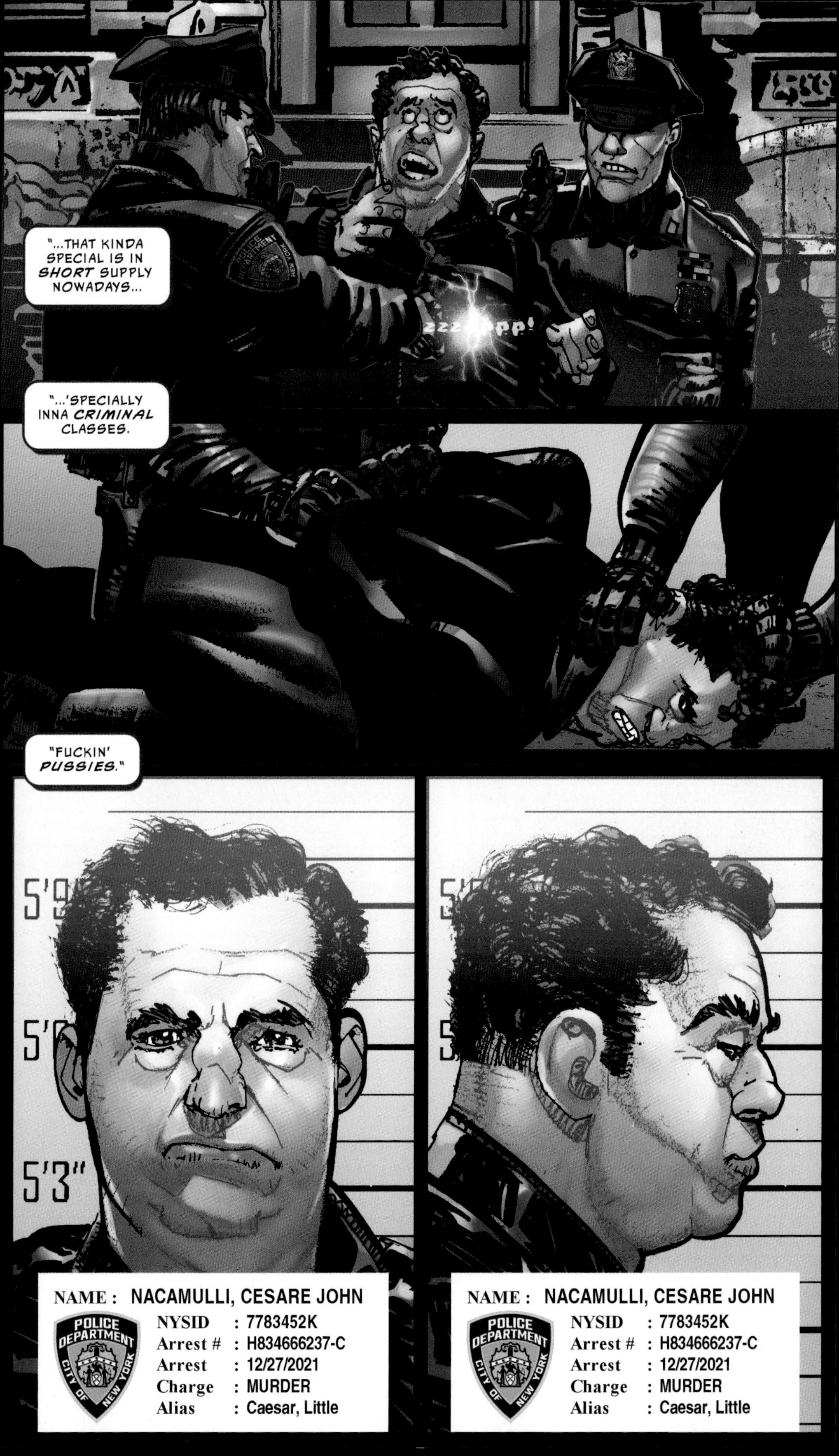
"...THAT KINDA SPECIAL IS IN SHORT SUPPLY NOWADAYS...
"...'SPECIALLY INNA CRIMINAL CLASSES.
"FUCKIN' PUSSIES."
5'3"
NAME : NACAMULLI, CESARE JOHN
POLICE DEPARTMENT CITY OF NEW YORK
NYSID : 7783452K
Arrest # : H834666237-C
Arrest : 12/27/2021
Charge : MURDER
Alias : Caesar, Little
NAME : NACAMULLI, CESARE JOHN
POLICE DEPARTMENT CITY OF NEW YORK
NYSID : 7783452K
Arrest # : H834666237-C
Arrest : 12/27/2021
Charge : MURDER
Alias : Caesar, Little

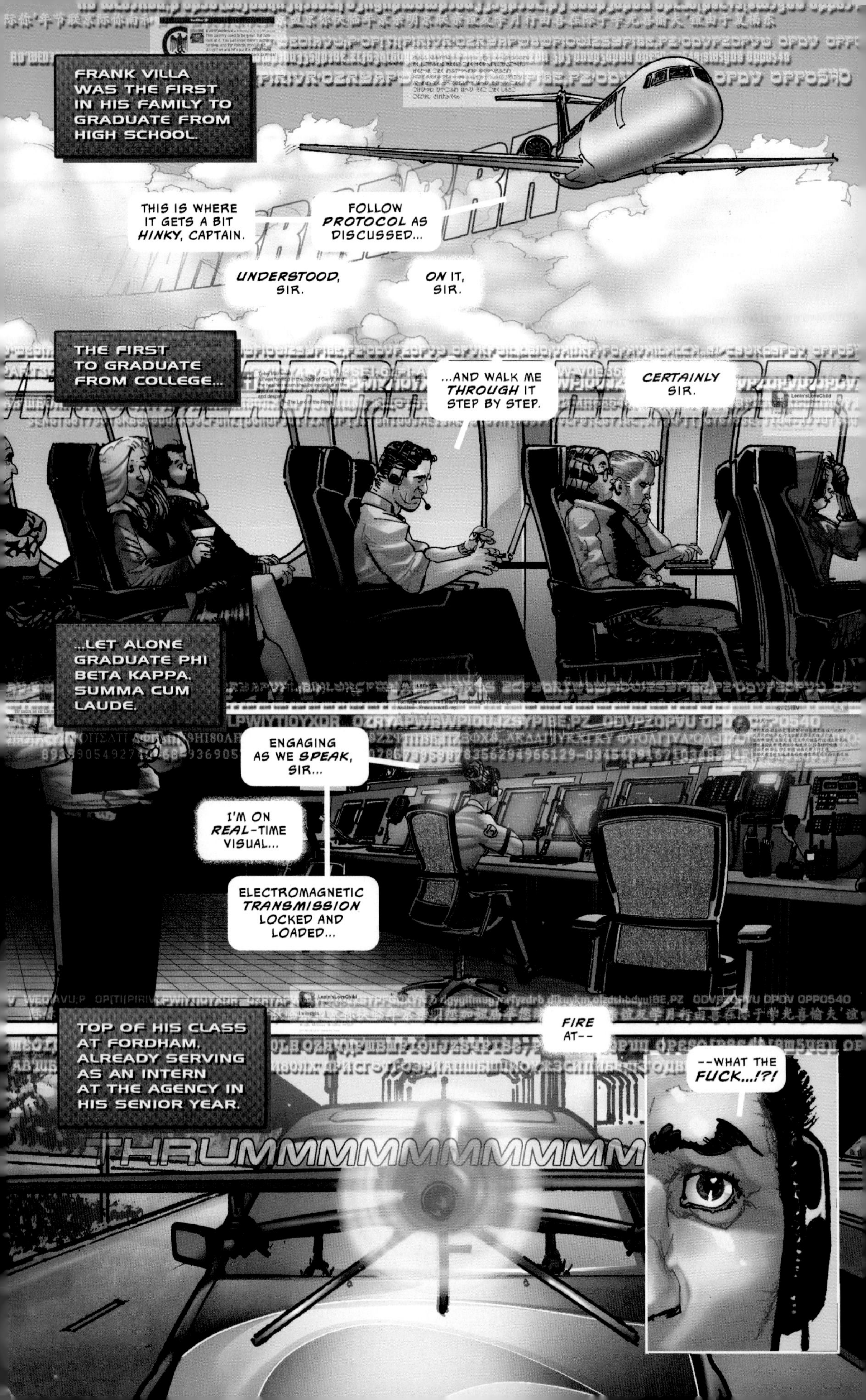
FRANK VILLA WAS THE FIRST IN HIS FAMILY TO GRADUATE FROM HIGH SCHOOL.
THIS IS WHERE IT GETS A BIT HINKY, CAPTAIN.
FOLLOW PROTOCOL AS DISCUSSED...
UNDERSTOOD, SIR.
ON IT, SIR.
THE FIRST TO GRADUATE FROM COLLEGE...
...AND WALK ME THROUGH IT STEP BY STEP.
CERTAINLY SIR.
...LET ALONE GRADUATE PHI BETA KAPPA. SUMMA CUM LAUDE.
ENGAGING AS WE SPEAK, SIR...
I'M ON REAL-TIME VISUAL...
ELECTROMAGNETIC TRANSMISSION LOCKED AND LOADED...
TOP OF HIS CLASS AT FORDHAM, ALREADY SERVING AS AN INTERN AT THE AGENCY IN HIS SENIOR YEAR.
FIRE AT--
--WHAT THE FUCK...!?!
THRUMMMMMMMMMMMM

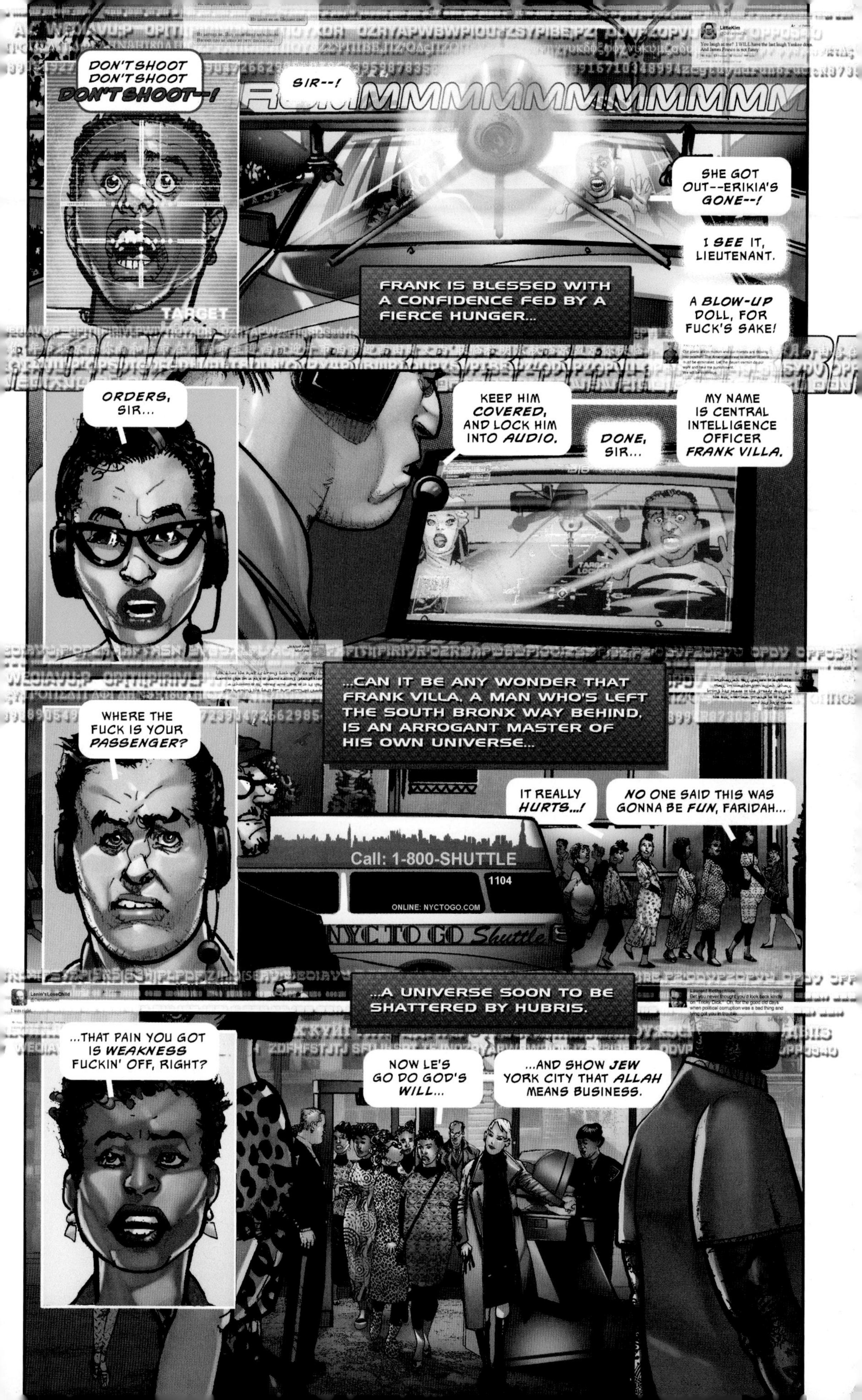
DON'T SHOOT DON'T SHOOT DON'T SHOOT--!
SIR--!
RRMMMMMMMMMMMMMMM
TARGET
SHE GOT OUT--ERIKIA'S GONE--!
I SEE IT, LIEUTENANT.
FRANK IS BLESSED WITH A CONFIDENCE FED BY A FIERCE HUNGER...
A BLOW-UP DOLL, FOR FUCK'S SAKE!
ORDERS, SIR...
KEEP HIM COVERED, AND LOCK HIM INTO AUDIO.
DONE, SIR...
MY NAME IS CENTRAL INTELLIGENCE OFFICER FRANK VILLA.
...CAN IT BE ANY WONDER THAT FRANK VILLA, A MAN WHO'S LEFT THE SOUTH BRONX WAY BEHIND, IS AN ARROGANT MASTER OF HIS OWN UNIVERSE...
WHERE THE FUCK IS YOUR PASSENGER?
IT REALLY HURTS...!
NO ONE SAID THIS WAS GONNA BE FUN, FARIDAH...
Call: 1-800-SHUTTLE
1104
ONLINE: NYCTOGO.COM
NYC TO GO Shuttle
...A UNIVERSE SOON TO BE SHATTERED BY HUBRIS.
...THAT PAIN YOU GOT IS WEAKNESS FUCKIN' OFF, RIGHT?
NOW LE'S GO DO GOD'S WILL...
...AND SHOW JEW YORK CITY THAT ALLAH MEANS BUSINESS.

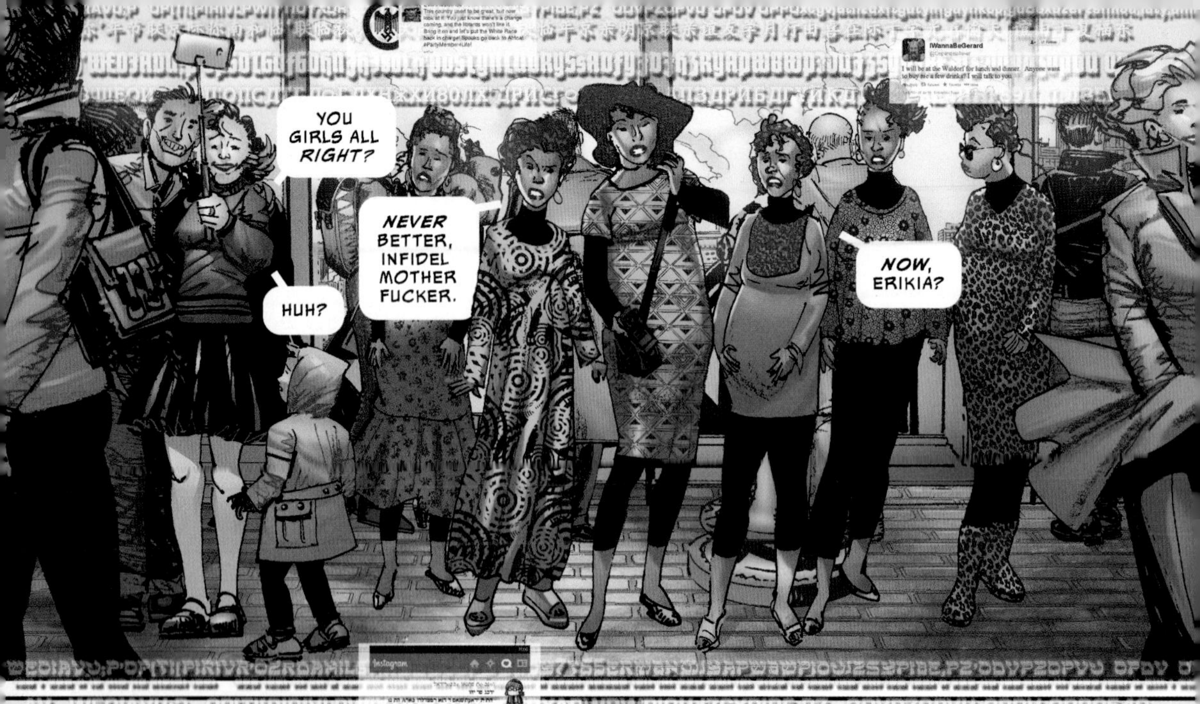
IWannaBeGerard
I will be at the Waldorf for lunch and dinner. Anyone want to buy me a few drinks? I will talk to you.
YOU GIRLS ALL RIGHT?
HUH?
NEVER BETTER, INFIDEL MOTHER FUCKER.
NOW, ERIKIA?

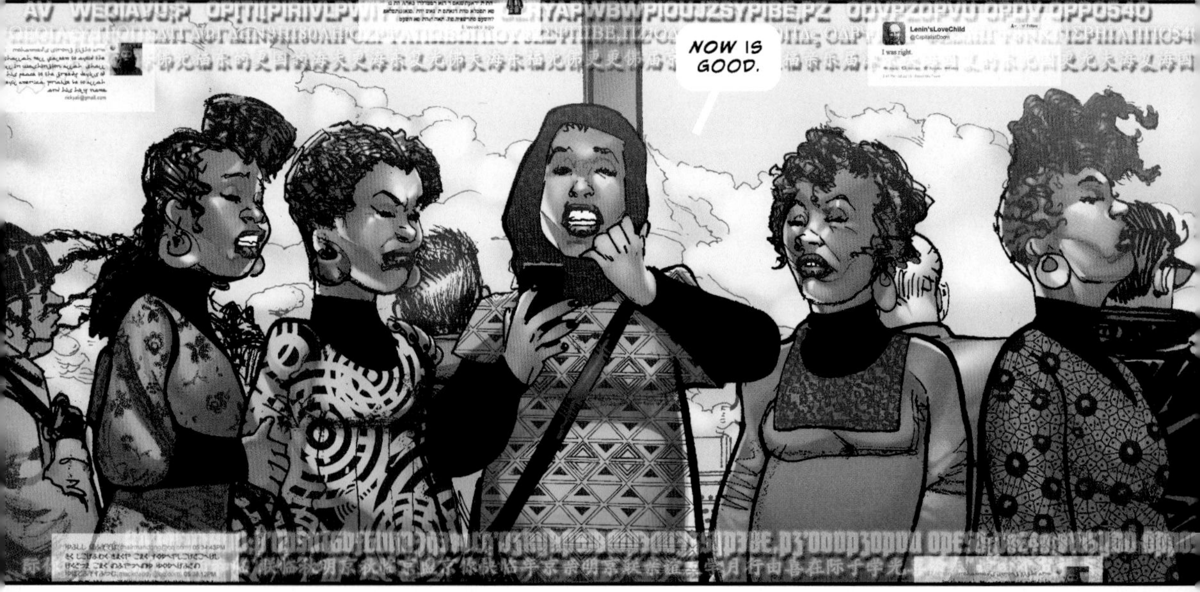
Lenin'sLoveChild
I was right.
NOW IS GOOD.

BOOM.

Drones

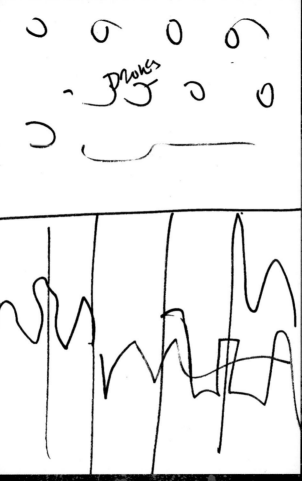

Part Two

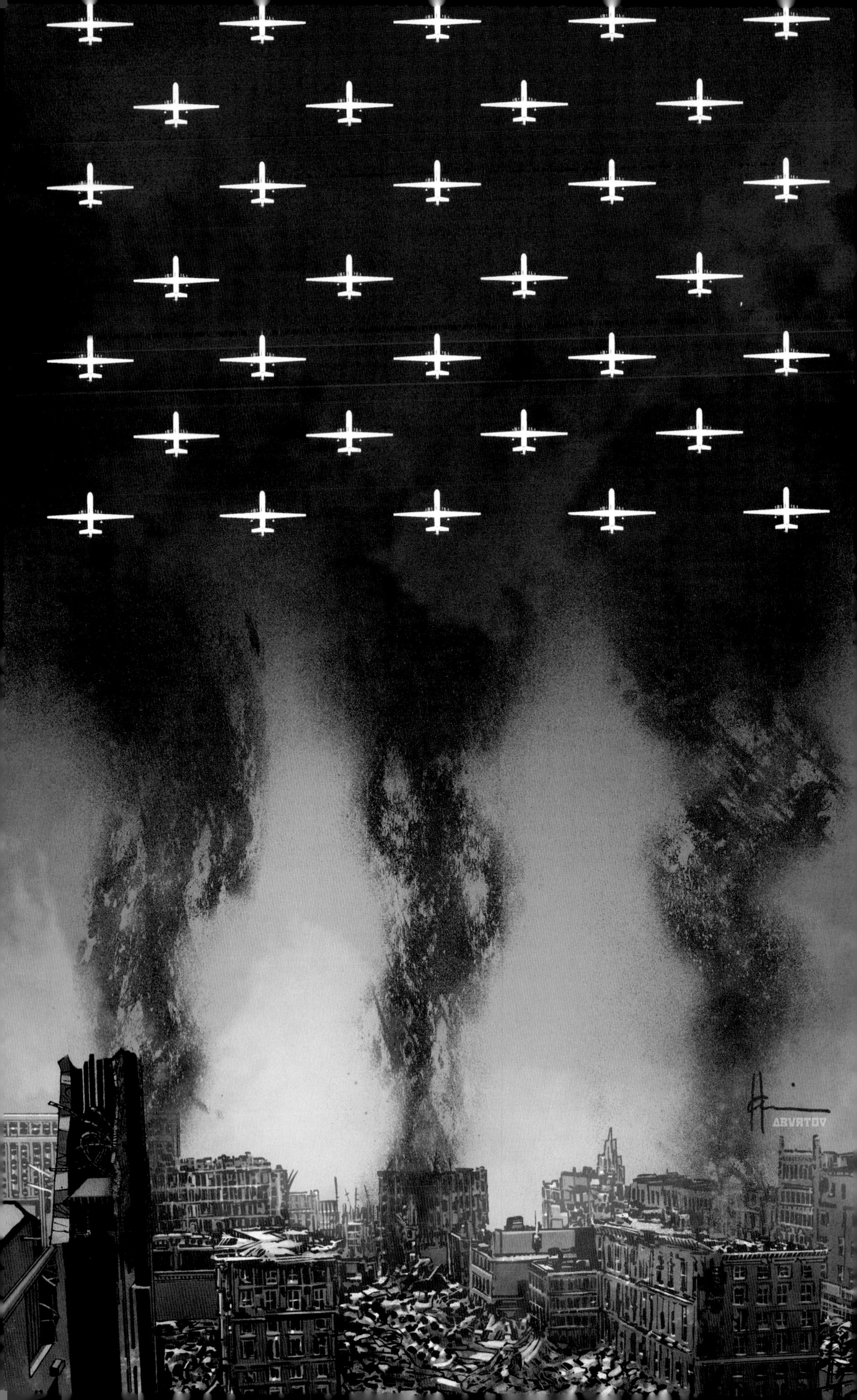

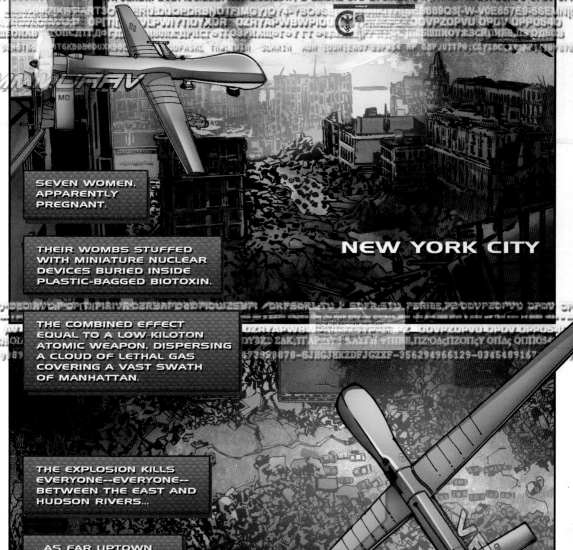

SEVEN WOMEN, APPARENTLY PREGNANT.

THEIR WOMBS STUFFED WITH MINIATURE NUCLEAR DEVICES BURIED INSIDE PLASTIC-BAGGED BIOTOXIN.

NEW YORK CITY

THE COMBINED EFFECT EQUAL TO A LOW KILOTON ATOMIC WEAPON, DISPERSING A CLOUD OF LETHAL GAS COVERING A VAST SWATH OF MANHATTAN.

THE EXPLOSION KILLS EVERYONE--EVERYONE-- BETWEEN THE EAST AND HUDSON RIVERS...

...AS FAR UPTOWN AS THE SHERRY- NETHERLAND HOTEL...

...AS FAR DOWNTOWN AS MACY'S, HERALD SQUARE.

YOU *SURE* YOU WANT TO *SEE* THIS, AGENT VILLA?

BUT IT IS THE AEROSOL DISPERSAL OF HEMOTOXIN THAT'S RESPONSIBLE FOR WHAT IS CONSERVATIVELY ESTIMATED AS TWO TO THREE MILLION DEATHS IN THE NEXT TWO WEEKS.

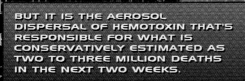

JUST KEEP *GOING*, LIEUTENANT.

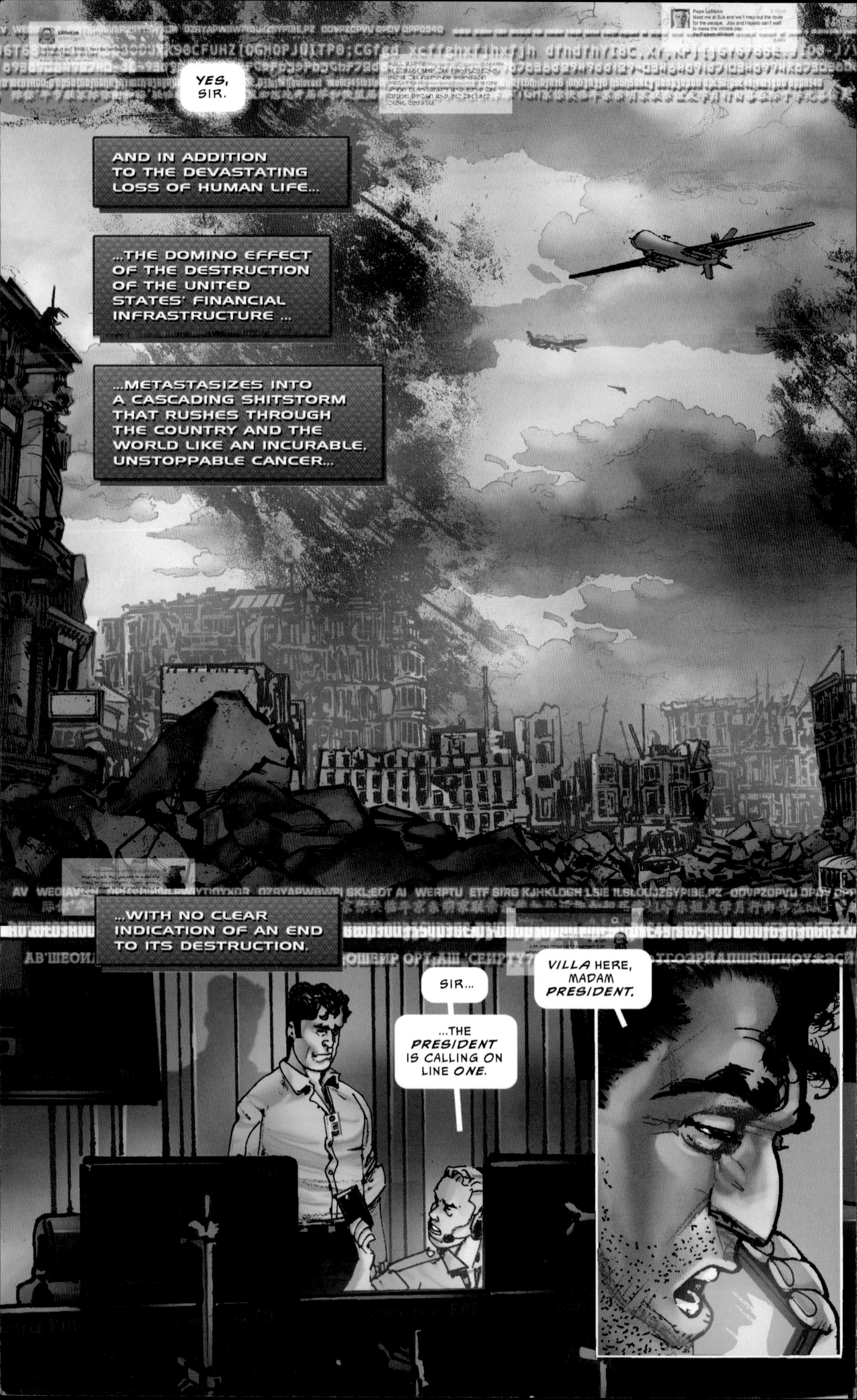
Meet me at BJs and we'll map out the route for the escape. Jojo and Hajeeb can't wait to make the infidels pay.
YES, SIR.
AND IN ADDITION TO THE DEVASTATING LOSS OF HUMAN LIFE...
...THE DOMINO EFFECT OF THE DESTRUCTION OF THE UNITED STATES' FINANCIAL INFRASTRUCTURE ...
...METASTASIZES INTO A CASCADING SHITSTORM THAT RUSHES THROUGH THE COUNTRY AND THE WORLD LIKE AN INCURABLE, UNSTOPPABLE CANCER...
...WITH NO CLEAR INDICATION OF AN END TO ITS DESTRUCTION.
SIR...
...THE PRESIDENT IS CALLING ON LINE ONE.
VILLA HERE, MADAM PRESIDENT.

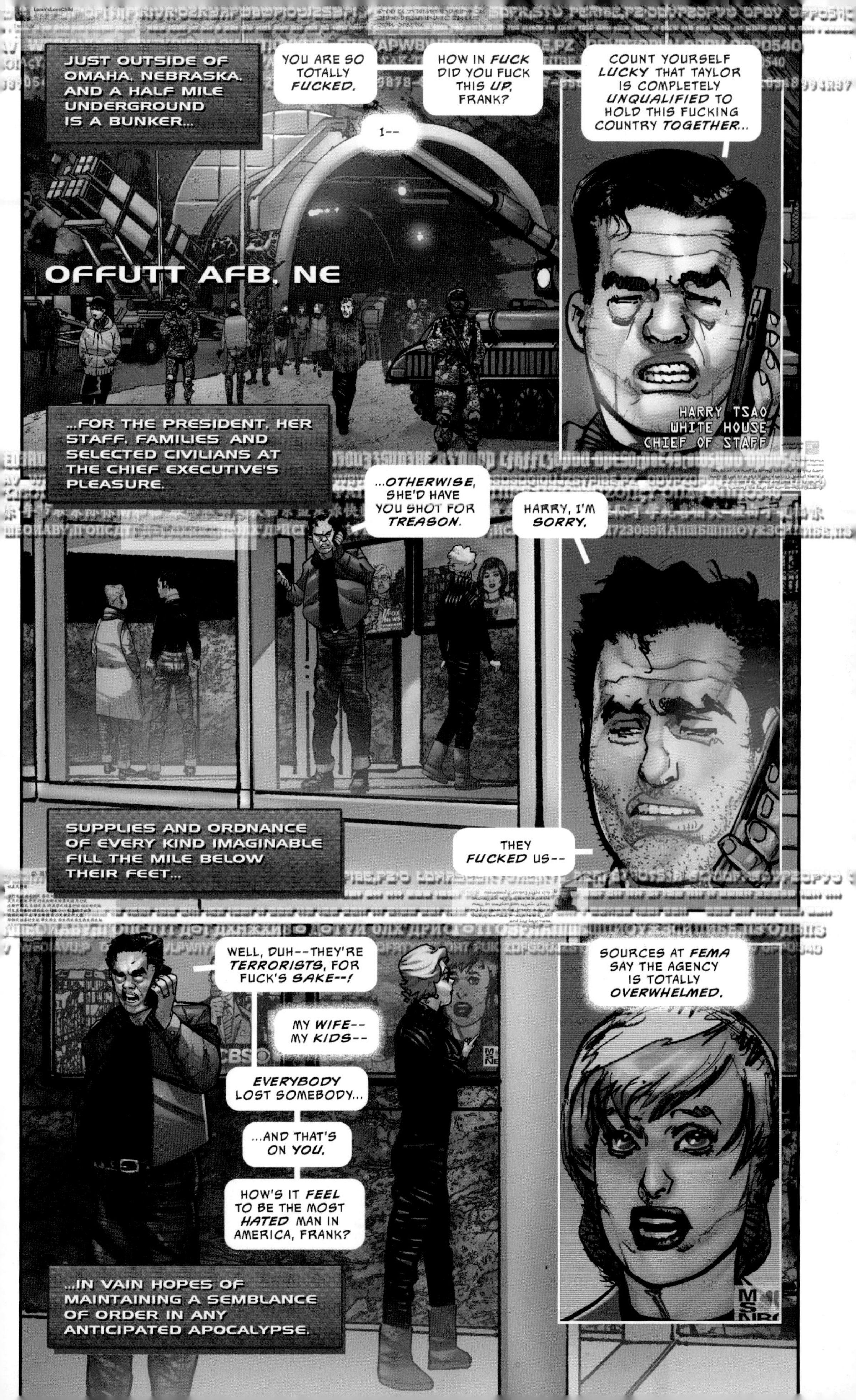
JUST OUTSIDE OF OMAHA, NEBRASKA, AND A HALF MILE UNDERGROUND IS A BUNKER...
YOU ARE SO TOTALLY FUCKED.
HOW IN FUCK DID YOU FUCK THIS UP, FRANK?
I--
COUNT YOURSELF LUCKY THAT TAYLOR IS COMPLETELY UNQUALIFIED TO HOLD THIS FUCKING COUNTRY TOGETHER...
OFFUTT AFB, NE
HARRY TSAO WHITE HOUSE CHIEF OF STAFF
...FOR THE PRESIDENT, HER STAFF, FAMILIES AND SELECTED CIVILIANS AT THE CHIEF EXECUTIVE'S PLEASURE.
...OTHERWISE, SHE'D HAVE YOU SHOT FOR TREASON.
HARRY, I'M SORRY.
THEY FUCKED US--
SUPPLIES AND ORDNANCE OF EVERY KIND IMAGINABLE FILL THE MILE BELOW THEIR FEET...
WELL, DUH--THEY'RE TERRORISTS, FOR FUCK'S SAKE--!
MY WIFE-- MY KIDS--
EVERYBODY LOST SOMEBODY...
...AND THAT'S ON YOU.
HOW'S IT FEEL TO BE THE MOST HATED MAN IN AMERICA, FRANK?
SOURCES AT FEMA SAY THE AGENCY IS TOTALLY OVERWHELMED.
...IN VAIN HOPES OF MAINTAINING A SEMBLANCE OF ORDER IN ANY ANTICIPATED APOCALYPSE.

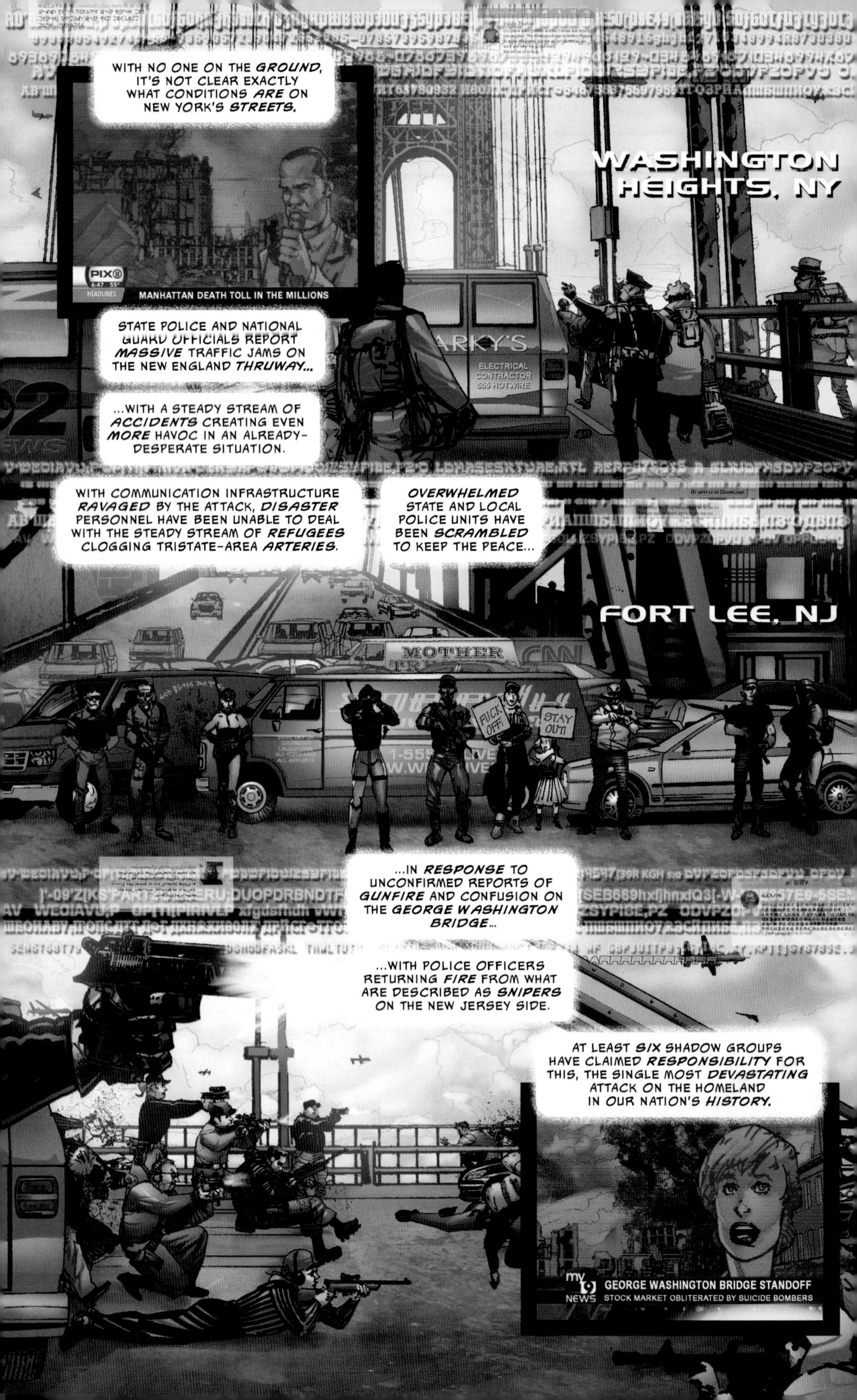

WITH NO ONE ON THE GROUND, IT'S NOT CLEAR EXACTLY WHAT CONDITIONS ARE ON NEW YORK'S STREETS.
PIX 11
HEADLINES
MANHATTAN DEATH TOLL IN THE MILLIONS
WASHINGTON HEIGHTS, NY
STATE POLICE AND NATIONAL GUARD OFFICIALS REPORT MASSIVE TRAFFIC JAMS ON THE NEW ENGLAND THRUWAY...
...WITH A STEADY STREAM OF ACCIDENTS CREATING EVEN MORE HAVOC IN AN ALREADY-DESPERATE SITUATION.
ELECTRICAL CONTRACTOR 555 HOTWIRE
WITH COMMUNICATION INFRASTRUCTURE RAVAGED BY THE ATTACK, DISASTER PERSONNEL HAVE BEEN UNABLE TO DEAL WITH THE STEADY STREAM OF REFUGEES CLOGGING TRISTATE-AREA ARTERIES.
OVERWHELMED STATE AND LOCAL POLICE UNITS HAVE BEEN SCRAMBLED TO KEEP THE PEACE...
FORT LEE, NJ
MOTHER
CNN
FUCK OFF
STAY OUT
...IN RESPONSE TO UNCONFIRMED REPORTS OF GUNFIRE AND CONFUSION ON THE GEORGE WASHINGTON BRIDGE...
...WITH POLICE OFFICERS RETURNING FIRE FROM WHAT ARE DESCRIBED AS SNIPERS ON THE NEW JERSEY SIDE.
AT LEAST SIX SHADOW GROUPS HAVE CLAIMED RESPONSIBILITY FOR THIS, THE SINGLE MOST DEVASTATING ATTACK ON THE HOMELAND IN OUR NATION'S HISTORY.
my 9 NEWS
GEORGE WASHINGTON BRIDGE STANDOFF
STOCK MARKET OBLITERATED BY SUICIDE BOMBERS

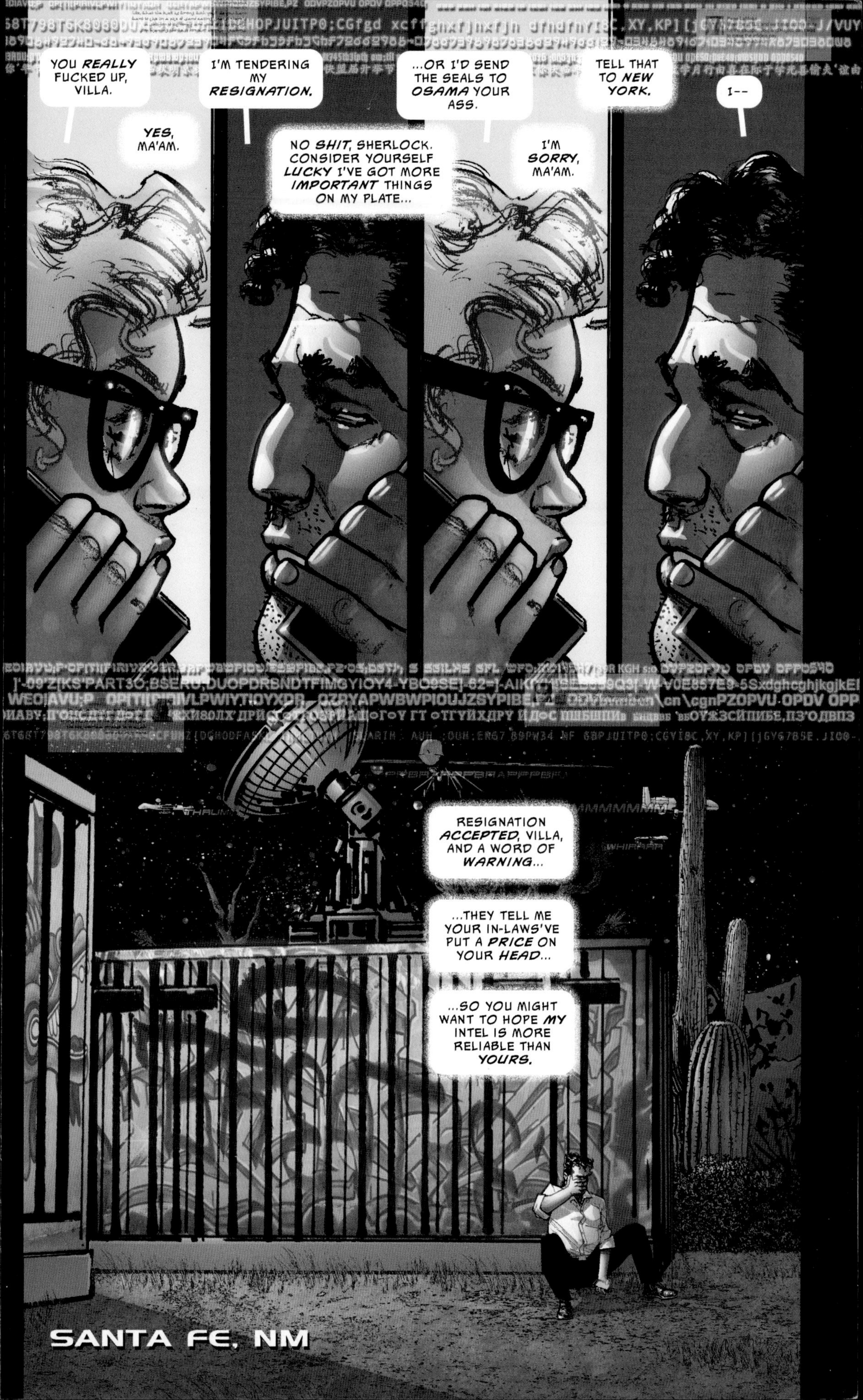

YOU *REALLY* FUCKED UP, VILLA.
YES, MA'AM.
I'M TENDERING MY *RESIGNATION.*
NO *SHIT,* SHERLOCK. CONSIDER YOURSELF *LUCKY* I'VE GOT MORE *IMPORTANT* THINGS ON MY PLATE...
...OR I'D SEND THE SEALS TO *OSAMA* YOUR ASS.
I'M *SORRY,* MA'AM.
TELL THAT TO *NEW YORK.*
I--
RESIGNATION *ACCEPTED,* VILLA, AND A WORD OF *WARNING*...
...THEY TELL ME YOUR IN-LAWS'VE PUT A *PRICE* ON YOUR *HEAD*...
...SO YOU MIGHT WANT TO HOPE *MY* INTEL IS MORE RELIABLE THAN *YOURS.*
SANTA FE, NM

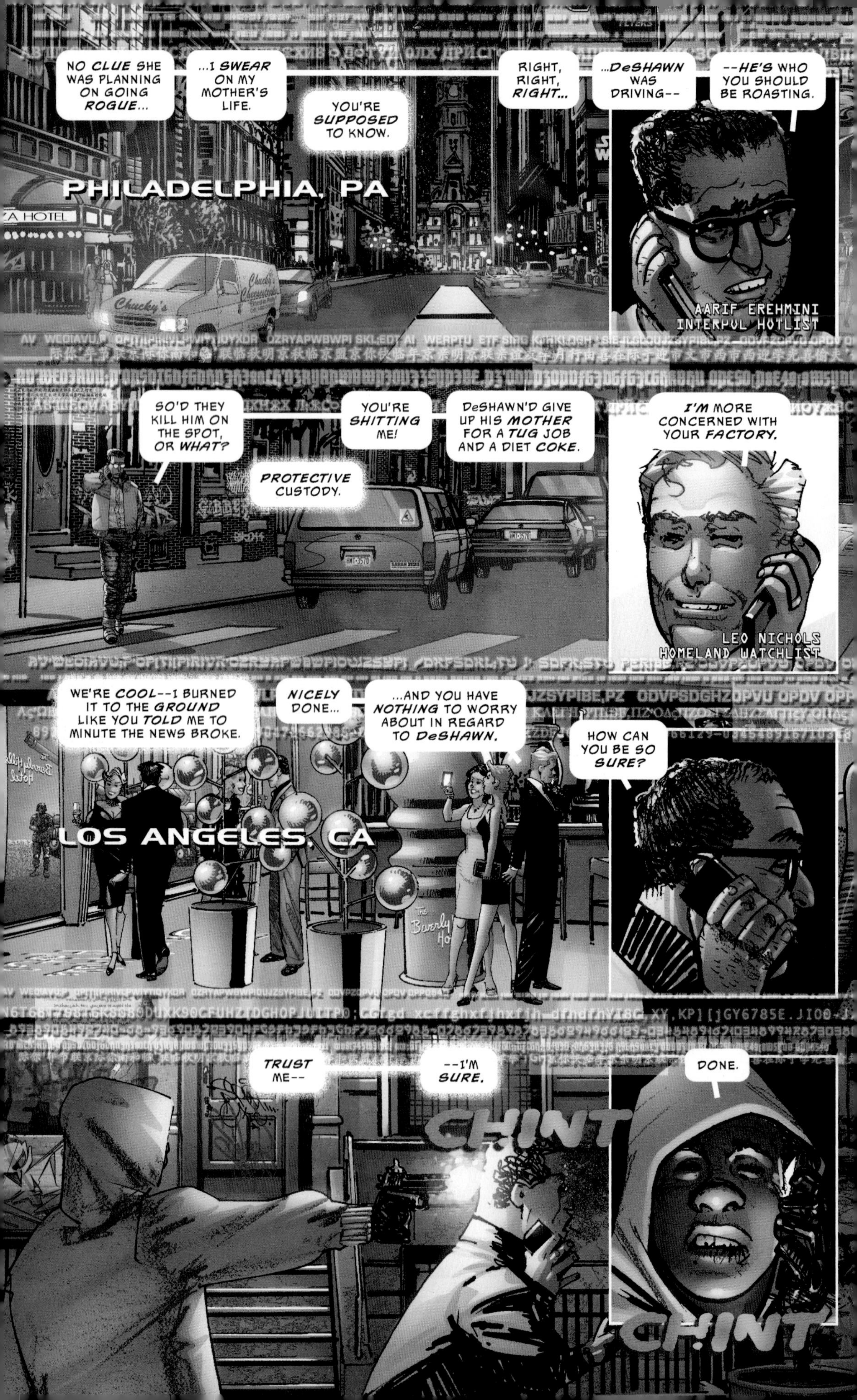
NO CLUE SHE WAS PLANNING ON GOING ROGUE...
...I SWEAR ON MY MOTHER'S LIFE.
YOU'RE SUPPOSED TO KNOW.
RIGHT, RIGHT, RIGHT...
...DeSHAWN WAS DRIVING--
--HE'S WHO YOU SHOULD BE ROASTING.
PHILADELPHIA, PA
AARIF EREHMINI
INTERPOL HOTLIST
SO'D THEY KILL HIM ON THE SPOT, OR WHAT?
YOU'RE SHITTING ME!
PROTECTIVE CUSTODY.
DeSHAWN'D GIVE UP HIS MOTHER FOR A TUG JOB AND A DIET COKE.
I'M MORE CONCERNED WITH YOUR FACTORY.
LEO NICHOLS
HOMELAND WATCHLIST
WE'RE COOL--I BURNED IT TO THE GROUND LIKE YOU TOLD ME TO MINUTE THE NEWS BROKE.
NICELY DONE...
...AND YOU HAVE NOTHING TO WORRY ABOUT IN REGARD TO DeSHAWN.
HOW CAN YOU BE SO SURE?
LOS ANGELES, CA
TRUST ME--
--I'M SURE.
DONE.
CHINT
CHINT

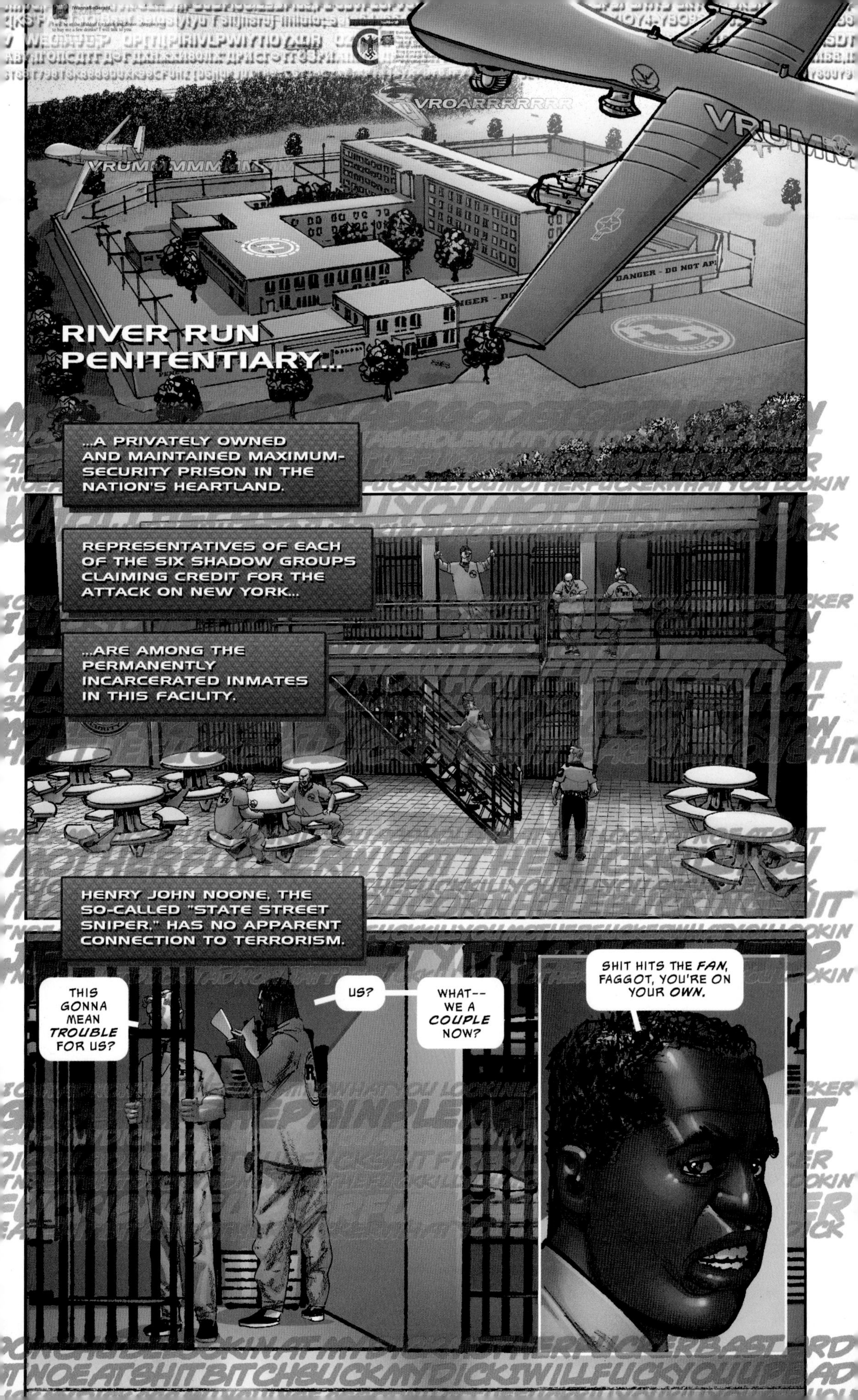
VROARRRRRRR
VRUM
RIVER RUN PENITENTIARY...
...A PRIVATELY OWNED AND MAINTAINED MAXIMUM-SECURITY PRISON IN THE NATION'S HEARTLAND.
REPRESENTATIVES OF EACH OF THE SIX SHADOW GROUPS CLAIMING CREDIT FOR THE ATTACK ON NEW YORK...
...ARE AMONG THE PERMANENTLY INCARCERATED INMATES IN THIS FACILITY.
HENRY JOHN NOONE, THE SO-CALLED "STATE STREET SNIPER," HAS NO APPARENT CONNECTION TO TERRORISM.
THIS GONNA MEAN TROUBLE FOR US?
US?
WHAT-- WE A COUPLE NOW?
SHIT HITS THE FAN, FAGGOT, YOU'RE ON YOUR OWN.

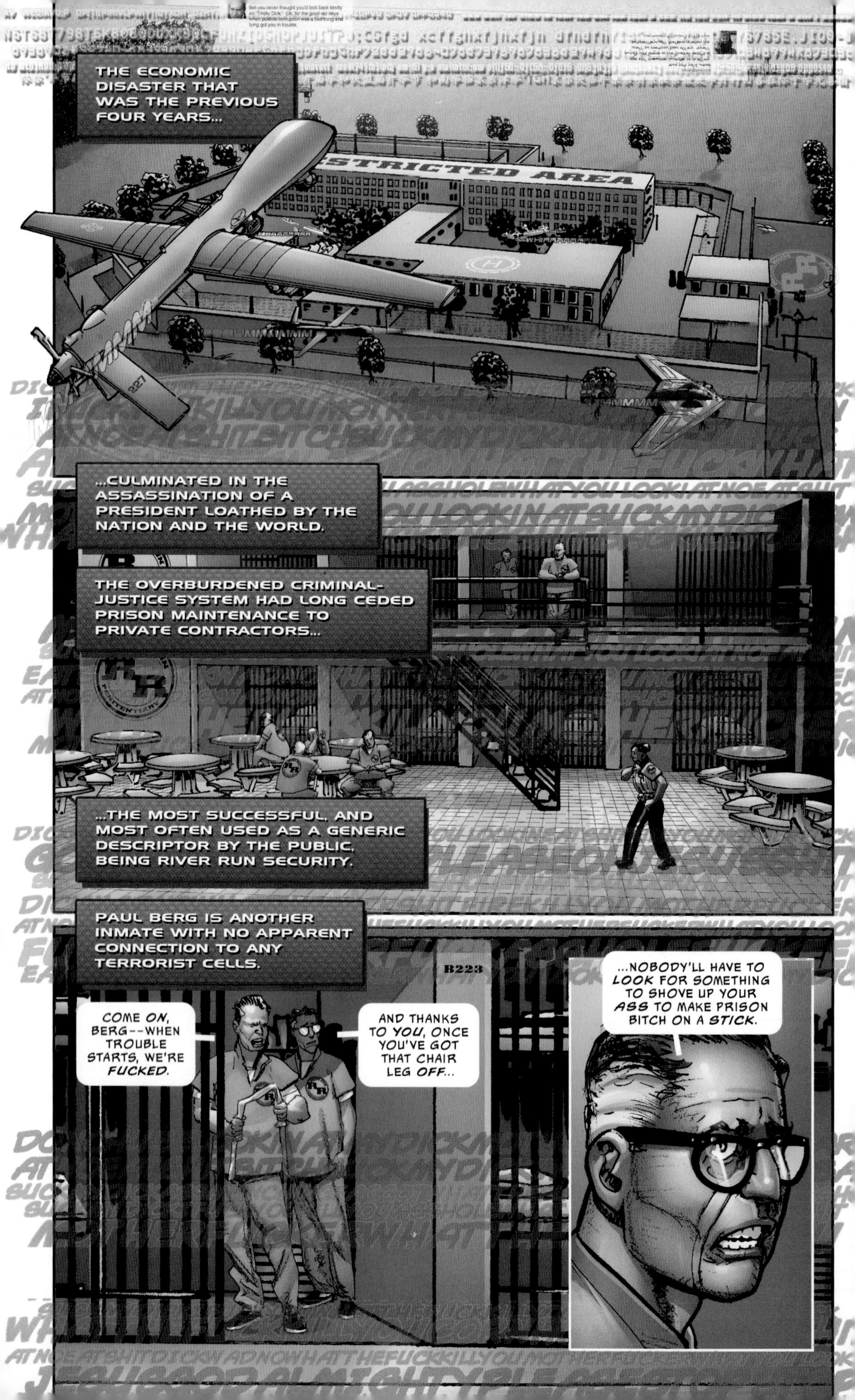
THE ECONOMIC DISASTER THAT WAS THE PREVIOUS FOUR YEARS...
STRICTED AREA
...CULMINATED IN THE ASSASSINATION OF A PRESIDENT LOATHED BY THE NATION AND THE WORLD.
THE OVERBURDENED CRIMINAL-JUSTICE SYSTEM HAD LONG CEDED PRISON MAINTENANCE TO PRIVATE CONTRACTORS...
...THE MOST SUCCESSFUL, AND MOST OFTEN USED AS A GENERIC DESCRIPTOR BY THE PUBLIC, BEING RIVER RUN SECURITY.
PAUL BERG IS ANOTHER INMATE WITH NO APPARENT CONNECTION TO ANY TERRORIST CELLS.
B223
COME ON, BERG--WHEN TROUBLE STARTS, WE'RE FUCKED.
AND THANKS TO YOU, ONCE YOU'VE GOT THAT CHAIR LEG OFF...
...NOBODY'LL HAVE TO LOOK FOR SOMETHING TO SHOVE UP YOUR ASS TO MAKE PRISON BITCH ON A STICK.

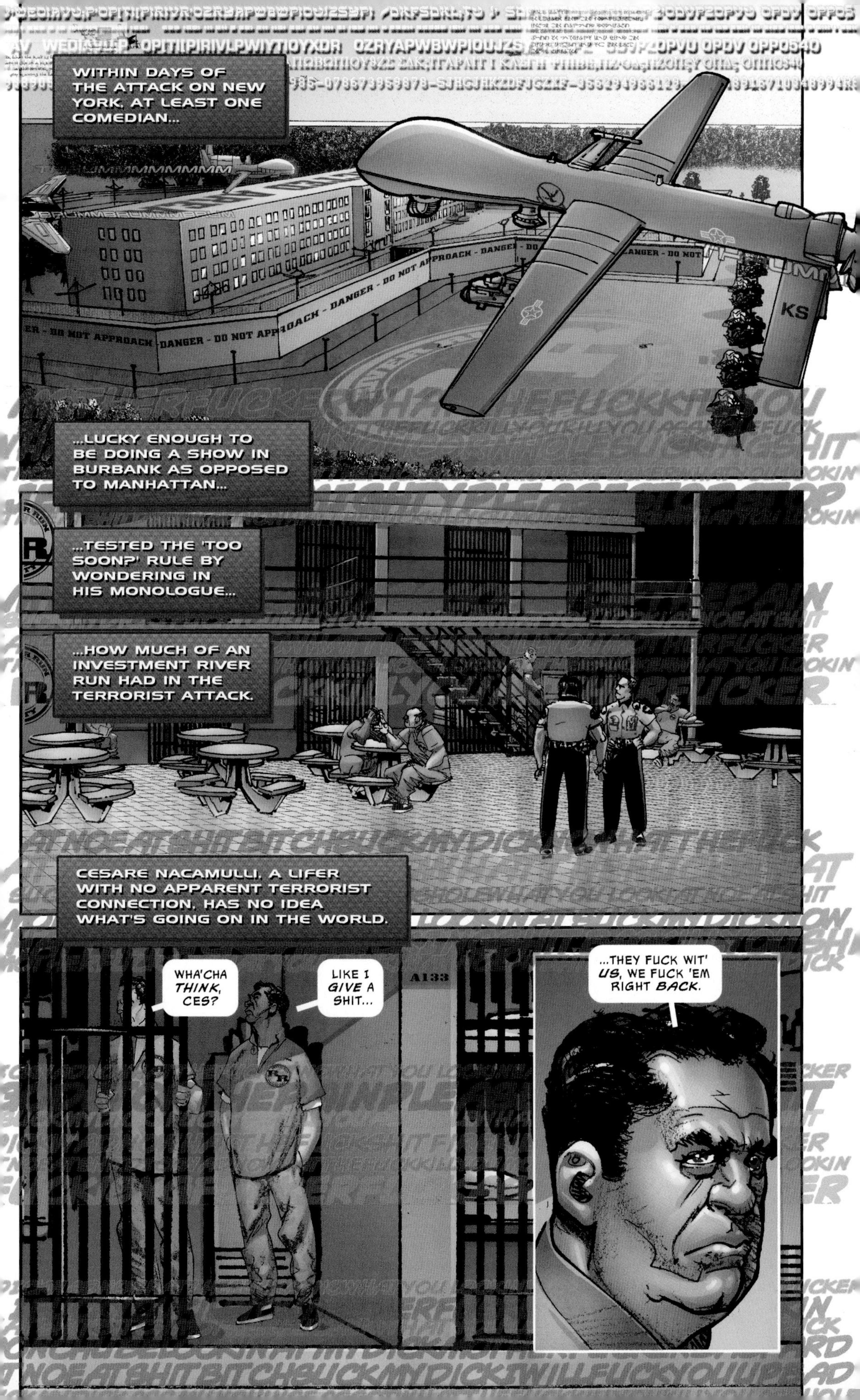

WITHIN DAYS OF THE ATTACK ON NEW YORK, AT LEAST ONE COMEDIAN...
DANGER - DO NOT APPROACH
KS
...LUCKY ENOUGH TO BE DOING A SHOW IN BURBANK AS OPPOSED TO MANHATTAN...
...TESTED THE 'TOO SOON?' RULE BY WONDERING IN HIS MONOLOGUE...
...HOW MUCH OF AN INVESTMENT RIVER RUN HAD IN THE TERRORIST ATTACK.
CESARE NACAMULLI, A LIFER WITH NO APPARENT TERRORIST CONNECTION, HAS NO IDEA WHAT'S GOING ON IN THE WORLD.
WHA'CHA *THINK*, CES?
LIKE I *GIVE* A SHIT...
A133
...THEY FUCK WIT' *US*, WE FUCK 'EM RIGHT *BACK*.

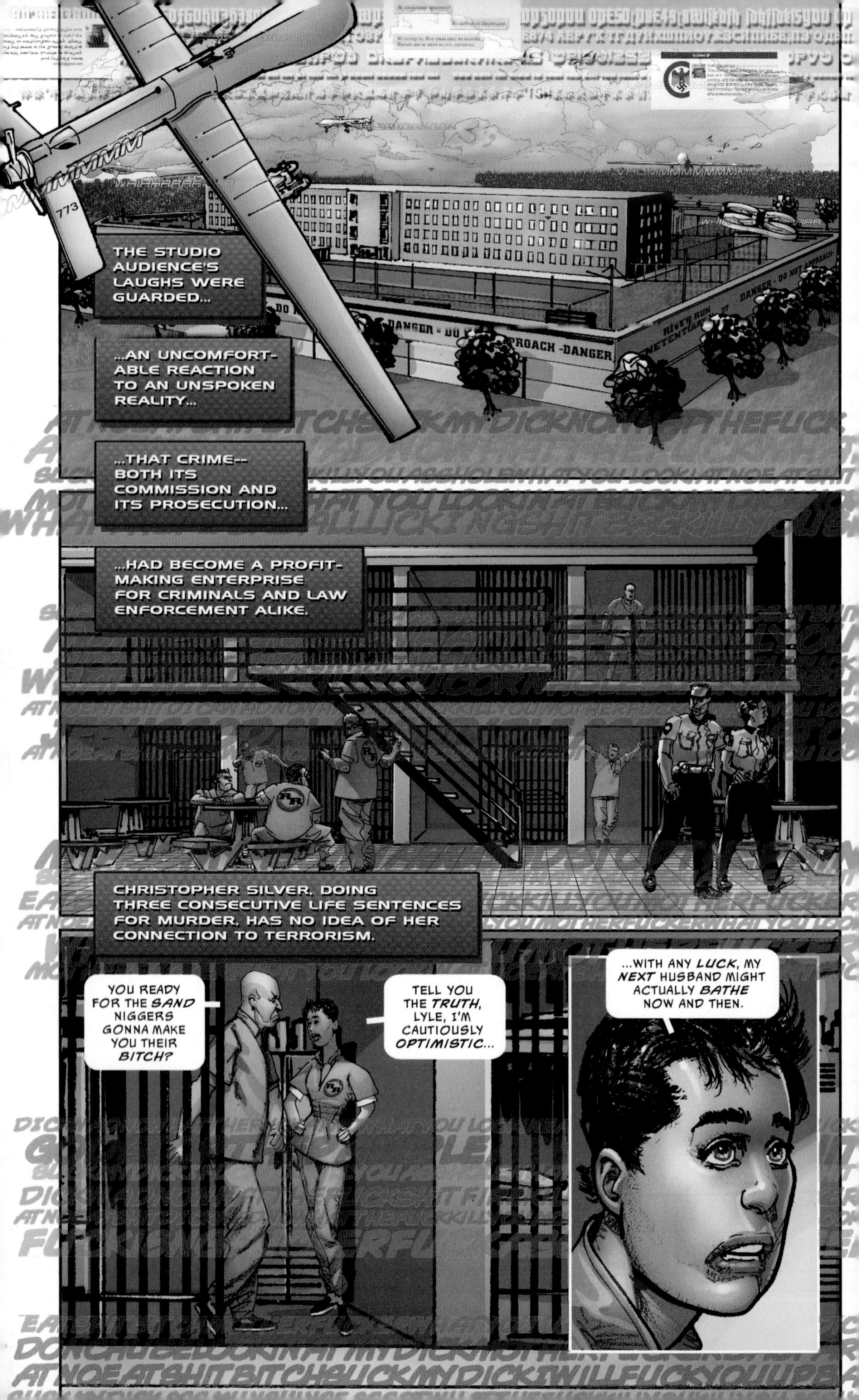
THE STUDIO AUDIENCE'S LAUGHS WERE GUARDED...
...AN UNCOMFORTABLE REACTION TO AN UNSPOKEN REALITY...
...THAT CRIME-- BOTH ITS COMMISSION AND ITS PROSECUTION...
...HAD BECOME A PROFIT-MAKING ENTERPRISE FOR CRIMINALS AND LAW ENFORCEMENT ALIKE.
CHRISTOPHER SILVER, DOING THREE CONSECUTIVE LIFE SENTENCES FOR MURDER, HAS NO IDEA OF HER CONNECTION TO TERRORISM.
YOU READY FOR THE SAND NIGGERS GONNA MAKE YOU THEIR BITCH?
TELL YOU THE TRUTH, LYLE, I'M CAUTIOUSLY OPTIMISTIC...
...WITH ANY LUCK, MY NEXT HUSBAND MIGHT ACTUALLY BATHE NOW AND THEN.

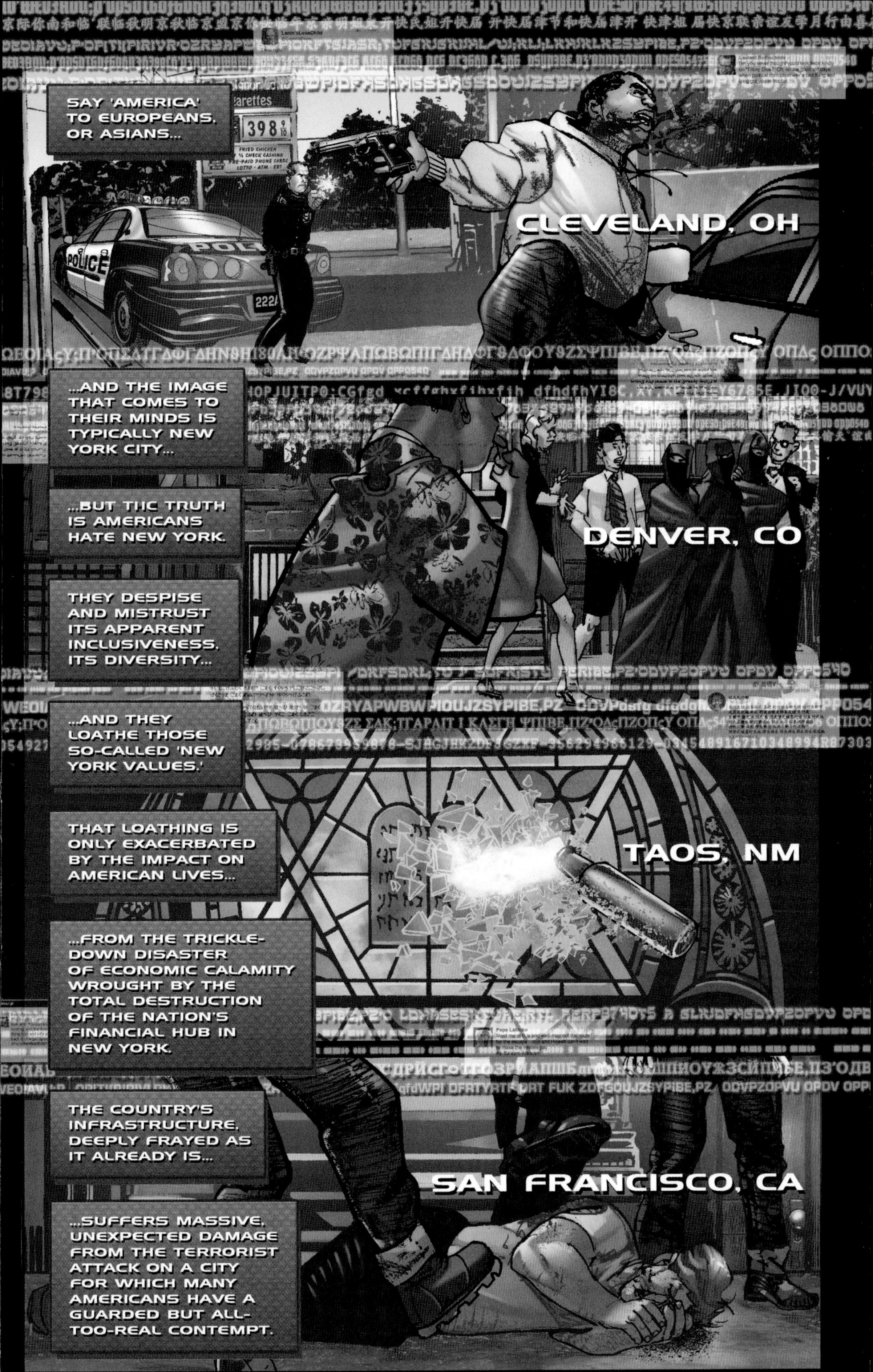

SAY 'AMERICA' TO EUROPEANS, OR ASIANS...
CLEVELAND, OH
...AND THE IMAGE THAT COMES TO THEIR MINDS IS TYPICALLY NEW YORK CITY...
...BUT THE TRUTH IS AMERICANS HATE NEW YORK.
DENVER, CO
THEY DESPISE AND MISTRUST ITS APPARENT INCLUSIVENESS, ITS DIVERSITY...
...AND THEY LOATHE THOSE SO-CALLED 'NEW YORK VALUES.'
THAT LOATHING IS ONLY EXACERBATED BY THE IMPACT ON AMERICAN LIVES...
TAOS, NM
...FROM THE TRICKLE-DOWN DISASTER OF ECONOMIC CALAMITY WROUGHT BY THE TOTAL DESTRUCTION OF THE NATION'S FINANCIAL HUB IN NEW YORK.
THE COUNTRY'S INFRASTRUCTURE, DEEPLY FRAYED AS IT ALREADY IS...
SAN FRANCISCO, CA
...SUFFERS MASSIVE, UNEXPECTED DAMAGE FROM THE TERRORIST ATTACK ON A CITY FOR WHICH MANY AMERICANS HAVE A GUARDED BUT ALL-TOO-REAL CONTEMPT.

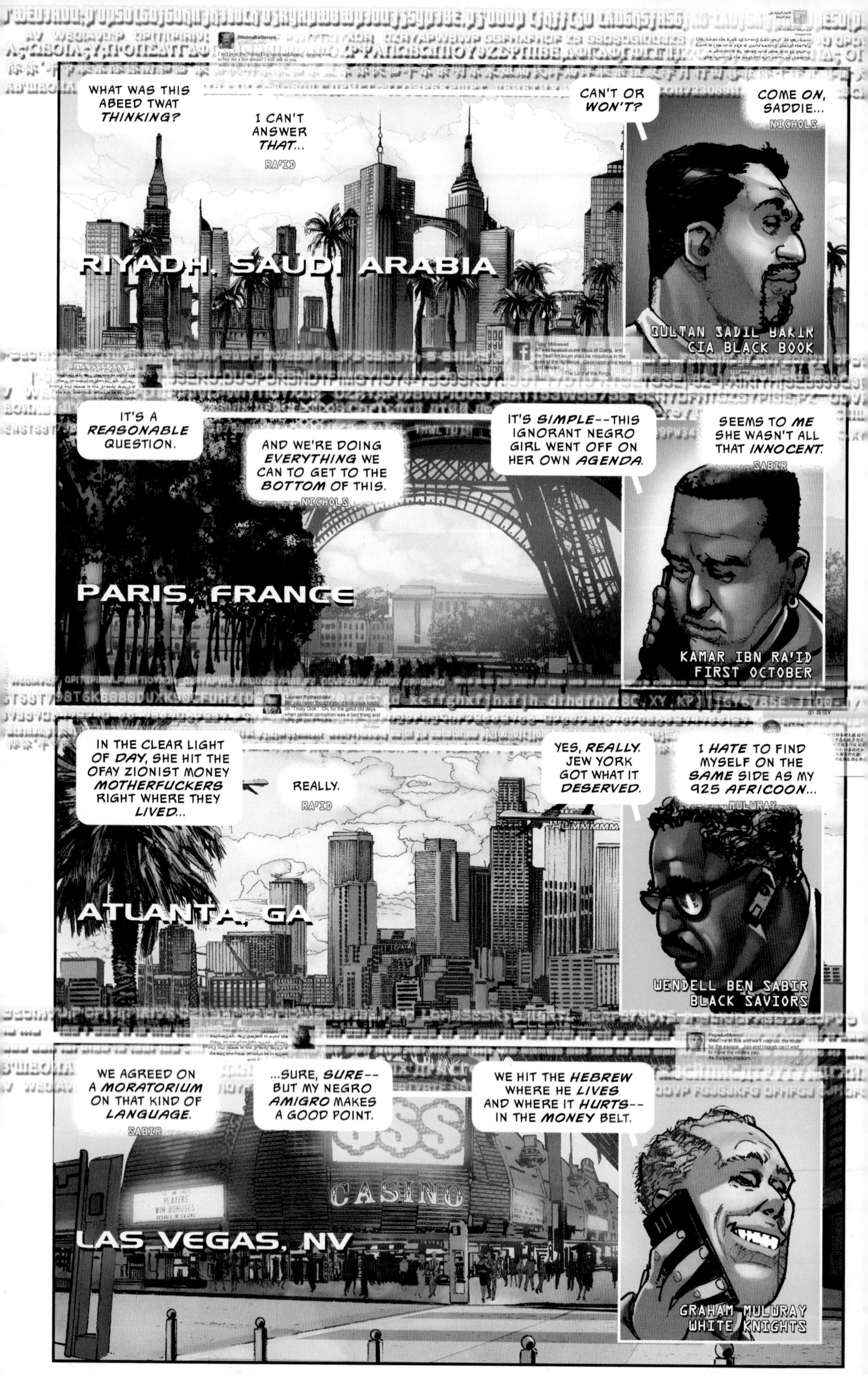
WHAT WAS THIS ABEED TWAT THINKING?
I CAN'T ANSWER THAT...
RA'ID
CAN'T OR WON'T?
COME ON, SADDIE...
NICHOLS
RIYADH, SAUDI ARABIA
SULTAN SADIL BAKIR
CIA BLACK BOOK
IT'S A REASONABLE QUESTION.
AND WE'RE DOING EVERYTHING WE CAN TO GET TO THE BOTTOM OF THIS.
NICHOLS
IT'S SIMPLE--THIS IGNORANT NEGRO GIRL WENT OFF ON HER OWN AGENDA.
SEEMS TO ME SHE WASN'T ALL THAT INNOCENT.
SABIR
PARIS, FRANCE
KAMAR IBN RA'ID
FIRST OCTOBER
IN THE CLEAR LIGHT OF DAY, SHE HIT THE OFAY ZIONIST MONEY MOTHERFUCKERS RIGHT WHERE THEY LIVED...
REALLY.
RA'ID
YES, REALLY. JEW YORK GOT WHAT IT DESERVED.
I HATE TO FIND MYSELF ON THE SAME SIDE AS MY 925 AFRICOON...
MULURAY
HMMMMM
ATLANTA, GA
WENDELL BEN SABIR
BLACK SAVIORS
WE AGREED ON A MORATORIUM ON THAT KIND OF LANGUAGE.
SABIR
...SURE, SURE--BUT MY NEGRO AMIGRO MAKES A GOOD POINT.
WE HIT THE HEBREW WHERE HE LIVES AND WHERE IT HURTS--IN THE MONEY BELT.
CASINO
PLAYERS WIN BONUSES
LAS VEGAS, NV
GRAHAM MULURAY
WHITE KNIGHTS

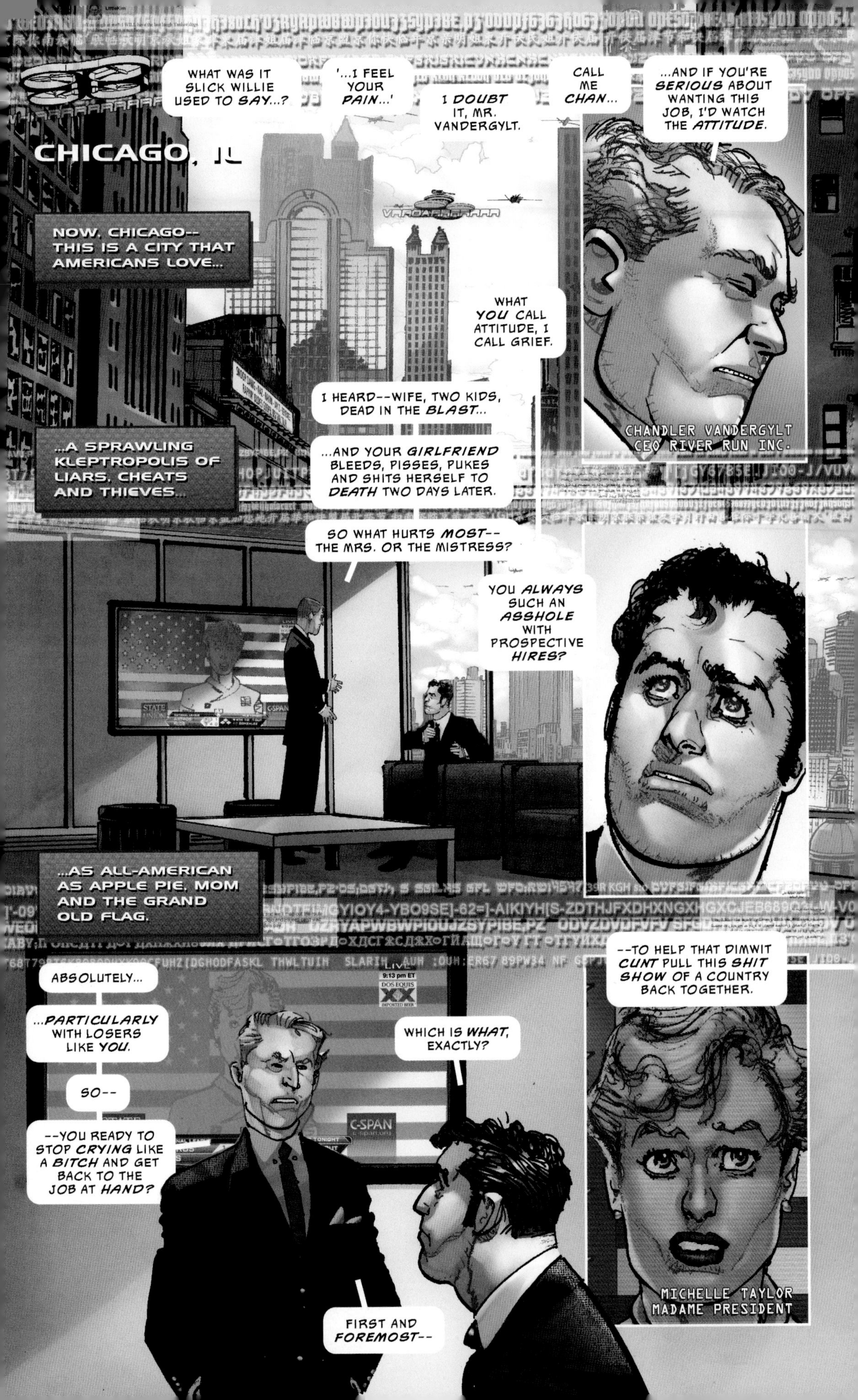
CHICAGO, IL
NOW, CHICAGO-- THIS IS A CITY THAT AMERICANS LOVE...
WHAT WAS IT SLICK WILLIE USED TO SAY...?
'...I FEEL YOUR PAIN...'
I DOUBT IT, MR. VANDERGYLT.
CALL ME CHAN...
...AND IF YOU'RE SERIOUS ABOUT WANTING THIS JOB, I'D WATCH THE ATTITUDE.
WHAT YOU CALL ATTITUDE, I CALL GRIEF.
CHANDLER VANDERGYLT
CEO RIVER RUN INC.
...A SPRAWLING KLEPTROPOLIS OF LIARS, CHEATS AND THIEVES...
I HEARD--WIFE, TWO KIDS, DEAD IN THE BLAST...
...AND YOUR GIRLFRIEND BLEEDS, PISSES, PUKES AND SHITS HERSELF TO DEATH TWO DAYS LATER.
SO WHAT HURTS MOST-- THE MRS. OR THE MISTRESS?
YOU ALWAYS SUCH AN ASSHOLE WITH PROSPECTIVE HIRES?
...AS ALL-AMERICAN AS APPLE PIE, MOM AND THE GRAND OLD FLAG.
LIVE
9:13 pm ET
DOS EQUIS XX
C-SPAN
ABSOLUTELY...
...PARTICULARLY WITH LOSERS LIKE YOU.
SO--
--YOU READY TO STOP CRYING LIKE A BITCH AND GET BACK TO THE JOB AT HAND?
WHICH IS WHAT, EXACTLY?
FIRST AND FOREMOST--
--TO HELP THAT DIMWIT CUNT PULL THIS SHIT SHOW OF A COUNTRY BACK TOGETHER.
MICHELLE TAYLOR
MADAME PRESIDENT

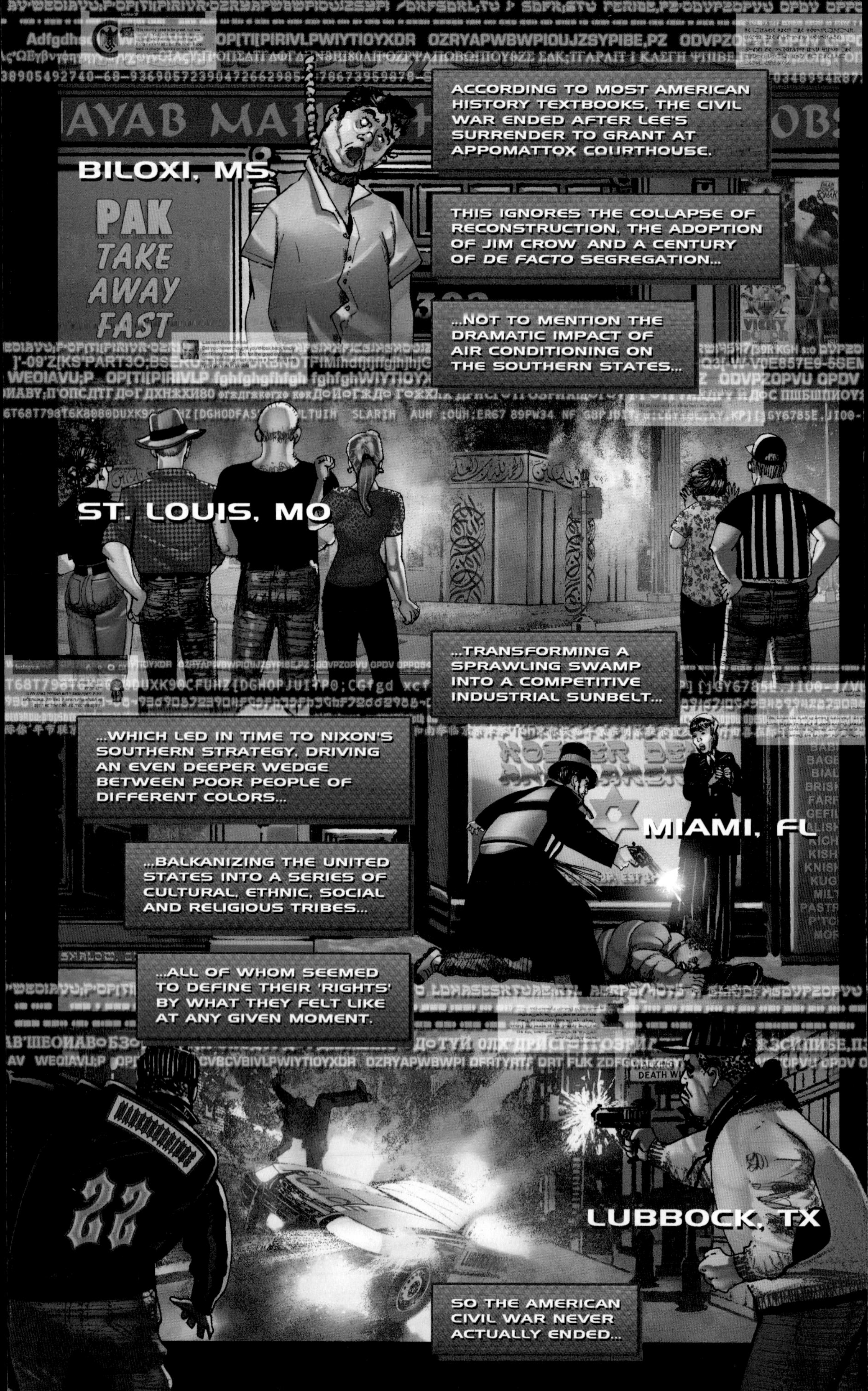
BILOXI, MS
ACCORDING TO MOST AMERICAN HISTORY TEXTBOOKS, THE CIVIL WAR ENDED AFTER LEE'S SURRENDER TO GRANT AT APPOMATTOX COURTHOUSE.
THIS IGNORES THE COLLAPSE OF RECONSTRUCTION, THE ADOPTION OF JIM CROW AND A CENTURY OF *DE FACTO* SEGREGATION...
...NOT TO MENTION THE DRAMATIC IMPACT OF AIR CONDITIONING ON THE SOUTHERN STATES...
PAK TAKE AWAY FAST
ST. LOUIS, MO
...TRANSFORMING A SPRAWLING SWAMP INTO A COMPETITIVE INDUSTRIAL SUNBELT...
...WHICH LED IN TIME TO NIXON'S SOUTHERN STRATEGY, DRIVING AN EVEN DEEPER WEDGE BETWEEN POOR PEOPLE OF DIFFERENT COLORS...
MIAMI, FL
...BALKANIZING THE UNITED STATES INTO A SERIES OF CULTURAL, ETHNIC, SOCIAL AND RELIGIOUS TRIBES...
...ALL OF WHOM SEEMED TO DEFINE THEIR 'RIGHTS' BY WHAT THEY FELT LIKE AT ANY GIVEN MOMENT.
LUBBOCK, TX
SO THE AMERICAN CIVIL WAR NEVER ACTUALLY ENDED...

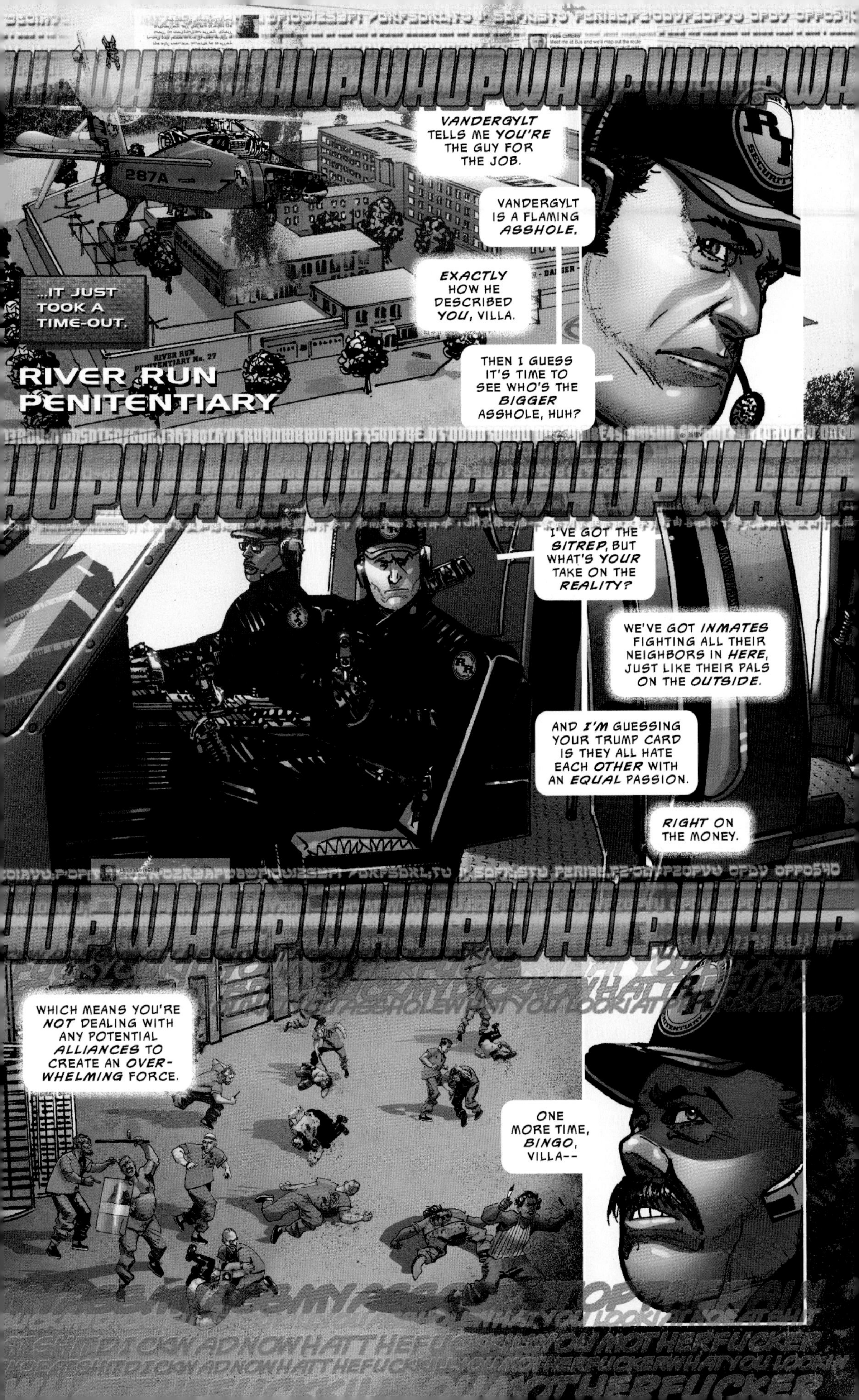
...IT JUST TOOK A TIME-OUT.
RIVER RUN PENITENTIARY
287A
RIVER RUN PENITENTIARY No. 27
VANDERGYLT TELLS ME YOU'RE THE GUY FOR THE JOB.
VANDERGYLT IS A FLAMING ASSHOLE.
EXACTLY HOW HE DESCRIBED YOU, VILLA.
THEN I GUESS IT'S TIME TO SEE WHO'S THE BIGGER ASSHOLE, HUH?
I'VE GOT THE SITREP, BUT WHAT'S YOUR TAKE ON THE REALITY?
WE'VE GOT INMATES FIGHTING ALL THEIR NEIGHBORS IN HERE, JUST LIKE THEIR PALS ON THE OUTSIDE.
AND I'M GUESSING YOUR TRUMP CARD IS THEY ALL HATE EACH OTHER WITH AN EQUAL PASSION.
RIGHT ON THE MONEY.
WHICH MEANS YOU'RE NOT DEALING WITH ANY POTENTIAL ALLIANCES TO CREATE AN OVER-WHELMING FORCE.
ONE MORE TIME, BINGO, VILLA--

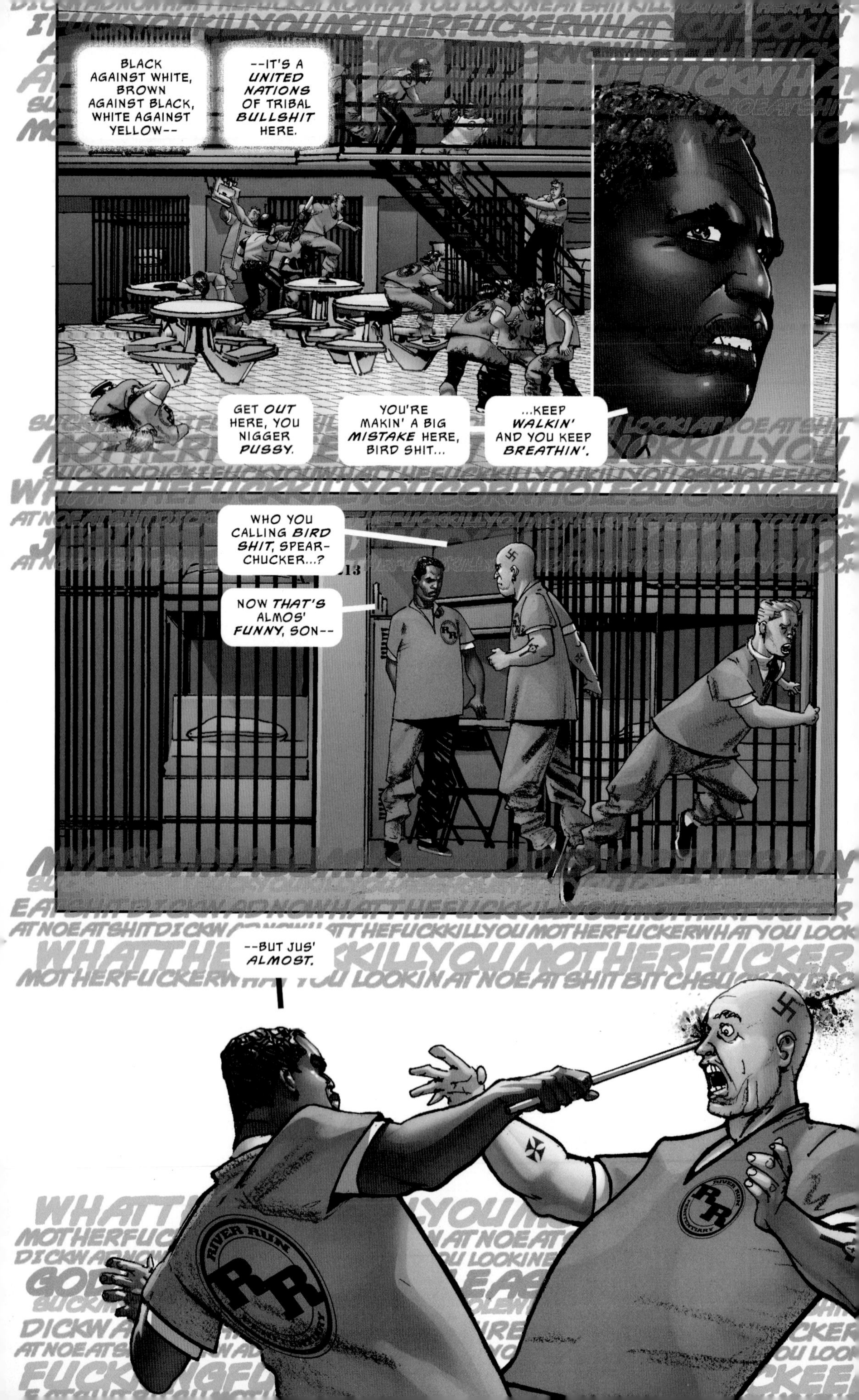
BLACK AGAINST WHITE, BROWN AGAINST BLACK, WHITE AGAINST YELLOW--
--IT'S A UNITED NATIONS OF TRIBAL BULLSHIT HERE.
GET OUT HERE, YOU NIGGER PUSSY.
YOU'RE MAKIN' A BIG MISTAKE HERE, BIRD SHIT...
...KEEP WALKIN' AND YOU KEEP BREATHIN'.
WHO YOU CALLING BIRD SHIT, SPEAR-CHUCKER...?
NOW THAT'S ALMOS' FUNNY, SON--
--BUT JUS' ALMOST.

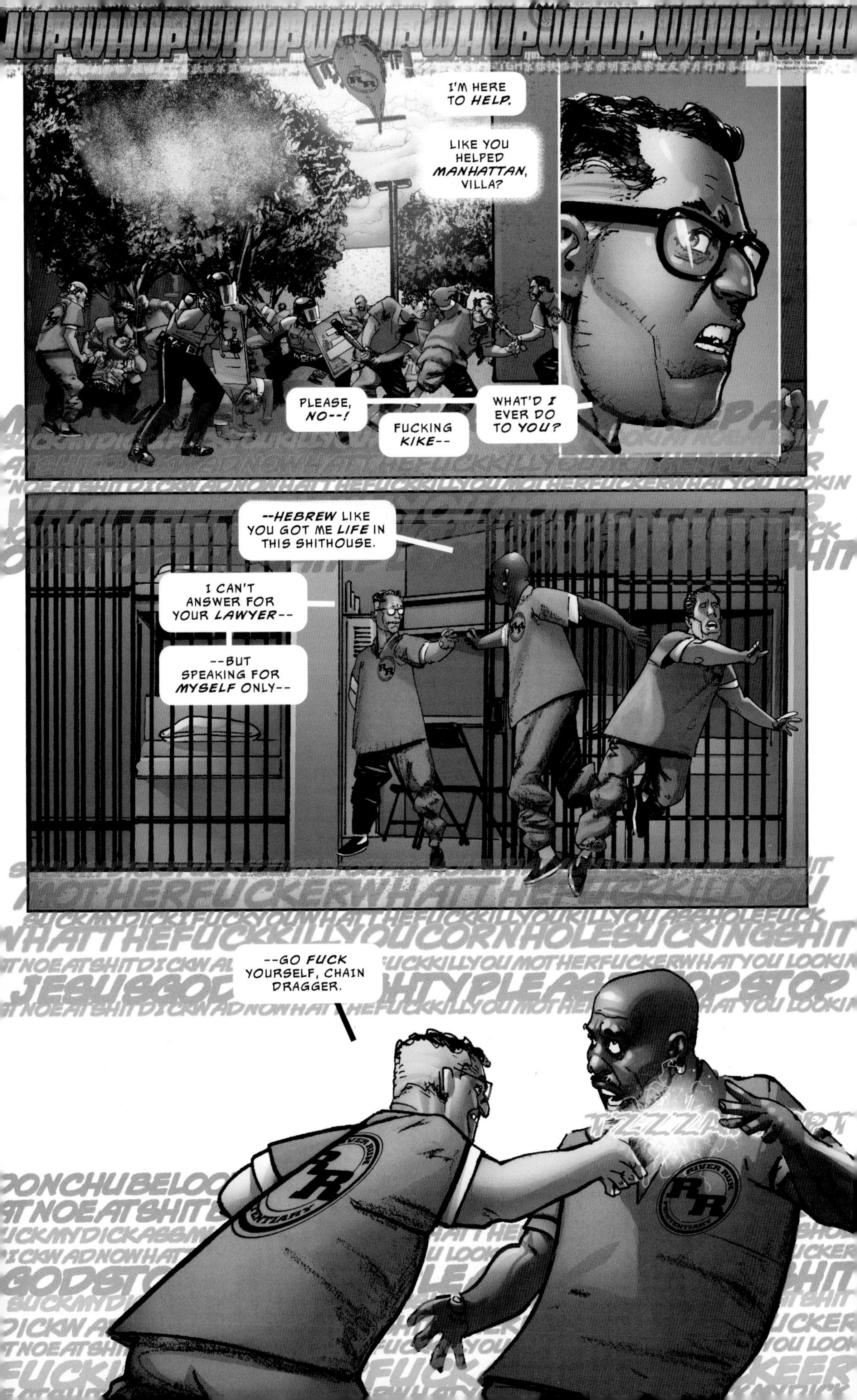
I'M HERE TO HELP.
LIKE YOU HELPED MANHATTAN, VILLA?
PLEASE, NO--!
FUCKING KIKE--
WHAT'D I EVER DO TO YOU?
--HEBREW LIKE YOU GOT ME LIFE IN THIS SHITHOUSE.
I CAN'T ANSWER FOR YOUR LAWYER--
--BUT SPEAKING FOR MYSELF ONLY--
--GO FUCK YOURSELF, CHAIN DRAGGER.

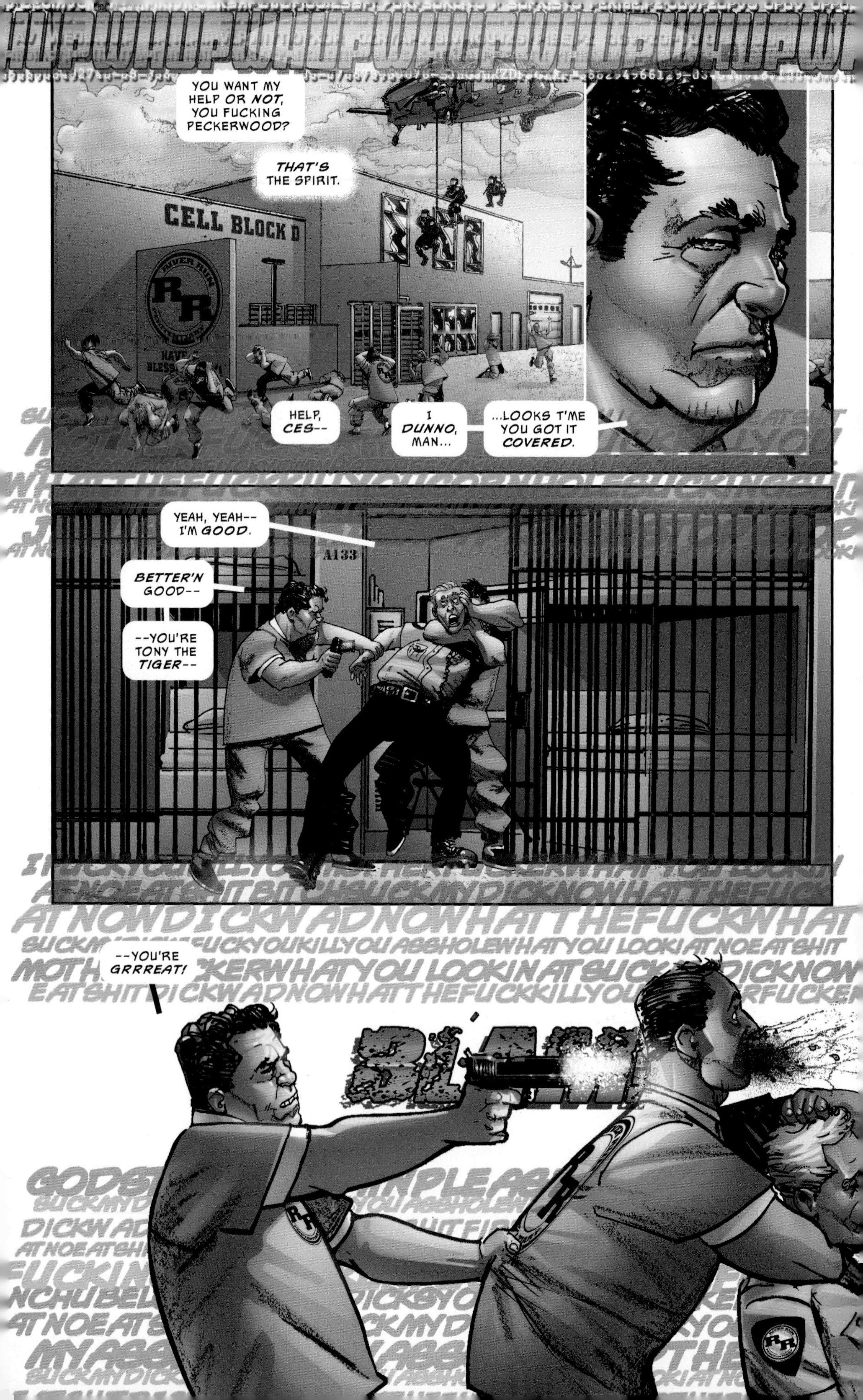
YOU WANT MY HELP OR NOT, YOU FUCKING PECKERWOOD?
THAT'S THE SPIRIT.
CELL BLOCK D
HELP, CES--
I DUNNO, MAN...
...LOOKS T'ME YOU GOT IT COVERED.
YEAH, YEAH-- I'M GOOD.
A133
BETTER'N GOOD--
--YOU'RE TONY THE TIGER--
--YOU'RE GRRREAT!

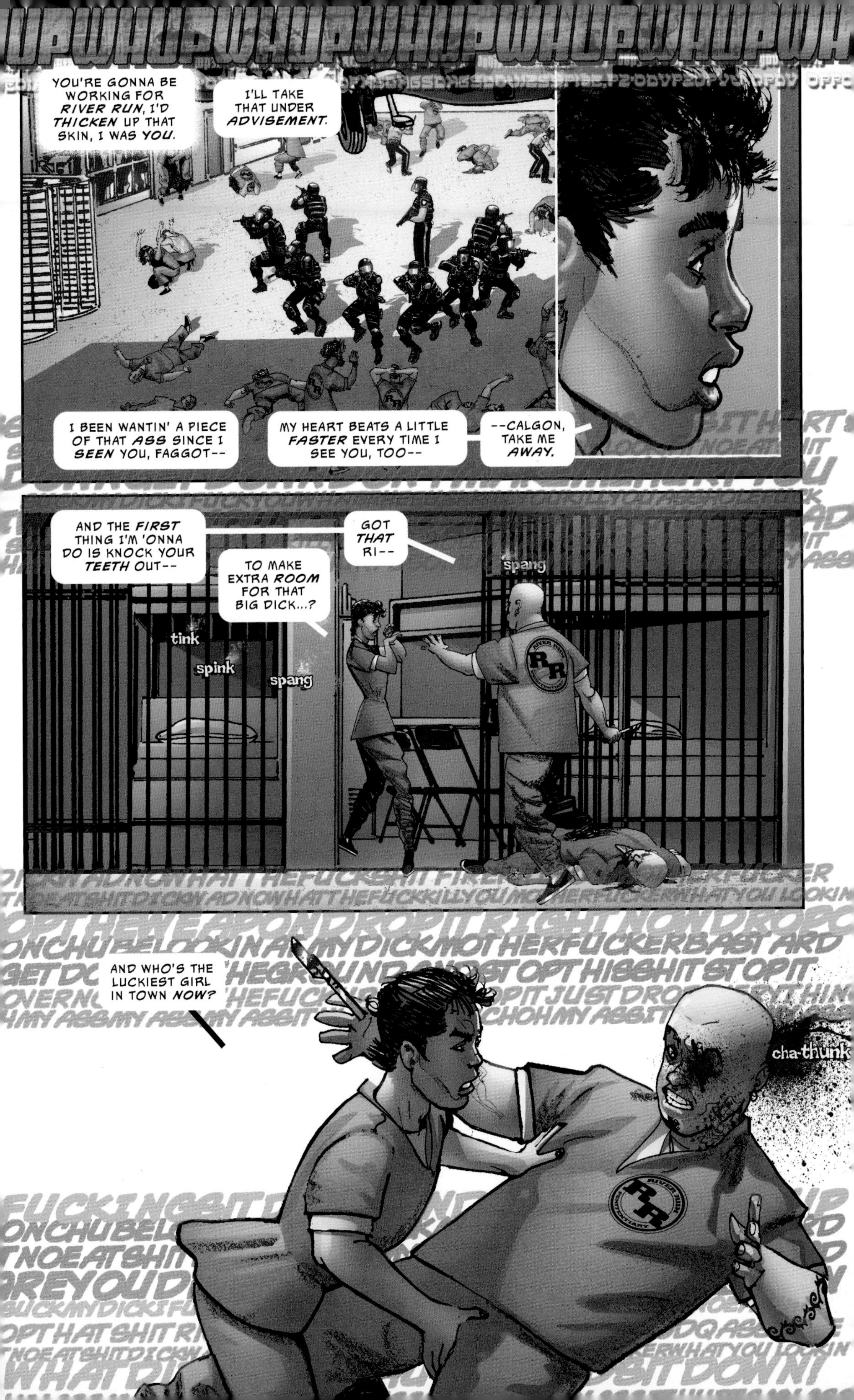
YOU'RE GONNA BE WORKING FOR RIVER RUN, I'D THICKEN UP THAT SKIN, I WAS YOU.
I'LL TAKE THAT UNDER ADVISEMENT.
I BEEN WANTIN' A PIECE OF THAT ASS SINCE I SEEN YOU, FAGGOT--
MY HEART BEATS A LITTLE FASTER EVERY TIME I SEE YOU, TOO--
--CALGON, TAKE ME AWAY.
AND THE FIRST THING I'M 'ONNA DO IS KNOCK YOUR TEETH OUT--
GOT THAT RI--
TO MAKE EXTRA ROOM FOR THAT BIG DICK...?
spang
tink
spink
spang
AND WHO'S THE LUCKIEST GIRL IN TOWN NOW?
cha-thunk

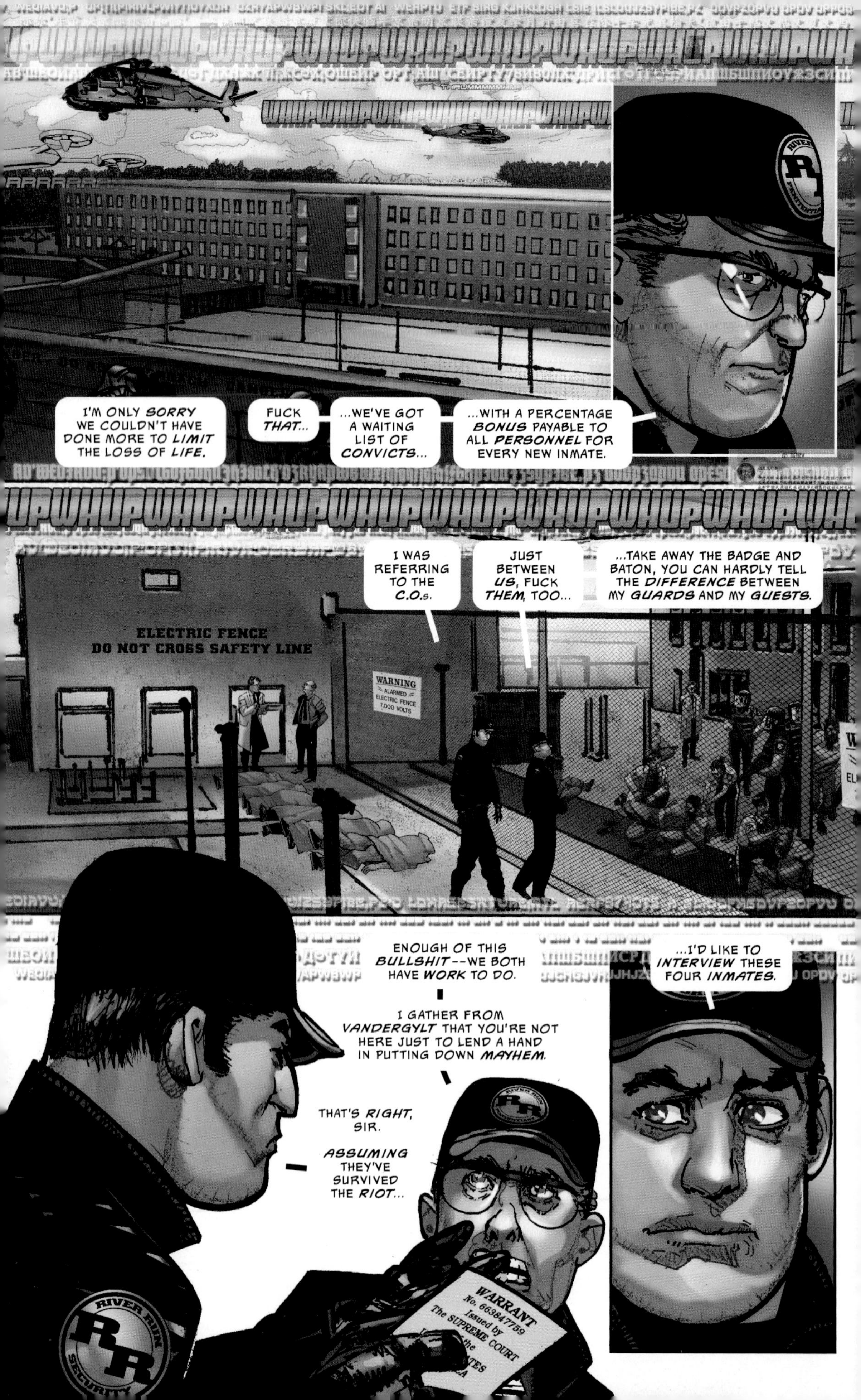
I'M ONLY SORRY WE COULDN'T HAVE DONE MORE TO LIMIT THE LOSS OF LIFE.
FUCK THAT...
...WE'VE GOT A WAITING LIST OF CONVICTS...
...WITH A PERCENTAGE BONUS PAYABLE TO ALL PERSONNEL FOR EVERY NEW INMATE.
I WAS REFERRING TO THE C.O.s.
JUST BETWEEN US, FUCK THEM, TOO...
...TAKE AWAY THE BADGE AND BATON, YOU CAN HARDLY TELL THE DIFFERENCE BETWEEN MY GUARDS AND MY GUESTS.
ELECTRIC FENCE
DO NOT CROSS SAFETY LINE
WARNING
ALARMED
ELECTRIC FENCE
7,000 VOLTS
ENOUGH OF THIS BULLSHIT--WE BOTH HAVE WORK TO DO.
I GATHER FROM VANDERGYLT THAT YOU'RE NOT HERE JUST TO LEND A HAND IN PUTTING DOWN MAYHEM.
THAT'S RIGHT, SIR.
ASSUMING THEY'VE SURVIVED THE RIOT...
...I'D LIKE TO INTERVIEW THESE FOUR INMATES.
WARRANT
No. 663847759
Issued by
The SUPREME COURT
RIVER RUN
SECURITY

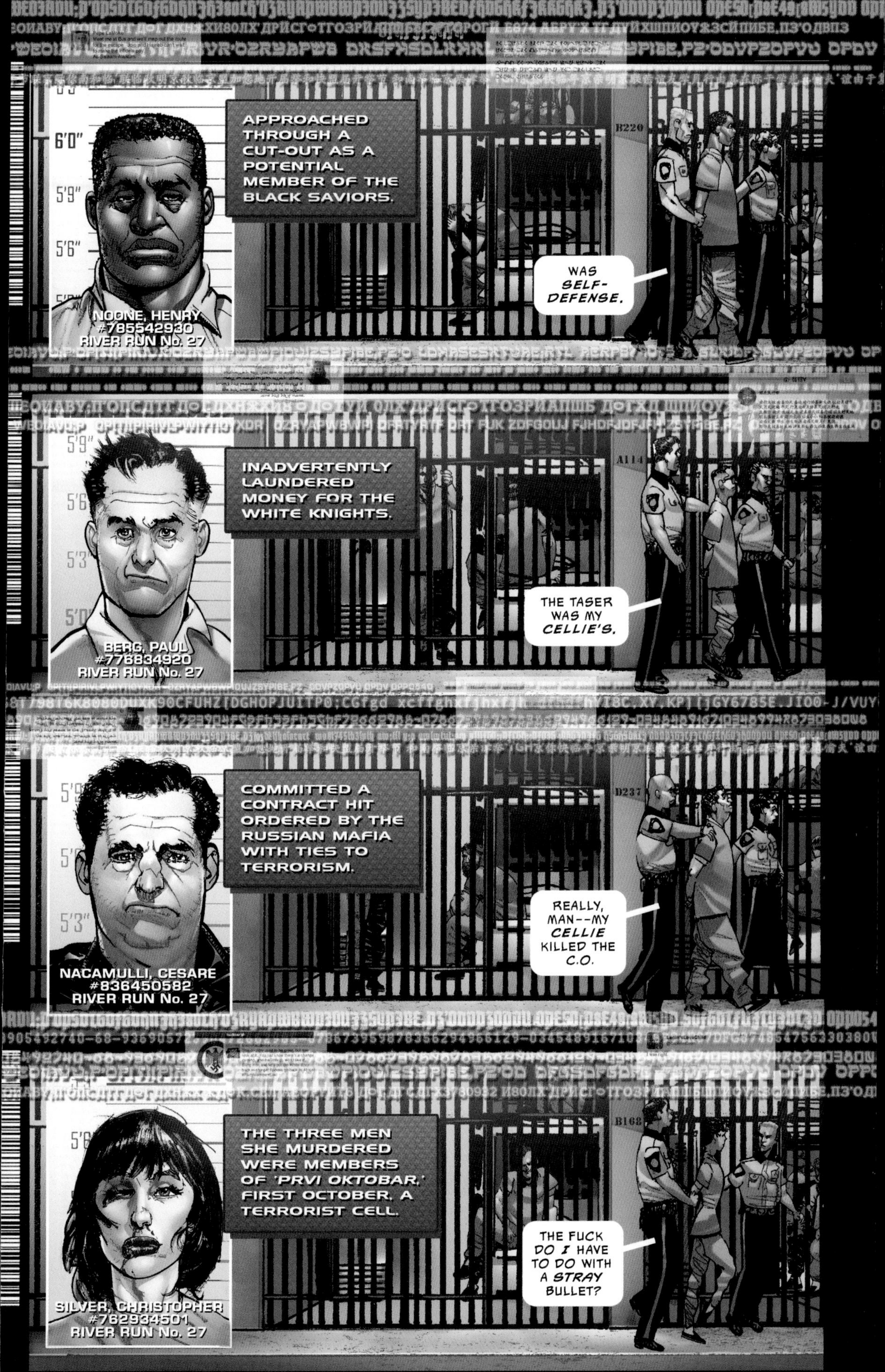

NOONE, HENRY
#785542930
RIVER RUN No. 27
APPROACHED THROUGH A CUT-OUT AS A POTENTIAL MEMBER OF THE BLACK SAVIORS.
WAS SELF-DEFENSE.
BERG, PAUL
#776834920
RIVER RUN No. 27
INADVERTENTLY LAUNDERED MONEY FOR THE WHITE KNIGHTS.
THE TASER WAS MY CELLIE'S.
NACAMULLI, CESARE
#836450582
RIVER RUN No. 27
COMMITTED A CONTRACT HIT ORDERED BY THE RUSSIAN MAFIA WITH TIES TO TERRORISM.
REALLY, MAN--MY CELLIE KILLED THE C.O.
SILVER, CHRISTOPHER
#762934501
RIVER RUN No. 27
THE THREE MEN SHE MURDERED WERE MEMBERS OF 'PRVI OKTOBAR,' FIRST OCTOBER, A TERRORIST CELL.
THE FUCK DO I HAVE TO DO WITH A STRAY BULLET?

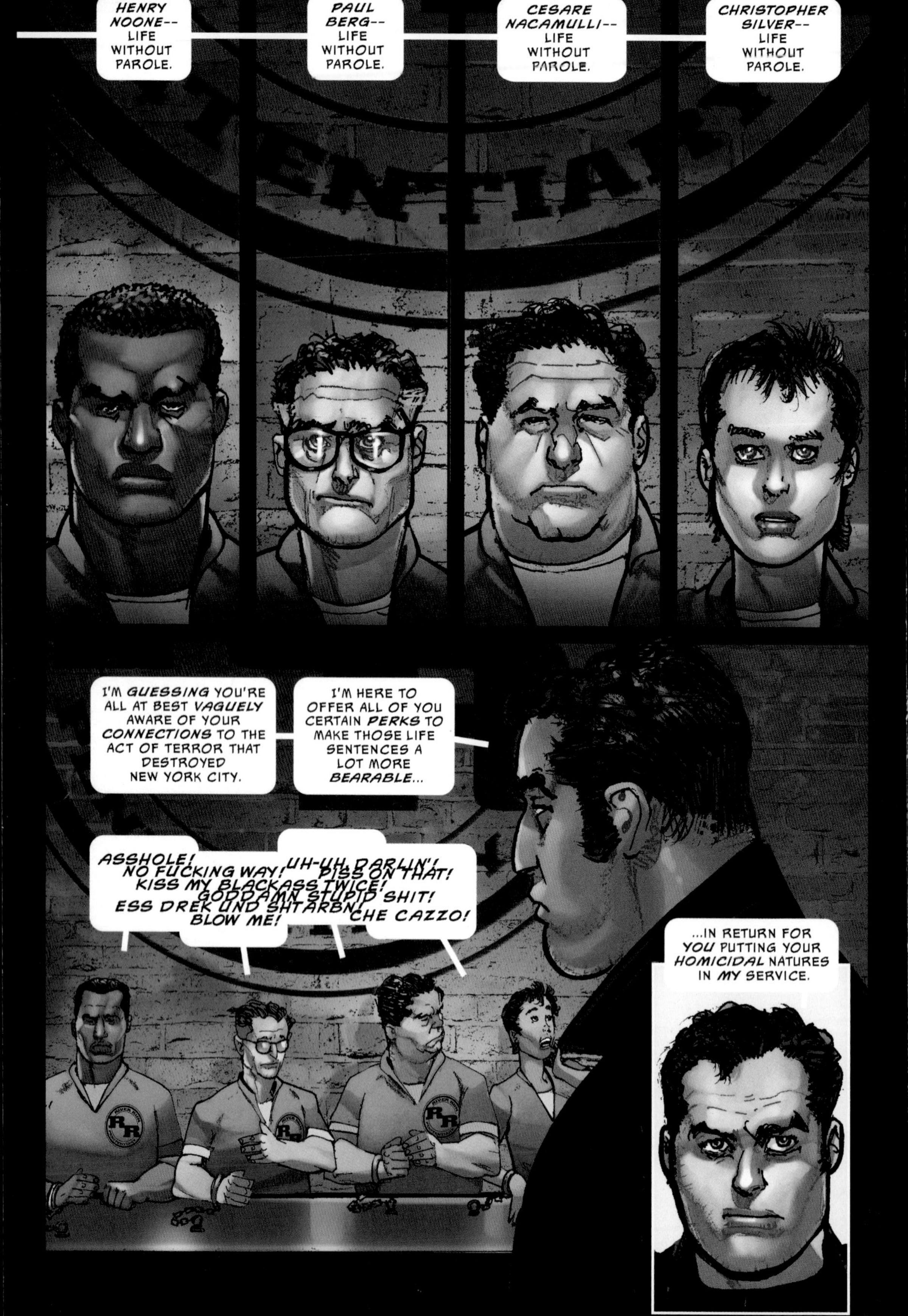
HENRY NOONE-- LIFE WITHOUT PAROLE.
PAUL BERG-- LIFE WITHOUT PAROLE.
CESARE NACAMULLI-- LIFE WITHOUT PAROLE.
CHRISTOPHER SILVER-- LIFE WITHOUT PAROLE.
I'M GUESSING YOU'RE ALL AT BEST VAGUELY AWARE OF YOUR CONNECTIONS TO THE ACT OF TERROR THAT DESTROYED NEW YORK CITY.
I'M HERE TO OFFER ALL OF YOU CERTAIN PERKS TO MAKE THOSE LIFE SENTENCES A LOT MORE BEARABLE...
ASSHOLE! NO FUCKING WAY! KISS MY BLACKASS TWICE! ESS DREK UND SHTARBN! BLOW ME!
UH-UH, DARLIN'! PISS ON THAT! GODDAMN STUPID SHIT! CHE CAZZO!
...IN RETURN FOR YOU PUTTING YOUR HOMICIDAL NATURES IN MY SERVICE.

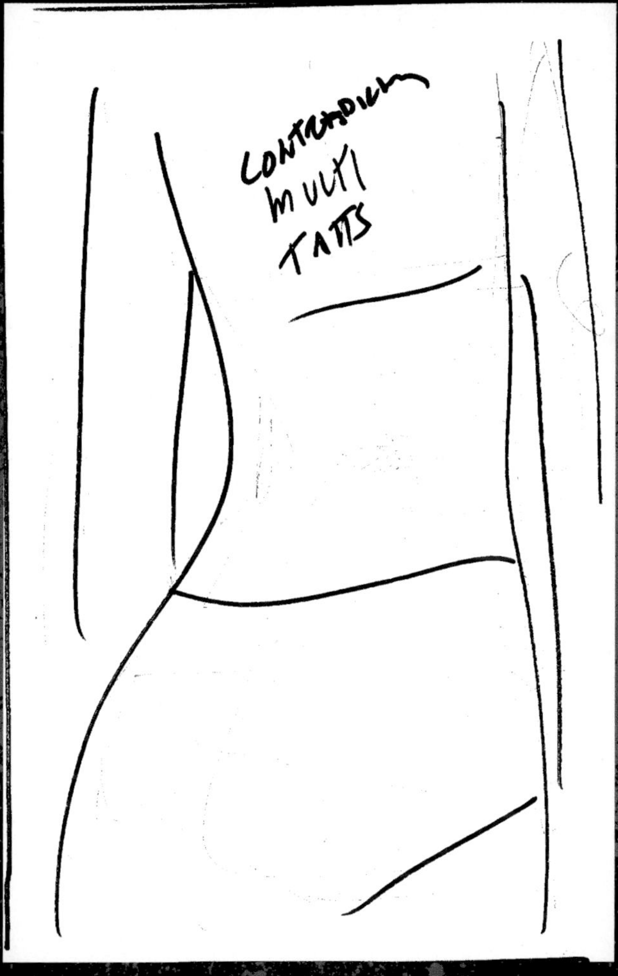
MULTI
TATTS

Part Three

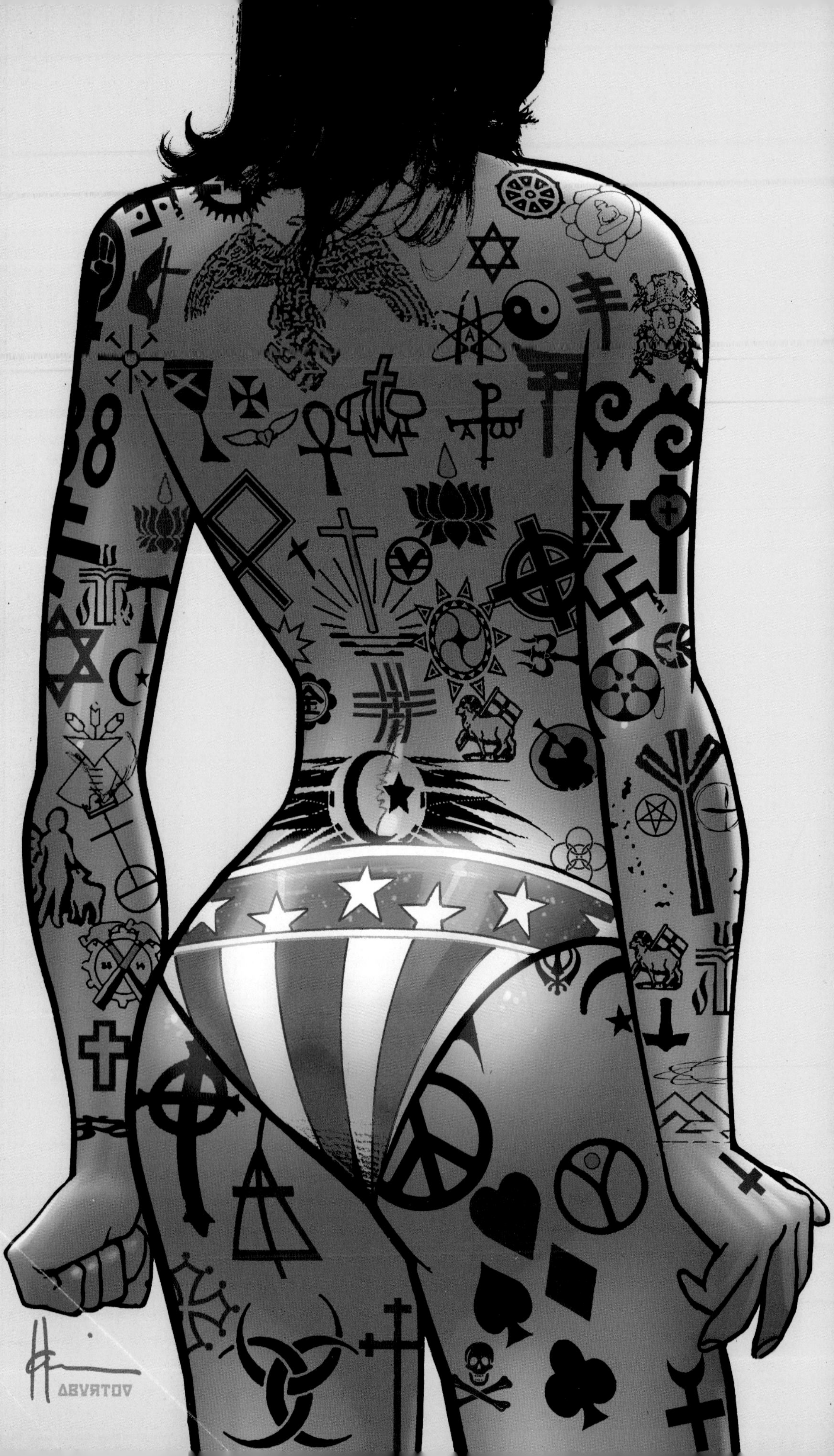

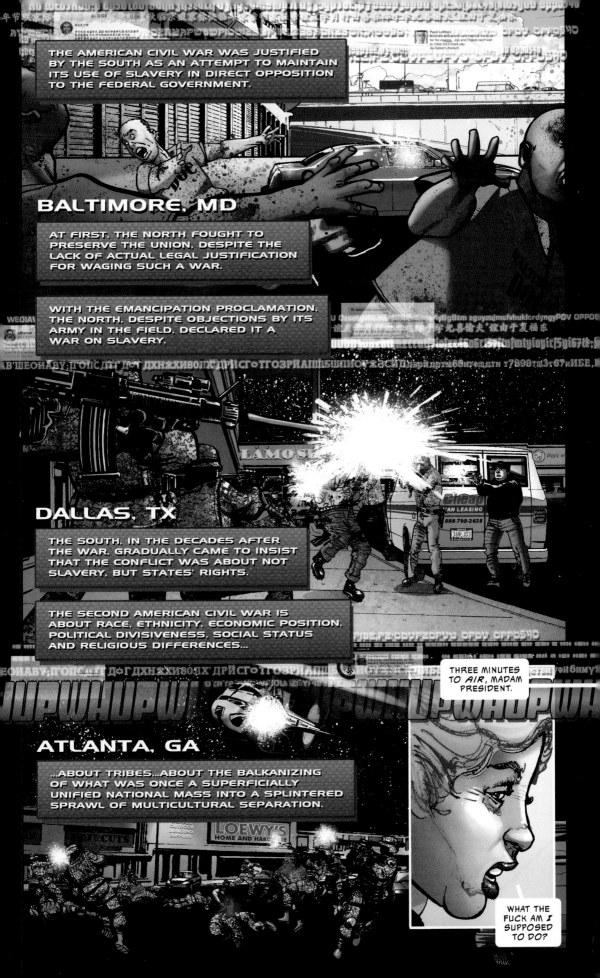

THE AMERICAN CIVIL WAR WAS JUSTIFIED BY THE SOUTH AS AN ATTEMPT TO MAINTAIN ITS USE OF SLAVERY IN DIRECT OPPOSITION TO THE FEDERAL GOVERNMENT.

BALTIMORE, MD

AT FIRST, THE NORTH FOUGHT TO PRESERVE THE UNION, DESPITE THE LACK OF ACTUAL LEGAL JUSTIFICATION FOR WAGING SUCH A WAR.

WITH THE EMANCIPATION PROCLAMATION, THE NORTH, DESPITE OBJECTIONS BY ITS ARMY IN THE FIELD, DECLARED IT A WAR ON SLAVERY.

DALLAS, TX

THE SOUTH, IN THE DECADES AFTER THE WAR, GRADUALLY CAME TO INSIST THAT THE CONFLICT WAS ABOUT NOT SLAVERY, BUT STATES' RIGHTS.

THE SECOND AMERICAN CIVIL WAR IS ABOUT RACE, ETHNICITY, ECONOMIC POSITION, POLITICAL DIVISIVENESS, SOCIAL STATUS AND RELIGIOUS DIFFERENCES...

THREE MINUTES TO *AIR*, MADAM PRESIDENT.

ATLANTA, GA

...ABOUT TRIBES...ABOUT THE BALKANIZING OF WHAT WAS ONCE A SUPERFICIALLY UNIFIED NATIONAL MASS INTO A SPLINTERED SPRAWL OF MULTICULTURAL SEPARATION.

WHAT THE FUCK AM *I* SUPPOSED TO DO?

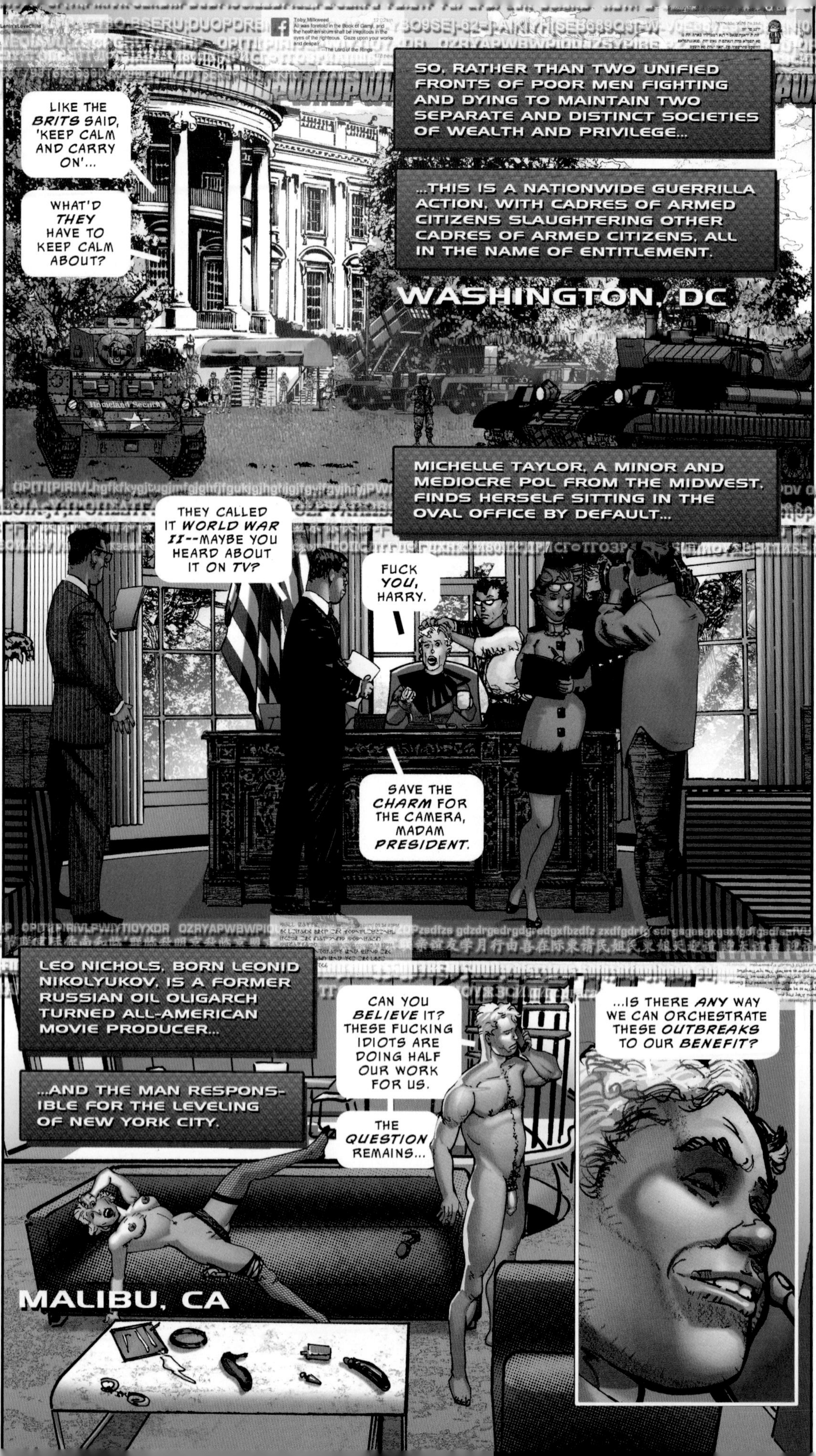
SO, RATHER THAN TWO UNIFIED FRONTS OF POOR MEN FIGHTING AND DYING TO MAINTAIN TWO SEPARATE AND DISTINCT SOCIETIES OF WEALTH AND PRIVILEGE...
...THIS IS A NATIONWIDE GUERRILLA ACTION, WITH CADRES OF ARMED CITIZENS SLAUGHTERING OTHER CADRES OF ARMED CITIZENS, ALL IN THE NAME OF ENTITLEMENT.
WASHINGTON, DC
LIKE THE BRITS SAID, 'KEEP CALM AND CARRY ON'...
WHAT'D THEY HAVE TO KEEP CALM ABOUT?
Homeland Security
MICHELLE TAYLOR, A MINOR AND MEDIOCRE POL FROM THE MIDWEST, FINDS HERSELF SITTING IN THE OVAL OFFICE BY DEFAULT...
THEY CALLED IT WORLD WAR II--MAYBE YOU HEARD ABOUT IT ON TV?
FUCK YOU, HARRY.
SAVE THE CHARM FOR THE CAMERA, MADAM PRESIDENT.
LEO NICHOLS, BORN LEONID NIKOLYUKOV, IS A FORMER RUSSIAN OIL OLIGARCH TURNED ALL-AMERICAN MOVIE PRODUCER...
...AND THE MAN RESPONSIBLE FOR THE LEVELING OF NEW YORK CITY.
MALIBU, CA
CAN YOU BELIEVE IT? THESE FUCKING IDIOTS ARE DOING HALF OUR WORK FOR US.
THE QUESTION REMAINS...
...IS THERE ANY WAY WE CAN ORCHESTRATE THESE OUTBREAKS TO OUR BENEFIT?

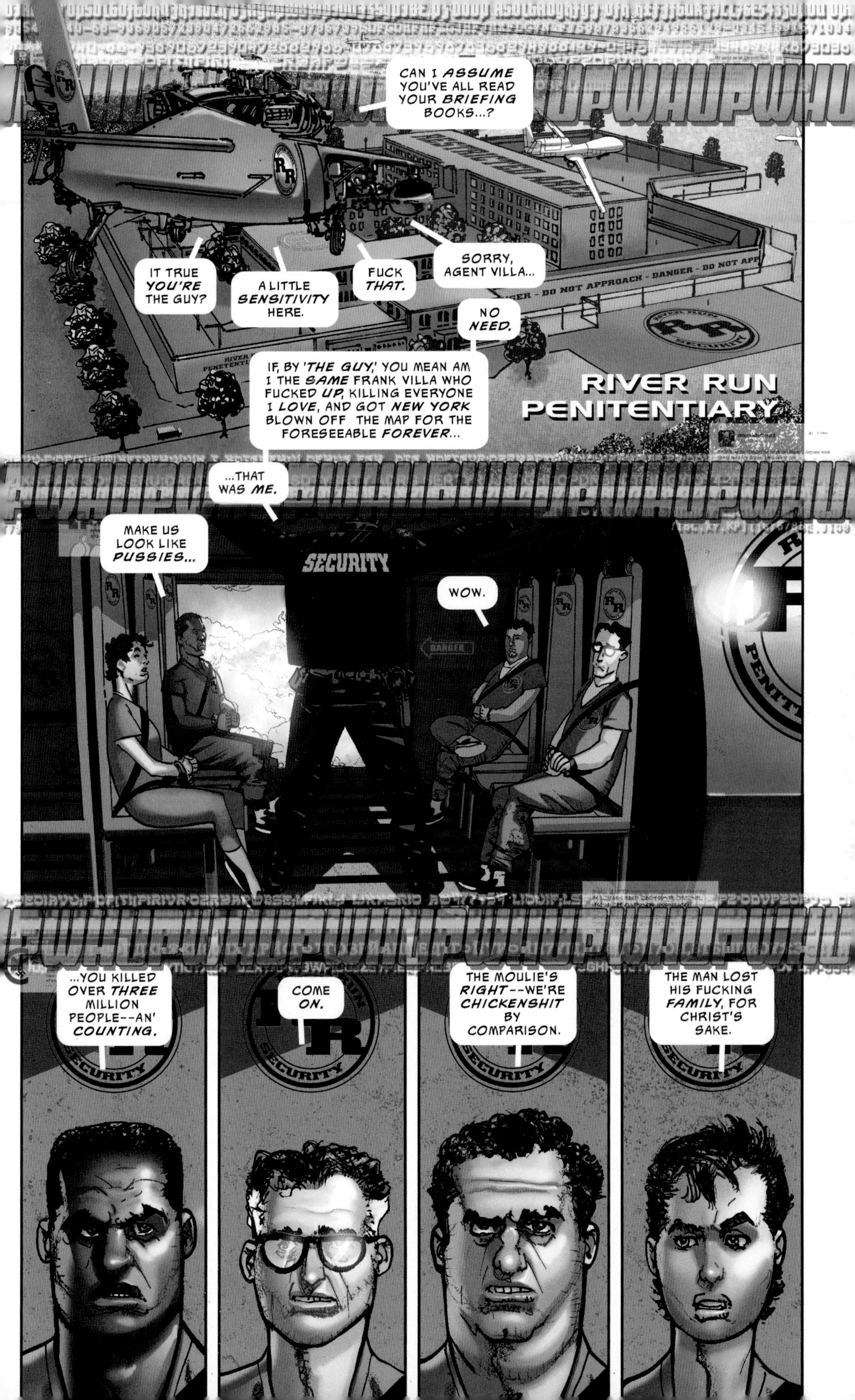
CAN I ASSUME YOU'VE ALL READ YOUR BRIEFING BOOKS...?
IT TRUE YOU'RE THE GUY?
A LITTLE SENSITIVITY HERE.
FUCK THAT.
SORRY, AGENT VILLA...
NO NEED.
IF, BY 'THE GUY,' YOU MEAN AM I THE SAME FRANK VILLA WHO FUCKED UP, KILLING EVERYONE I LOVE, AND GOT NEW YORK BLOWN OFF THE MAP FOR THE FORESEEABLE FOREVER...
RIVER RUN PENITENTIARY
DANGER - DO NOT APPROACH - DANGER - DO NOT APP
...THAT WAS ME.
MAKE US LOOK LIKE PUSSIES...
SECURITY
WOW.
DANGER
...YOU KILLED OVER THREE MILLION PEOPLE--AN' COUNTING.
COME ON.
THE MOULIE'S RIGHT--WE'RE CHICKENSHIT BY COMPARISON.
THE MAN LOST HIS FUCKING FAMILY, FOR CHRIST'S SAKE.

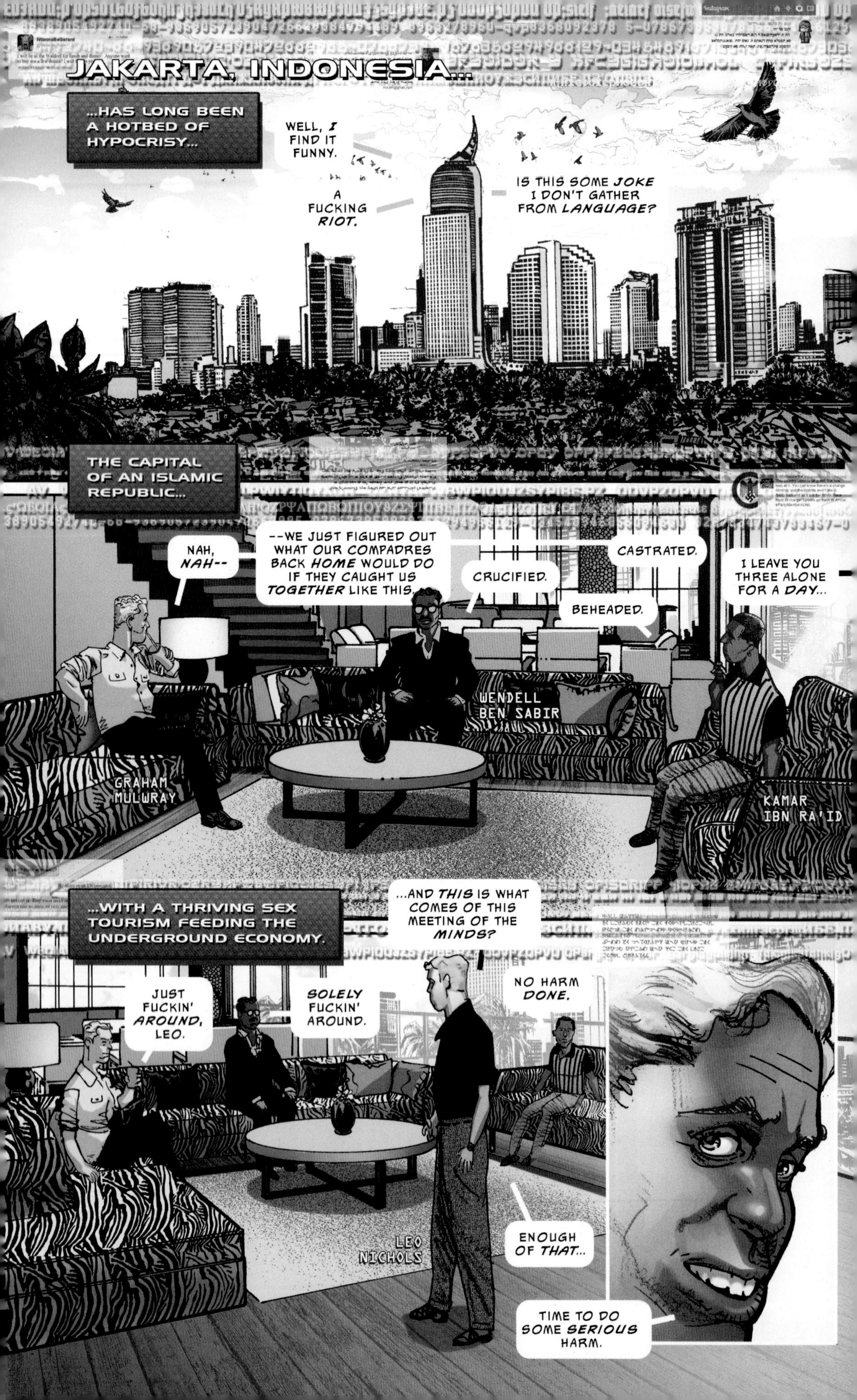
JAKARTA, INDONESIA...
...HAS LONG BEEN A HOTBED OF HYPOCRISY...
WELL, *I* FIND IT FUNNY.
A FUCKING *RIOT.*
IS THIS SOME *JOKE* I DON'T GATHER FROM *LANGUAGE?*
THE CAPITAL OF AN ISLAMIC REPUBLIC...
NAH, *NAH*--
--WE JUST FIGURED OUT WHAT OUR COMPADRES BACK *HOME* WOULD DO IF THEY CAUGHT US *TOGETHER* LIKE THIS.
CRUCIFIED.
CASTRATED.
BEHEADED.
I LEAVE YOU THREE ALONE FOR A *DAY*...
GRAHAM MULWRAY
WENDELL BEN SABIR
KAMAR IBN RA'ID
...WITH A THRIVING SEX TOURISM FEEDING THE UNDERGROUND ECONOMY.
...AND *THIS* IS WHAT COMES OF THIS MEETING OF THE *MINDS?*
JUST FUCKIN' *AROUND,* LEO.
SOLELY FUCKIN' AROUND.
NO HARM *DONE.*
LEO NICHOLS
ENOUGH OF *THAT*...
TIME TO DO SOME *SERIOUS* HARM.

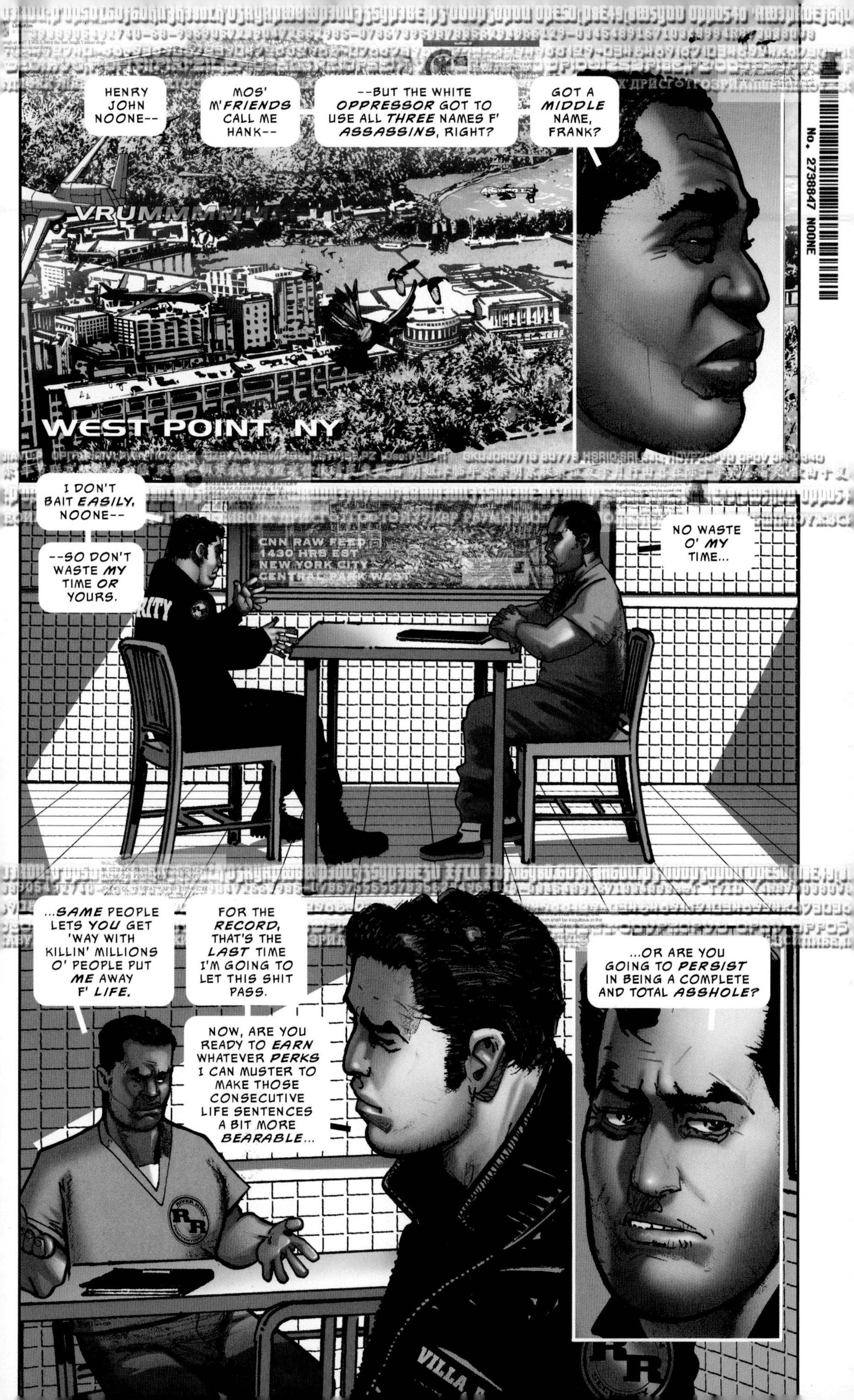

HENRY JOHN NOONE--
MOS' M'FRIENDS CALL ME HANK--
--BUT THE WHITE OPPRESSOR GOT TO USE ALL THREE NAMES F' ASSASSINS, RIGHT?
GOT A MIDDLE NAME, FRANK?
No. 2738847 NOONE
WEST POINT, NY
I DON'T BAIT EASILY, NOONE--
--SO DON'T WASTE MY TIME OR YOURS.
CNN RAW FEED
1430 HRS EST
NEW YORK CITY
CENTRAL PARK WEST
NO WASTE O' MY TIME...
...SAME PEOPLE LETS YOU GET 'WAY WITH KILLIN' MILLIONS O' PEOPLE PUT ME AWAY F' LIFE.
FOR THE RECORD, THAT'S THE LAST TIME I'M GOING TO LET THIS SHIT PASS.
NOW, ARE YOU READY TO EARN WHATEVER PERKS I CAN MUSTER TO MAKE THOSE CONSECUTIVE LIFE SENTENCES A BIT MORE BEARABLE...
...OR ARE YOU GOING TO PERSIST IN BEING A COMPLETE AND TOTAL ASSHOLE?

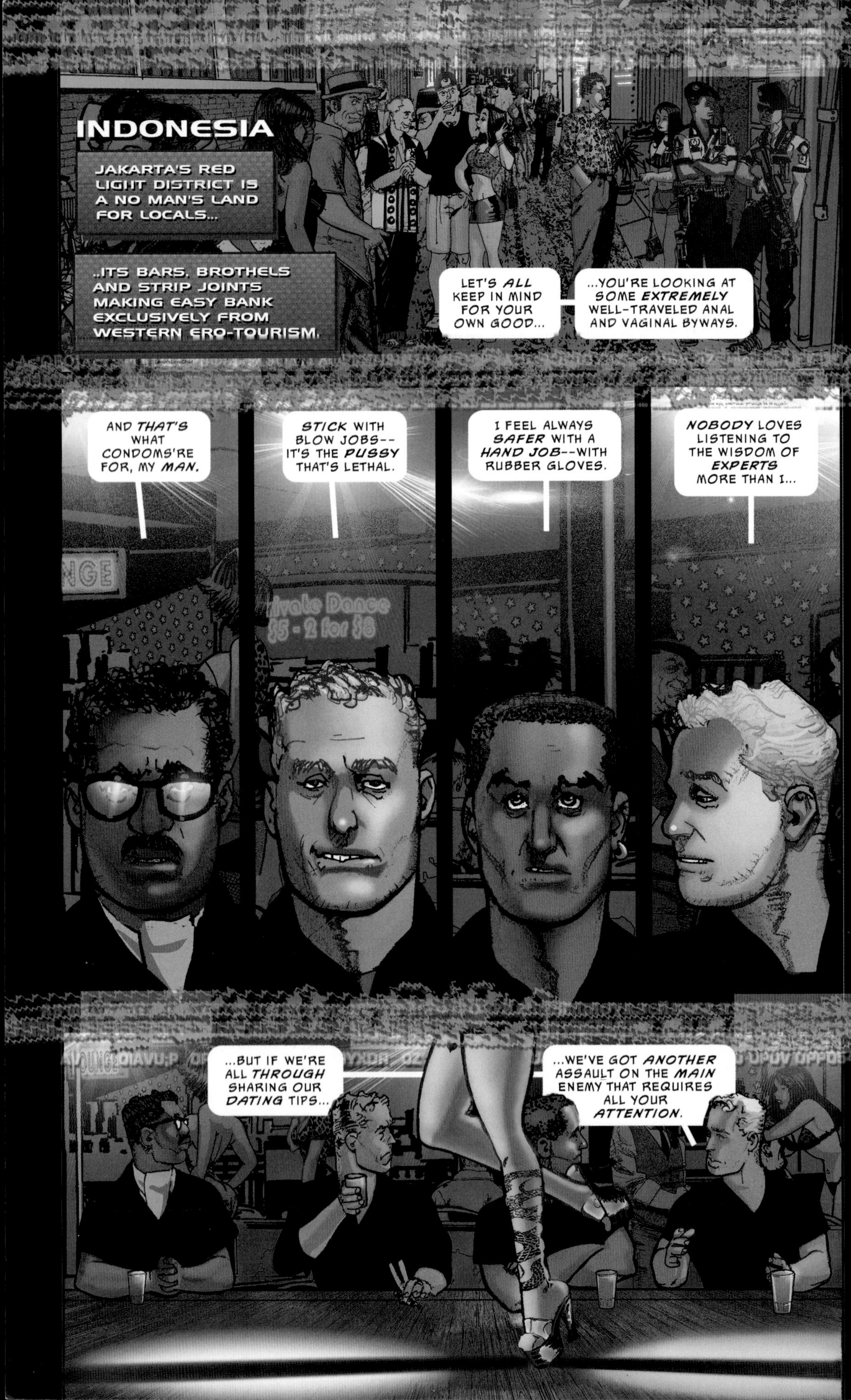
INDONESIA
JAKARTA'S RED LIGHT DISTRICT IS A NO MAN'S LAND FOR LOCALS...
..ITS BARS, BROTHELS AND STRIP JOINTS MAKING EASY BANK EXCLUSIVELY FROM WESTERN ERO-TOURISM.
LET'S ALL KEEP IN MIND FOR YOUR OWN GOOD...
...YOU'RE LOOKING AT SOME EXTREMELY WELL-TRAVELED ANAL AND VAGINAL BYWAYS.
AND THAT'S WHAT CONDOMS'RE FOR, MY MAN.
STICK WITH BLOW JOBS--IT'S THE PUSSY THAT'S LETHAL.
I FEEL ALWAYS SAFER WITH A HAND JOB--WITH RUBBER GLOVES.
NOBODY LOVES LISTENING TO THE WISDOM OF EXPERTS MORE THAN I...
NGE
ivate Dance
$5 - 2 for $8
...BUT IF WE'RE ALL THROUGH SHARING OUR DATING TIPS...
...WE'VE GOT ANOTHER ASSAULT ON THE MAIN ENEMY THAT REQUIRES ALL YOUR ATTENTION.

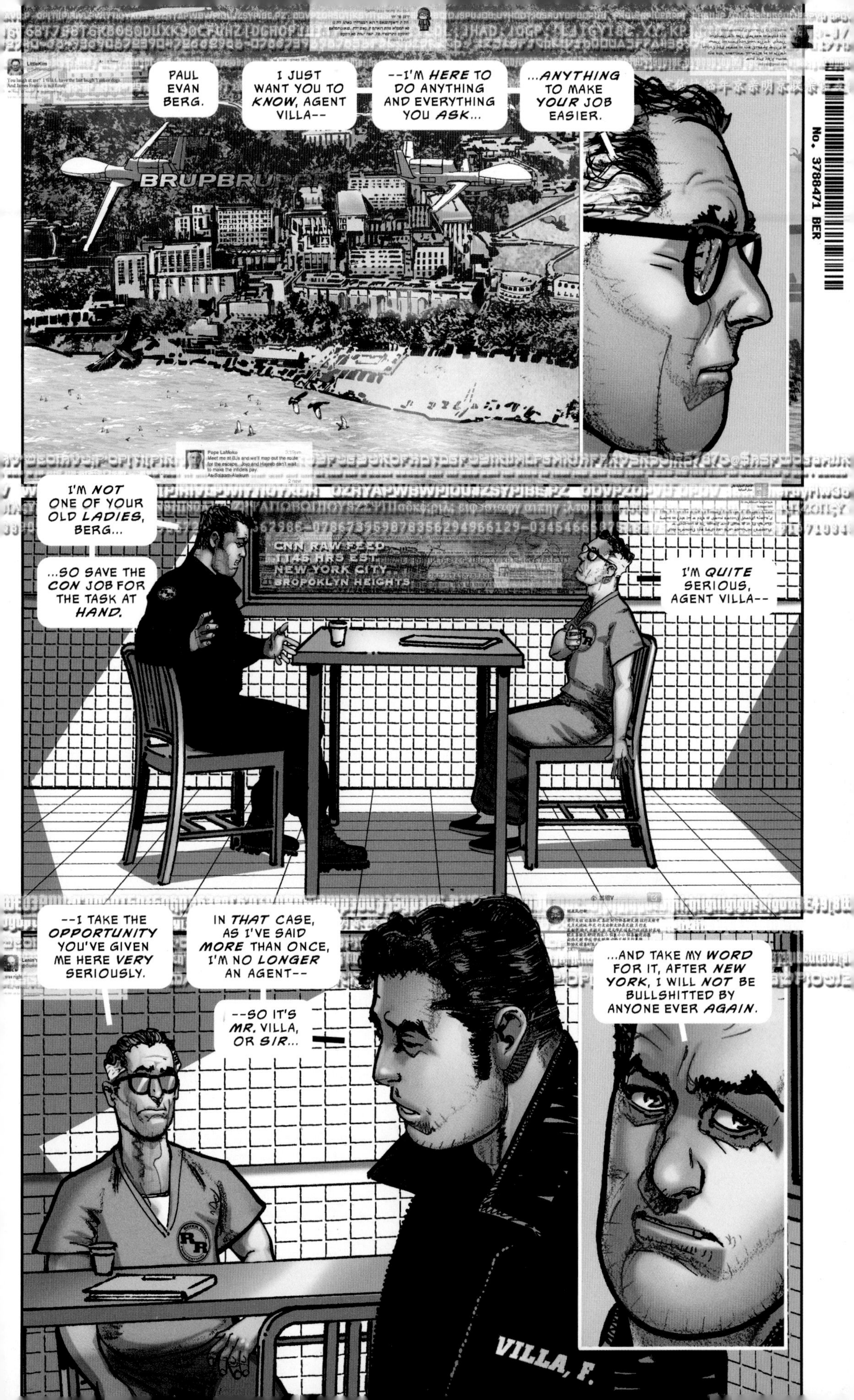
PAUL EVAN BERG.
I JUST WANT YOU TO KNOW, AGENT VILLA--
--I'M HERE TO DO ANYTHING AND EVERYTHING YOU ASK...
...ANYTHING TO MAKE YOUR JOB EASIER.
BRUPBRU
No. 3788471 BER
I'M NOT ONE OF YOUR OLD LADIES, BERG...
...SO SAVE THE CON JOB FOR THE TASK AT HAND.
CNN RAW FEED
1145 HRS EST
NEW YORK CITY
BROOKLYN HEIGHTS
I'M QUITE SERIOUS, AGENT VILLA--
--I TAKE THE OPPORTUNITY YOU'VE GIVEN ME HERE VERY SERIOUSLY.
IN THAT CASE, AS I'VE SAID MORE THAN ONCE, I'M NO LONGER AN AGENT--
--SO IT'S MR. VILLA, OR SIR...
...AND TAKE MY WORD FOR IT, AFTER NEW YORK, I WILL NOT BE BULLSHITTED BY ANYONE EVER AGAIN.
VILLA, F.

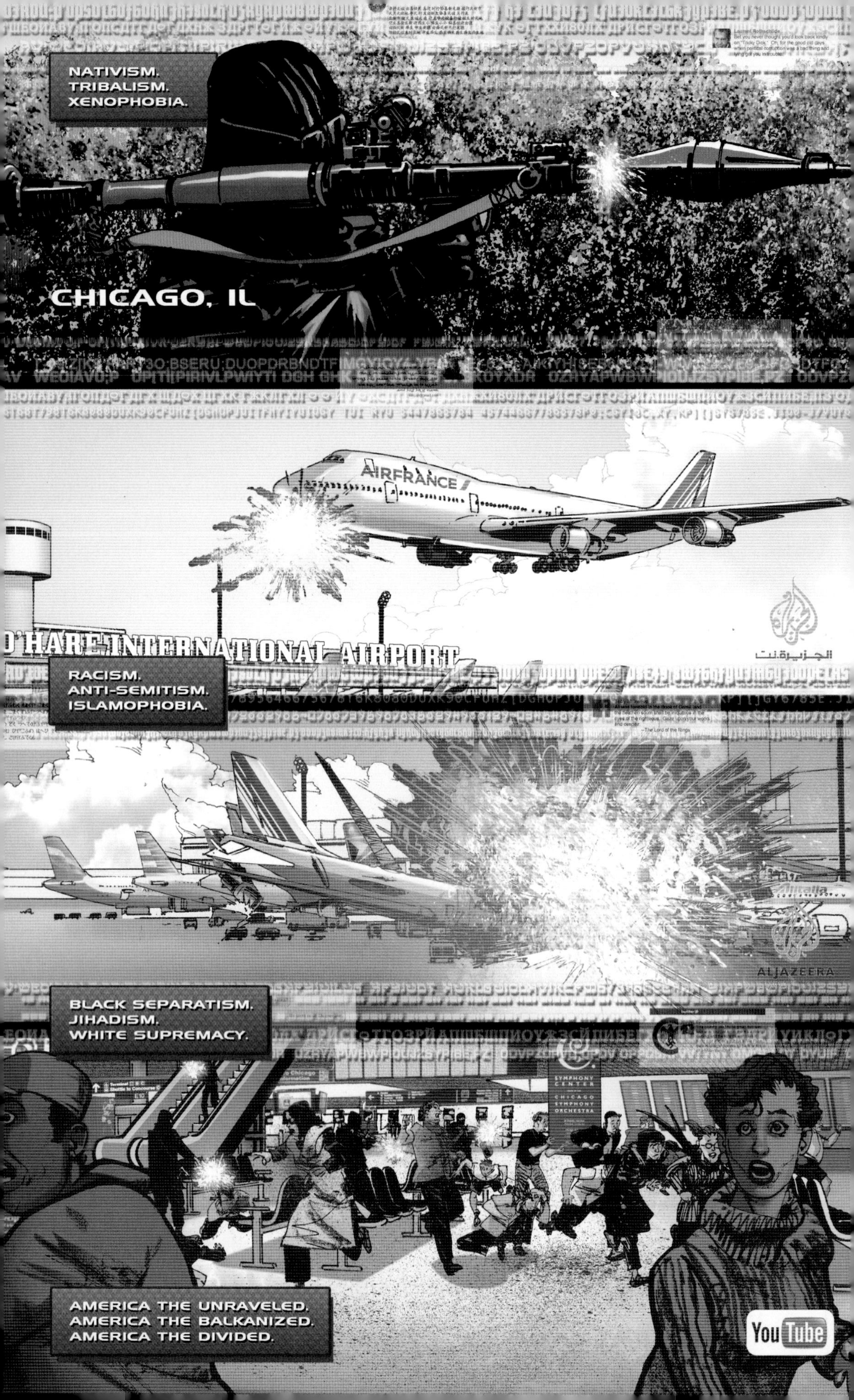

NATIVISM.
TRIBALISM.
XENOPHOBIA.
CHICAGO, IL
AIRFRANCE
O'HARE INTERNATIONAL AIRPORT
الجزيرة.نت
RACISM.
ANTI-SEMITISM.
ISLAMOPHOBIA.
ALJAZEERA
BLACK SEPARATISM.
JIHADISM.
WHITE SUPREMACY.
SYMPHONY CENTER
CHICAGO SYMPHONY ORCHESTRA
AMERICA THE UNRAVELED.
AMERICA THE BALKANIZED.
AMERICA THE DIVIDED.
YouTube

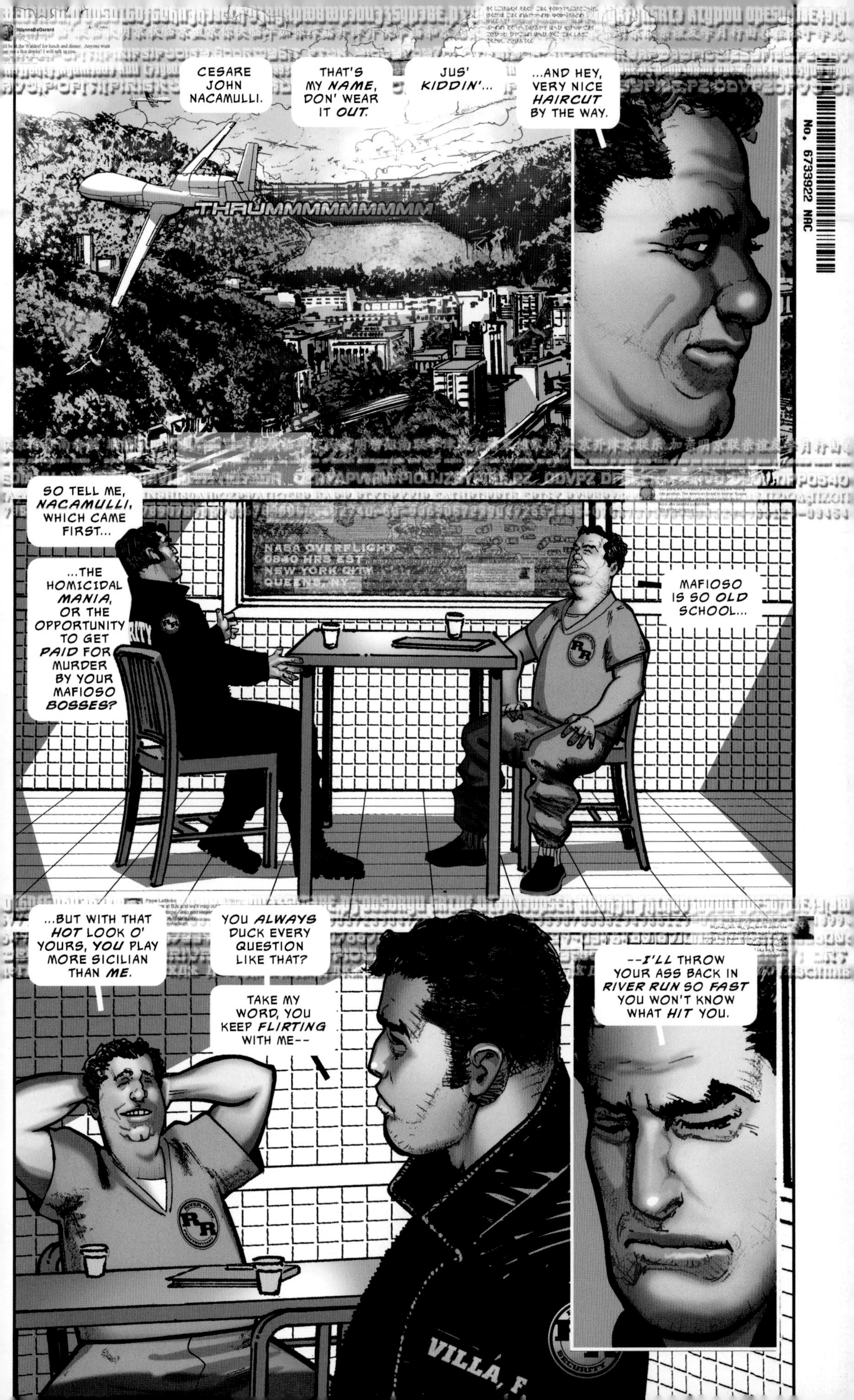

CESARE JOHN NACAMULLI.
THAT'S MY NAME, DON' WEAR IT OUT.
JUS' KIDDIN'...
...AND HEY, VERY NICE HAIRCUT BY THE WAY.
THRUMMMMMMMMMM
No. 6733922 NRC
SO TELL ME, NACAMULLI, WHICH CAME FIRST...
...THE HOMICIDAL MANIA, OR THE OPPORTUNITY TO GET PAID FOR MURDER BY YOUR MAFIOSO BOSSES?
NASA OVERFLIGHT
0840 HRS EST
NEW YORK CITY
QUEENS, NY
MAFIOSO IS SO OLD SCHOOL...
...BUT WITH THAT HOT LOOK O' YOURS, YOU PLAY MORE SICILIAN THAN ME.
YOU ALWAYS DUCK EVERY QUESTION LIKE THAT?
TAKE MY WORD, YOU KEEP FLIRTING WITH ME--
--I'LL THROW YOUR ASS BACK IN RIVER RUN SO FAST YOU WON'T KNOW WHAT HIT YOU.
VILLA, F

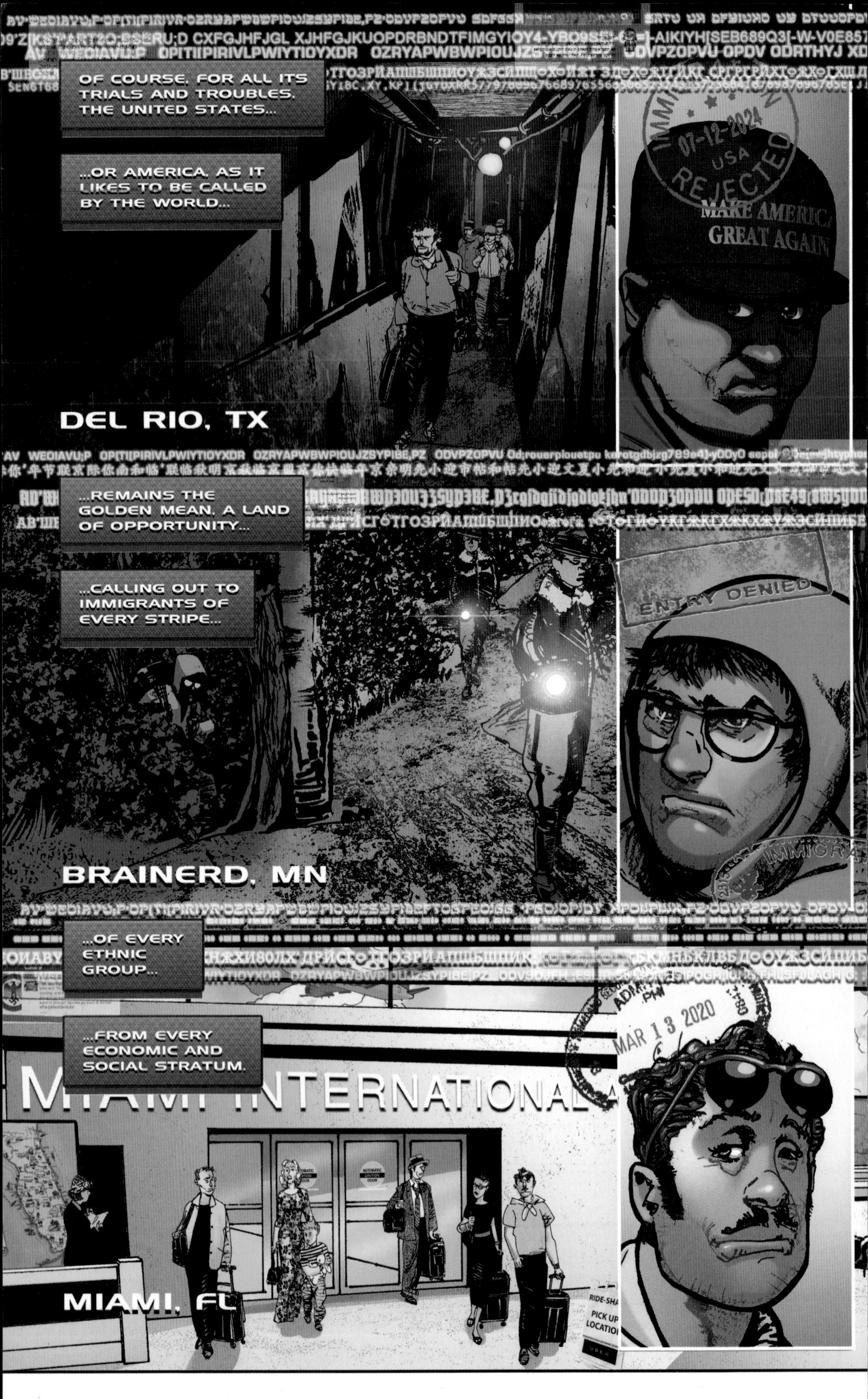
OF COURSE, FOR ALL ITS TRIALS AND TROUBLES, THE UNITED STATES...
...OR AMERICA, AS IT LIKES TO BE CALLED BY THE WORLD...
DEL RIO, TX
07-12-2024
USA
REJECTED
MAKE AMERICA GREAT AGAIN
...REMAINS THE GOLDEN MEAN, A LAND OF OPPORTUNITY...
...CALLING OUT TO IMMIGRANTS OF EVERY STRIPE...
ENTRY DENIED
BRAINERD, MN
...OF EVERY ETHNIC GROUP...
...FROM EVERY ECONOMIC AND SOCIAL STRATUM.
MAR 13 2020
MIAMI, FL

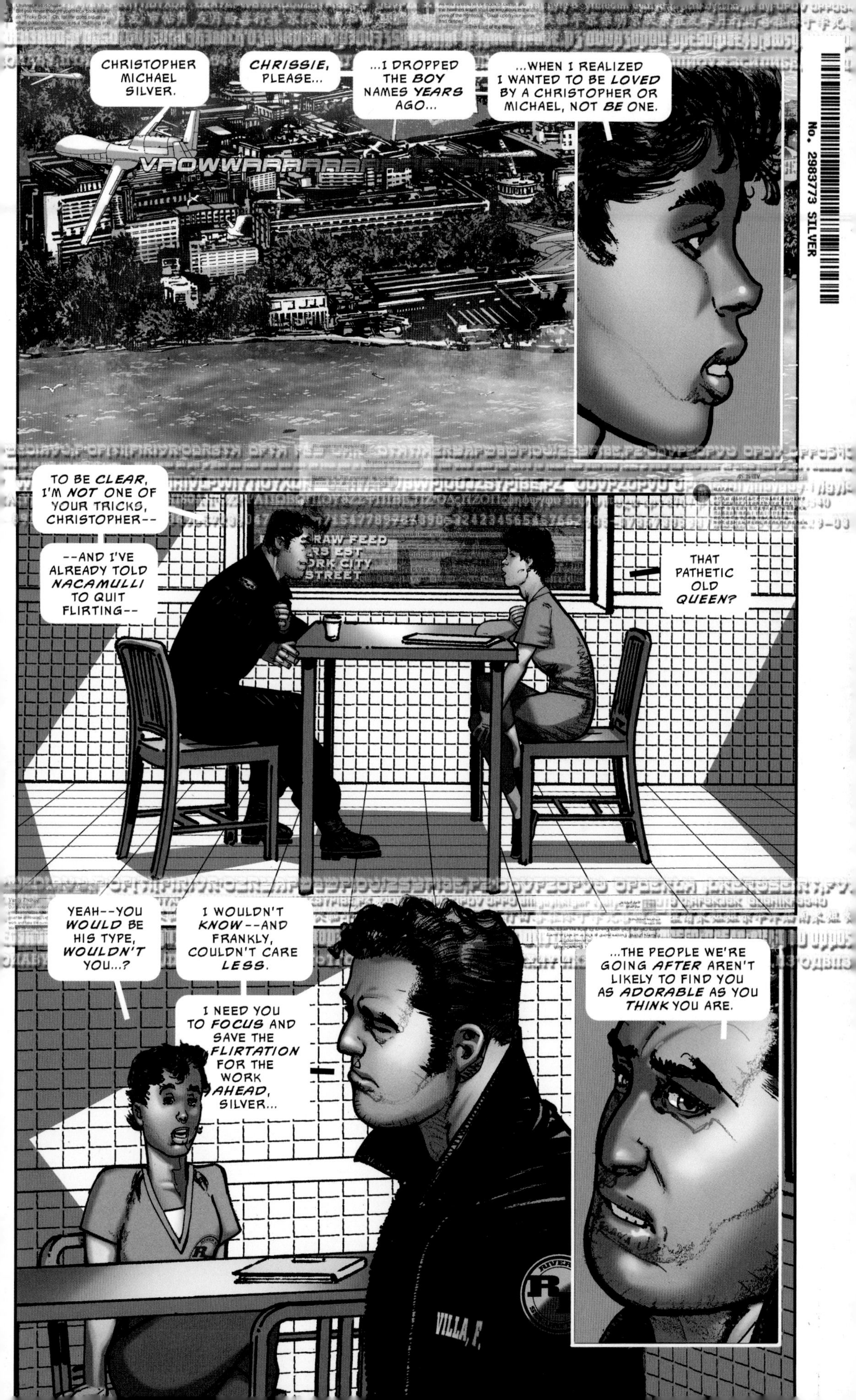

CHRISTOPHER MICHAEL SILVER.
CHRISSIE, PLEASE...
...I DROPPED THE BOY NAMES YEARS AGO...
...WHEN I REALIZED I WANTED TO BE LOVED BY A CHRISTOPHER OR MICHAEL, NOT BE ONE.
VROWWRRRRRR
No. 2983773 SILVER
TO BE CLEAR, I'M NOT ONE OF YOUR TRICKS, CHRISTOPHER--
--AND I'VE ALREADY TOLD NACAMULLI TO QUIT FLIRTING--
THAT PATHETIC OLD QUEEN?
YEAH--YOU WOULD BE HIS TYPE, WOULDN'T YOU...?
I WOULDN'T KNOW--AND FRANKLY, COULDN'T CARE LESS.
I NEED YOU TO FOCUS AND SAVE THE FLIRTATION FOR THE WORK AHEAD, SILVER...
...THE PEOPLE WE'RE GOING AFTER AREN'T LIKELY TO FIND YOU AS ADORABLE AS YOU THINK YOU ARE.
VILLA, F.

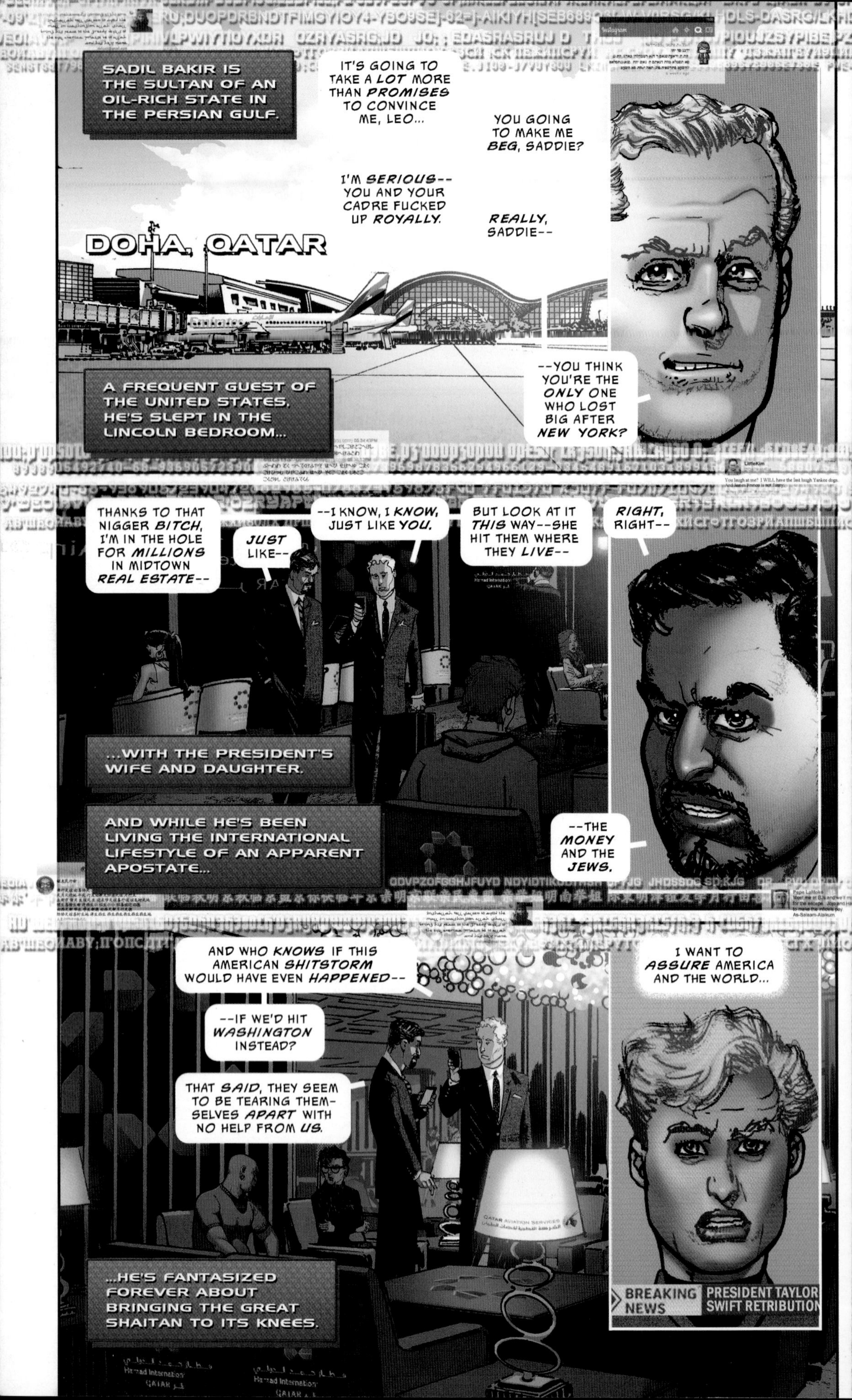

SADIL BAKIR IS THE SULTAN OF AN OIL-RICH STATE IN THE PERSIAN GULF.
IT'S GOING TO TAKE A LOT MORE THAN PROMISES TO CONVINCE ME, LEO...
YOU GOING TO MAKE ME BEG, SADDIE?
I'M SERIOUS-- YOU AND YOUR CADRE FUCKED UP ROYALLY.
REALLY, SADDIE--
DOHA, QATAR
A FREQUENT GUEST OF THE UNITED STATES, HE'S SLEPT IN THE LINCOLN BEDROOM...
--YOU THINK YOU'RE THE ONLY ONE WHO LOST BIG AFTER NEW YORK?
THANKS TO THAT NIGGER BITCH, I'M IN THE HOLE FOR MILLIONS IN MIDTOWN REAL ESTATE--
JUST LIKE--
--I KNOW, I KNOW, JUST LIKE YOU.
BUT LOOK AT IT THIS WAY--SHE HIT THEM WHERE THEY LIVE--
RIGHT, RIGHT--
--THE MONEY AND THE JEWS.
...WITH THE PRESIDENT'S WIFE AND DAUGHTER.
AND WHILE HE'S BEEN LIVING THE INTERNATIONAL LIFESTYLE OF AN APPARENT APOSTATE...
AND WHO KNOWS IF THIS AMERICAN SHITSTORM WOULD HAVE EVEN HAPPENED--
--IF WE'D HIT WASHINGTON INSTEAD?
THAT SAID, THEY SEEM TO BE TEARING THEMSELVES APART WITH NO HELP FROM US.
I WANT TO ASSURE AMERICA AND THE WORLD...
BREAKING NEWS
PRESIDENT TAYLOR SWIFT RETRIBUTION
...HE'S FANTASIZED FOREVER ABOUT BRINGING THE GREAT SHAITAN TO ITS KNEES.

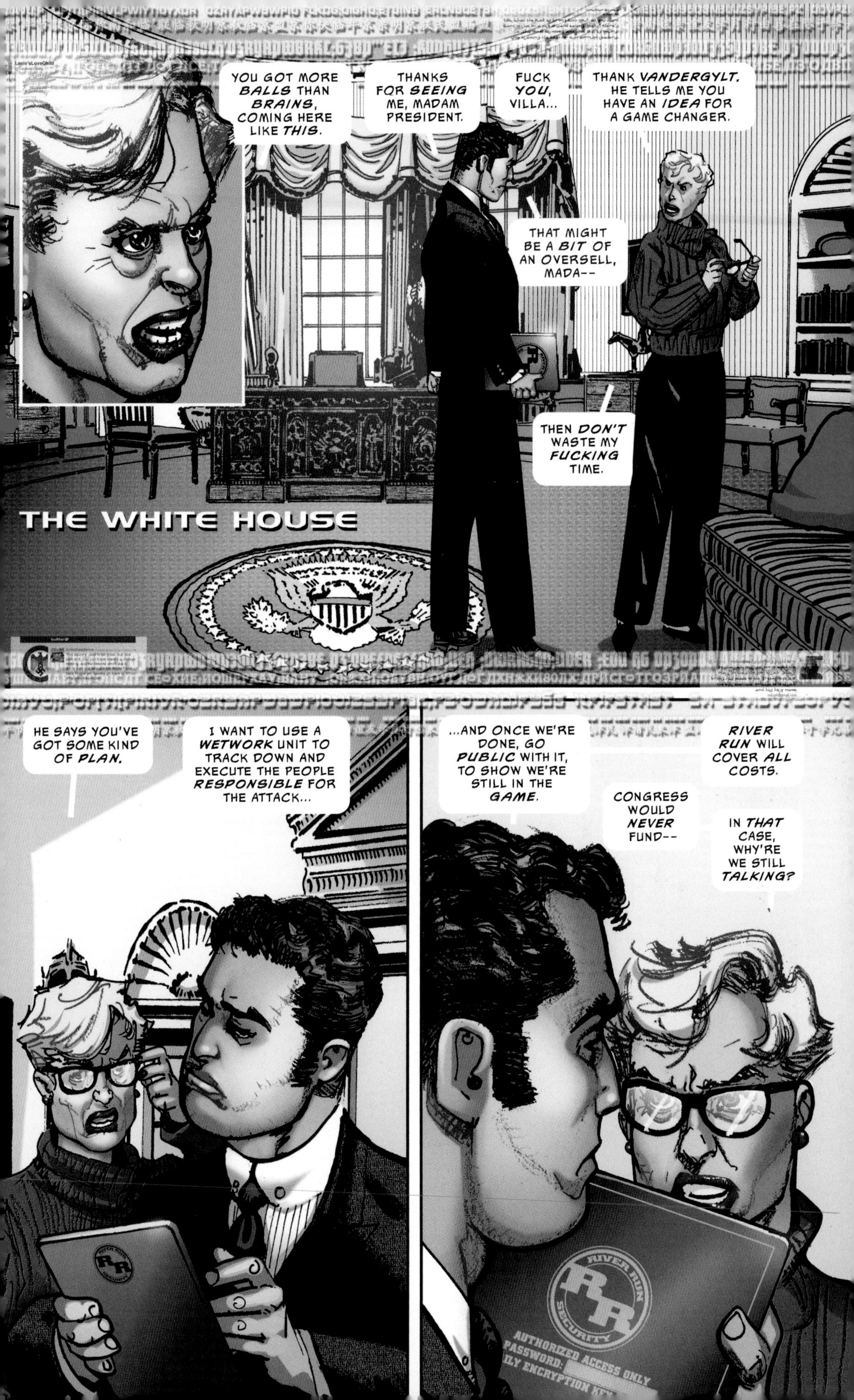
YOU GOT MORE BALLS THAN BRAINS, COMING HERE LIKE THIS.
THANKS FOR SEEING ME, MADAM PRESIDENT.
FUCK YOU, VILLA...
THANK VANDERGYLT. HE TELLS ME YOU HAVE AN IDEA FOR A GAME CHANGER.
THAT MIGHT BE A BIT OF AN OVERSELL, MADA--
THEN DON'T WASTE MY FUCKING TIME.
THE WHITE HOUSE
HE SAYS YOU'VE GOT SOME KIND OF PLAN.
I WANT TO USE A WETWORK UNIT TO TRACK DOWN AND EXECUTE THE PEOPLE RESPONSIBLE FOR THE ATTACK...
...AND ONCE WE'RE DONE, GO PUBLIC WITH IT, TO SHOW WE'RE STILL IN THE GAME.
CONGRESS WOULD NEVER FUND--
RIVER RUN WILL COVER ALL COSTS.
IN THAT CASE, WHY'RE WE STILL TALKING?
RIVER RUN SECURITY
AUTHORIZED ACCESS ONLY
PASSWORD: [redacted]

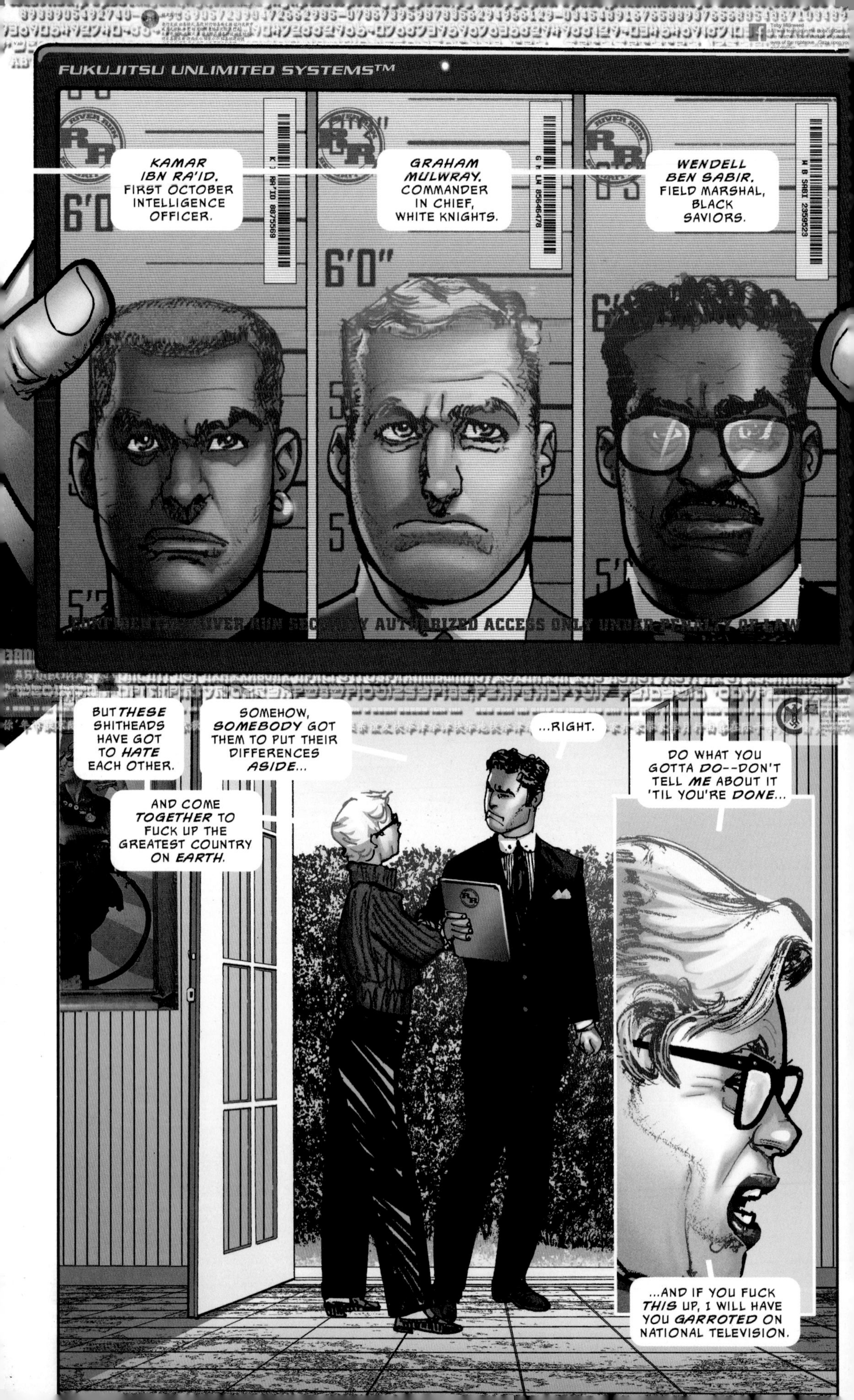

FUKUJITSU UNLIMITED SYSTEMS™
KAMAR IBN RA'ID. FIRST OCTOBER INTELLIGENCE OFFICER.
GRAHAM MULWRAY. COMMANDER IN CHIEF, WHITE KNIGHTS.
WENDELL BEN SABIR. FIELD MARSHAL, BLACK SAVIORS.
BUT THESE SHITHEADS HAVE GOT TO HATE EACH OTHER.
SOMEHOW, SOMEBODY GOT THEM TO PUT THEIR DIFFERENCES ASIDE...
AND COME TOGETHER TO FUCK UP THE GREATEST COUNTRY ON EARTH.
...RIGHT.
DO WHAT YOU GOTTA DO--DON'T TELL ME ABOUT IT 'TIL YOU'RE DONE...
...AND IF YOU FUCK THIS UP, I WILL HAVE YOU GARROTED ON NATIONAL TELEVISION.

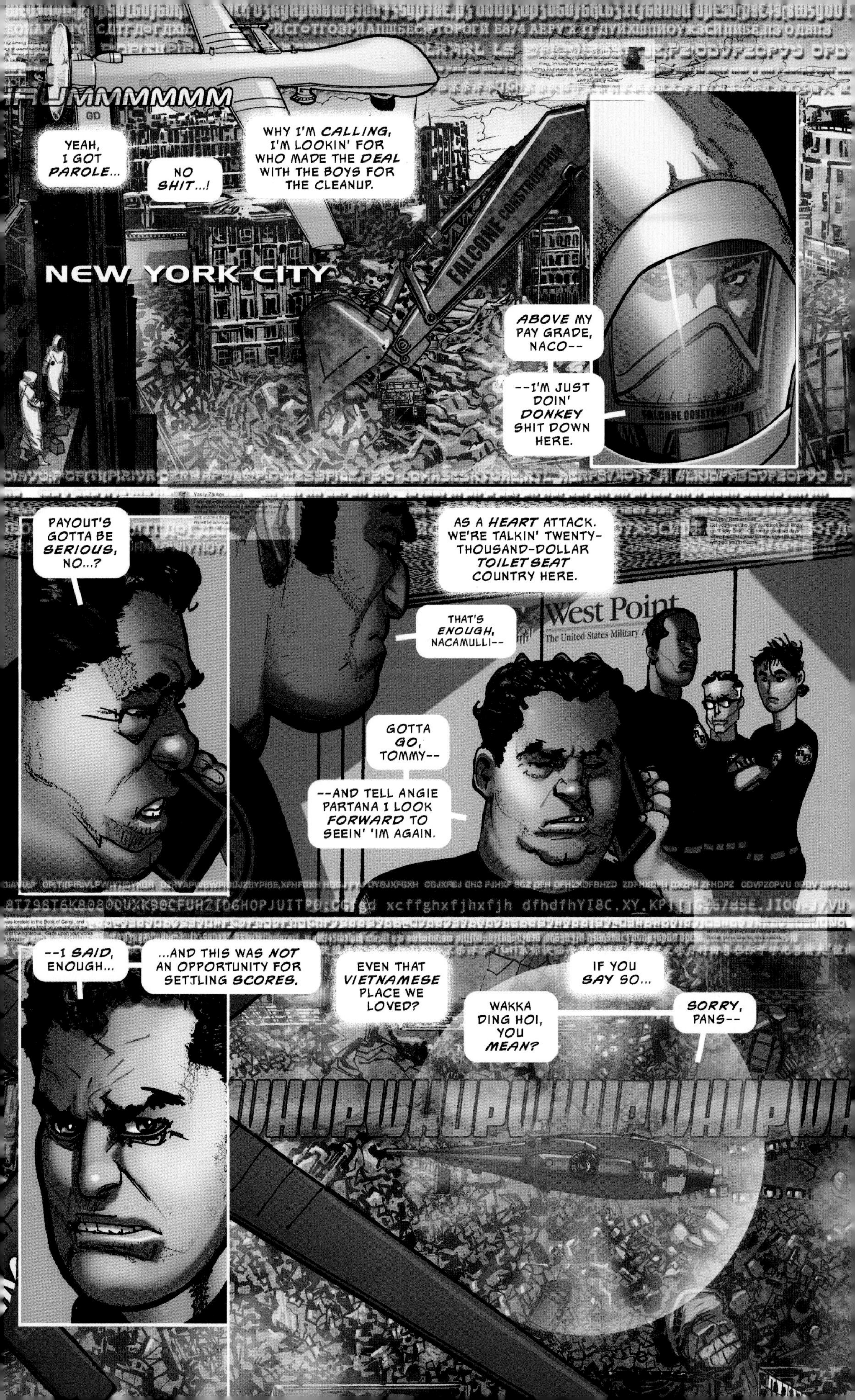
HUMMMMMMM
YEAH, I GOT PAROLE...
NO SHIT...!
WHY I'M CALLING, I'M LOOKIN' FOR WHO MADE THE DEAL WITH THE BOYS FOR THE CLEANUP.
NEW YORK CITY
FALCONE CONSTRUCTION
ABOVE MY PAY GRADE, NACO--
--I'M JUST DOIN' DONKEY SHIT DOWN HERE.
PAYOUT'S GOTTA BE SERIOUS, NO...?
AS A HEART ATTACK. WE'RE TALKIN' TWENTY-THOUSAND-DOLLAR TOILET SEAT COUNTRY HERE.
West Point
The United States Military A
THAT'S ENOUGH, NACAMULLI--
GOTTA GO, TOMMY--
--AND TELL ANGIE PARTANA I LOOK FORWARD TO SEEIN' 'IM AGAIN.
--I SAID, ENOUGH...
...AND THIS WAS NOT AN OPPORTUNITY FOR SETTLING SCORES.
EVEN THAT VIETNAMESE PLACE WE LOVED?
IF YOU SAY SO...
WAKKA DING HOI, YOU MEAN?
SORRY, PANS--
WHUPWHUPWHUPWHUPWH

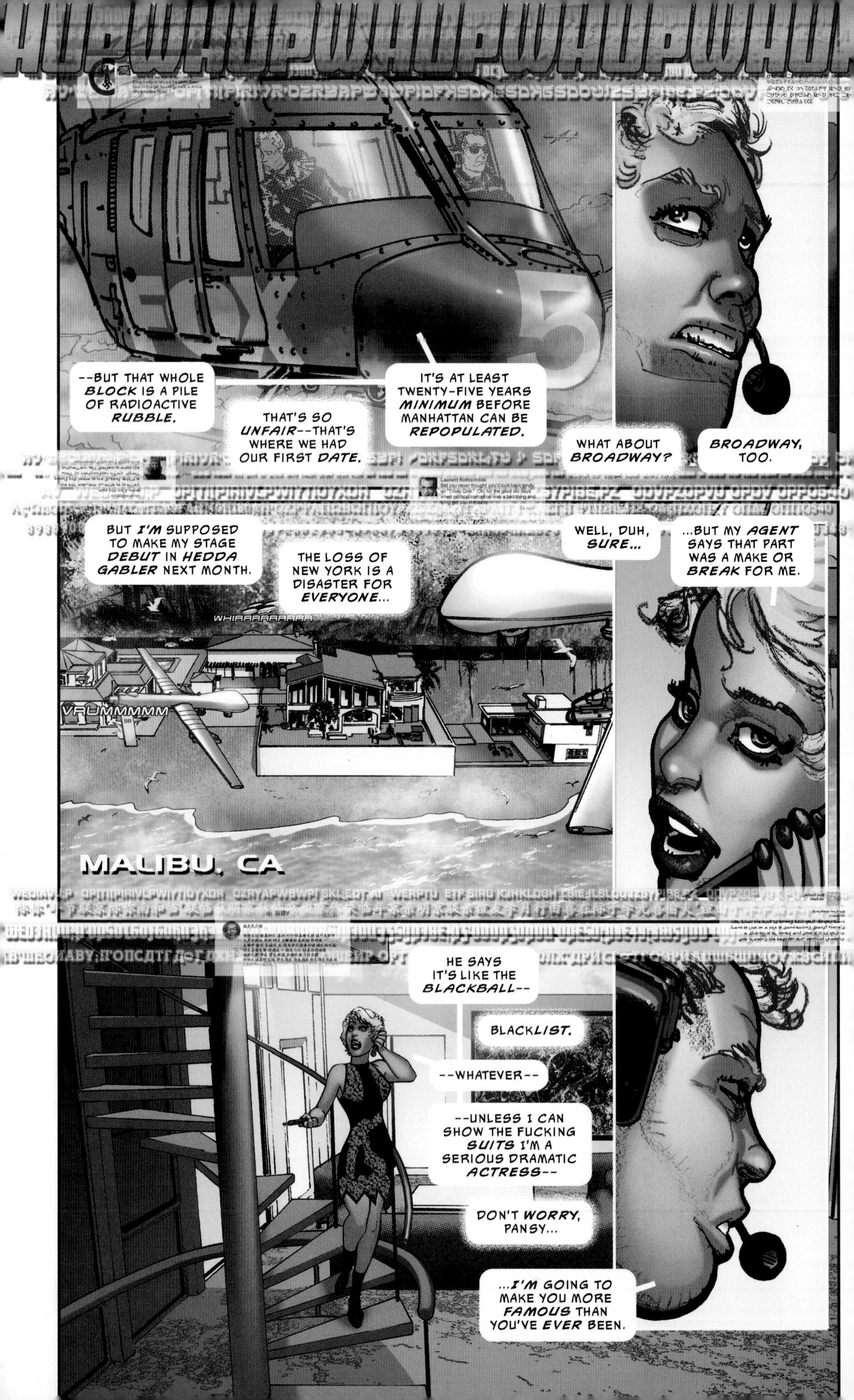
--BUT THAT WHOLE BLOCK IS A PILE OF RADIOACTIVE RUBBLE.
THAT'S SO UNFAIR--THAT'S WHERE WE HAD OUR FIRST DATE.
IT'S AT LEAST TWENTY-FIVE YEARS MINIMUM BEFORE MANHATTAN CAN BE REPOPULATED.
WHAT ABOUT BROADWAY?
BROADWAY, TOO.
BUT I'M SUPPOSED TO MAKE MY STAGE DEBUT IN HEDDA GABLER NEXT MONTH.
THE LOSS OF NEW YORK IS A DISASTER FOR EVERYONE...
WELL, DUH, SURE...
...BUT MY AGENT SAYS THAT PART WAS A MAKE OR BREAK FOR ME.
WHIRRRRRRRRRR
VRUMMMMMM
MALIBU, CA
HE SAYS IT'S LIKE THE BLACKBALL--
BLACKLIST.
--WHATEVER--
--UNLESS I CAN SHOW THE FUCKING SUITS I'M A SERIOUS DRAMATIC ACTRESS--
DON'T WORRY, PANSY...
...I'M GOING TO MAKE YOU MORE FAMOUS THAN YOU'VE EVER BEEN.

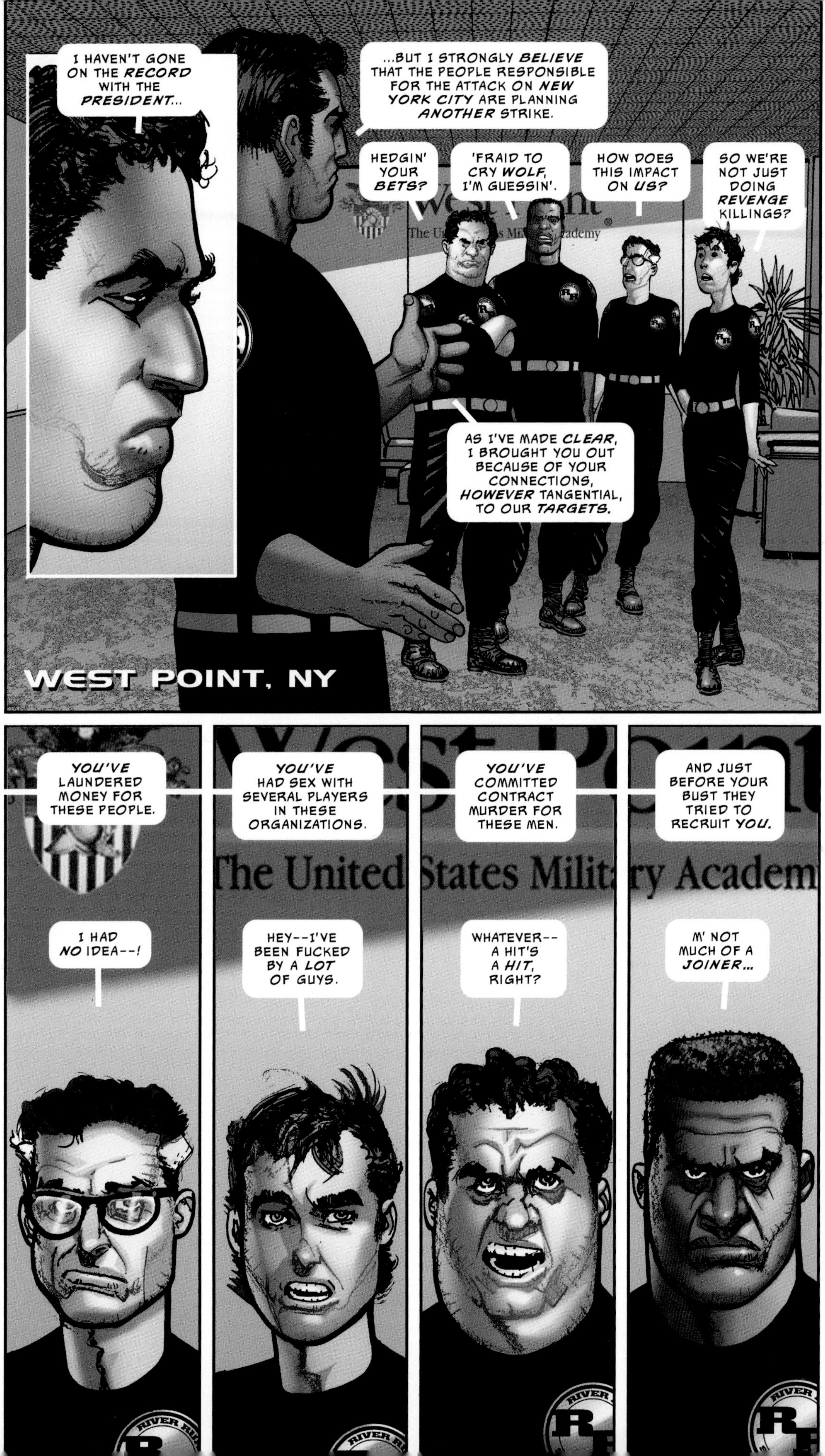
I HAVEN'T GONE ON THE RECORD WITH THE PRESIDENT...
...BUT I STRONGLY BELIEVE THAT THE PEOPLE RESPONSIBLE FOR THE ATTACK ON NEW YORK CITY ARE PLANNING ANOTHER STRIKE.
HEDGIN' YOUR BETS?
'FRAID TO CRY WOLF, I'M GUESSIN'.
HOW DOES THIS IMPACT ON US?
SO WE'RE NOT JUST DOING REVENGE KILLINGS?
AS I'VE MADE CLEAR, I BROUGHT YOU OUT BECAUSE OF YOUR CONNECTIONS, HOWEVER TANGENTIAL, TO OUR TARGETS.
WEST POINT, NY
YOU'VE LAUNDERED MONEY FOR THESE PEOPLE.
I HAD NO IDEA--!
YOU'VE HAD SEX WITH SEVERAL PLAYERS IN THESE ORGANIZATIONS.
HEY--I'VE BEEN FUCKED BY A LOT OF GUYS.
YOU'VE COMMITTED CONTRACT MURDER FOR THESE MEN.
WHATEVER-- A HIT'S A HIT, RIGHT?
AND JUST BEFORE YOUR BUST THEY TRIED TO RECRUIT YOU.
M' NOT MUCH OF A JOINER...

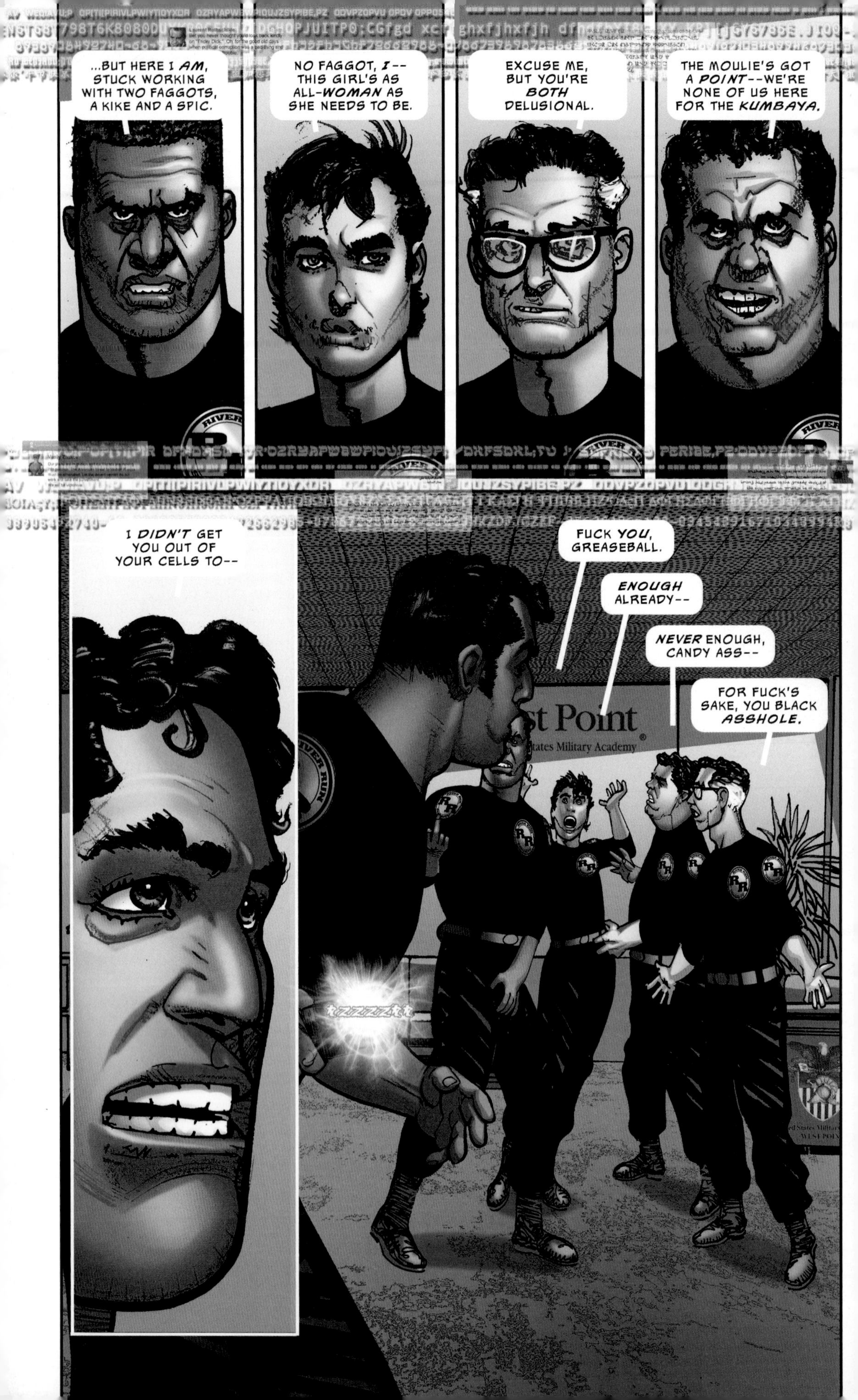
...BUT HERE I AM, STUCK WORKING WITH TWO FAGGOTS, A KIKE AND A SPIC.
NO FAGGOT, I -- THIS GIRL'S AS ALL-WOMAN AS SHE NEEDS TO BE.
EXCUSE ME, BUT YOU'RE BOTH DELUSIONAL.
THE MOULIE'S GOT A POINT--WE'RE NONE OF US HERE FOR THE KUMBAYA.
I DIDN'T GET YOU OUT OF YOUR CELLS TO--
FUCK YOU, GREASEBALL.
ENOUGH ALREADY--
NEVER ENOUGH, CANDY ASS--
FOR FUCK'S SAKE, YOU BLACK ASSHOLE.

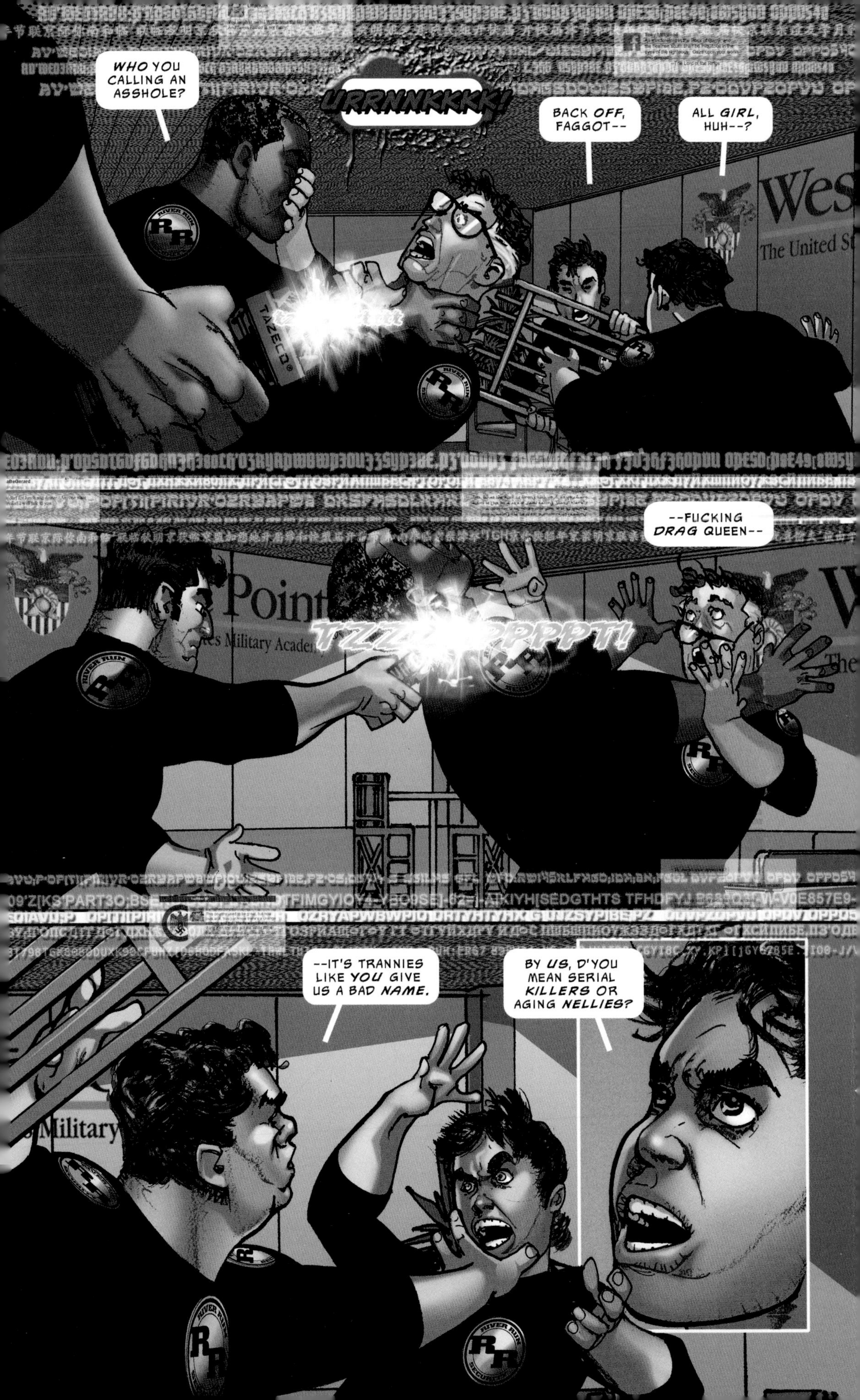
WHO YOU CALLING AN ASSHOLE?
URRNNKKKK!
BACK OFF, FAGGOT--
ALL GIRL, HUH--?
TAZECO
--FUCKING DRAG QUEEN--
Point
es Military Academy
TZZZ
PPPPT!
--IT'S TRANNIES LIKE YOU GIVE US A BAD NAME.
BY US, D'YOU MEAN SERIAL KILLERS OR AGING NELLIES?
Military

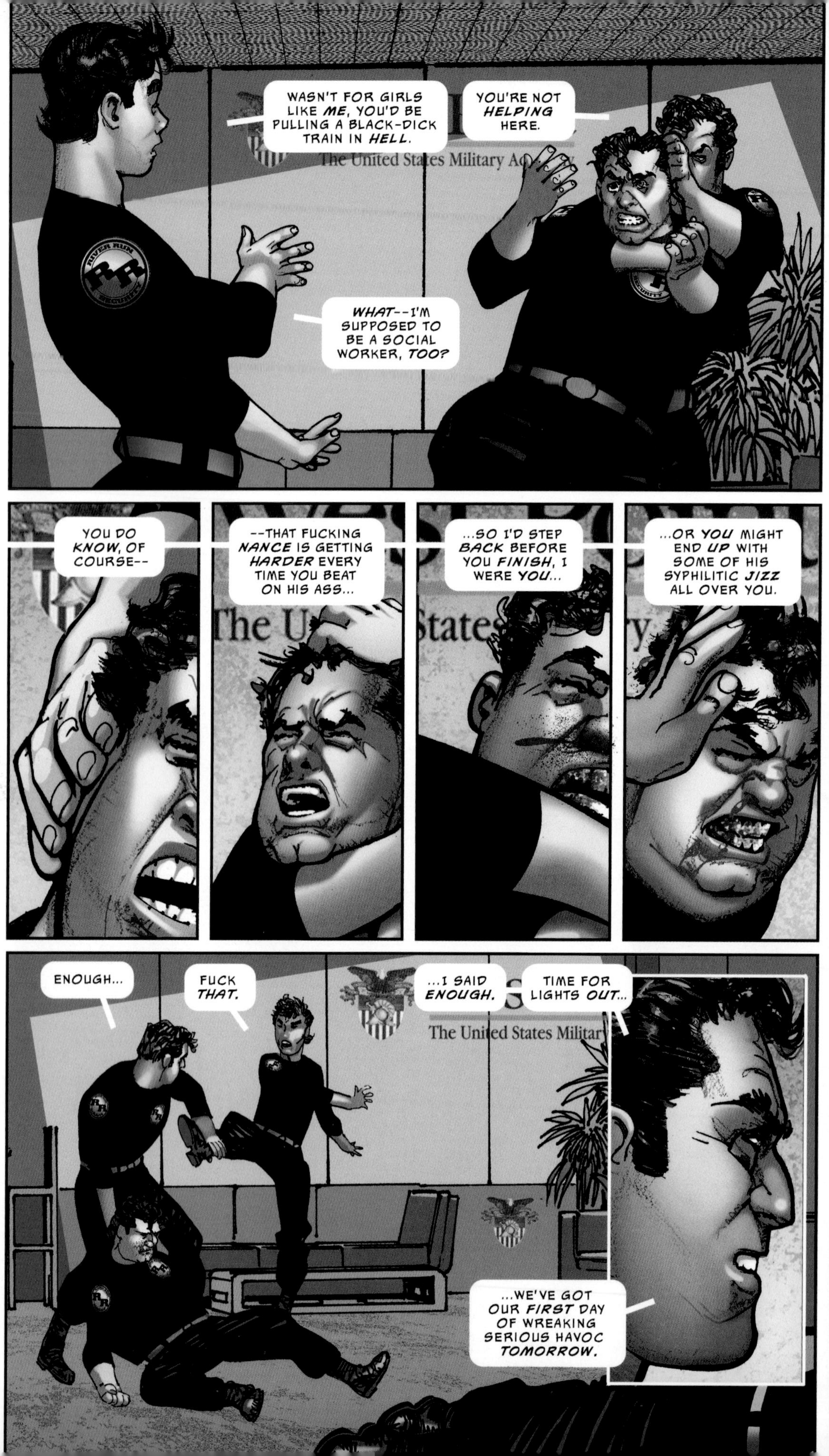
WASN'T FOR GIRLS LIKE *ME*, YOU'D BE PULLING A BLACK-DICK TRAIN IN *HELL*.
YOU'RE NOT *HELPING* HERE.
The United States Military Academy
WHAT--I'M SUPPOSED TO BE A SOCIAL WORKER, *TOO?*
YOU DO *KNOW*, OF COURSE--
--THAT FUCKING *NANCE* IS GETTING *HARDER* EVERY TIME YOU BEAT ON HIS ASS...
...SO I'D STEP *BACK* BEFORE YOU *FINISH*, I WERE *YOU*...
...OR *YOU* MIGHT END *UP* WITH SOME OF HIS SYPHILITIC *JIZZ* ALL OVER YOU.
ENOUGH...
FUCK *THAT*.
...I SAID *ENOUGH*.
TIME FOR LIGHTS *OUT*...
...WE'VE GOT OUR *FIRST* DAY OF WREAKING SERIOUS HAVOC *TOMORROW*.

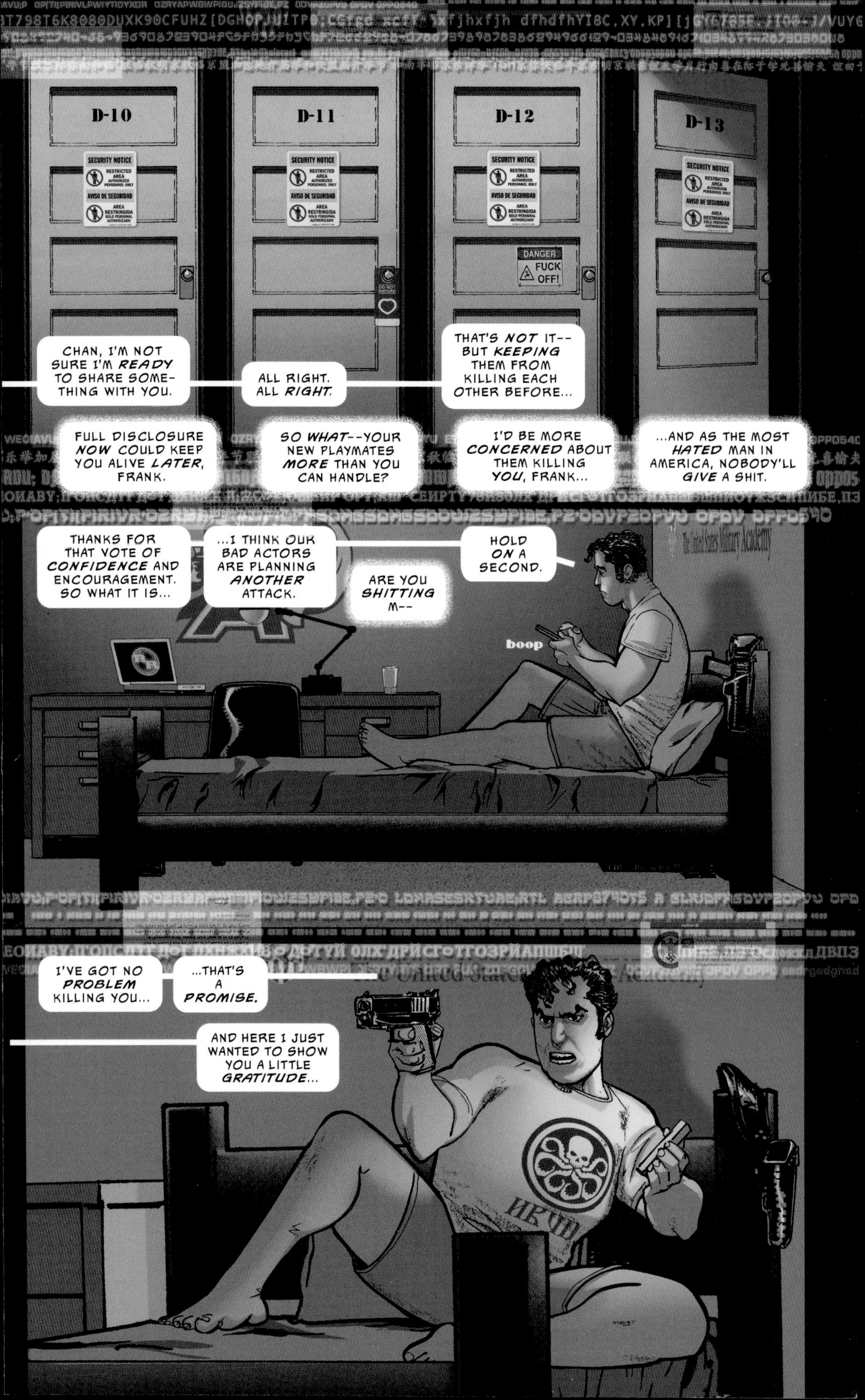
D-10
D-11
D-12
D-13
SECURITY NOTICE
RESTRICTED AREA AUTHORIZED PERSONNEL ONLY
AVISO DE SEGURIDAD
AREA RESTRINGIDA SOLO PERSONAL AUTORIZADO
DANGER
FUCK OFF!
CHAN, I'M NOT SURE I'M *READY* TO SHARE SOMETHING WITH YOU.
ALL RIGHT. ALL *RIGHT*.
THAT'S *NOT* IT--BUT *KEEPING* THEM FROM KILLING EACH OTHER BEFORE...
FULL DISCLOSURE *NOW* COULD KEEP YOU ALIVE *LATER*, FRANK.
SO *WHAT*--YOUR NEW PLAYMATES *MORE* THAN YOU CAN HANDLE?
I'D BE MORE *CONCERNED* ABOUT THEM KILLING *YOU*, FRANK...
...AND AS THE MOST *HATED* MAN IN AMERICA, NOBODY'LL *GIVE* A SHIT.
THANKS FOR THAT VOTE OF *CONFIDENCE* AND ENCOURAGEMENT. SO WHAT IT IS...
...I THINK OUR BAD ACTORS ARE PLANNING *ANOTHER* ATTACK.
ARE YOU *SHITTING* M--
HOLD *ON* A SECOND.
boop
The United States Military Academy
I'VE GOT NO *PROBLEM* KILLING YOU...
...THAT'S A *PROMISE.*
AND HERE I JUST WANTED TO SHOW YOU A LITTLE *GRATITUDE*...

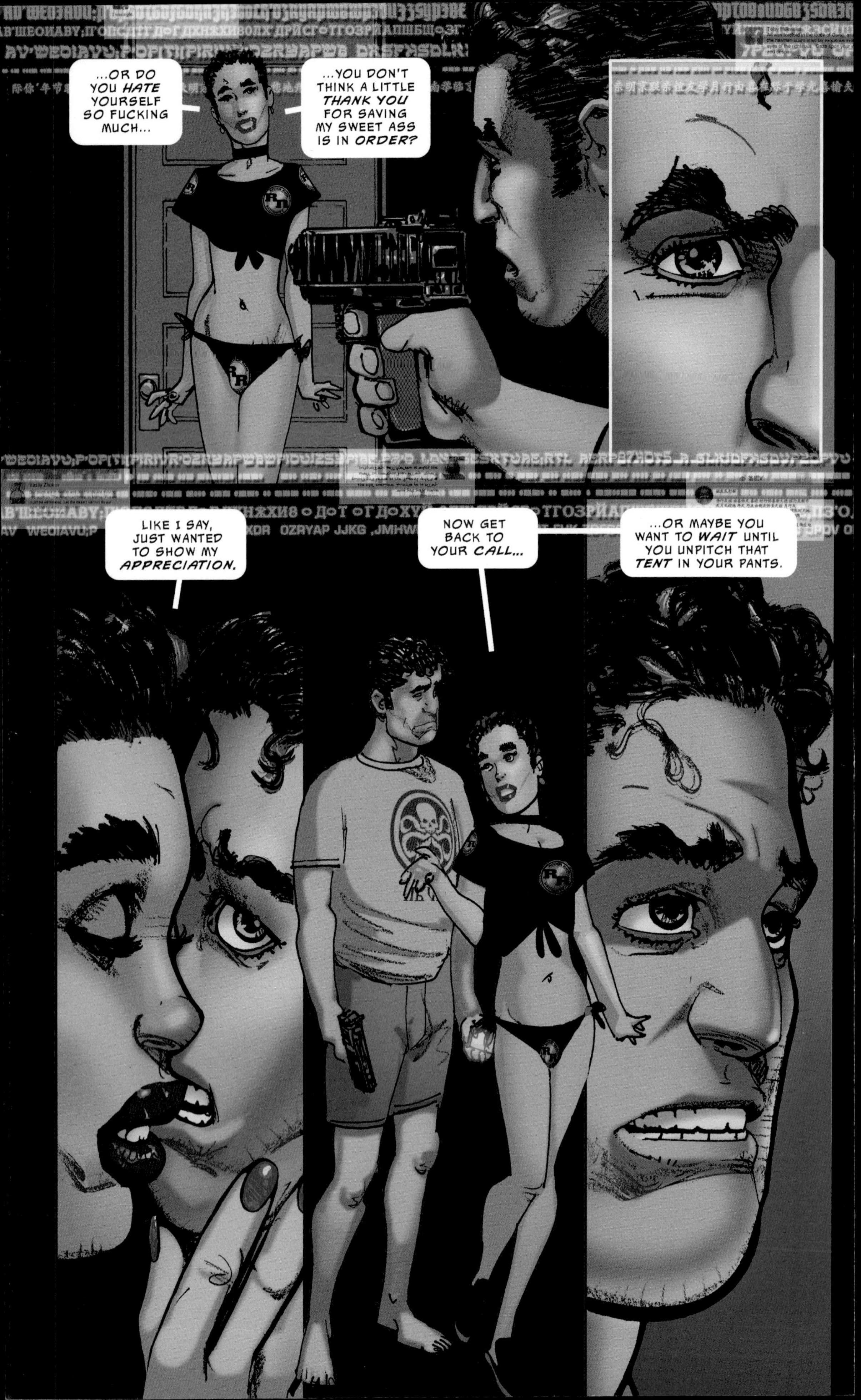
...OR DO YOU HATE YOURSELF SO FUCKING MUCH...
...YOU DON'T THINK A LITTLE THANK YOU FOR SAVING MY SWEET ASS IS IN ORDER?
LIKE I SAY, JUST WANTED TO SHOW MY APPRECIATION.
NOW GET BACK TO YOUR CALL...
...OR MAYBE YOU WANT TO WAIT UNTIL YOU UNPITCH THAT TENT IN YOUR PANTS.

Part Four

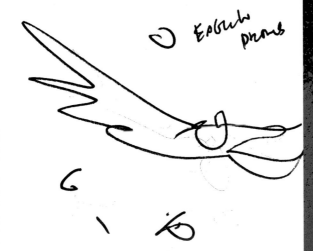

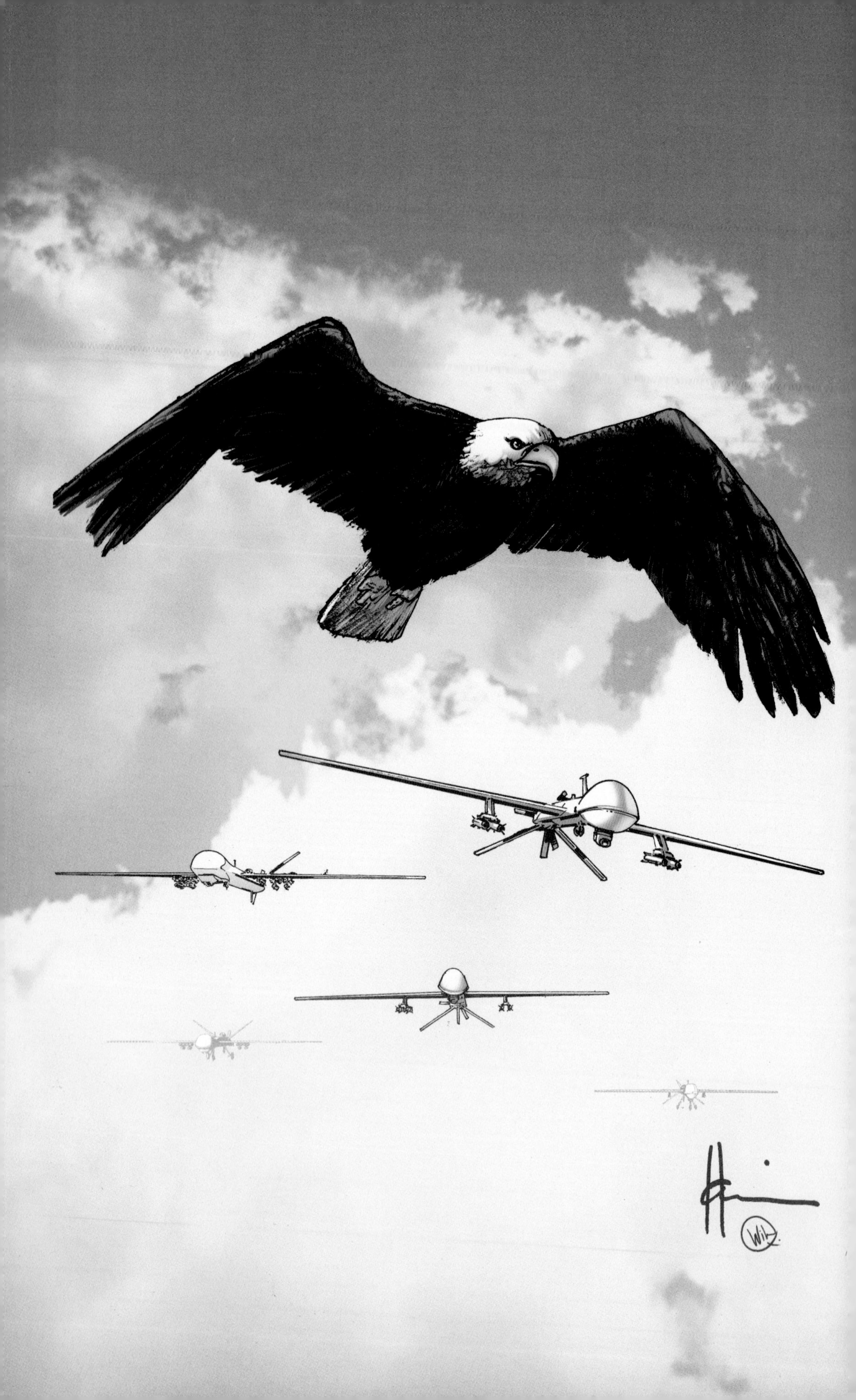

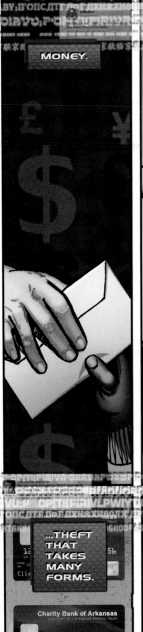

MONEY.
IT COMES FROM EVERYWHERE.
THE BENEVOLENT SISTERS OF MERCY SHELTER FOR HOMELESS MOTHERS AND ORPHANS
FROM LEGITIMATE SOURCES...
than 10 availa
uy it now
dd basket
d to Watch list
d Delivery | s
rdington, Bridg
ingdom
2-3 working d
...AND FROM THEFT...
Record
RECORDING
ATM
STOP
...THEFT THAT TAKES MANY FORMS.
Charity Bank of Arkansas
1234 5678 9012 3456
Client Name
Charity Bank of Arkansas
1234 5678 9012 3456
Client Name
Charity Bank of Arkansas
1234 5678 9012 3456
Client Name
Charity Bank of Arkansas
1234 5678 9012 3456
Client Name
SOME LOUD, TERRIFYING AND VIOLENT...
...AND SOME SO SILENT AND SUBTLE AS TO BE NEARLY INVISIBLE.
ARLES, CHUCK 0.00
BOT, SEBASTIAN 0.00
RISTOPHER, LEE 0.00
HN, GUS 0.00
ISP, QUENTIN 0.00
UZ, PENNY 0.00
SHING, PETE 0.00
ECHURIN, ARPOD 0.00
Y, DORINDA 0.00
ILY, WILLIAM 0.00
SH, SLAP N. 0.00
UGHERTY, DICK 0.00
STRY, TOM 0.00
MERGUE, AMY 0.00
URY, PETER 0.00
UZE, ANTON 0.00
CK, DAPHNE 0.00
RKA, HABIR 0.00
LAN, ROBERT 0.00
SART, RICHARD 0.00
KINS, THOMAS 0.00
MES, WILLARD 0.00
WOOD, JAKE 0.00
MY, R. LEE 0.00
TES, SAUL 0.00
TEVEZ, EMILIO 0.00
CUCHA, MEI 0.00
IN, SAMMY 0.00
MILIA, SUE 0.00
MONEY.

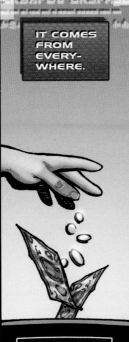

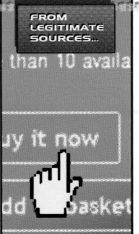

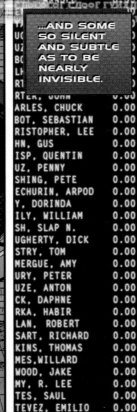

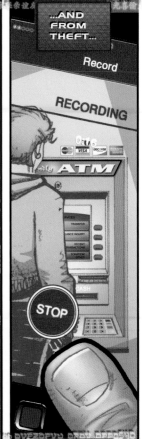

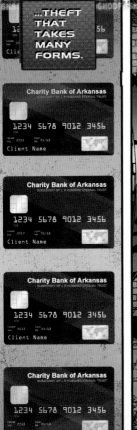

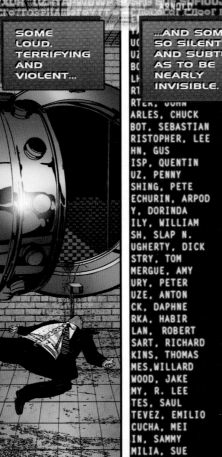

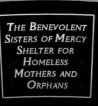

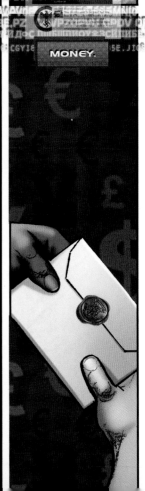

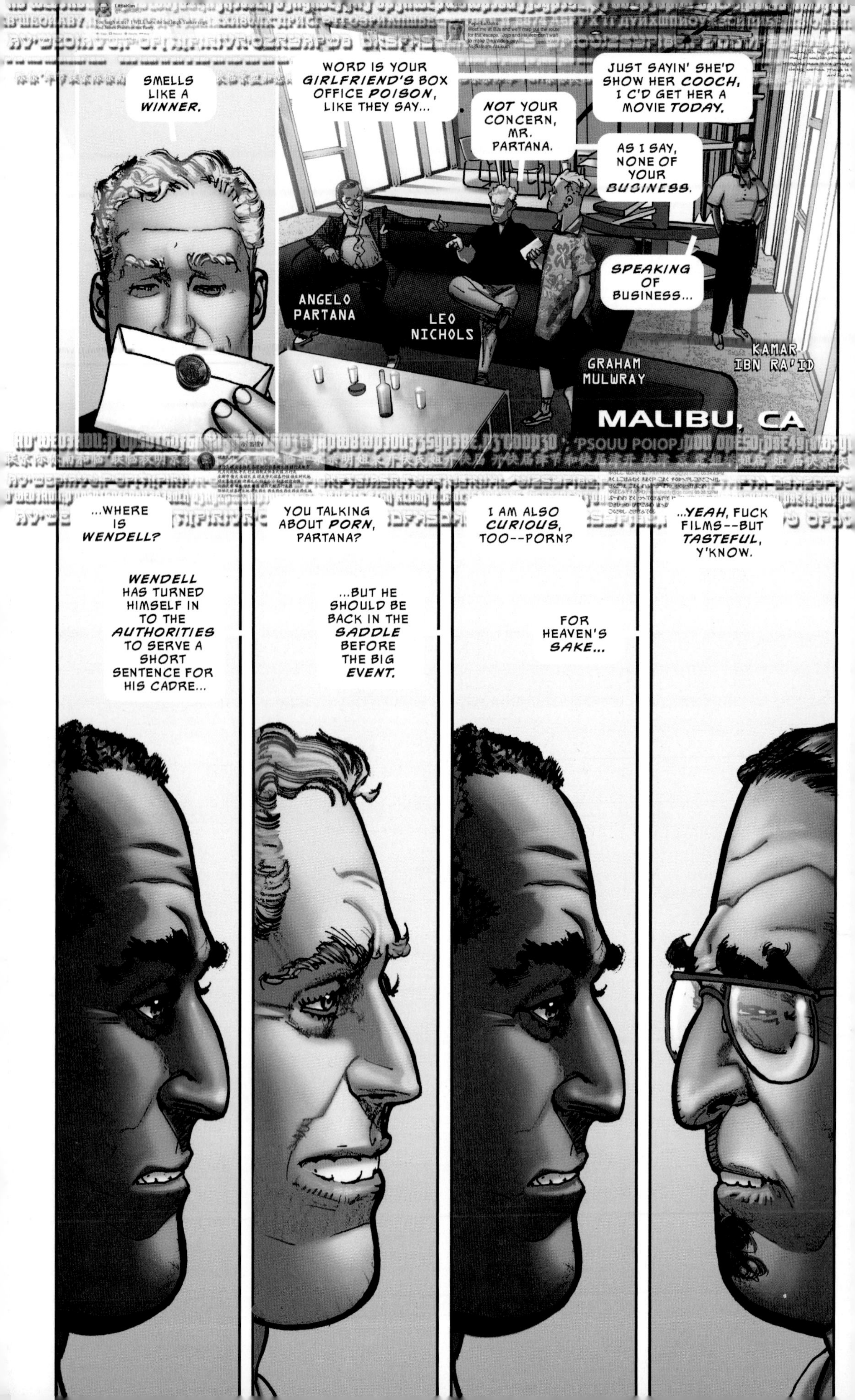

SMELLS LIKE A WINNER.
WORD IS YOUR GIRLFRIEND'S BOX OFFICE POISON, LIKE THEY SAY...
NOT YOUR CONCERN, MR. PARTANA.
JUST SAYIN' SHE'D SHOW HER COOCH, I C'D GET HER A MOVIE TODAY.
AS I SAY, NONE OF YOUR BUSINESS.
SPEAKING OF BUSINESS...
ANGELO PARTANA
LEO NICHOLS
GRAHAM MULWRAY
KAMAR IBN RA'ID
MALIBU, CA
...WHERE IS WENDELL?
YOU TALKING ABOUT PORN, PARTANA?
I AM ALSO CURIOUS, TOO--PORN?
...YEAH, FUCK FILMS--BUT TASTEFUL, Y'KNOW.
WENDELL HAS TURNED HIMSELF IN TO THE AUTHORITIES TO SERVE A SHORT SENTENCE FOR HIS CADRE...
...BUT HE SHOULD BE BACK IN THE SADDLE BEFORE THE BIG EVENT.
FOR HEAVEN'S SAKE...

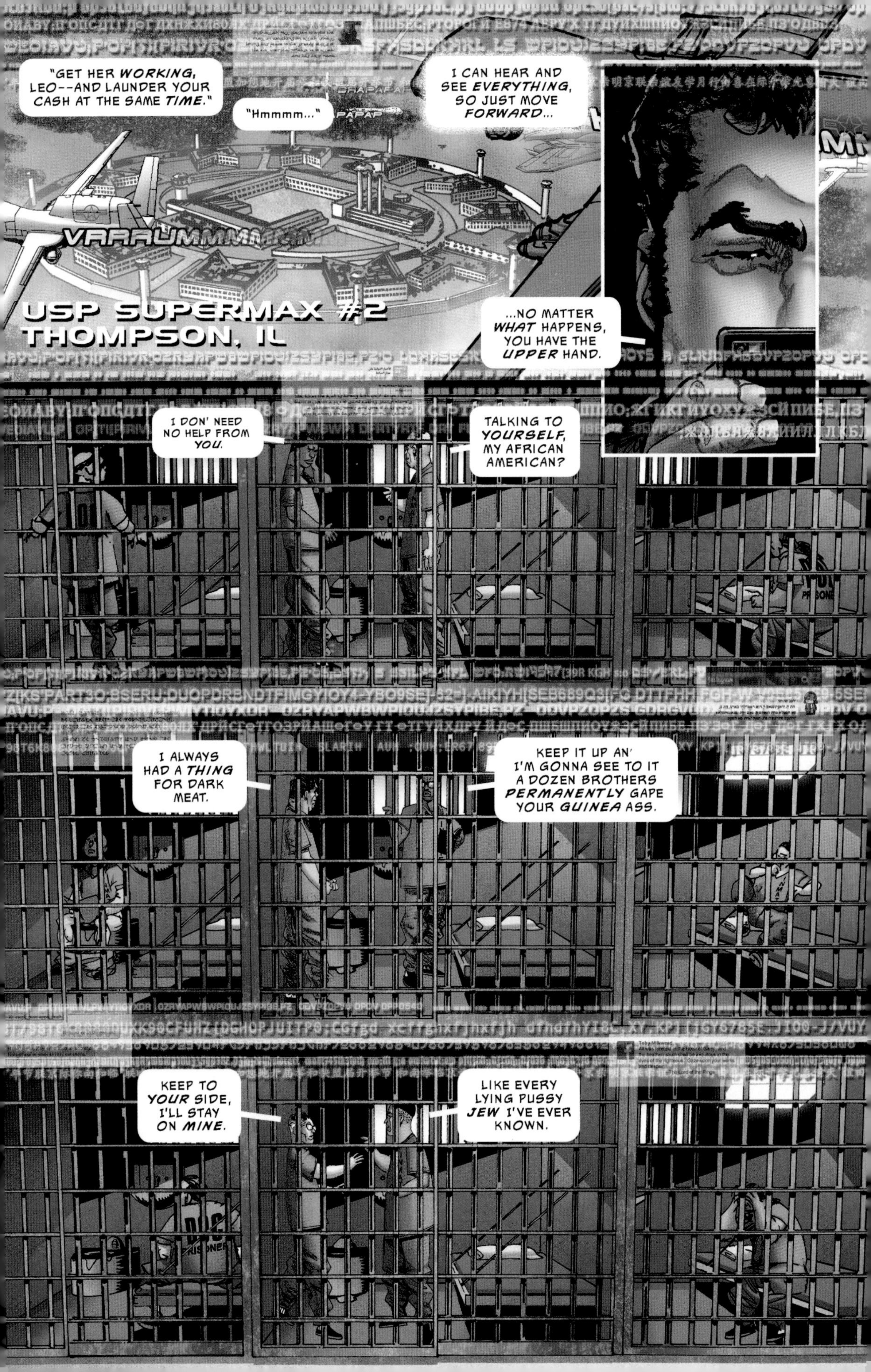
"GET HER WORKING, LEO--AND LAUNDER YOUR CASH AT THE SAME TIME."
"Hmmmm..."
I CAN HEAR AND SEE EVERYTHING, SO JUST MOVE FORWARD...
VRRRUMMMM
USP SUPERMAX #2 THOMPSON, IL
...NO MATTER WHAT HAPPENS, YOU HAVE THE UPPER HAND.
I DON' NEED NO HELP FROM YOU.
TALKING TO YOURSELF, MY AFRICAN AMERICAN?
I ALWAYS HAD A THING FOR DARK MEAT.
KEEP IT UP AN' I'M GONNA SEE TO IT A DOZEN BROTHERS PERMANENTLY GAPE YOUR GUINEA ASS.
KEEP TO YOUR SIDE, I'LL STAY ON MINE.
LIKE EVERY LYING PUSSY JEW I'VE EVER KNOWN.

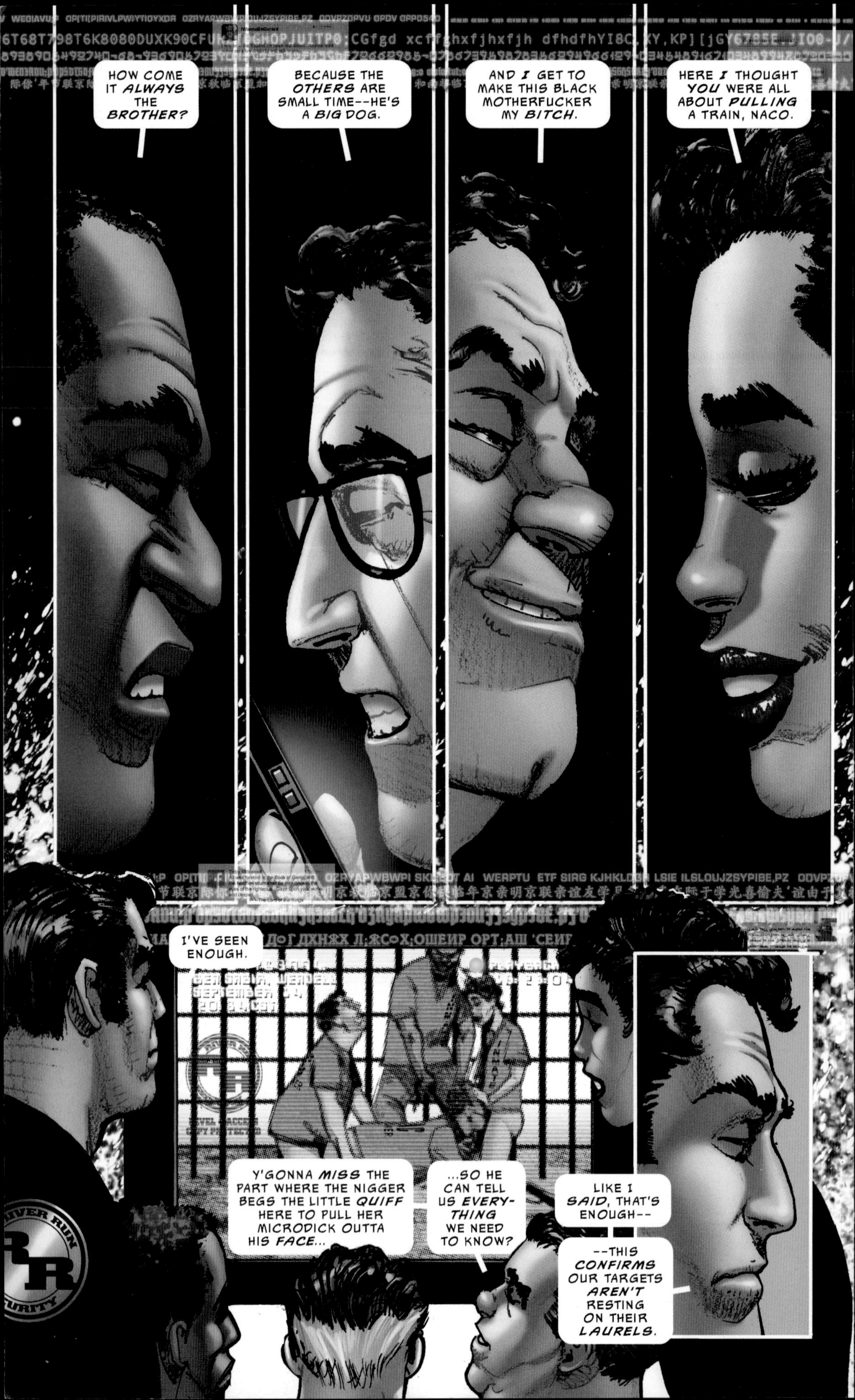
HOW COME IT ALWAYS THE BROTHER?
BECAUSE THE OTHERS ARE SMALL TIME--HE'S A BIG DOG.
AND I GET TO MAKE THIS BLACK MOTHERFUCKER MY BITCH.
HERE I THOUGHT YOU WERE ALL ABOUT PULLING A TRAIN, NACO.
I'VE SEEN ENOUGH.
Y'GONNA MISS THE PART WHERE THE NIGGER BEGS THE LITTLE QUIFF HERE TO PULL HER MICRODICK OUTTA HIS FACE...
...SO HE CAN TELL US EVERYTHING WE NEED TO KNOW?
LIKE I SAID, THAT'S ENOUGH--
--THIS CONFIRMS OUR TARGETS AREN'T RESTING ON THEIR LAURELS.

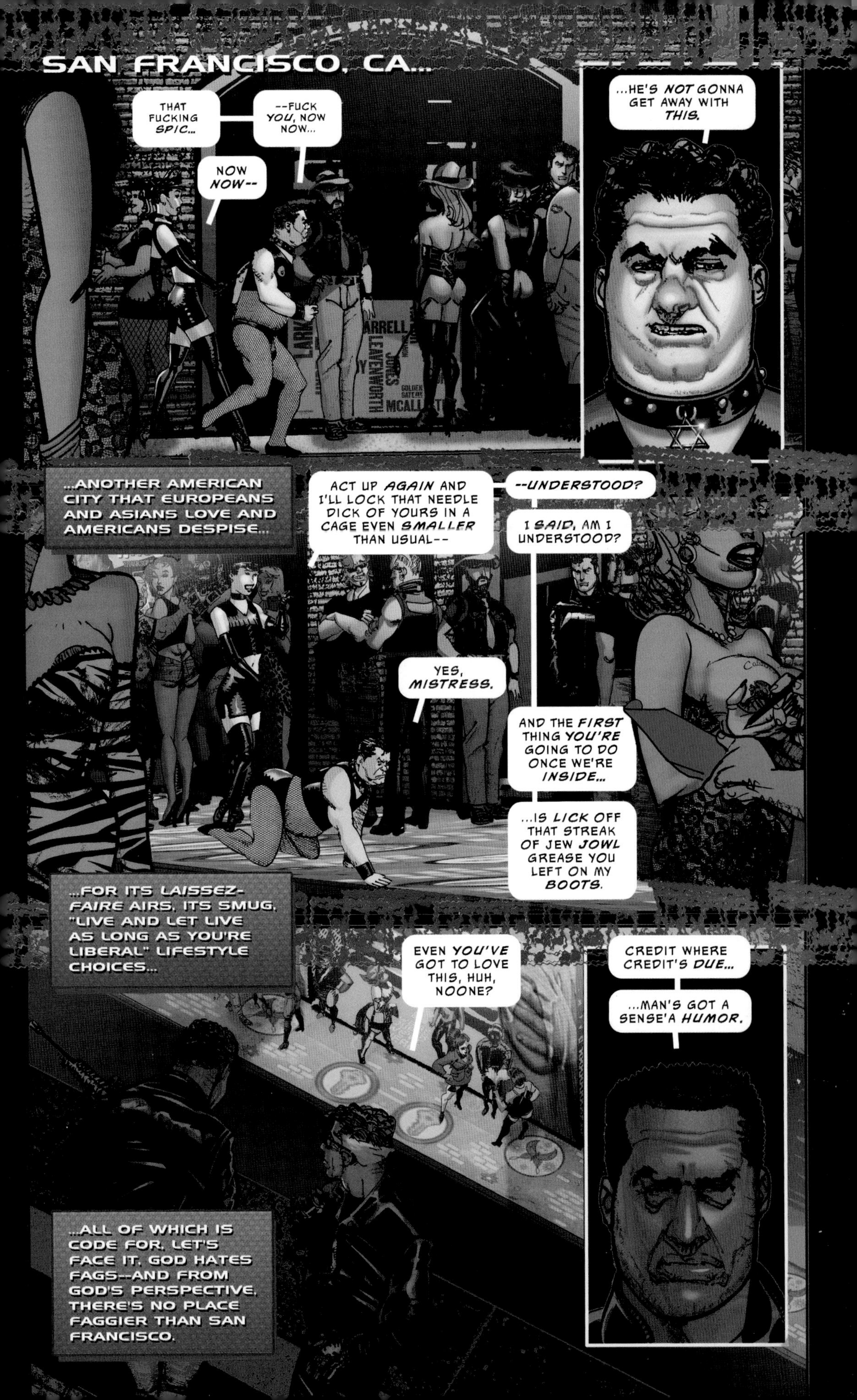
SAN FRANCISCO, CA...
THAT FUCKING SPIC...
--FUCK YOU, NOW NOW...
NOW NOW--
...HE'S NOT GONNA GET AWAY WITH THIS.
...ANOTHER AMERICAN CITY THAT EUROPEANS AND ASIANS LOVE AND AMERICANS DESPISE...
ACT UP AGAIN AND I'LL LOCK THAT NEEDLE DICK OF YOURS IN A CAGE EVEN SMALLER THAN USUAL--
--UNDERSTOOD?
I SAID, AM I UNDERSTOOD?
YES, MISTRESS.
AND THE FIRST THING YOU'RE GOING TO DO ONCE WE'RE INSIDE...
...IS LICK OFF THAT STREAK OF JEW JOWL GREASE YOU LEFT ON MY BOOTS.
...FOR ITS LAISSEZ-FAIRE AIRS, ITS SMUG, "LIVE AND LET LIVE AS LONG AS YOU'RE LIBERAL" LIFESTYLE CHOICES...
EVEN YOU'VE GOT TO LOVE THIS, HUH, NOONE?
...ALL OF WHICH IS CODE FOR, LET'S FACE IT, GOD HATES FAGS--AND FROM GOD'S PERSPECTIVE, THERE'S NO PLACE FAGGIER THAN SAN FRANCISCO.
CREDIT WHERE CREDIT'S DUE...
...MAN'S GOT A SENSE'A HUMOR.

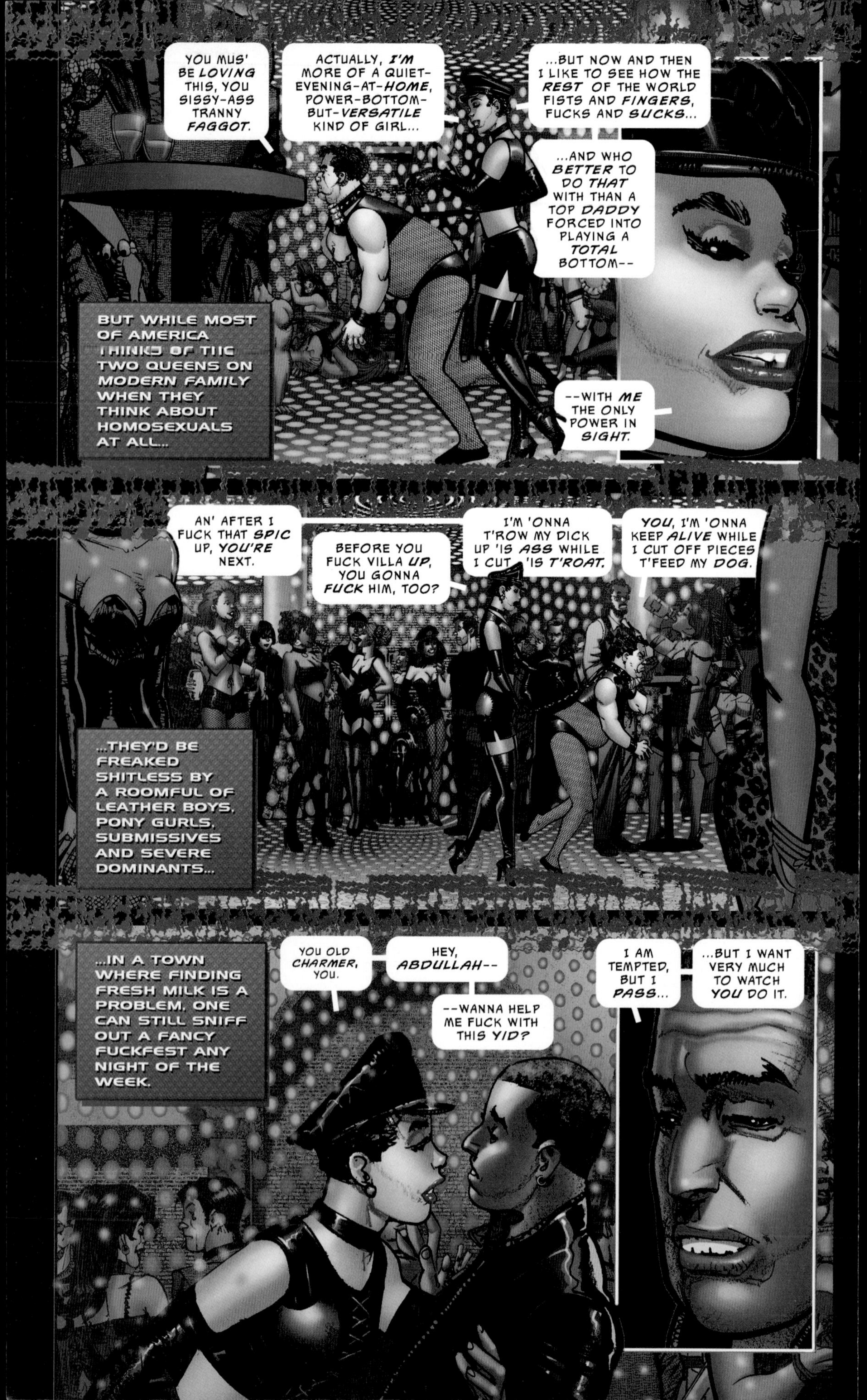
YOU MUS' BE LOVING THIS, YOU SISSY-ASS TRANNY FAGGOT.
ACTUALLY, I'M MORE OF A QUIET-EVENING-AT-HOME, POWER-BOTTOM-BUT-VERSATILE KIND OF GIRL...
...BUT NOW AND THEN I LIKE TO SEE HOW THE REST OF THE WORLD FISTS AND FINGERS, FUCKS AND SUCKS...
...AND WHO BETTER TO DO THAT WITH THAN A TOP DADDY FORCED INTO PLAYING A TOTAL BOTTOM--
--WITH ME THE ONLY POWER IN SIGHT.
BUT WHILE MOST OF AMERICA THINKS OF THE TWO QUEENS ON MODERN FAMILY WHEN THEY THINK ABOUT HOMOSEXUALS AT ALL...
AN' AFTER I FUCK THAT SPIC UP, YOU'RE NEXT.
BEFORE YOU FUCK VILLA UP, YOU GONNA FUCK HIM, TOO?
I'M 'ONNA T'ROW MY DICK UP 'IS ASS WHILE I CUT 'IS T'ROAT.
YOU, I'M 'ONNA KEEP ALIVE WHILE I CUT OFF PIECES T'FEED MY DOG.
...THEY'D BE FREAKED SHITLESS BY A ROOMFUL OF LEATHER BOYS, PONY GURLS, SUBMISSIVES AND SEVERE DOMINANTS...
...IN A TOWN WHERE FINDING FRESH MILK IS A PROBLEM, ONE CAN STILL SNIFF OUT A FANCY FUCKFEST ANY NIGHT OF THE WEEK.
YOU OLD CHARMER, YOU.
HEY, ABDULLAH--
--WANNA HELP ME FUCK WITH THIS YID?
I AM TEMPTED, BUT I PASS...
...BUT I WANT VERY MUCH TO WATCH YOU DO IT.

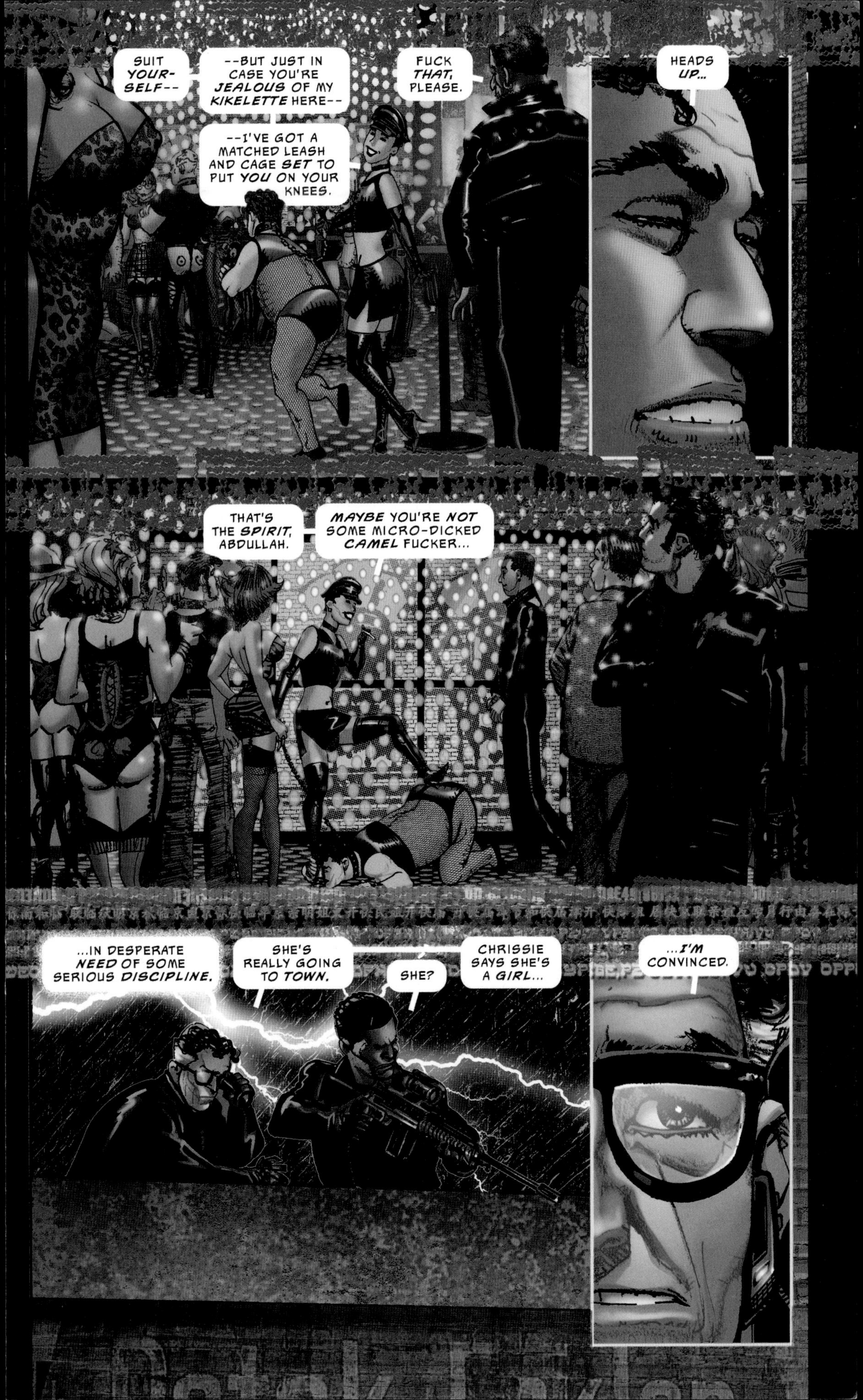
SUIT YOUR-SELF--
--BUT JUST IN CASE YOU'RE JEALOUS OF MY KIKELETTE HERE--
--I'VE GOT A MATCHED LEASH AND CAGE SET TO PUT YOU ON YOUR KNEES.
FUCK THAT, PLEASE.
HEADS UP...
THAT'S THE SPIRIT, ABDULLAH.
MAYBE YOU'RE NOT SOME MICRO-DICKED CAMEL FUCKER...
...IN DESPERATE NEED OF SOME SERIOUS DISCIPLINE.
SHE'S REALLY GOING TO TOWN.
SHE?
CHRISSIE SAYS SHE'S A GIRL...
...I'M CONVINCED.

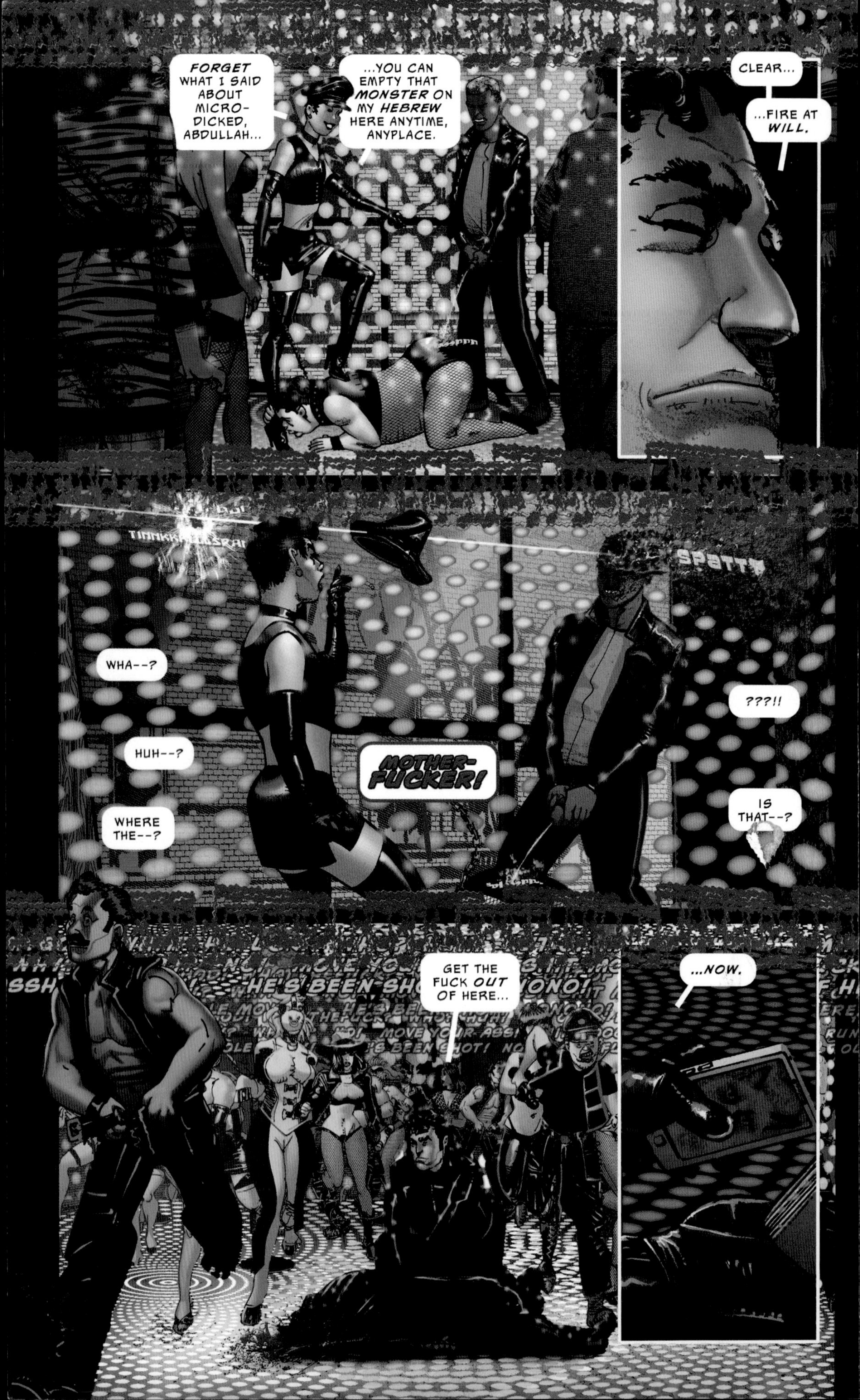
FORGET WHAT I SAID ABOUT MICRO-DICKED, ABDULLAH...
...YOU CAN EMPTY THAT MONSTER ON MY HEBREW HERE ANYTIME, ANYPLACE.
CLEAR...
...FIRE AT WILL.
SPATT
WHA--?
HUH--?
WHERE THE--?
MOTHER-FUCKER!
???!!
IS THAT--?
HE'S BEEN SHOT!
GET THE FUCK OUT OF HERE...
...NOW.

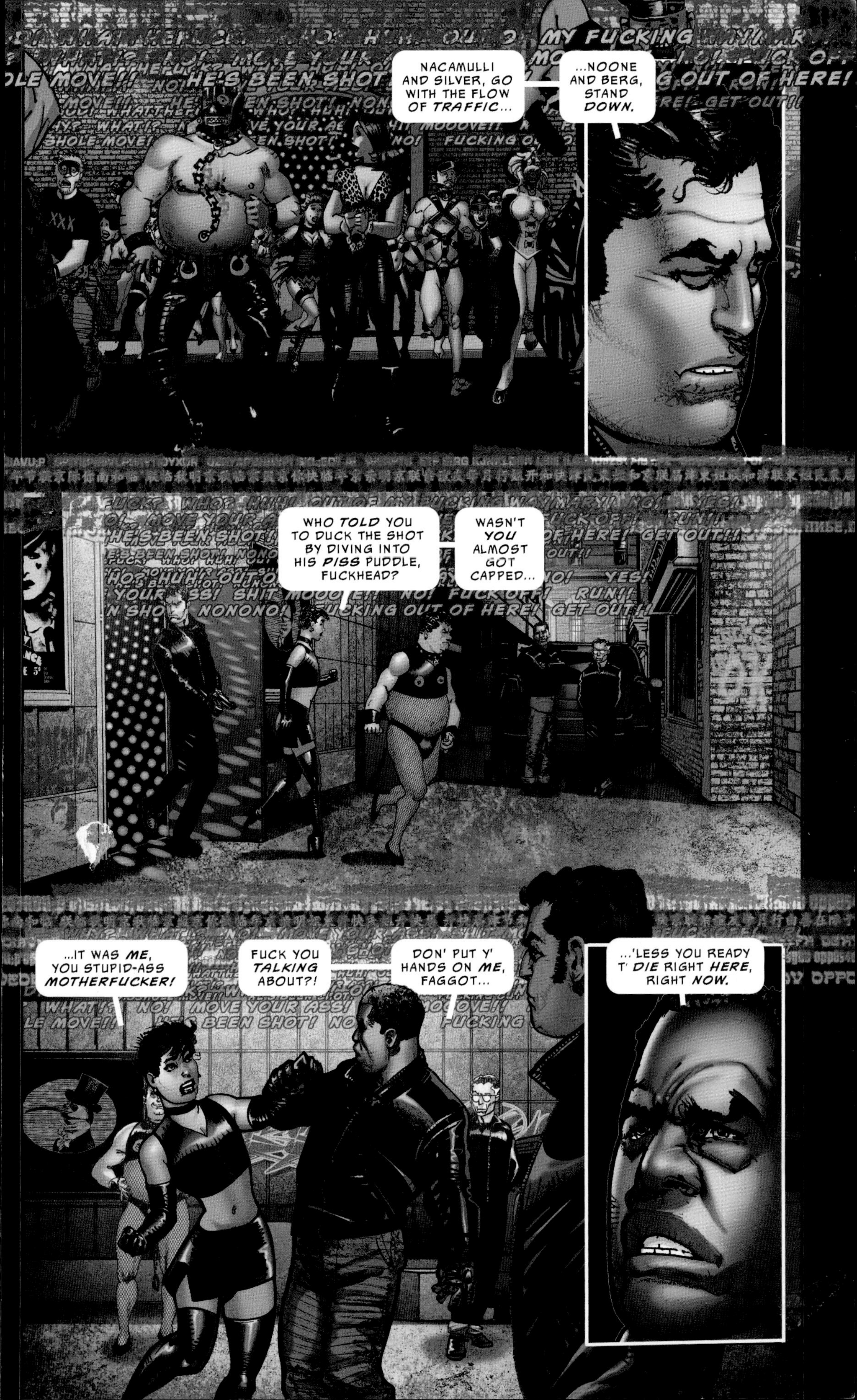
NACAMULLI AND SILVER, GO WITH THE FLOW OF TRAFFIC...
...NOONE AND BERG, STAND DOWN.
WHO TOLD YOU TO DUCK THE SHOT BY DIVING INTO HIS PISS PUDDLE, FUCKHEAD?
WASN'T YOU ALMOST GOT CAPPED...
...IT WAS ME, YOU STUPID-ASS MOTHERFUCKER!
FUCK YOU TALKING ABOUT?!
DON' PUT Y' HANDS ON ME, FAGGOT...
...'LESS YOU READY T' DIE RIGHT HERE, RIGHT NOW.

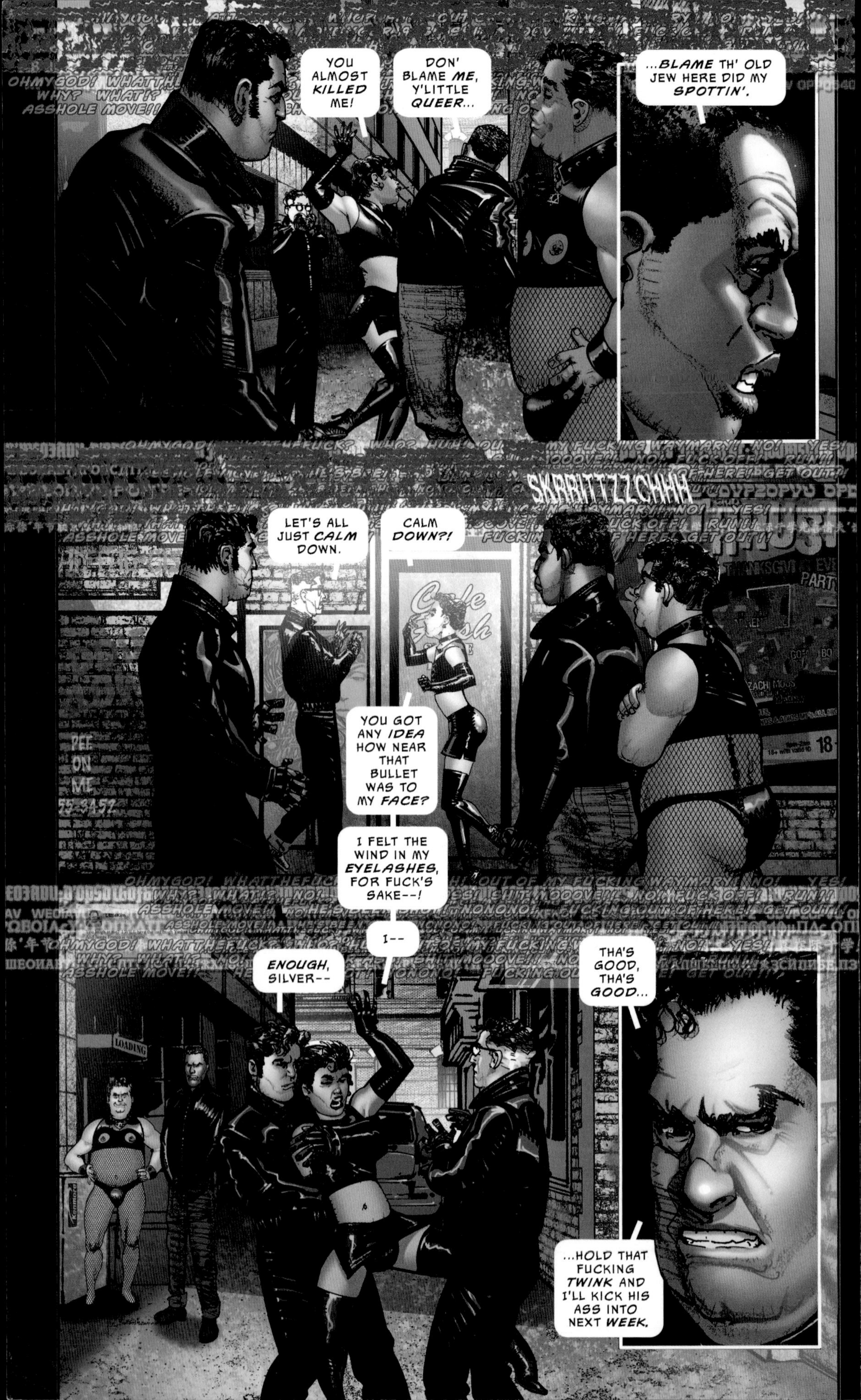
YOU ALMOST KILLED ME!
DON' BLAME ME, Y'LITTLE QUEER...
...BLAME TH' OLD JEW HERE DID MY SPOTTIN'.
SKRRITTZZCHHH
LET'S ALL JUST CALM DOWN.
CALM DOWN?!
YOU GOT ANY IDEA HOW NEAR THAT BULLET WAS TO MY FACE?
I FELT THE WIND IN MY EYELASHES, FOR FUCK'S SAKE--!
I--
ENOUGH, SILVER--
THA'S GOOD, THA'S GOOD...
...HOLD THAT FUCKING TWINK AND I'LL KICK HIS ASS INTO NEXT WEEK.
PEE ON ME
LOADING

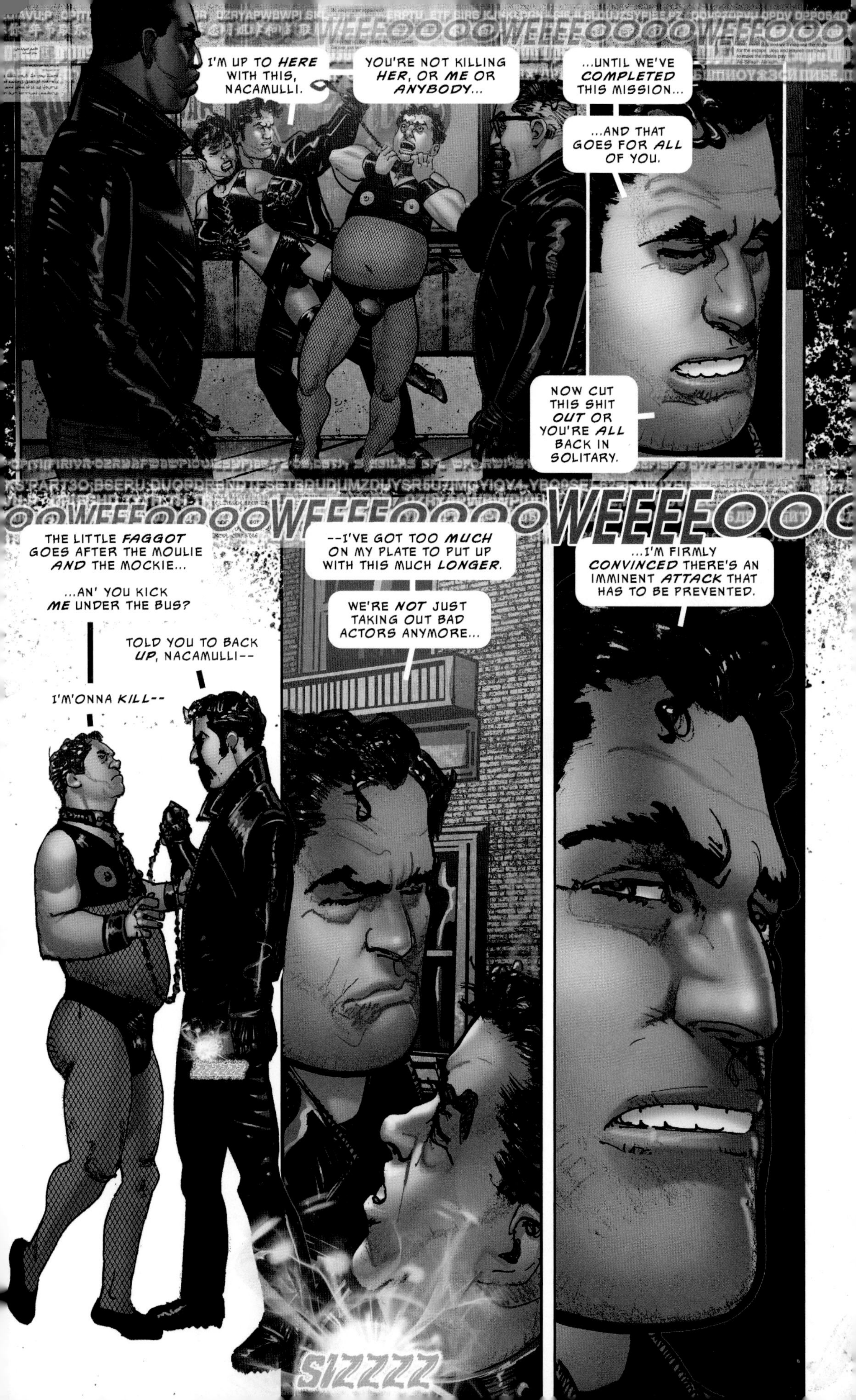

I'M UP TO HERE WITH THIS, NACAMULLI.
YOU'RE NOT KILLING HER, OR ME OR ANYBODY...
...UNTIL WE'VE COMPLETED THIS MISSION...
...AND THAT GOES FOR ALL OF YOU.
NOW CUT THIS SHIT OUT OR YOU'RE ALL BACK IN SOLITARY.
THE LITTLE FAGGOT GOES AFTER THE MOULIE AND THE MOCKIE...
...AN' YOU KICK ME UNDER THE BUS?
TOLD YOU TO BACK UP, NACAMULLI--
I'M'ONNA KILL--
--I'VE GOT TOO MUCH ON MY PLATE TO PUT UP WITH THIS MUCH LONGER.
WE'RE NOT JUST TAKING OUT BAD ACTORS ANYMORE...
...I'M FIRMLY CONVINCED THERE'S AN IMMINENT ATTACK THAT HAS TO BE PREVENTED.
SIZZZZ

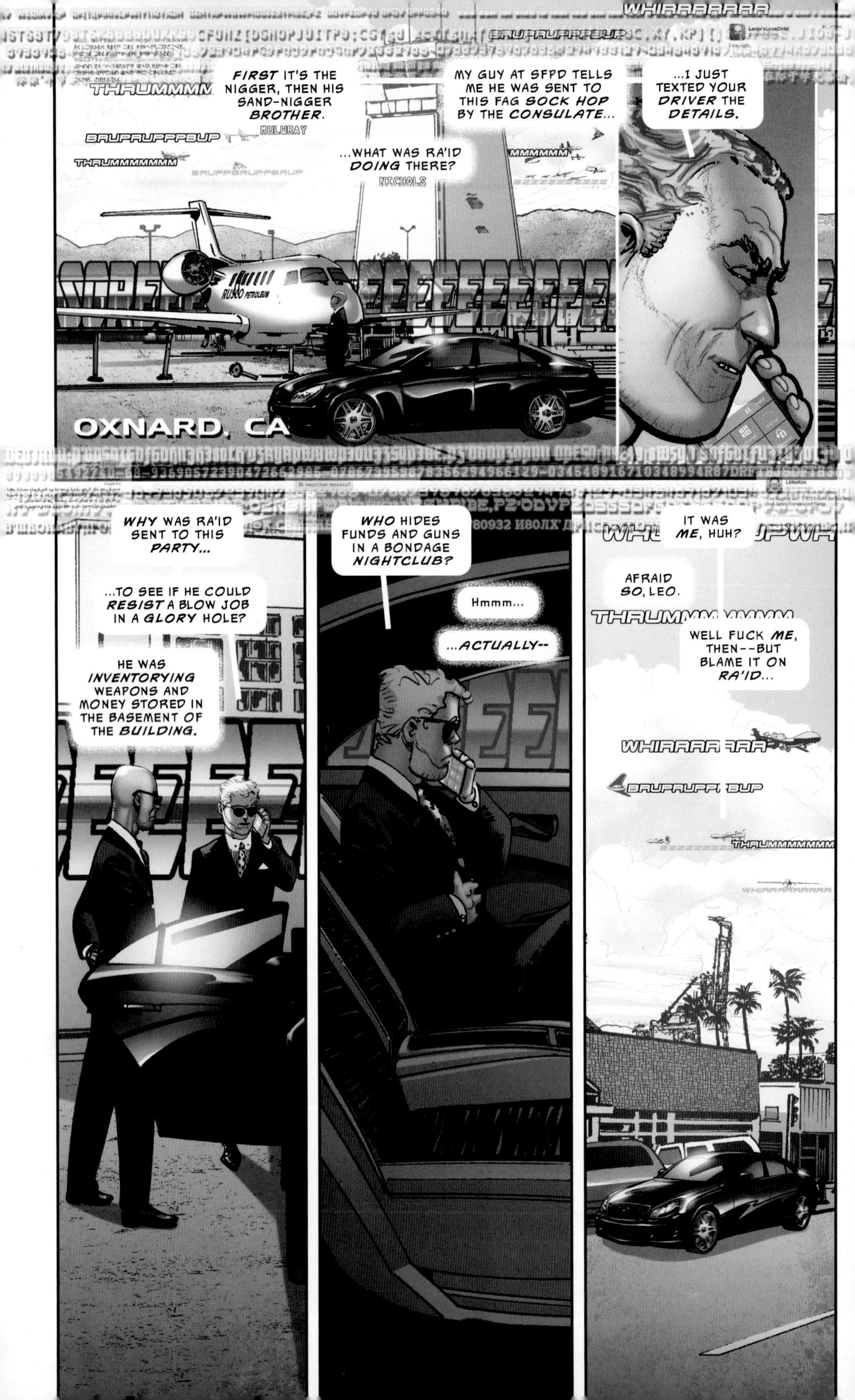
WHIRRRRRRRR
BRUPRUPPPBUP
THRUMMMM
FIRST IT'S THE NIGGER, THEN HIS SAND-NIGGER BROTHER.
MULURAY
...WHAT WAS RA'ID DOING THERE?
NICHOLS
MY GUY AT SFPD TELLS ME HE WAS SENT TO THIS FAG SOCK HOP BY THE CONSULATE...
...I JUST TEXTED YOUR DRIVER THE DETAILS.
BRUPRUPPPBUP
THRUMMMMMMM
RUSCO PETROLEUM
OXNARD, CA
WHY WAS RA'ID SENT TO THIS PARTY...
...TO SEE IF HE COULD RESIST A BLOW JOB IN A GLORY HOLE?
HE WAS INVENTORYING WEAPONS AND MONEY STORED IN THE BASEMENT OF THE BUILDING.
WHO HIDES FUNDS AND GUNS IN A BONDAGE NIGHTCLUB?
Hmmm...
...ACTUALLY--
IT WAS ME, HUH?
AFRAID SO, LEO.
THRUMMMMMMMM
WELL FUCK ME, THEN--BUT BLAME IT ON RA'ID...
WHIRRRRRRRR
BRUPRUPPPBUP
THRUMMMMMMM

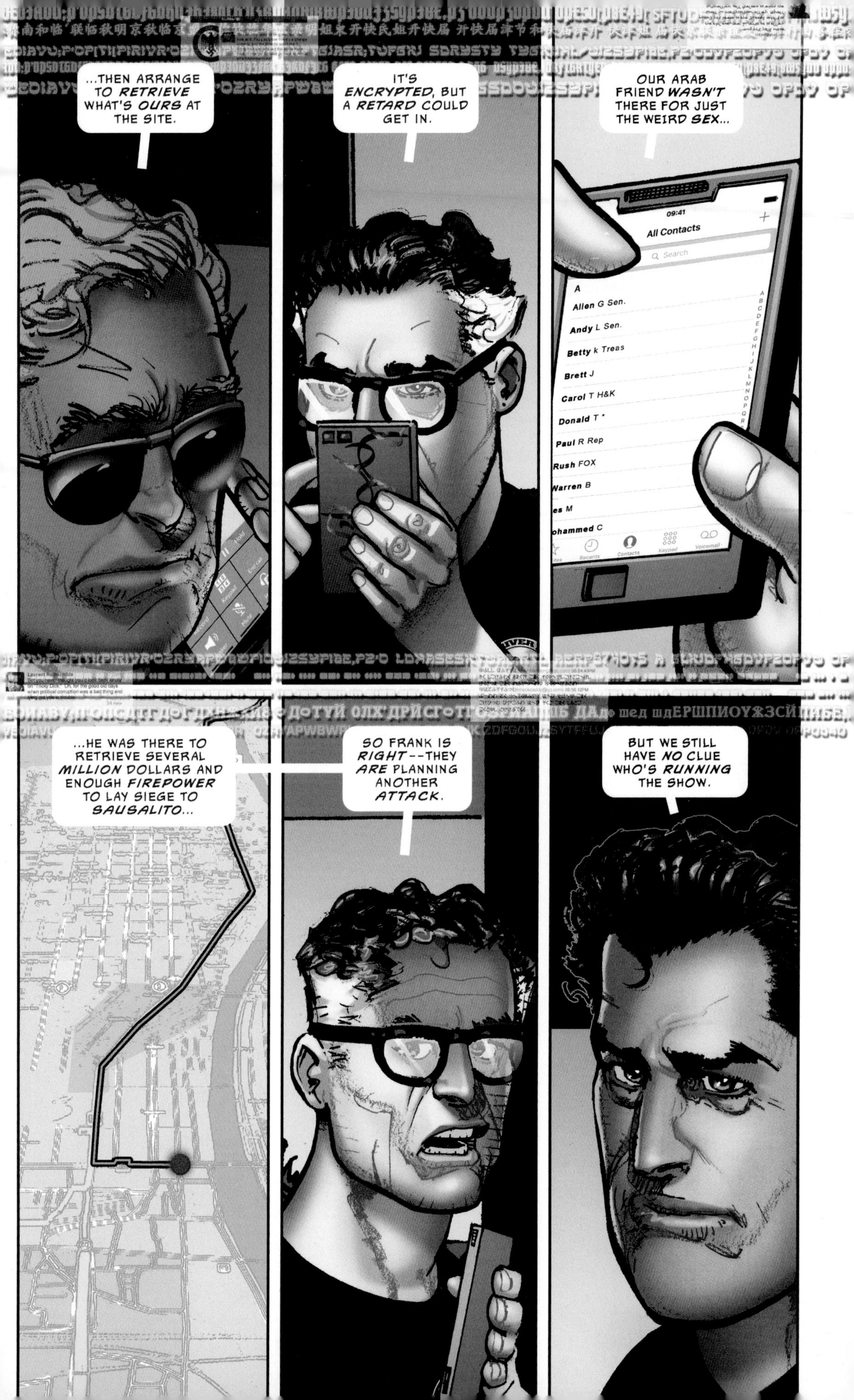
...THEN ARRANGE TO RETRIEVE WHAT'S OURS AT THE SITE.
IT'S ENCRYPTED, BUT A RETARD COULD GET IN.
OUR ARAB FRIEND WASN'T THERE FOR JUST THE WEIRD SEX...
09:41
All Contacts
Search
A
Allen G Sen.
Andy L Sen.
Betty k Treas
Brett J
Carol T H&K
Donald T *
Paul R Rep
Rush FOX
Warren B
Recents
Contacts
Keypad
Voicemail
...HE WAS THERE TO RETRIEVE SEVERAL MILLION DOLLARS AND ENOUGH FIREPOWER TO LAY SIEGE TO SAUSALITO...
SO FRANK IS RIGHT--THEY ARE PLANNING ANOTHER ATTACK.
BUT WE STILL HAVE NO CLUE WHO'S RUNNING THE SHOW.

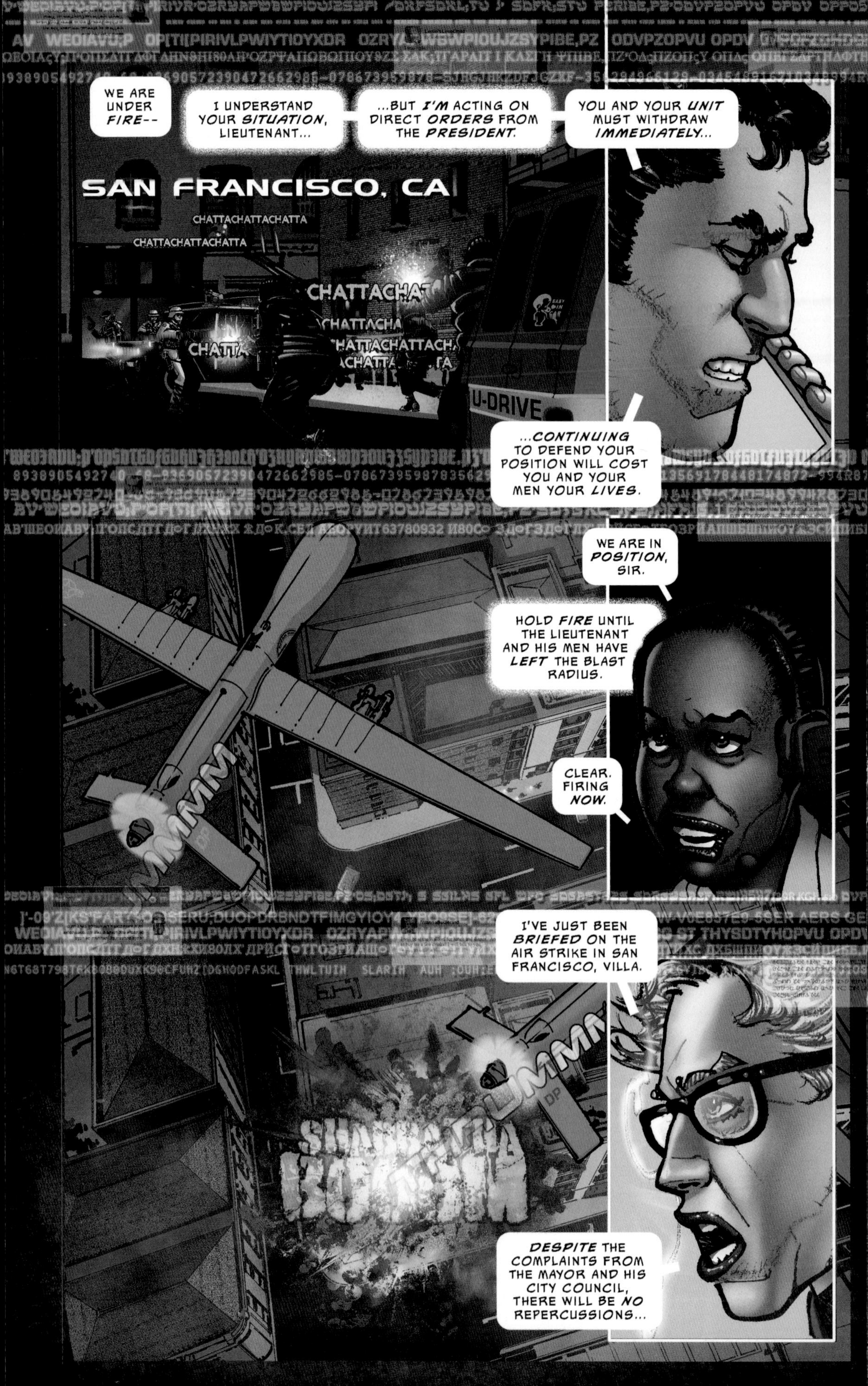
WE ARE UNDER FIRE--
I UNDERSTAND YOUR SITUATION, LIEUTENANT...
...BUT I'M ACTING ON DIRECT ORDERS FROM THE PRESIDENT.
YOU AND YOUR UNIT MUST WITHDRAW IMMEDIATELY...
SAN FRANCISCO, CA
CHATTACHATTACHATTA
CHATTACHATTACHATTA
U-DRIVE
...CONTINUING TO DEFEND YOUR POSITION WILL COST YOU AND YOUR MEN YOUR LIVES.
WE ARE IN POSITION, SIR.
HOLD FIRE UNTIL THE LIEUTENANT AND HIS MEN HAVE LEFT THE BLAST RADIUS.
CLEAR. FIRING NOW.
I'VE JUST BEEN BRIEFED ON THE AIR STRIKE IN SAN FRANCISCO, VILLA.
DESPITE THE COMPLAINTS FROM THE MAYOR AND HIS CITY COUNCIL, THERE WILL BE NO REPERCUSSIONS...

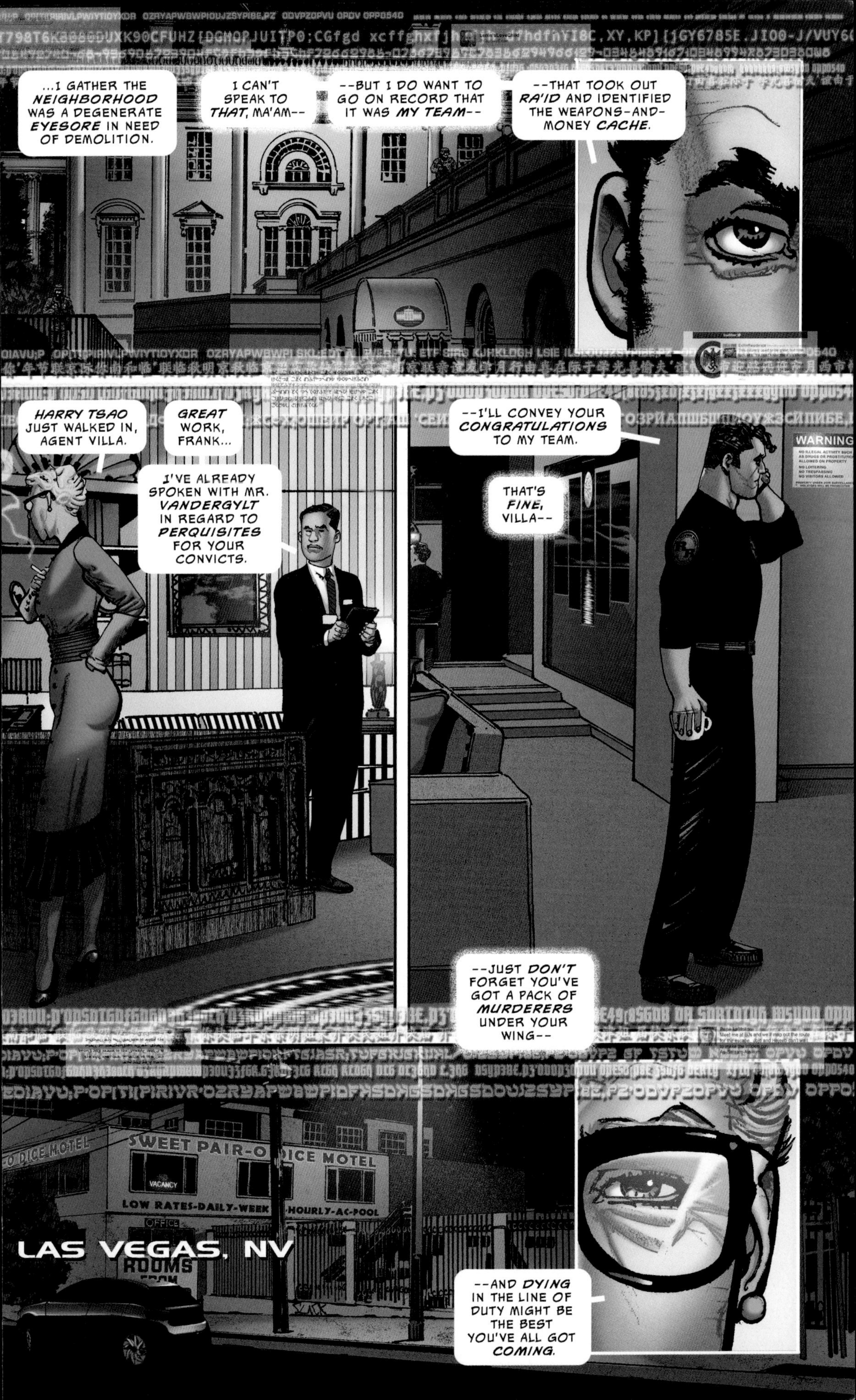

...I GATHER THE NEIGHBORHOOD WAS A DEGENERATE EYESORE IN NEED OF DEMOLITION.
I CAN'T SPEAK TO THAT, MA'AM--
--BUT I DO WANT TO GO ON RECORD THAT IT WAS MY TEAM--
--THAT TOOK OUT RA'ID AND IDENTIFIED THE WEAPONS-AND-MONEY CACHE.
HARRY TSAO JUST WALKED IN, AGENT VILLA.
GREAT WORK, FRANK...
I'VE ALREADY SPOKEN WITH MR. VANDERGYLT IN REGARD TO PERQUISITES FOR YOUR CONVICTS.
--I'LL CONVEY YOUR CONGRATULATIONS TO MY TEAM.
WARNING
THAT'S FINE, VILLA--
--JUST DON'T FORGET YOU'VE GOT A PACK OF MURDERERS UNDER YOUR WING--
SWEET PAIR-O-DICE MOTEL
VACANCY
LOW RATES-DAILY-WEEK-HOURLY-AC-POOL
OFFICE
ROOMS
LAS VEGAS, NV
--AND DYING IN THE LINE OF DUTY MIGHT BE THE BEST YOU'VE ALL GOT COMING.

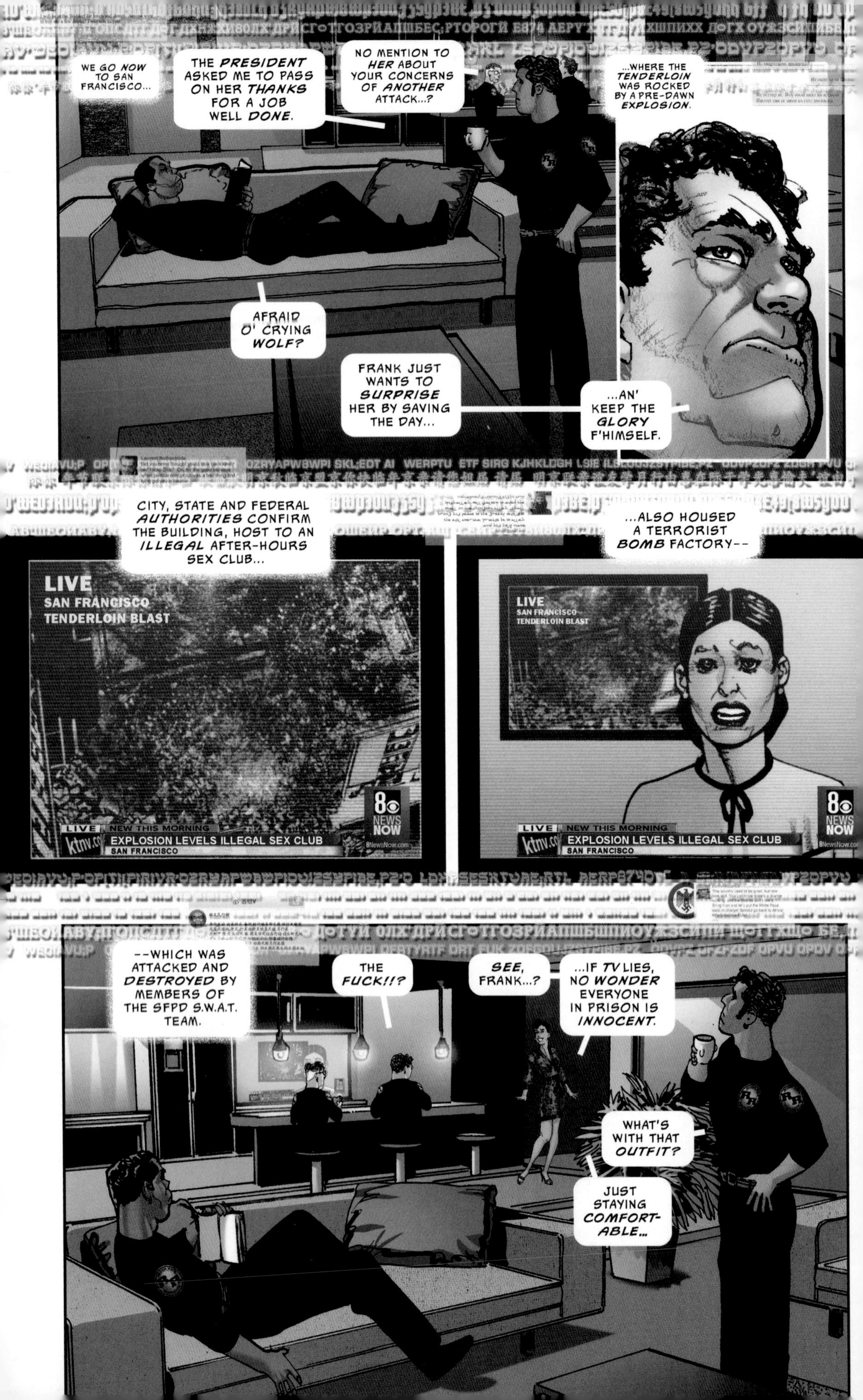

WE GO NOW TO SAN FRANCISCO...
THE PRESIDENT ASKED ME TO PASS ON HER THANKS FOR A JOB WELL DONE.
NO MENTION TO HER ABOUT YOUR CONCERNS OF ANOTHER ATTACK...?
...WHERE THE TENDERLOIN WAS ROCKED BY A PRE-DAWN EXPLOSION.
AFRAID O' CRYING WOLF?
FRANK JUST WANTS TO SURPRISE HER BY SAVING THE DAY...
...AN' KEEP THE GLORY F'HIMSELF.
CITY, STATE AND FEDERAL AUTHORITIES CONFIRM THE BUILDING, HOST TO AN ILLEGAL AFTER-HOURS SEX CLUB...
LIVE
SAN FRANCISCO
TENDERLOIN BLAST
LIVE
NEW THIS MORNING
EXPLOSION LEVELS ILLEGAL SEX CLUB
SAN FRANCISCO
8 NEWS NOW
8NewsNow.com
...ALSO HOUSED A TERRORIST BOMB FACTORY--
LIVE
SAN FRANCISCO
TENDERLOIN BLAST
LIVE
NEW THIS MORNING
EXPLOSION LEVELS ILLEGAL SEX CLUB
SAN FRANCISCO
8 NEWS NOW
8NewsNow.com
--WHICH WAS ATTACKED AND DESTROYED BY MEMBERS OF THE SFPD S.W.A.T. TEAM.
THE FUCK!!?
SEE, FRANK...?
...IF TV LIES, NO WONDER EVERYONE IN PRISON IS INNOCENT.
WHAT'S WITH THAT OUTFIT?
JUST STAYING COMFORT-ABLE...

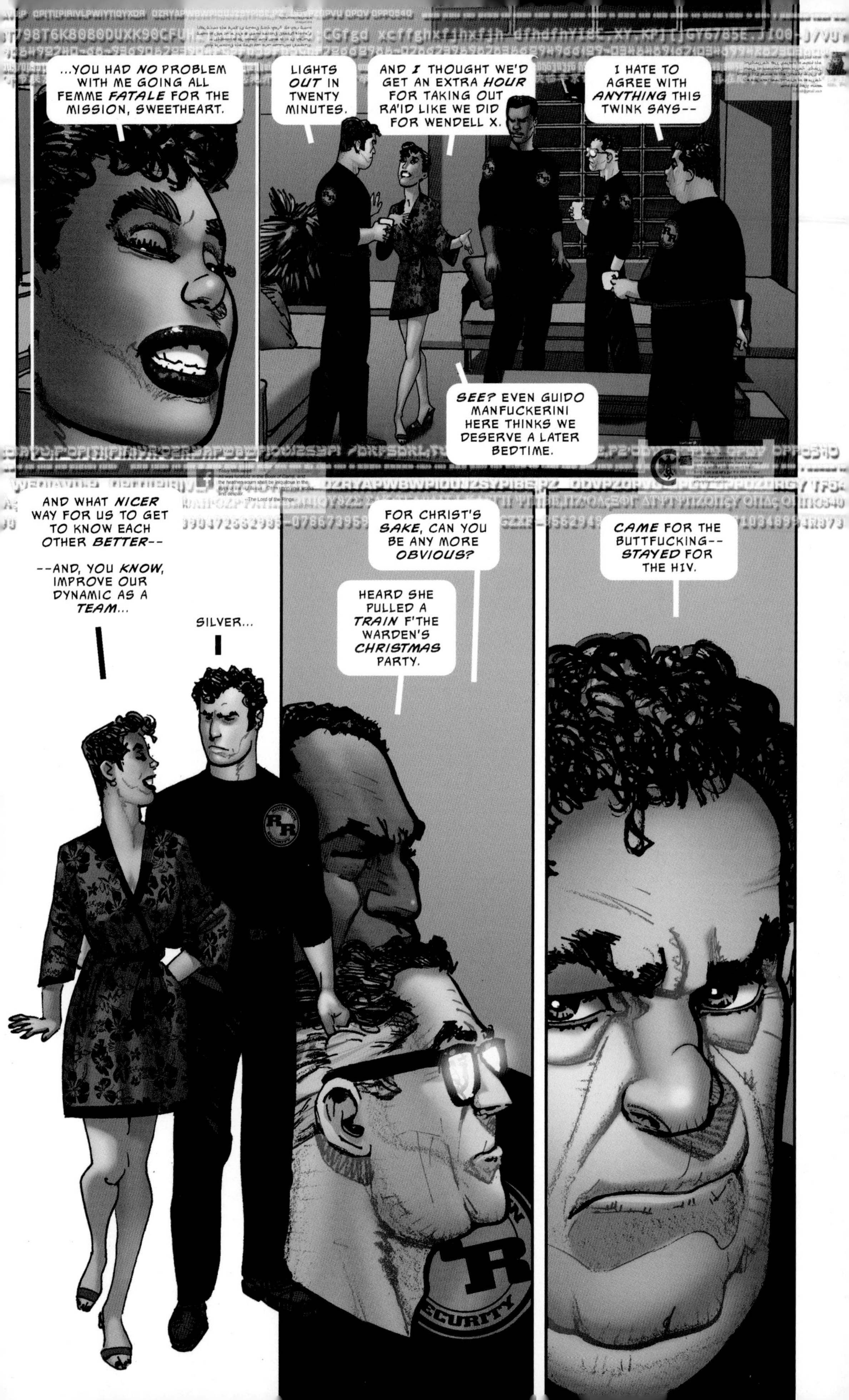
...YOU HAD NO PROBLEM WITH ME GOING ALL FEMME FATALE FOR THE MISSION, SWEETHEART.
LIGHTS OUT IN TWENTY MINUTES.
AND I THOUGHT WE'D GET AN EXTRA HOUR FOR TAKING OUT RA'ID LIKE WE DID FOR WENDELL X.
I HATE TO AGREE WITH ANYTHING THIS TWINK SAYS--
SEE? EVEN GUIDO MANFUCKERINI HERE THINKS WE DESERVE A LATER BEDTIME.
AND WHAT NICER WAY FOR US TO GET TO KNOW EACH OTHER BETTER--
--AND, YOU KNOW, IMPROVE OUR DYNAMIC AS A TEAM...
SILVER...
FOR CHRIST'S SAKE, CAN YOU BE ANY MORE OBVIOUS?
HEARD SHE PULLED A TRAIN F'THE WARDEN'S CHRISTMAS PARTY.
CAME FOR THE BUTTFUCKING--STAYED FOR THE HIV.

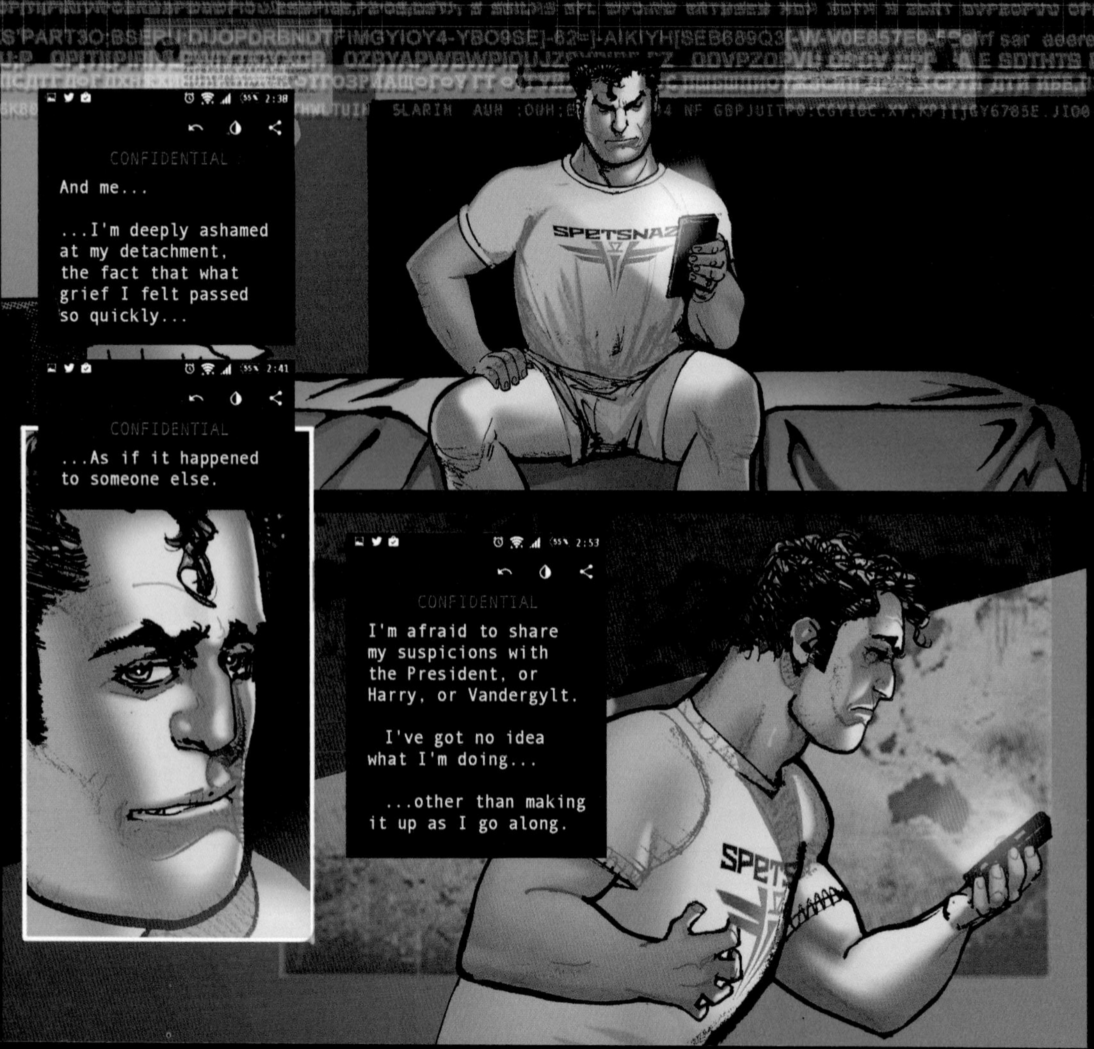

CONFIDENTIAL
And me...
...I'm deeply ashamed at my detachment, the fact that what grief I felt passed so quickly...
CONFIDENTIAL
...As if it happened to someone else.
CONFIDENTIAL
I'm afraid to share my suspicions with the President, or Harry, or Vandergylt.
I've got no idea what I'm doing...
...other than making it up as I go along.
SPETSNAZ

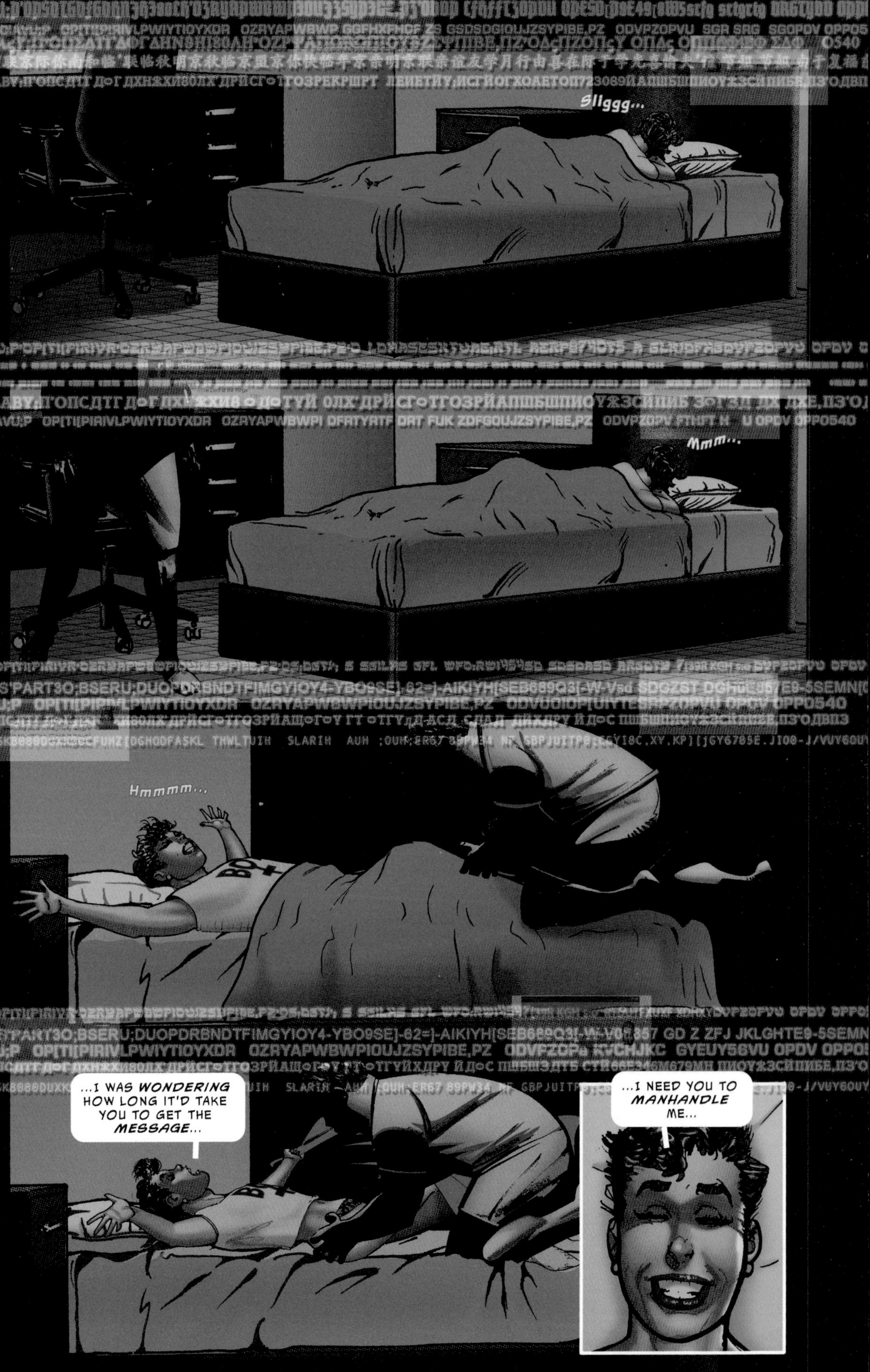
Sliggg...
Mmm...
Hmmmm...
...I WAS WONDERING HOW LONG IT'D TAKE YOU TO GET THE MESSAGE...
...I NEED YOU TO MANHANDLE ME...

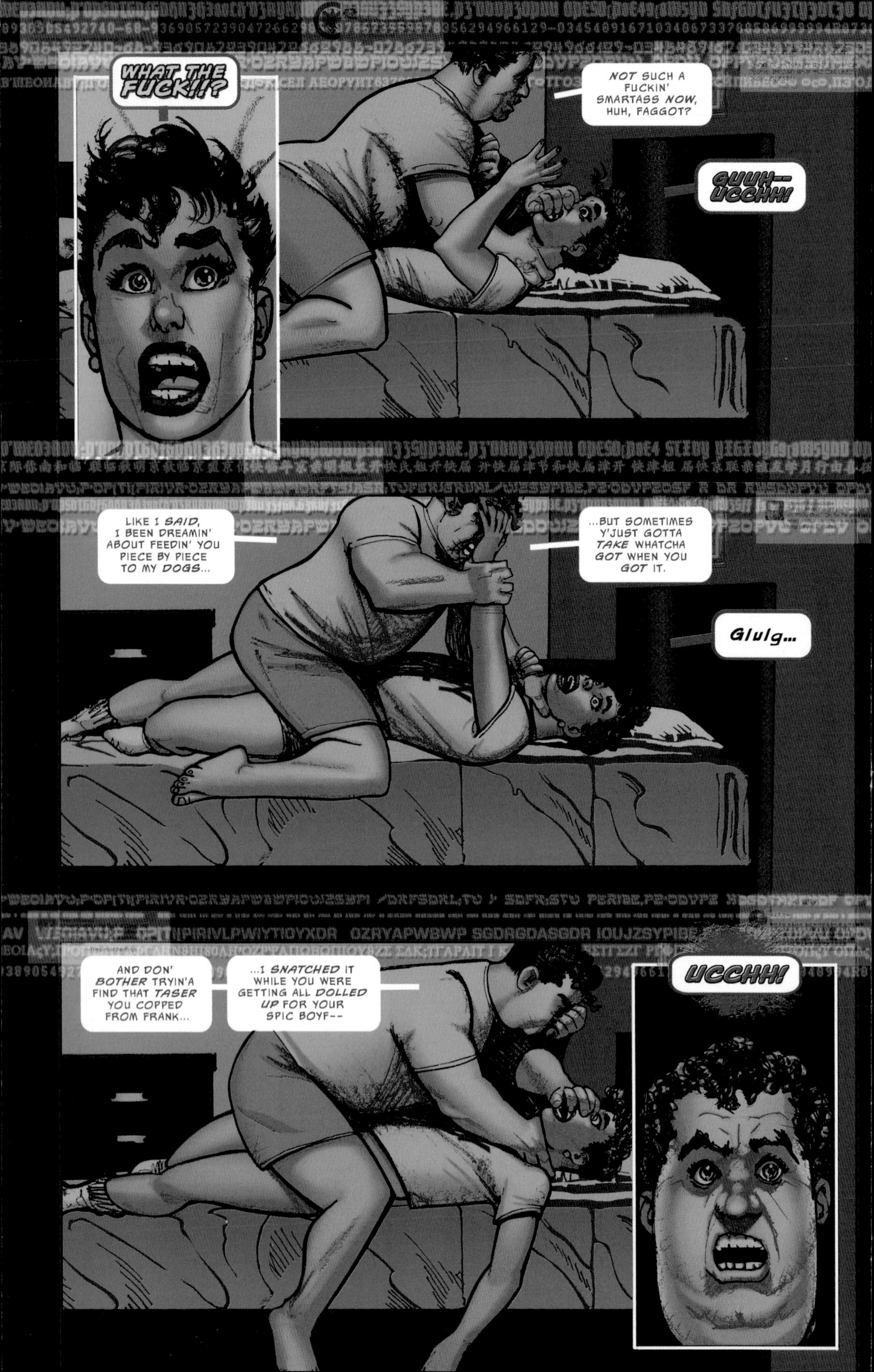
WHAT THE FUCK!!?
NOT SUCH A FUCKIN' SMARTASS NOW, HUH, FAGGOT?
GUUH-- UCCHH!
LIKE I SAID, I BEEN DREAMIN' ABOUT FEEDIN' YOU PIECE BY PIECE TO MY DOGS...
...BUT SOMETIMES Y'JUST GOTTA TAKE WHATCHA GOT WHEN YOU GOT IT.
Glulg...
AND DON' BOTHER TRYIN'A FIND THAT TASER YOU COPPED FROM FRANK...
...I SNATCHED IT WHILE YOU WERE GETTING ALL DOLLED UP FOR YOUR SPIC BOYF--
UCCHH!

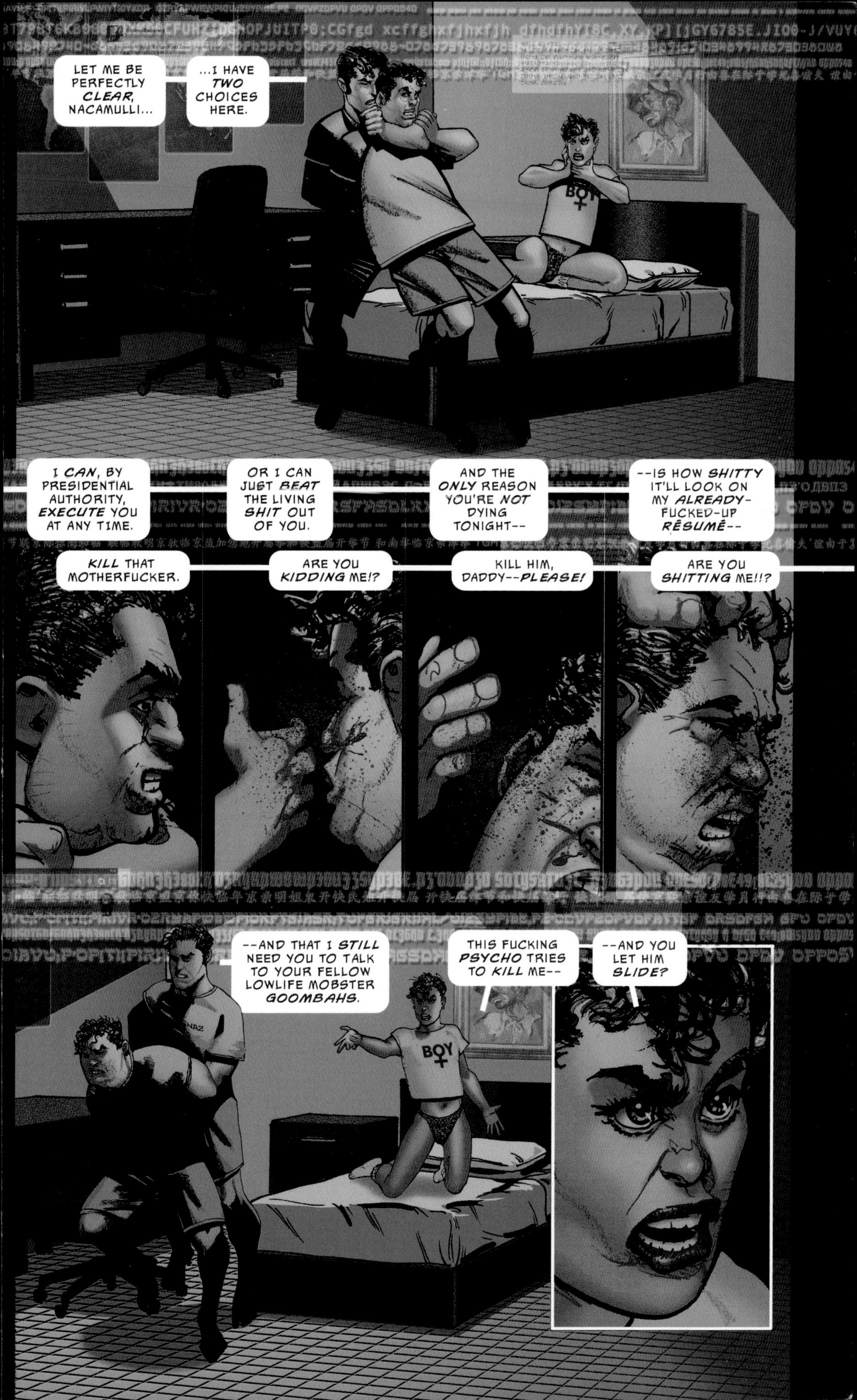
LET ME BE PERFECTLY CLEAR, NACAMULLI...
...I HAVE TWO CHOICES HERE.
I CAN, BY PRESIDENTIAL AUTHORITY, EXECUTE YOU AT ANY TIME.
OR I CAN JUST BEAT THE LIVING SHIT OUT OF YOU.
AND THE ONLY REASON YOU'RE NOT DYING TONIGHT--
--IS HOW SHITTY IT'LL LOOK ON MY ALREADY-FUCKED-UP RÉSUMÉ--
KILL THAT MOTHERFUCKER.
ARE YOU KIDDING ME!?
KILL HIM, DADDY--PLEASE!
ARE YOU SHITTING ME!!?
--AND THAT I STILL NEED YOU TO TALK TO YOUR FELLOW LOWLIFE MOBSTER GOOMBAHS.
THIS FUCKING PSYCHO TRIES TO KILL ME--
--AND YOU LET HIM SLIDE?

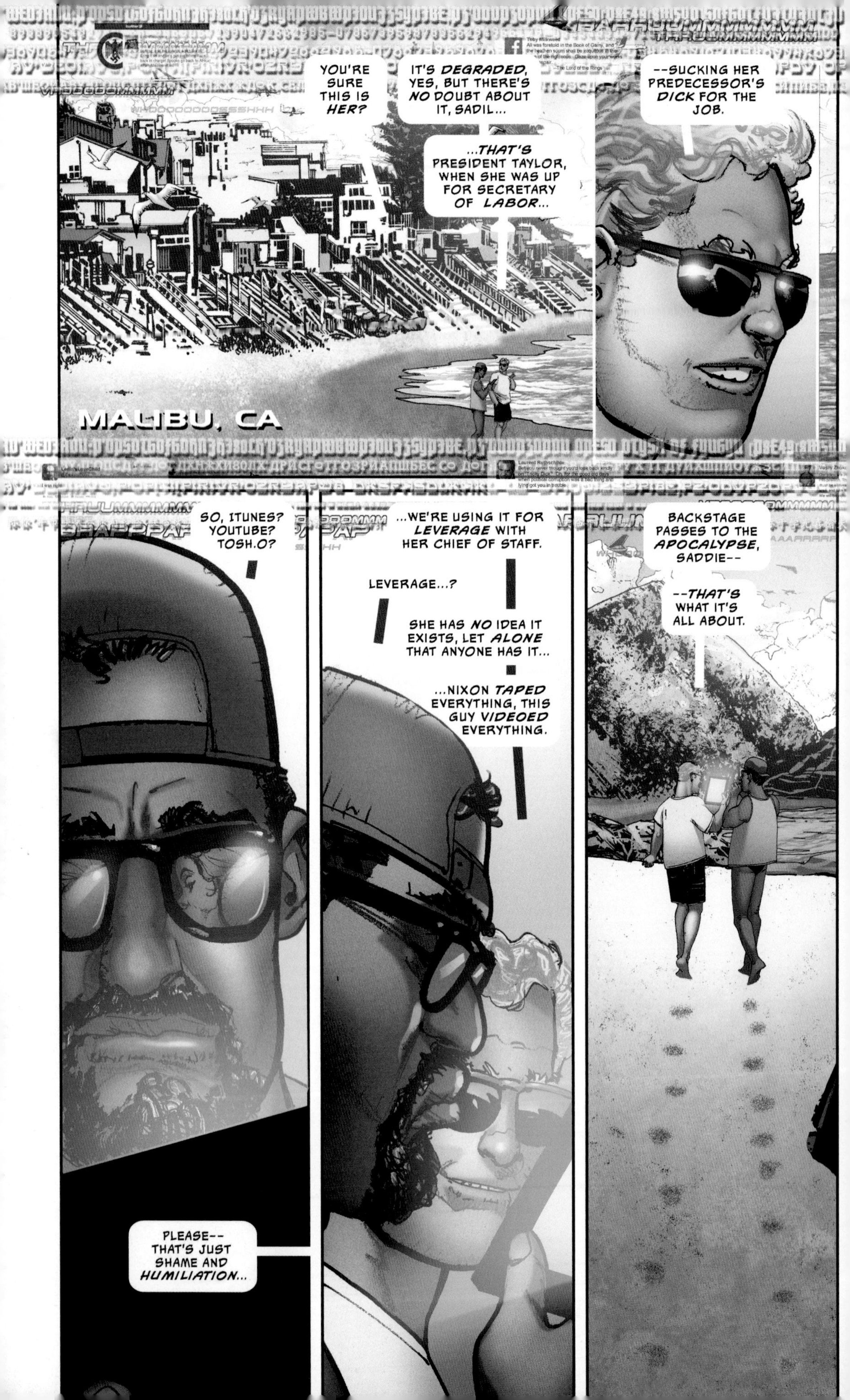
YOU'RE SURE THIS IS HER?
IT'S DEGRADED, YES, BUT THERE'S NO DOUBT ABOUT IT, SADIL...
...THAT'S PRESIDENT TAYLOR, WHEN SHE WAS UP FOR SECRETARY OF LABOR...
MALIBU, CA
--SUCKING HER PREDECESSOR'S DICK FOR THE JOB.
SO, ITUNES? YOUTUBE? TOSH.O?
PLEASE-- THAT'S JUST SHAME AND HUMILIATION...
...WE'RE USING IT FOR LEVERAGE WITH HER CHIEF OF STAFF.
LEVERAGE...?
SHE HAS NO IDEA IT EXISTS, LET ALONE THAT ANYONE HAS IT...
...NIXON TAPED EVERYTHING, THIS GUY VIDEOED EVERYTHING.
BACKSTAGE PASSES TO THE APOCALYPSE, SADDIE--
--THAT'S WHAT IT'S ALL ABOUT.

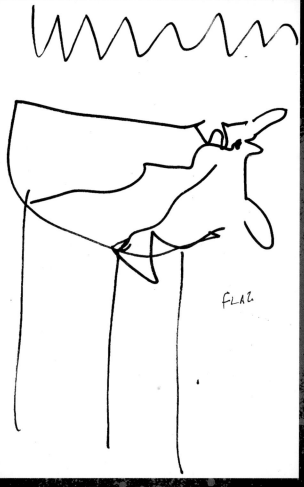

FLAG

Part Five

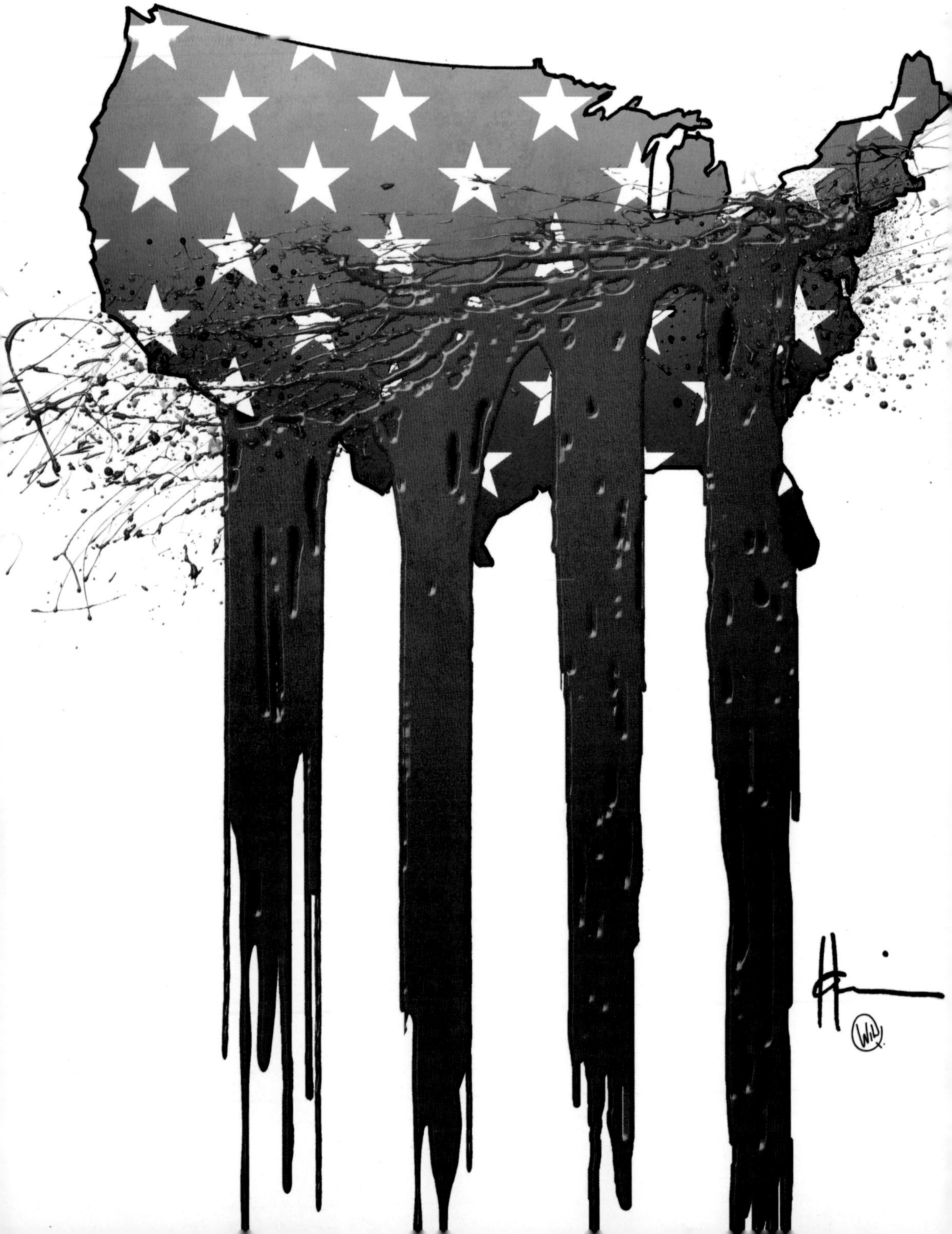

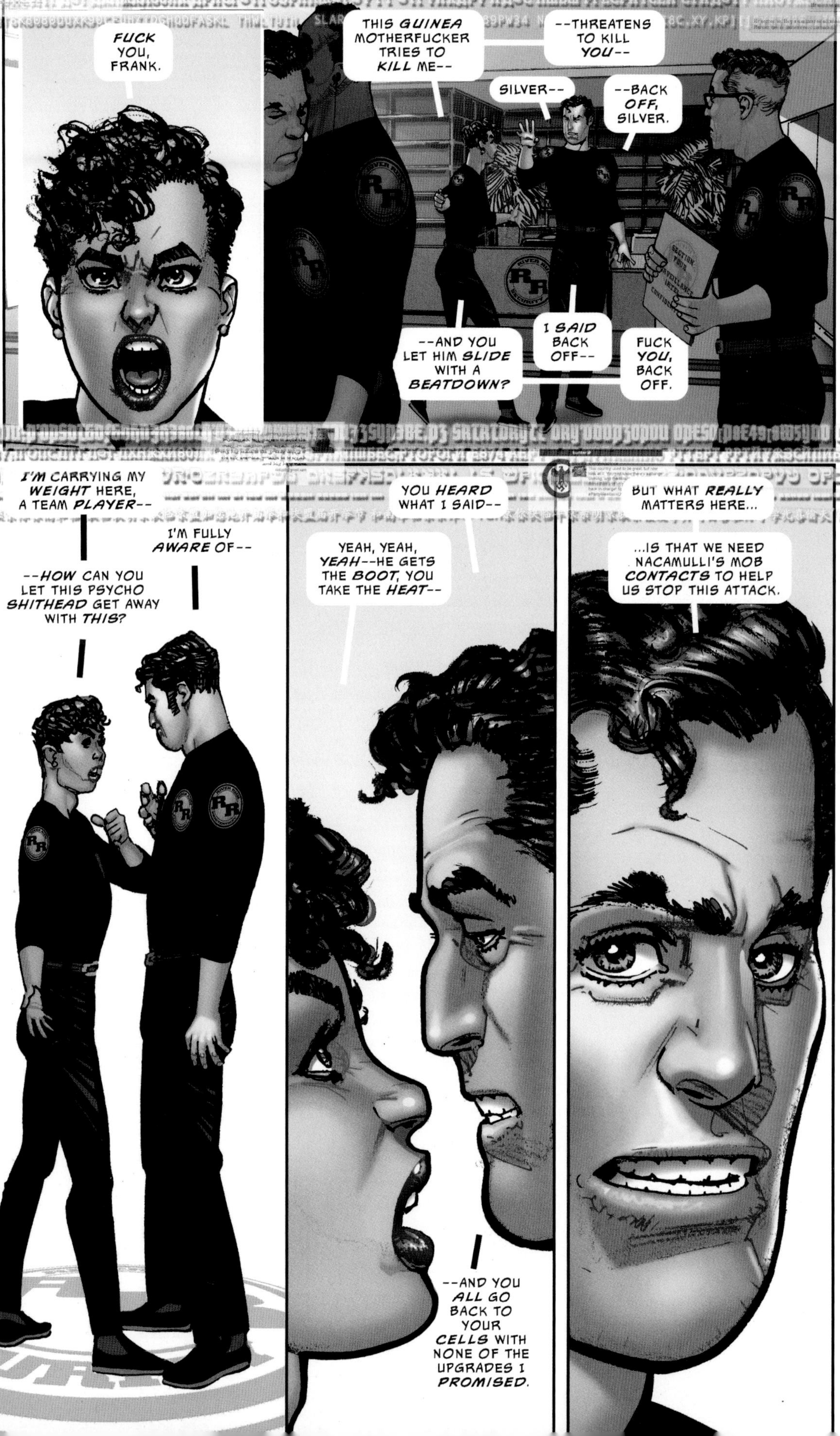
FUCK YOU, FRANK.
THIS GUINEA MOTHERFUCKER TRIES TO KILL ME--
--THREATENS TO KILL YOU--
SILVER--
--BACK OFF, SILVER.
--AND YOU LET HIM SLIDE WITH A BEATDOWN?
I SAID BACK OFF--
FUCK YOU, BACK OFF.
I'M CARRYING MY WEIGHT HERE, A TEAM PLAYER--
I'M FULLY AWARE OF--
--HOW CAN YOU LET THIS PSYCHO SHITHEAD GET AWAY WITH THIS?
YOU HEARD WHAT I SAID--
YEAH, YEAH, YEAH--HE GETS THE BOOT, YOU TAKE THE HEAT--
--AND YOU ALL GO BACK TO YOUR CELLS WITH NONE OF THE UPGRADES I PROMISED.
BUT WHAT REALLY MATTERS HERE...
...IS THAT WE NEED NACAMULLI'S MOB CONTACTS TO HELP US STOP THIS ATTACK.

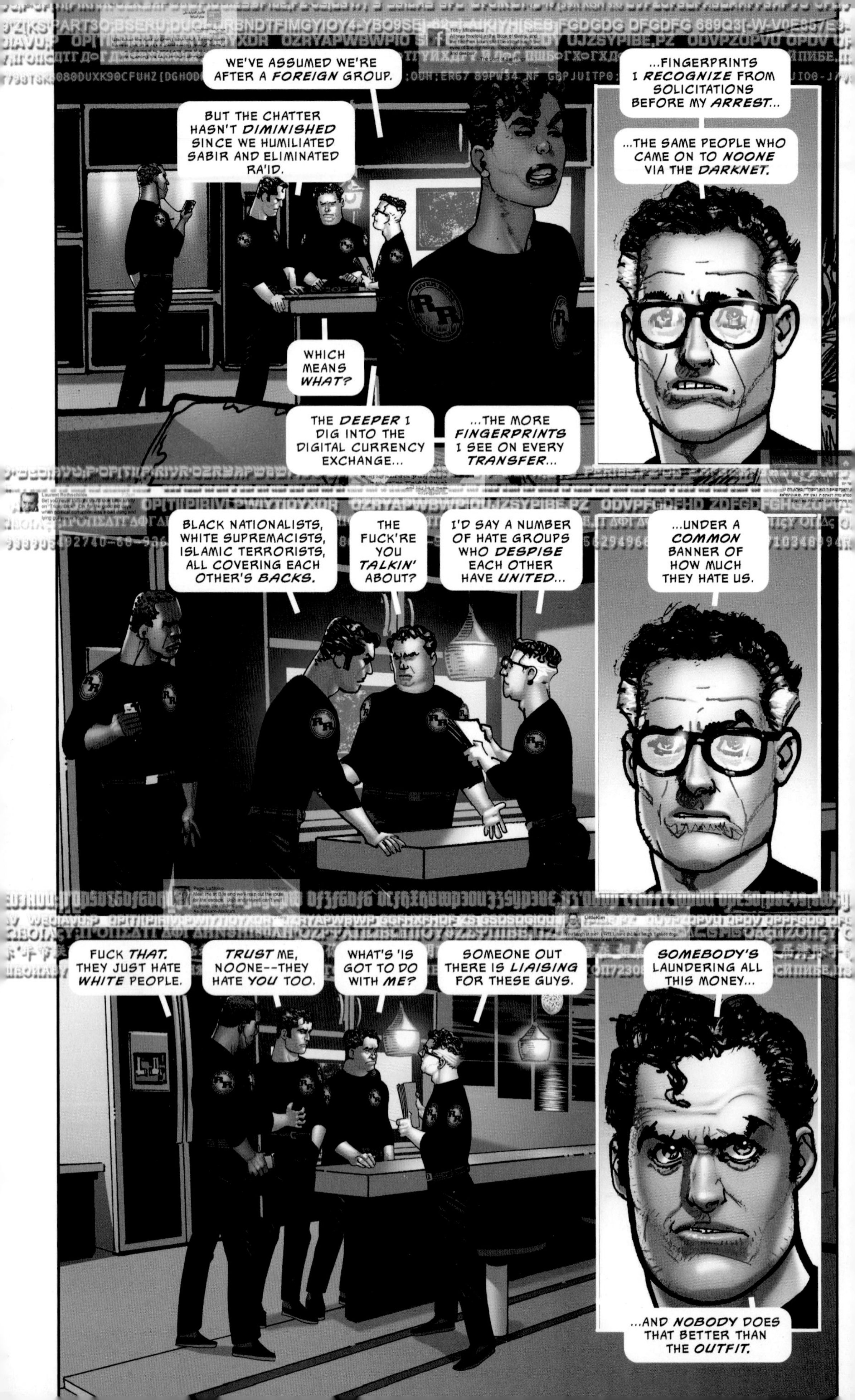
WE'VE ASSUMED WE'RE AFTER A FOREIGN GROUP.
BUT THE CHATTER HASN'T DIMINISHED SINCE WE HUMILIATED SABIR AND ELIMINATED RA'ID.
WHICH MEANS WHAT?
THE DEEPER I DIG INTO THE DIGITAL CURRENCY EXCHANGE...
...THE MORE FINGERPRINTS I SEE ON EVERY TRANSFER...
...FINGERPRINTS I RECOGNIZE FROM SOLICITATIONS BEFORE MY ARREST...
...THE SAME PEOPLE WHO CAME ON TO NOONE VIA THE DARKNET.
BLACK NATIONALISTS, WHITE SUPREMACISTS, ISLAMIC TERRORISTS, ALL COVERING EACH OTHER'S BACKS.
THE FUCK'RE YOU TALKIN' ABOUT?
I'D SAY A NUMBER OF HATE GROUPS WHO DESPISE EACH OTHER HAVE UNITED...
...UNDER A COMMON BANNER OF HOW MUCH THEY HATE US.
FUCK THAT. THEY JUST HATE WHITE PEOPLE.
TRUST ME, NOONE--THEY HATE YOU TOO.
WHAT'S 'IS GOT TO DO WITH ME?
SOMEONE OUT THERE IS LIAISING FOR THESE GUYS.
SOMEBODY'S LAUNDERING ALL THIS MONEY...
...AND NOBODY DOES THAT BETTER THAN THE OUTFIT.

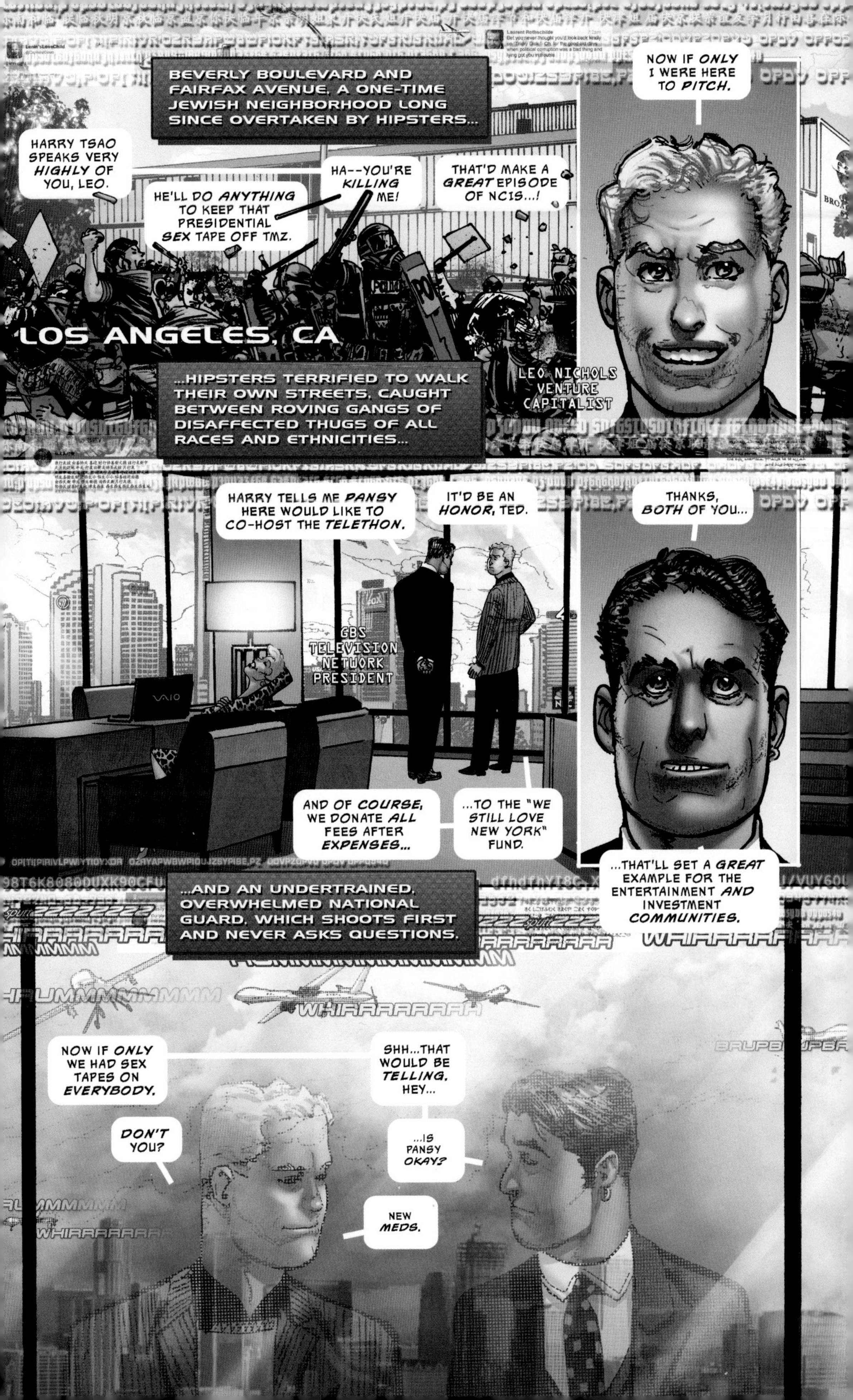
BEVERLY BOULEVARD AND FAIRFAX AVENUE, A ONE-TIME JEWISH NEIGHBORHOOD LONG SINCE OVERTAKEN BY HIPSTERS...
HARRY TSAO SPEAKS VERY HIGHLY OF YOU, LEO.
HE'LL DO ANYTHING TO KEEP THAT PRESIDENTIAL SEX TAPE OFF TMZ.
HA--YOU'RE KILLING ME!
THAT'D MAKE A GREAT EPISODE OF NCIS...!
NOW IF ONLY I WERE HERE TO PITCH.
LOS ANGELES, CA
...HIPSTERS TERRIFIED TO WALK THEIR OWN STREETS, CAUGHT BETWEEN ROVING GANGS OF DISAFFECTED THUGS OF ALL RACES AND ETHNICITIES...
LEO NICHOLS VENTURE CAPITALIST
HARRY TELLS ME PANSY HERE WOULD LIKE TO CO-HOST THE TELETHON.
IT'D BE AN HONOR, TED.
THANKS, BOTH OF YOU...
GBS TELEVISION NETWORK PRESIDENT
AND OF COURSE, WE DONATE ALL FEES AFTER EXPENSES...
...TO THE "WE STILL LOVE NEW YORK" FUND.
...THAT'LL SET A GREAT EXAMPLE FOR THE ENTERTAINMENT AND INVESTMENT COMMUNITIES.
...AND AN UNDERTRAINED, OVERWHELMED NATIONAL GUARD, WHICH SHOOTS FIRST AND NEVER ASKS QUESTIONS.
WHIRRRRRRRRR
HUMMMMMMMMMM
NOW IF ONLY WE HAD SEX TAPES ON EVERYBODY.
SHH...THAT WOULD BE TELLING, HEY...
DON'T YOU?
...IS PANSY OKAY?
NEW MEDS.

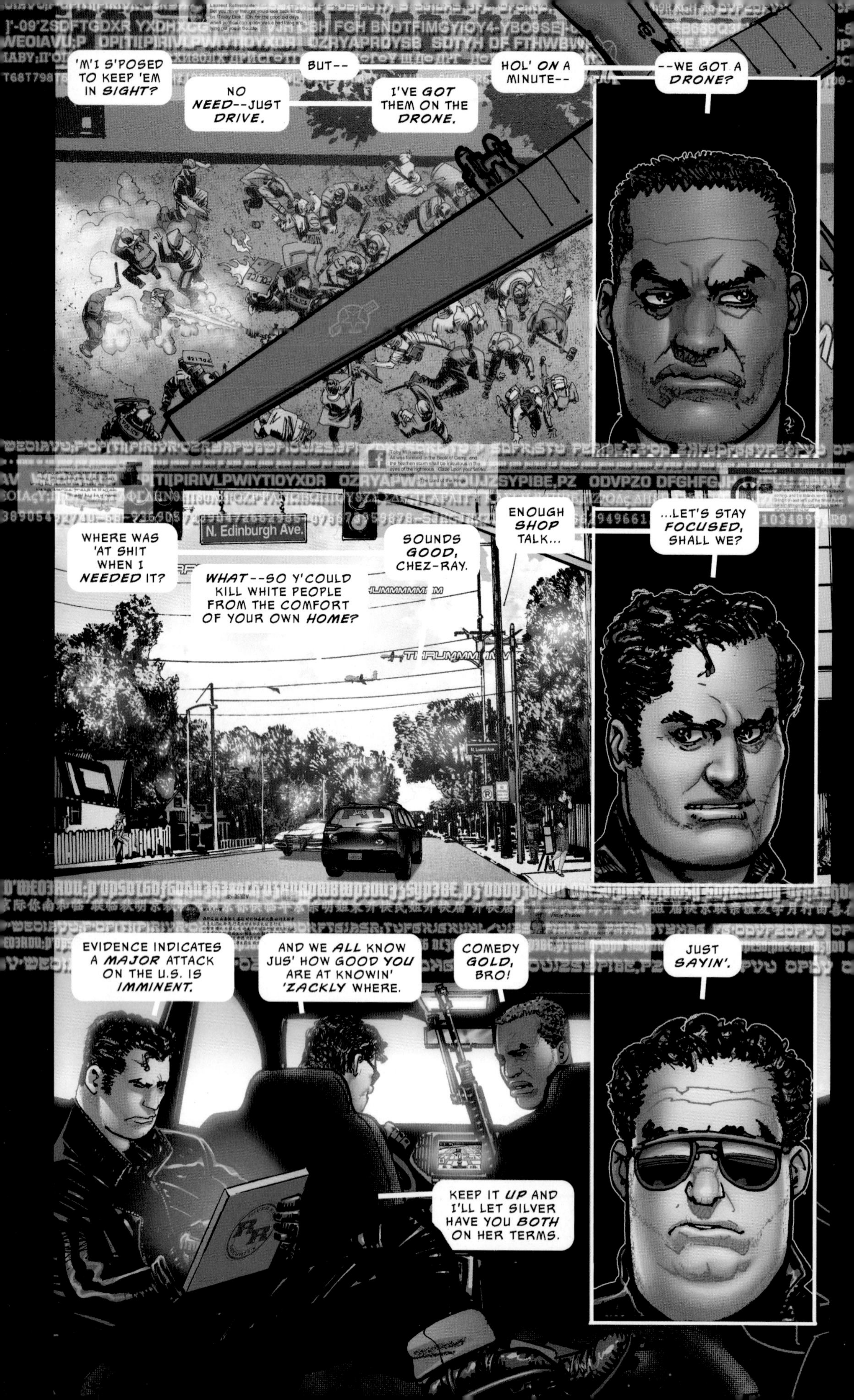

'M'I S'POSED TO KEEP 'EM IN SIGHT?
BUT--
NO NEED--JUST DRIVE.
I'VE GOT THEM ON THE DRONE.
HOL' ON A MINUTE--
--WE GOT A DRONE?
N. Edinburgh Ave.
WHERE WAS 'AT SHIT WHEN I NEEDED IT?
WHAT--SO Y'COULD KILL WHITE PEOPLE FROM THE COMFORT OF YOUR OWN HOME?
SOUNDS GOOD, CHEZ-RAY.
ENOUGH SHOP TALK...
...LET'S STAY FOCUSED, SHALL WE?
THRUMMMMM
EVIDENCE INDICATES A MAJOR ATTACK ON THE U.S. IS IMMINENT.
AND WE ALL KNOW JUS' HOW GOOD YOU ARE AT KNOWIN' 'ZACKLY WHERE.
COMEDY GOLD, BRO!
JUST SAYIN'.
KEEP IT UP AND I'LL LET SILVER HAVE YOU BOTH ON HER TERMS.

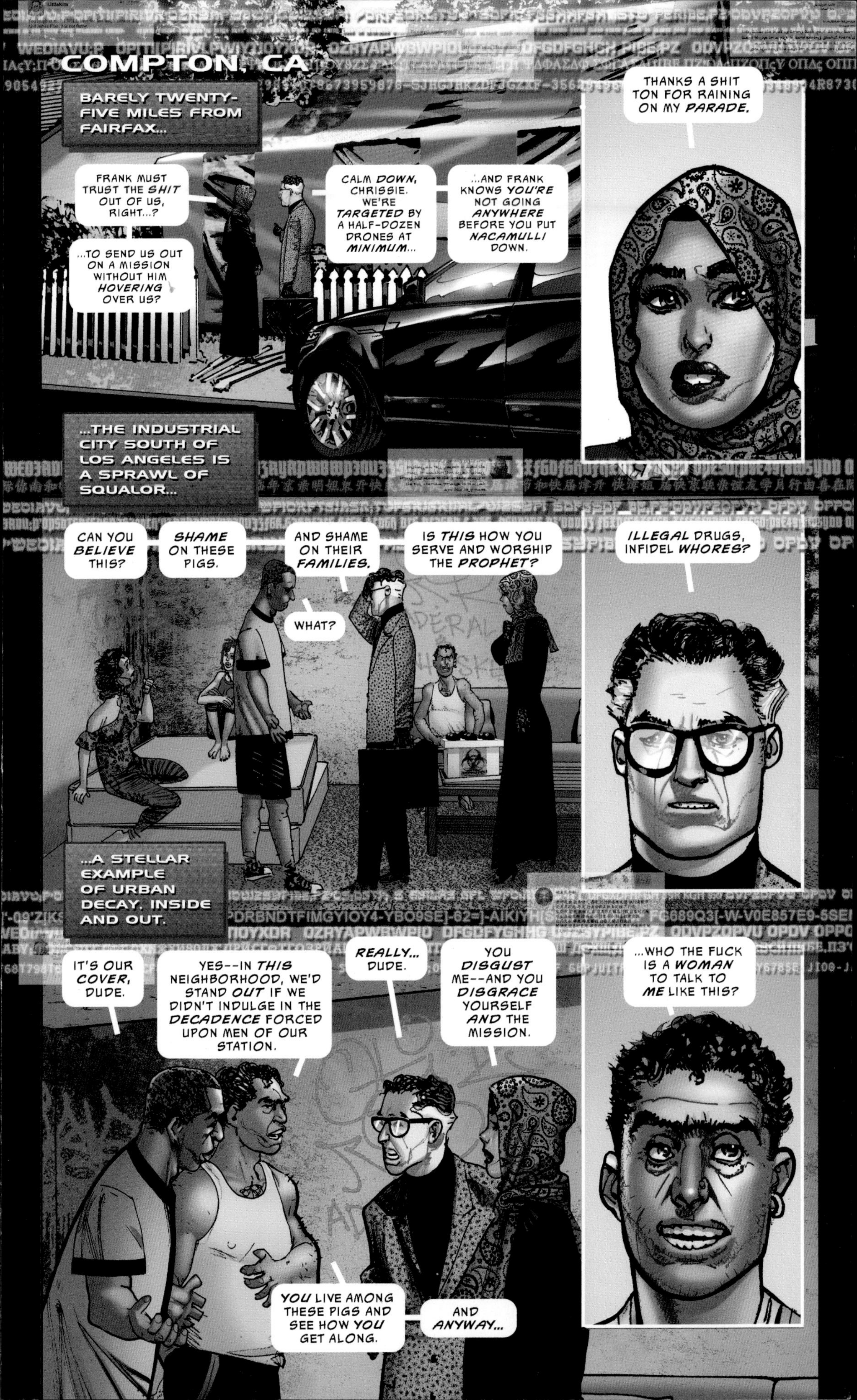
COMPTON, CA
BARELY TWENTY-FIVE MILES FROM FAIRFAX...
FRANK MUST TRUST THE SHIT OUT OF US, RIGHT...?
...TO SEND US OUT ON A MISSION WITHOUT HIM HOVERING OVER US?
CALM DOWN, CHRISSIE. WE'RE TARGETED BY A HALF-DOZEN DRONES AT MINIMUM...
...AND FRANK KNOWS YOU'RE NOT GOING ANYWHERE BEFORE YOU PUT NACAMULLI DOWN.
THANKS A SHIT TON FOR RAINING ON MY PARADE.
...THE INDUSTRIAL CITY SOUTH OF LOS ANGELES IS A SPRAWL OF SQUALOR...
CAN YOU BELIEVE THIS?
SHAME ON THESE PIGS.
AND SHAME ON THEIR FAMILIES.
IS THIS HOW YOU SERVE AND WORSHIP THE PROPHET?
WHAT?
ILLEGAL DRUGS, INFIDEL WHORES?
...A STELLAR EXAMPLE OF URBAN DECAY, INSIDE AND OUT.
IT'S OUR COVER, DUDE.
YES--IN THIS NEIGHBORHOOD, WE'D STAND OUT IF WE DIDN'T INDULGE IN THE DECADENCE FORCED UPON MEN OF OUR STATION.
REALLY... DUDE.
YOU DISGUST ME--AND YOU DISGRACE YOURSELF AND THE MISSION.
YOU LIVE AMONG THESE PIGS AND SEE HOW YOU GET ALONG.
AND ANYWAY...
...WHO THE FUCK IS A WOMAN TO TALK TO ME LIKE THIS?

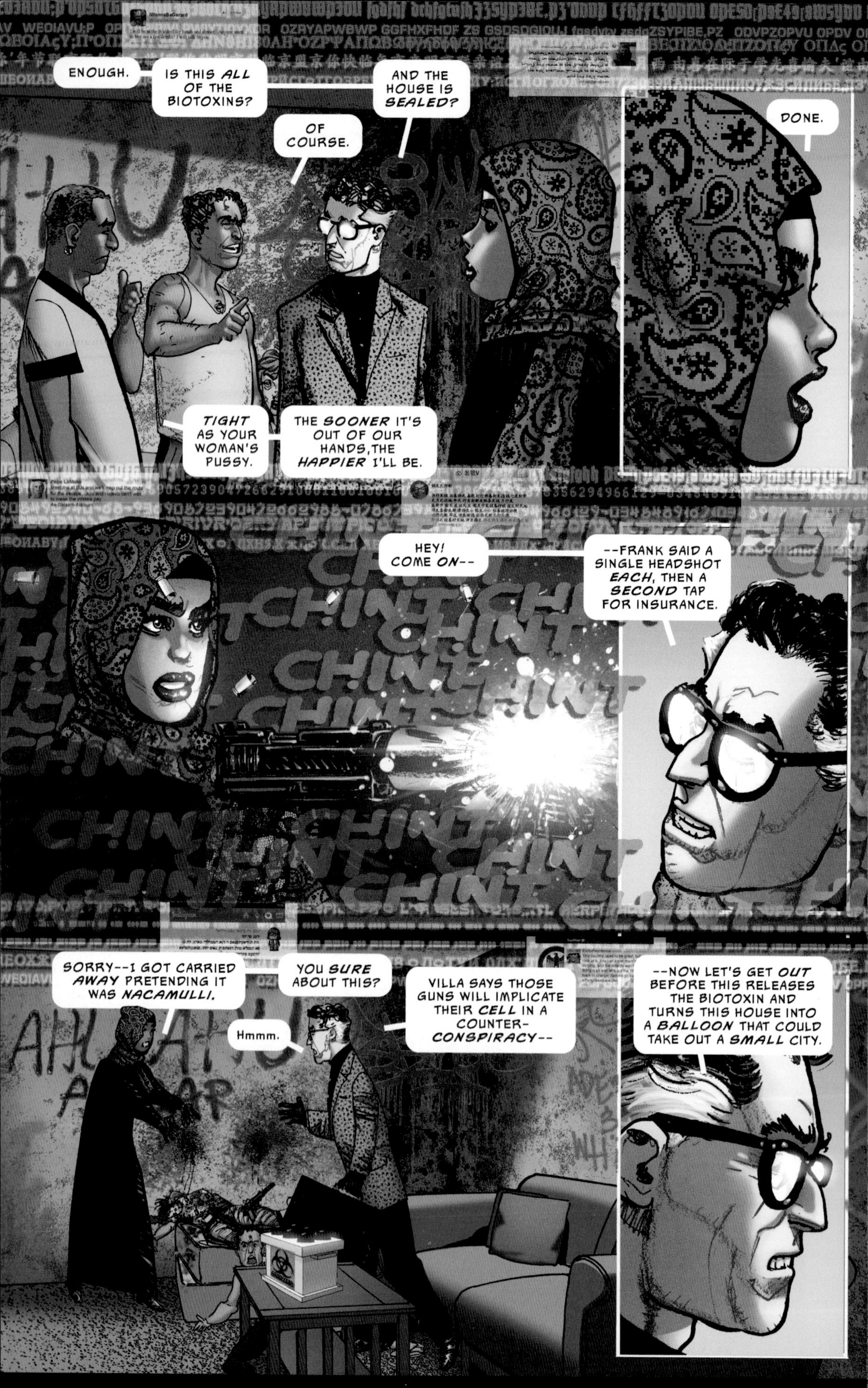
ENOUGH.
IS THIS ALL OF THE BIOTOXINS?
AND THE HOUSE IS SEALED?
OF COURSE.
DONE.
TIGHT AS YOUR WOMAN'S PUSSY.
THE SOONER IT'S OUT OF OUR HANDS, THE HAPPIER I'LL BE.
HEY! COME ON--
--FRANK SAID A SINGLE HEADSHOT EACH, THEN A SECOND TAP FOR INSURANCE.
CHINT CHINT CHINT CHINT CHINT CHINT
SORRY--I GOT CARRIED AWAY PRETENDING IT WAS NACAMULLI.
YOU SURE ABOUT THIS?
Hmmm.
VILLA SAYS THOSE GUNS WILL IMPLICATE THEIR CELL IN A COUNTER-CONSPIRACY--
--NOW LET'S GET OUT BEFORE THIS RELEASES THE BIOTOXIN AND TURNS THIS HOUSE INTO A BALLOON THAT COULD TAKE OUT A SMALL CITY.

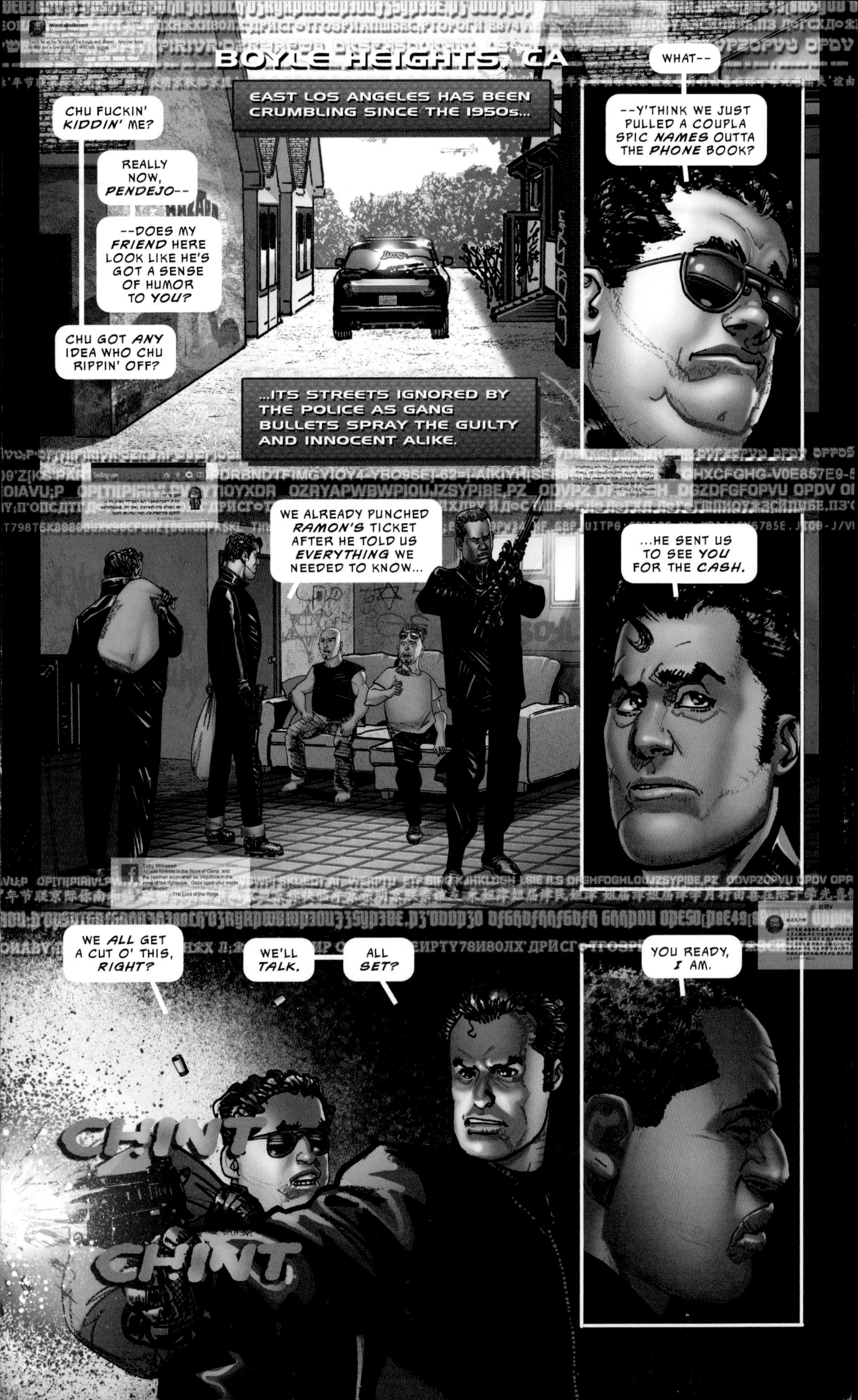
BOYLE HEIGHTS, CA
EAST LOS ANGELES HAS BEEN CRUMBLING SINCE THE 1950s...
CHU FUCKIN' KIDDIN' ME?
REALLY NOW, PENDEJO--
--DOES MY FRIEND HERE LOOK LIKE HE'S GOT A SENSE OF HUMOR TO YOU?
CHU GOT ANY IDEA WHO CHU RIPPIN' OFF?
...ITS STREETS IGNORED BY THE POLICE AS GANG BULLETS SPRAY THE GUILTY AND INNOCENT ALIKE.
WHAT--
--Y'THINK WE JUST PULLED A COUPLA SPIC NAMES OUTTA THE PHONE BOOK?
WE ALREADY PUNCHED RAMON'S TICKET AFTER HE TOLD US EVERYTHING WE NEEDED TO KNOW...
...HE SENT US TO SEE YOU FOR THE CASH.
WE ALL GET A CUT O' THIS, RIGHT?
WE'LL TALK.
ALL SET?
YOU READY, I AM.
CHINT
CHINT

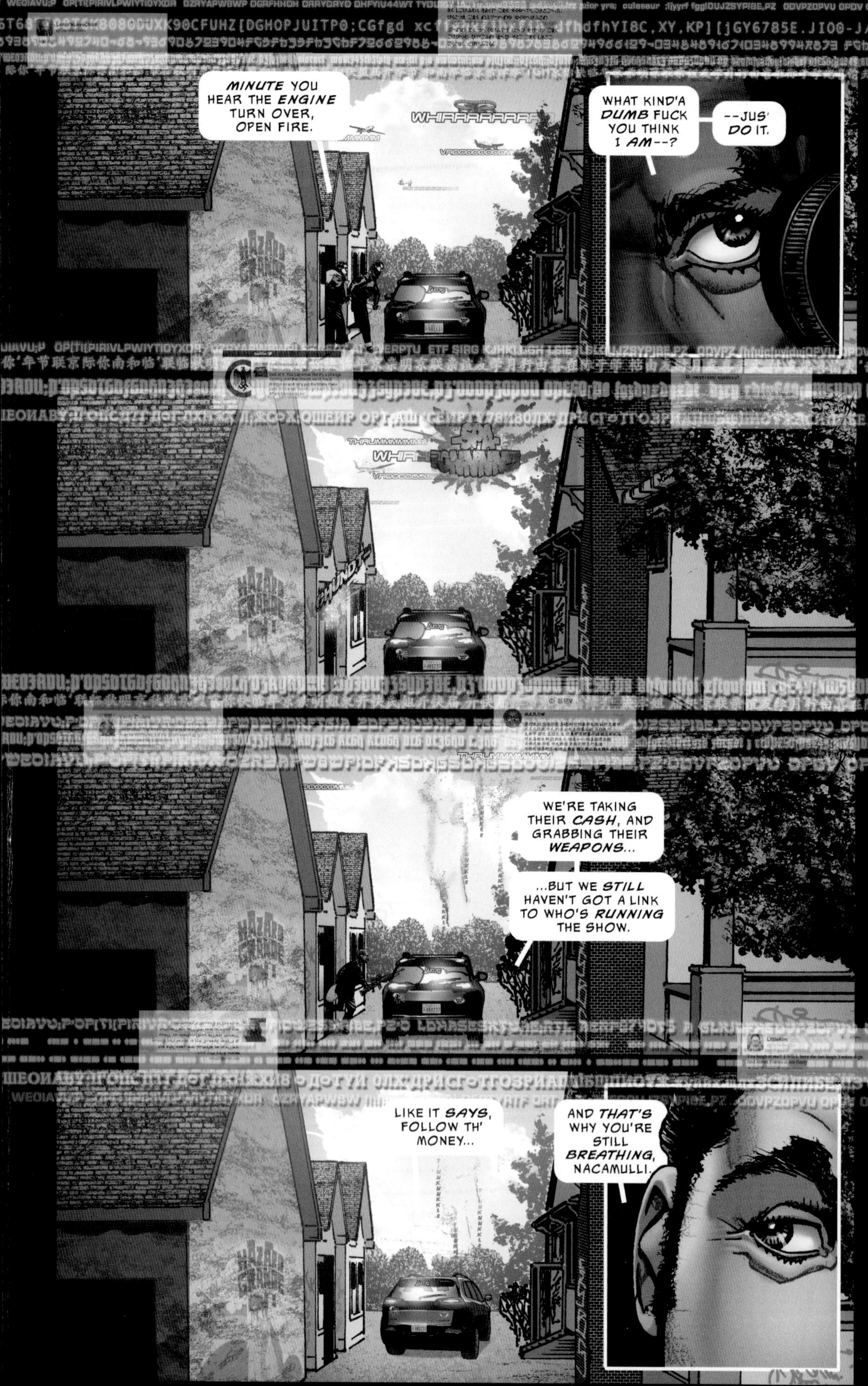
MINUTE YOU HEAR THE ENGINE TURN OVER, OPEN FIRE.
WHIRRRRRRRR
VROOOOOOOM
WHAT KIND'A DUMB FUCK YOU THINK I AM--?
--JUS' DO IT.
THRUMMMMMM
CHUNK
WE'RE TAKING THEIR CASH, AND GRABBING THEIR WEAPONS...
...BUT WE STILL HAVEN'T GOT A LINK TO WHO'S RUNNING THE SHOW.
LIKE IT SAYS, FOLLOW TH' MONEY...
AND THAT'S WHY YOU'RE STILL BREATHING, NACAMULLI.

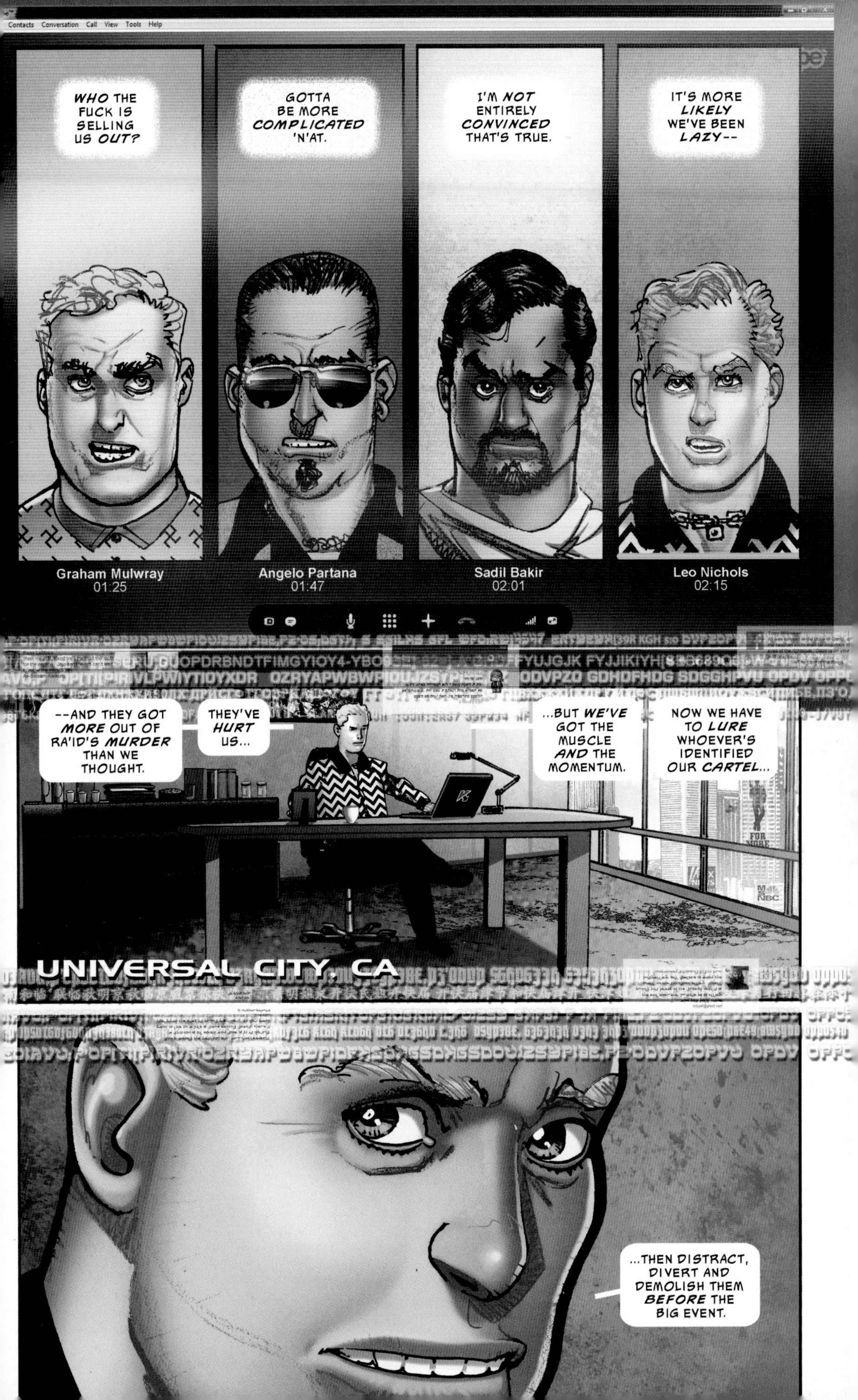
Contacts Conversation Call View Tools Help
WHO THE FUCK IS SELLING US OUT?
GOTTA BE MORE COMPLICATED 'N'AT.
I'M NOT ENTIRELY CONVINCED THAT'S TRUE.
IT'S MORE LIKELY WE'VE BEEN LAZY--
Graham Mulwray 01:25
Angelo Partana 01:47
Sadil Bakir 02:01
Leo Nichols 02:15
--AND THEY GOT MORE OUT OF RA'ID'S MURDER THAN WE THOUGHT.
THEY'VE HURT US...
...BUT WE'VE GOT THE MUSCLE AND THE MOMENTUM.
NOW WE HAVE TO LURE WHOEVER'S IDENTIFIED OUR CARTEL...
UNIVERSAL CITY, CA
...THEN DISTRACT, DIVERT AND DEMOLISH THEM BEFORE THE BIG EVENT.

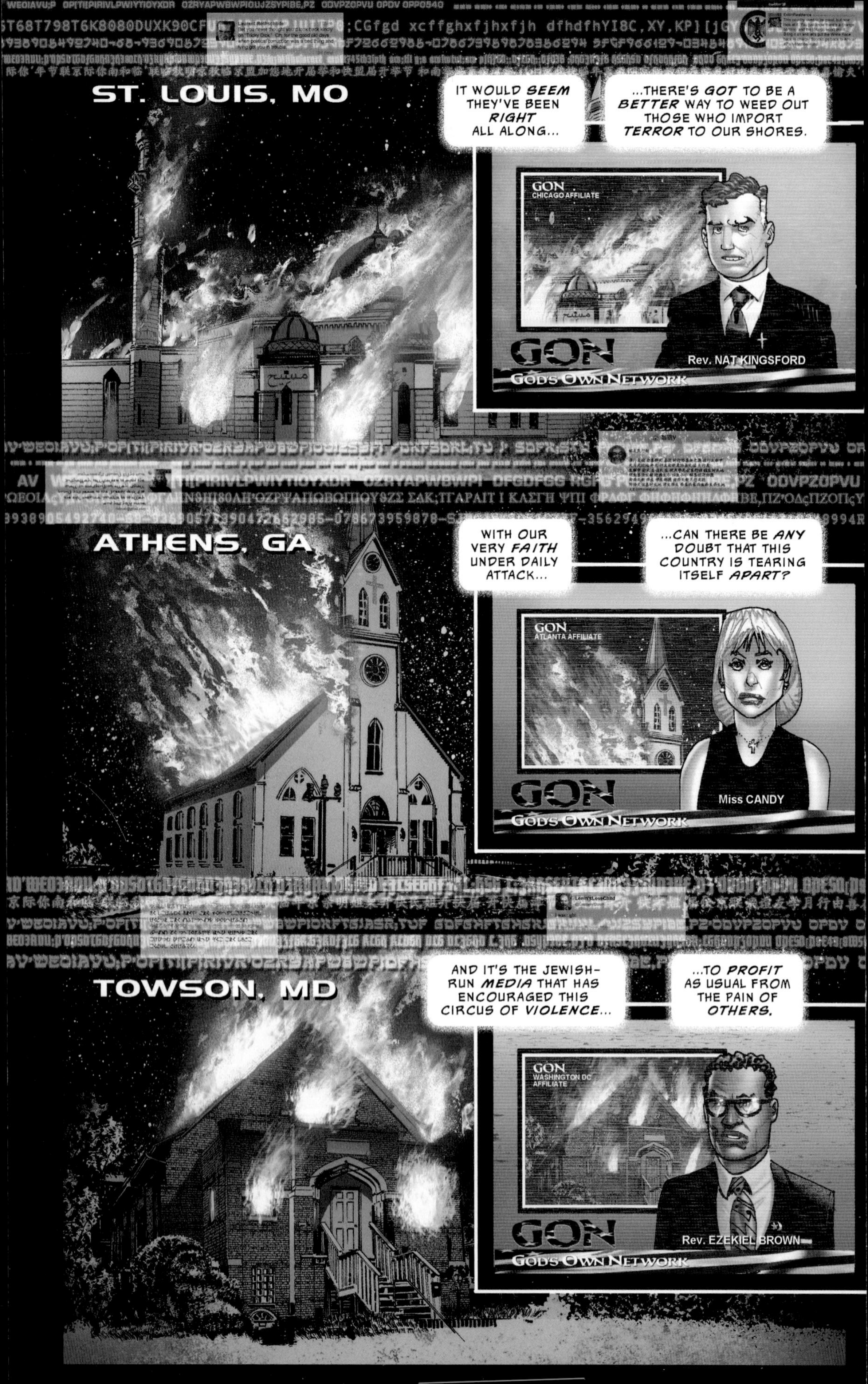
ST. LOUIS, MO
IT WOULD SEEM THEY'VE BEEN RIGHT ALL ALONG...
...THERE'S GOT TO BE A BETTER WAY TO WEED OUT THOSE WHO IMPORT TERROR TO OUR SHORES.
GON CHICAGO AFFILIATE
Rev. NAT KINGSFORD
GON GOD'S OWN NETWORK
ATHENS, GA
WITH OUR VERY FAITH UNDER DAILY ATTACK...
...CAN THERE BE ANY DOUBT THAT THIS COUNTRY IS TEARING ITSELF APART?
GON ATLANTA AFFILIATE
Miss CANDY
GON GOD'S OWN NETWORK
TOWSON, MD
AND IT'S THE JEWISH-RUN MEDIA THAT HAS ENCOURAGED THIS CIRCUS OF VIOLENCE...
...TO PROFIT AS USUAL FROM THE PAIN OF OTHERS.
GON WASHINGTON DC AFFILIATE
Rev. EZEKIEL BROWN
GON GOD'S OWN NETWORK

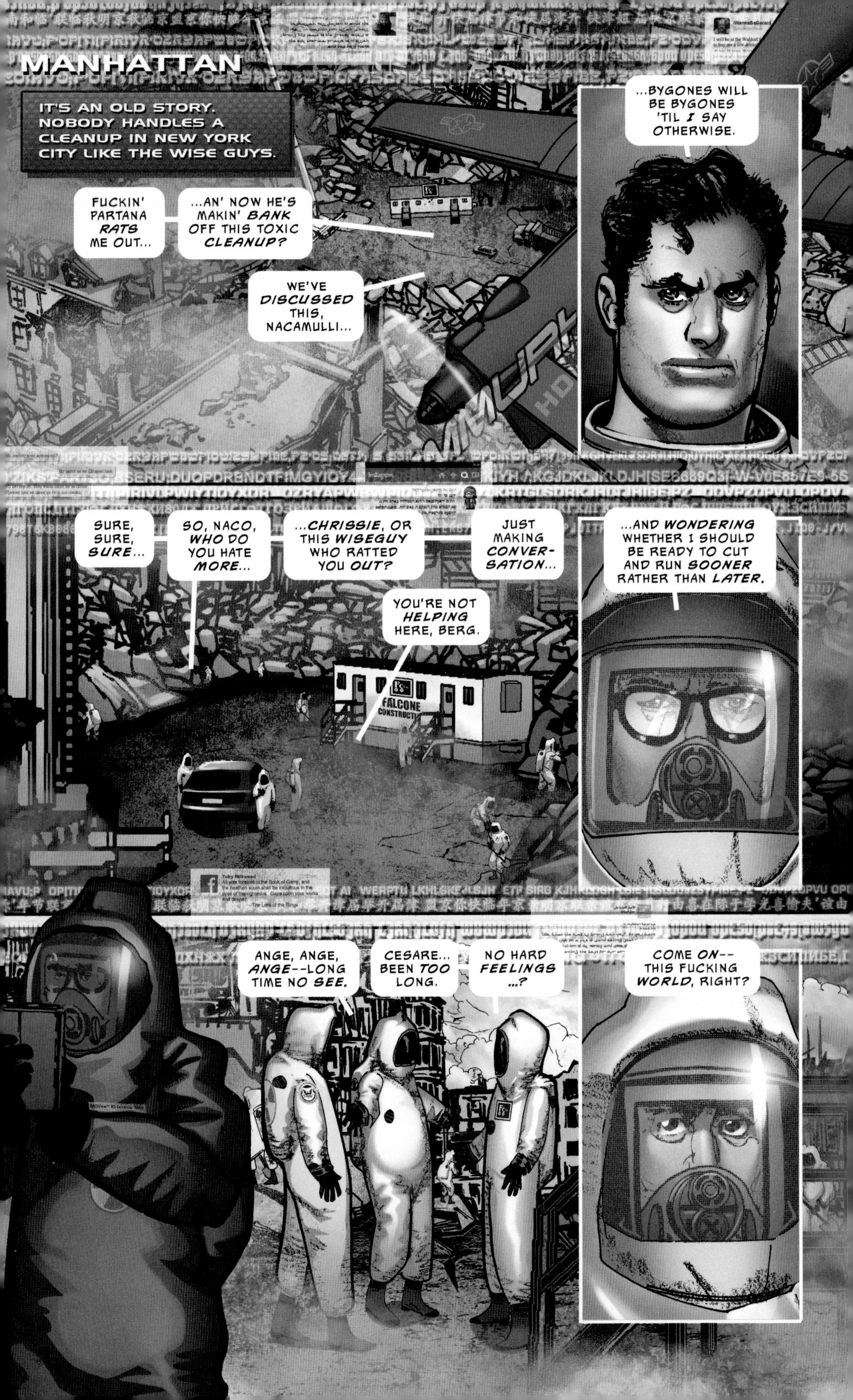
MANHATTAN
IT'S AN OLD STORY. NOBODY HANDLES A CLEANUP IN NEW YORK CITY LIKE THE WISE GUYS.
FUCKIN' PARTANA RATS ME OUT...
...AN' NOW HE'S MAKIN' BANK OFF THIS TOXIC CLEANUP?
WE'VE DISCUSSED THIS, NACAMULLI...
...BYGONES WILL BE BYGONES 'TIL I SAY OTHERWISE.
SURE, SURE, SURE...
SO, NACO, WHO DO YOU HATE MORE...
...CHRISSIE, OR THIS WISEGUY WHO RATTED YOU OUT?
JUST MAKING CONVERSATION...
YOU'RE NOT HELPING HERE, BERG.
FALCONE CONSTRUCTI
...AND WONDERING WHETHER I SHOULD BE READY TO CUT AND RUN SOONER RATHER THAN LATER.
ANGE, ANGE, ANGE--LONG TIME NO SEE.
CESARE... BEEN TOO LONG.
NO HARD FEELINGS ...?
COME ON-- THIS FUCKING WORLD, RIGHT?

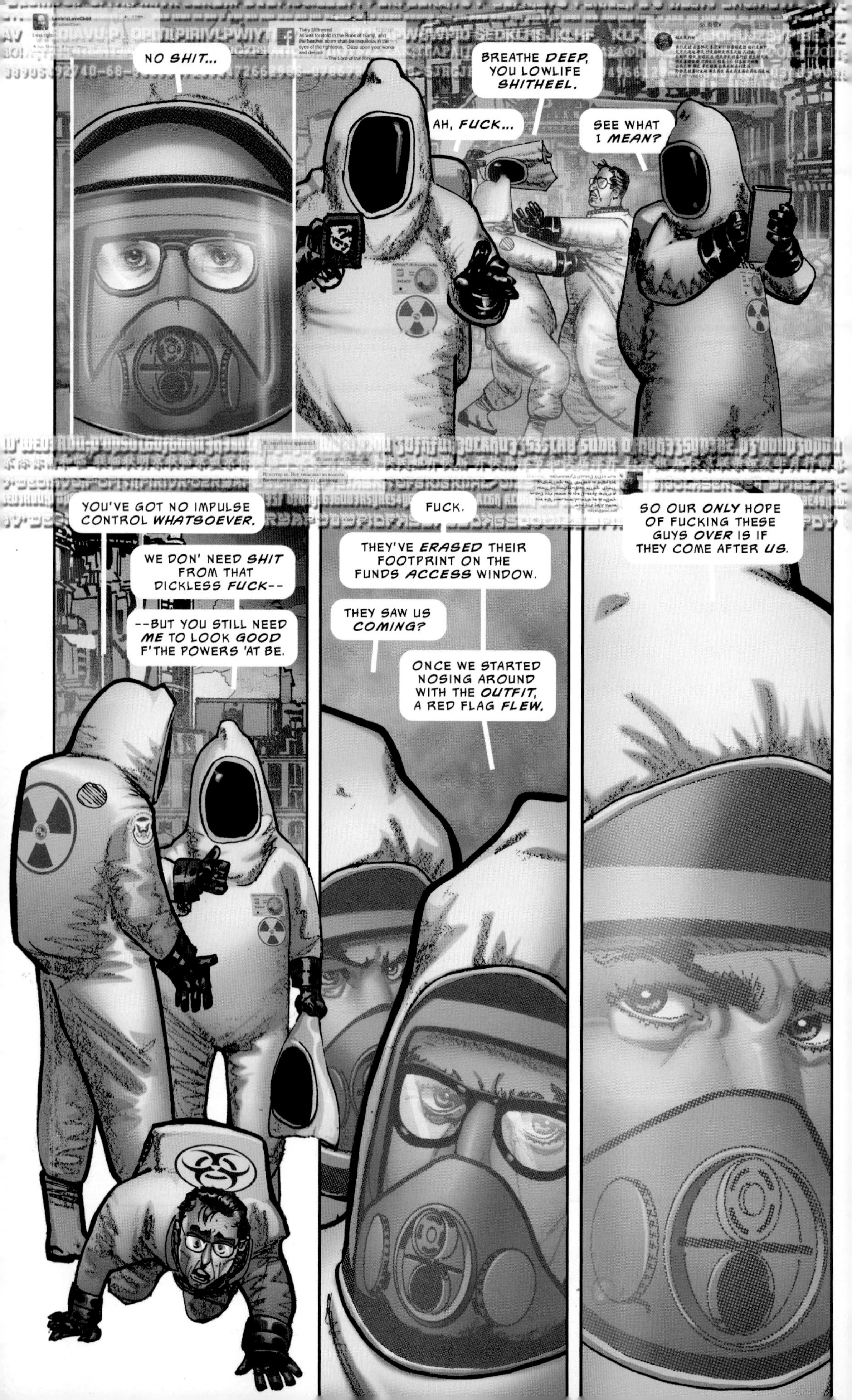
NO SHIT...
AH, FUCK...
BREATHE DEEP, YOU LOWLIFE SHITHEEL.
SEE WHAT I MEAN?
YOU'VE GOT NO IMPULSE CONTROL WHATSOEVER.
WE DON' NEED SHIT FROM THAT DICKLESS FUCK--
--BUT YOU STILL NEED ME TO LOOK GOOD F'THE POWERS 'AT BE.
FUCK.
THEY'VE ERASED THEIR FOOTPRINT ON THE FUNDS ACCESS WINDOW.
THEY SAW US COMING?
ONCE WE STARTED NOSING AROUND WITH THE OUTFIT, A RED FLAG FLEW.
SO OUR ONLY HOPE OF FUCKING THESE GUYS OVER IS IF THEY COME AFTER US.

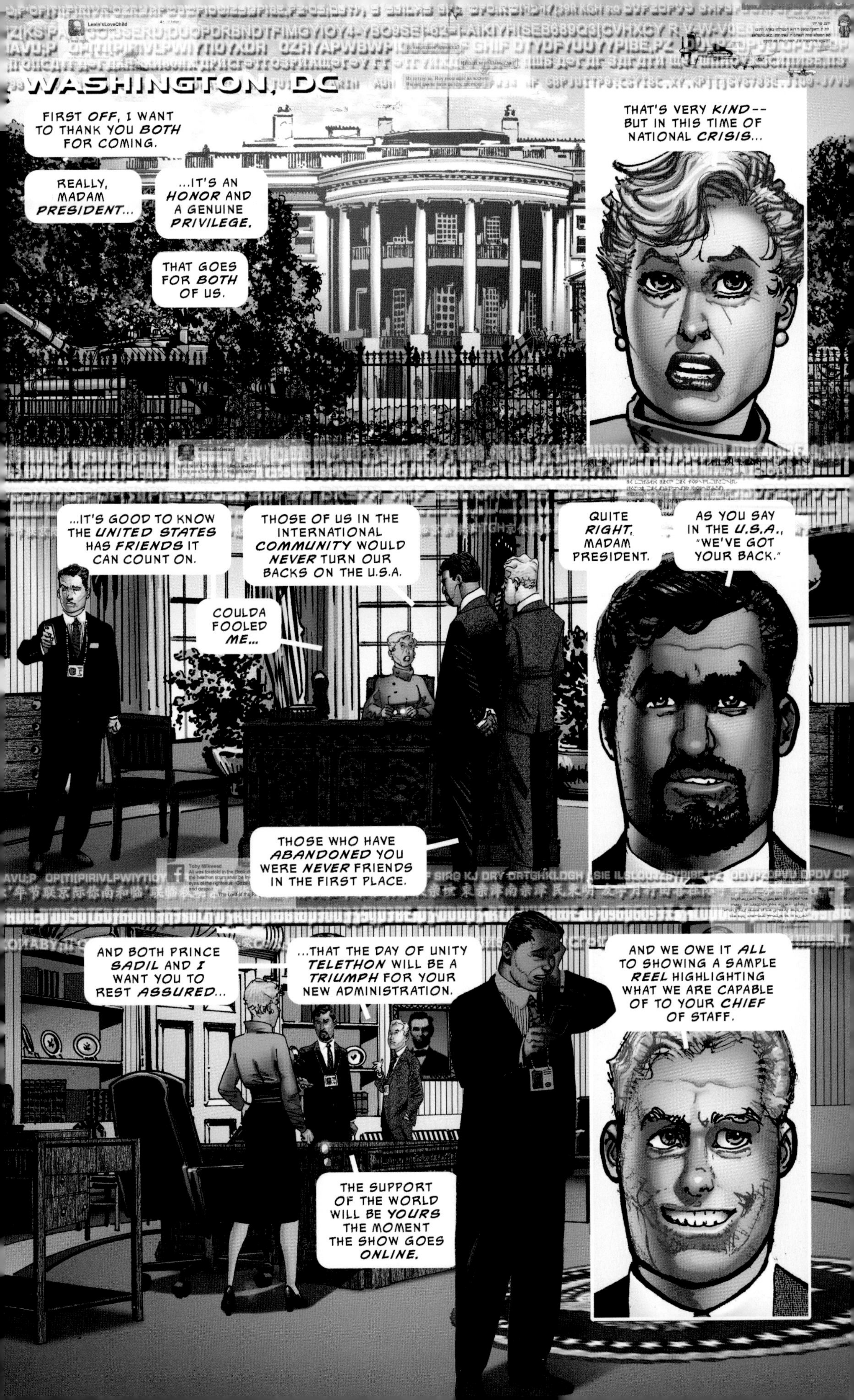
WASHINGTON, DC
FIRST OFF, I WANT TO THANK YOU BOTH FOR COMING.
REALLY, MADAM PRESIDENT...
...IT'S AN HONOR AND A GENUINE PRIVILEGE.
THAT GOES FOR BOTH OF US.
THAT'S VERY KIND-- BUT IN THIS TIME OF NATIONAL CRISIS...
...IT'S GOOD TO KNOW THE UNITED STATES HAS FRIENDS IT CAN COUNT ON.
THOSE OF US IN THE INTERNATIONAL COMMUNITY WOULD NEVER TURN OUR BACKS ON THE U.S.A.
COULDA FOOLED ME...
QUITE RIGHT, MADAM PRESIDENT.
AS YOU SAY IN THE U.S.A., "WE'VE GOT YOUR BACK."
THOSE WHO HAVE ABANDONED YOU WERE NEVER FRIENDS IN THE FIRST PLACE.
AND BOTH PRINCE SADIL AND I WANT YOU TO REST ASSURED...
...THAT THE DAY OF UNITY TELETHON WILL BE A TRIUMPH FOR YOUR NEW ADMINISTRATION.
THE SUPPORT OF THE WORLD WILL BE YOURS THE MOMENT THE SHOW GOES ONLINE.
AND WE OWE IT ALL TO SHOWING A SAMPLE REEL HIGHLIGHTING WHAT WE ARE CAPABLE OF TO YOUR CHIEF OF STAFF.

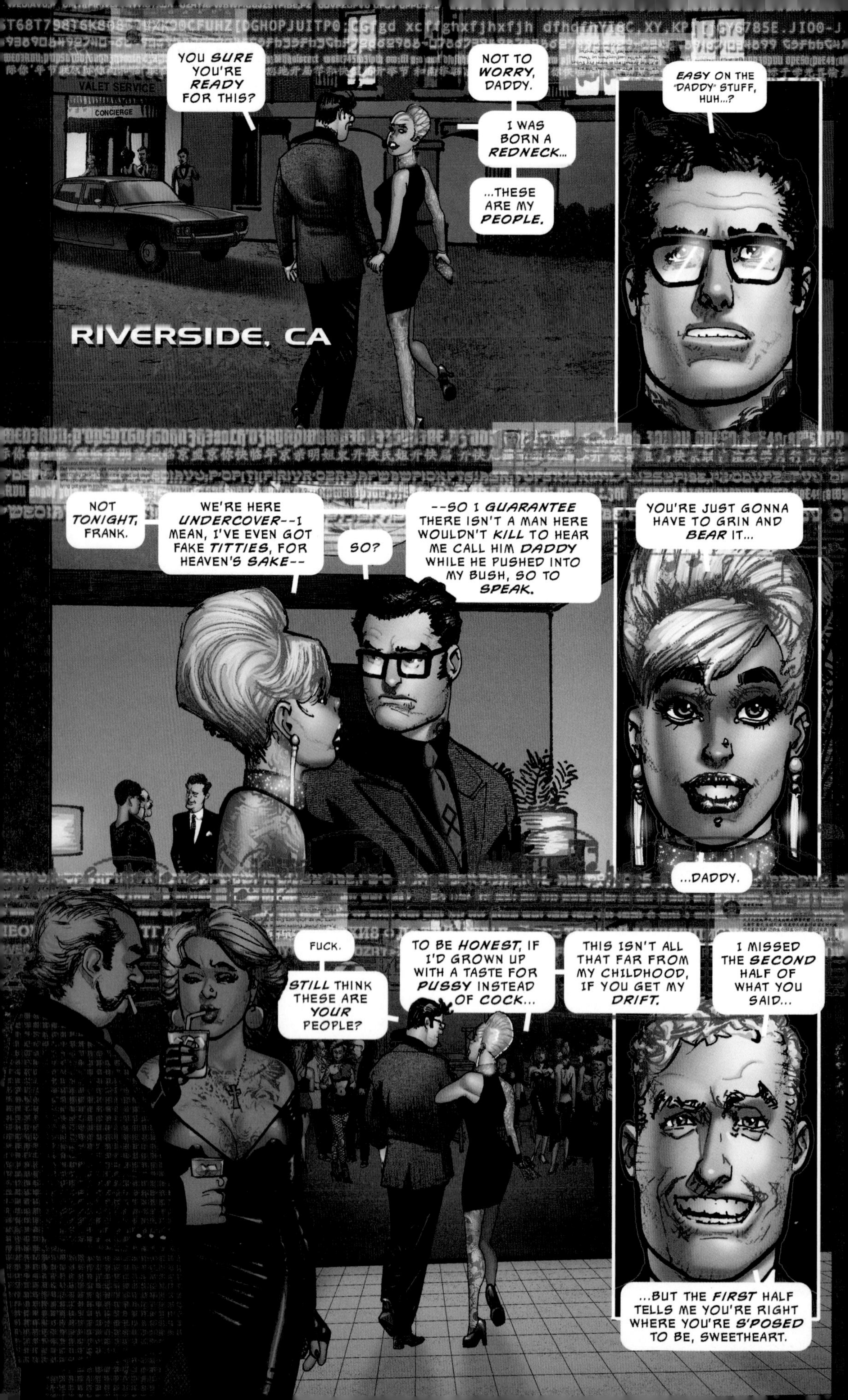
YOU SURE YOU'RE READY FOR THIS?
NOT TO WORRY, DADDY.
I WAS BORN A REDNECK...
...THESE ARE MY PEOPLE.
EASY ON THE "DADDY" STUFF, HUH...?
RIVERSIDE, CA
NOT TONIGHT, FRANK.
WE'RE HERE UNDERCOVER--I MEAN, I'VE EVEN GOT FAKE TITTIES, FOR HEAVEN'S SAKE--
SO?
--SO I GUARANTEE THERE ISN'T A MAN HERE WOULDN'T KILL TO HEAR ME CALL HIM DADDY WHILE HE PUSHED INTO MY BUSH, SO TO SPEAK.
YOU'RE JUST GONNA HAVE TO GRIN AND BEAR IT...
...DADDY.
FUCK.
STILL THINK THESE ARE YOUR PEOPLE?
TO BE HONEST, IF I'D GROWN UP WITH A TASTE FOR PUSSY INSTEAD OF COCK...
THIS ISN'T ALL THAT FAR FROM MY CHILDHOOD, IF YOU GET MY DRIFT.
I MISSED THE SECOND HALF OF WHAT YOU SAID...
...BUT THE FIRST HALF TELLS ME YOU'RE RIGHT WHERE YOU'RE S'POSED TO BE, SWEETHEART.

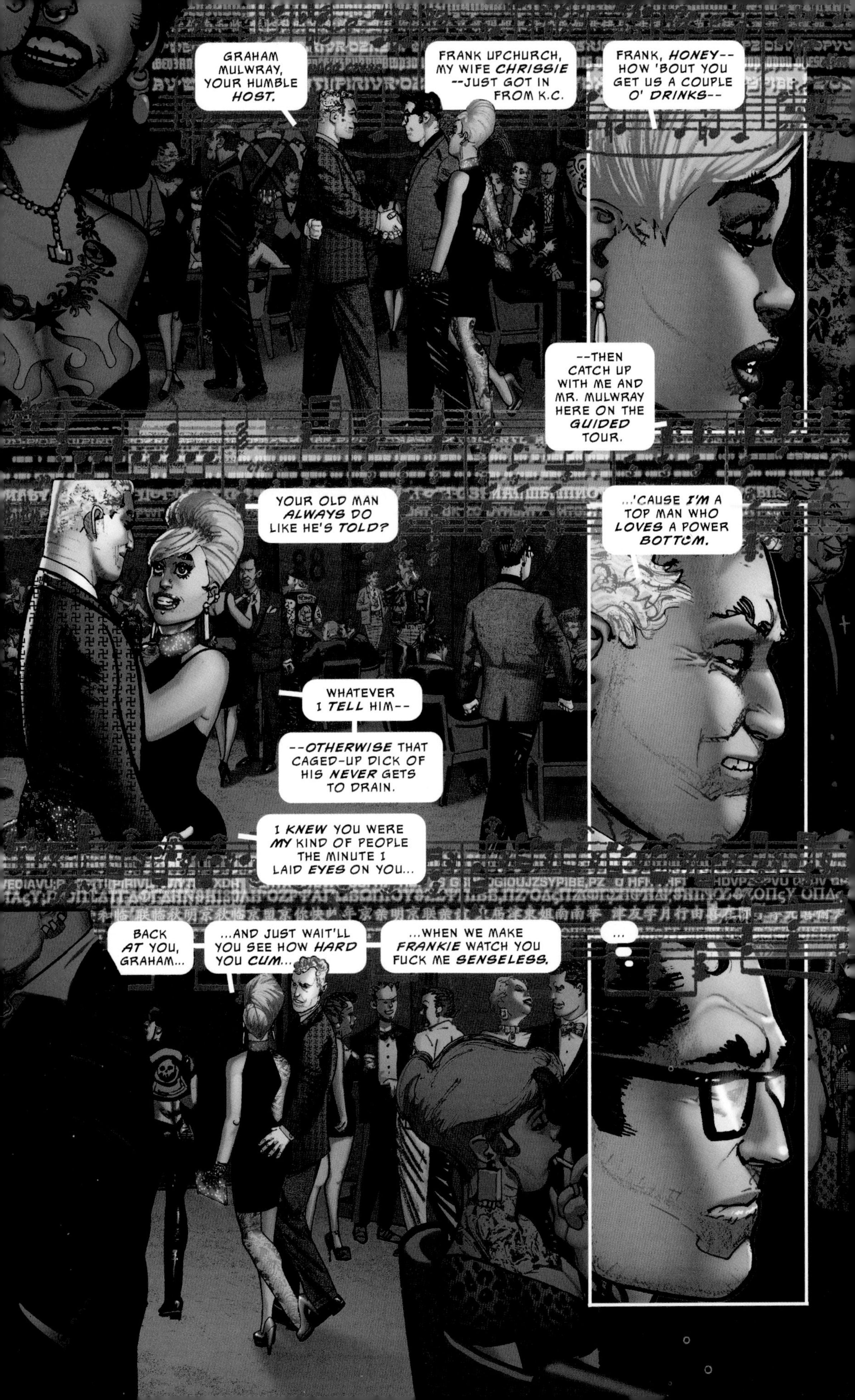
GRAHAM MULWRAY, YOUR HUMBLE HOST.
FRANK UPCHURCH, MY WIFE CHRISSIE --JUST GOT IN FROM K.C.
FRANK, HONEY-- HOW 'BOUT YOU GET US A COUPLE O' DRINKS--
--THEN CATCH UP WITH ME AND MR. MULWRAY HERE ON THE GUIDED TOUR.
YOUR OLD MAN ALWAYS DO LIKE HE'S TOLD?
...'CAUSE I'M A TOP MAN WHO LOVES A POWER BOTTOM.
WHATEVER I TELL HIM--
--OTHERWISE THAT CAGED-UP DICK OF HIS NEVER GETS TO DRAIN.
I KNEW YOU WERE MY KIND OF PEOPLE THE MINUTE I LAID EYES ON YOU...
BACK AT YOU, GRAHAM...
...AND JUST WAIT'LL YOU SEE HOW HARD YOU CUM...
...WHEN WE MAKE FRANKIE WATCH YOU FUCK ME SENSELESS.
...

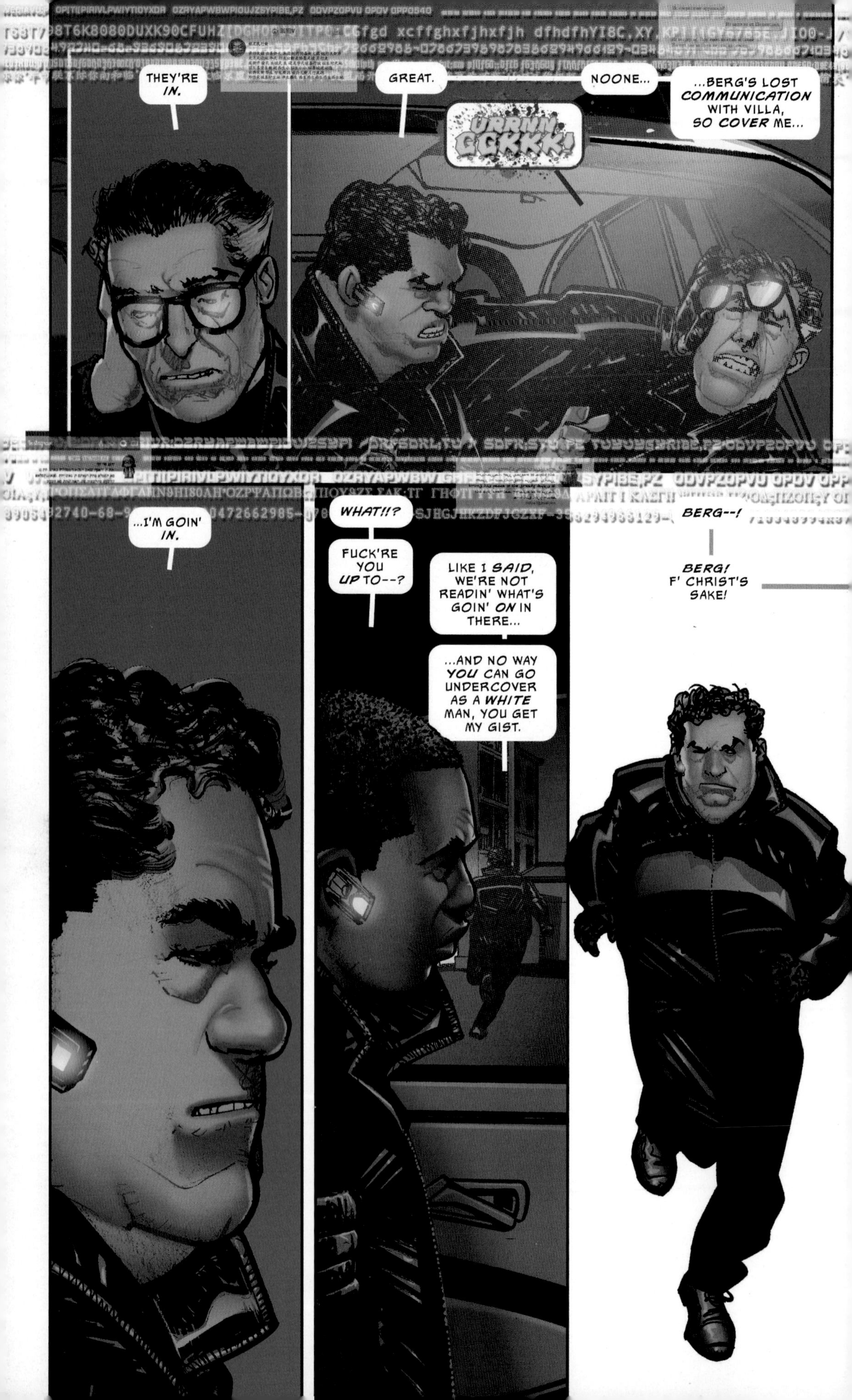

THEY'RE IN.
GREAT.
URRNN GGKKK!
NOONE...
...BERG'S LOST COMMUNICATION WITH VILLA, SO COVER ME...
...I'M GOIN' IN.
WHAT!!?
FUCK'RE YOU UP TO--?
LIKE I SAID, WE'RE NOT READIN' WHAT'S GOIN' ON IN THERE...
...AND NO WAY YOU CAN GO UNDERCOVER AS A WHITE MAN, YOU GET MY GIST.
BERG--!
BERG! F' CHRIST'S SAKE!

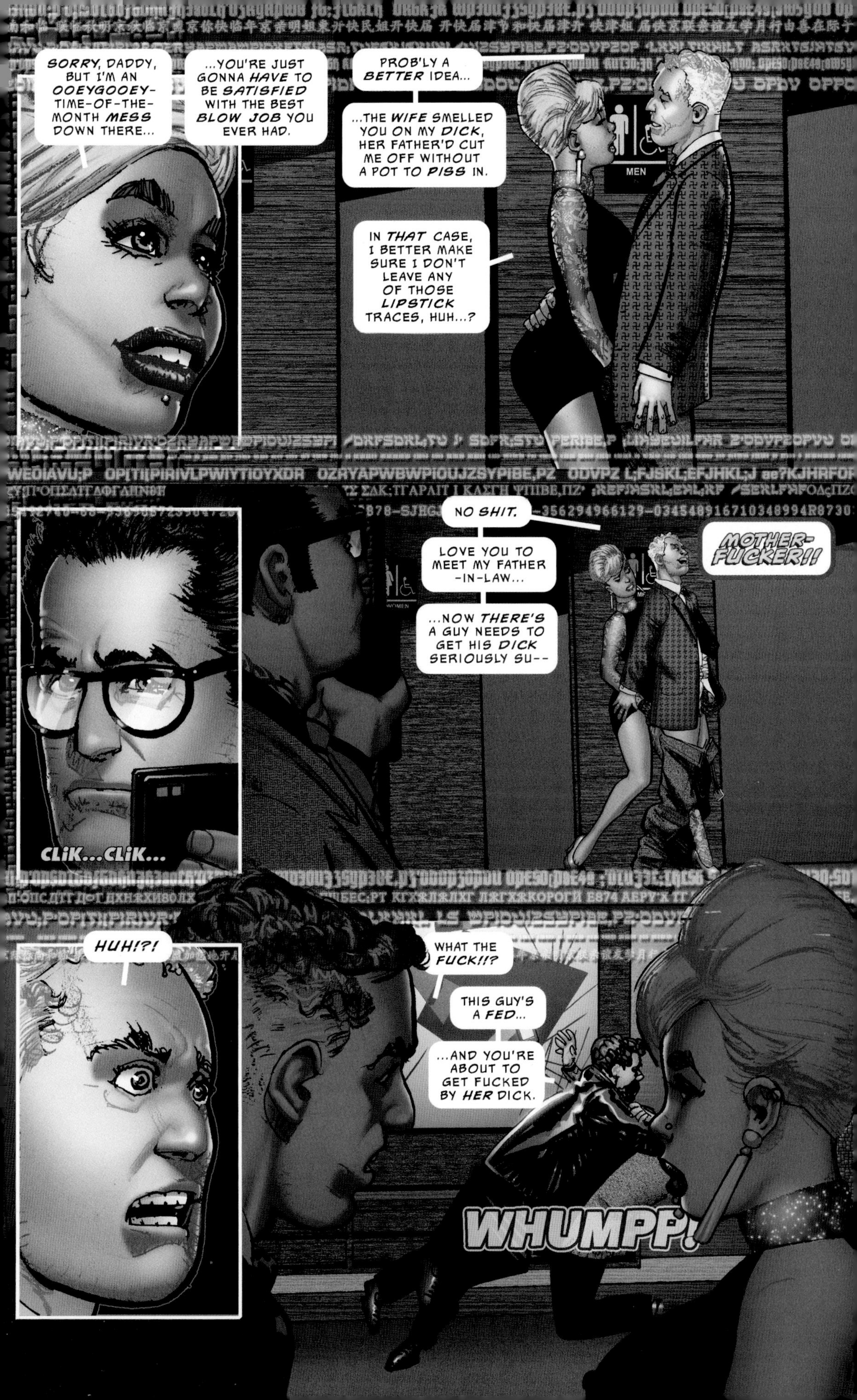
SORRY, DADDY, BUT I'M AN OOEYGOOEY-TIME-OF-THE-MONTH MESS DOWN THERE...
...YOU'RE JUST GONNA HAVE TO BE SATISFIED WITH THE BEST BLOW JOB YOU EVER HAD.
PROB'LY A BETTER IDEA...
...THE WIFE SMELLED YOU ON MY DICK, HER FATHER'D CUT ME OFF WITHOUT A POT TO PISS IN.
MEN
IN THAT CASE, I BETTER MAKE SURE I DON'T LEAVE ANY OF THOSE LIPSTICK TRACES, HUH...?
NO SHIT.
LOVE YOU TO MEET MY FATHER-IN-LAW...
...NOW THERE'S A GUY NEEDS TO GET HIS DICK SERIOUSLY SU--
MOTHER-FUCKER!!
WOMEN
CLiK...CLiK...
HUH!?!
WHAT THE FUCK!!?
THIS GUY'S A FED...
...AND YOU'RE ABOUT TO GET FUCKED BY HER DICK.
WHUMPP!

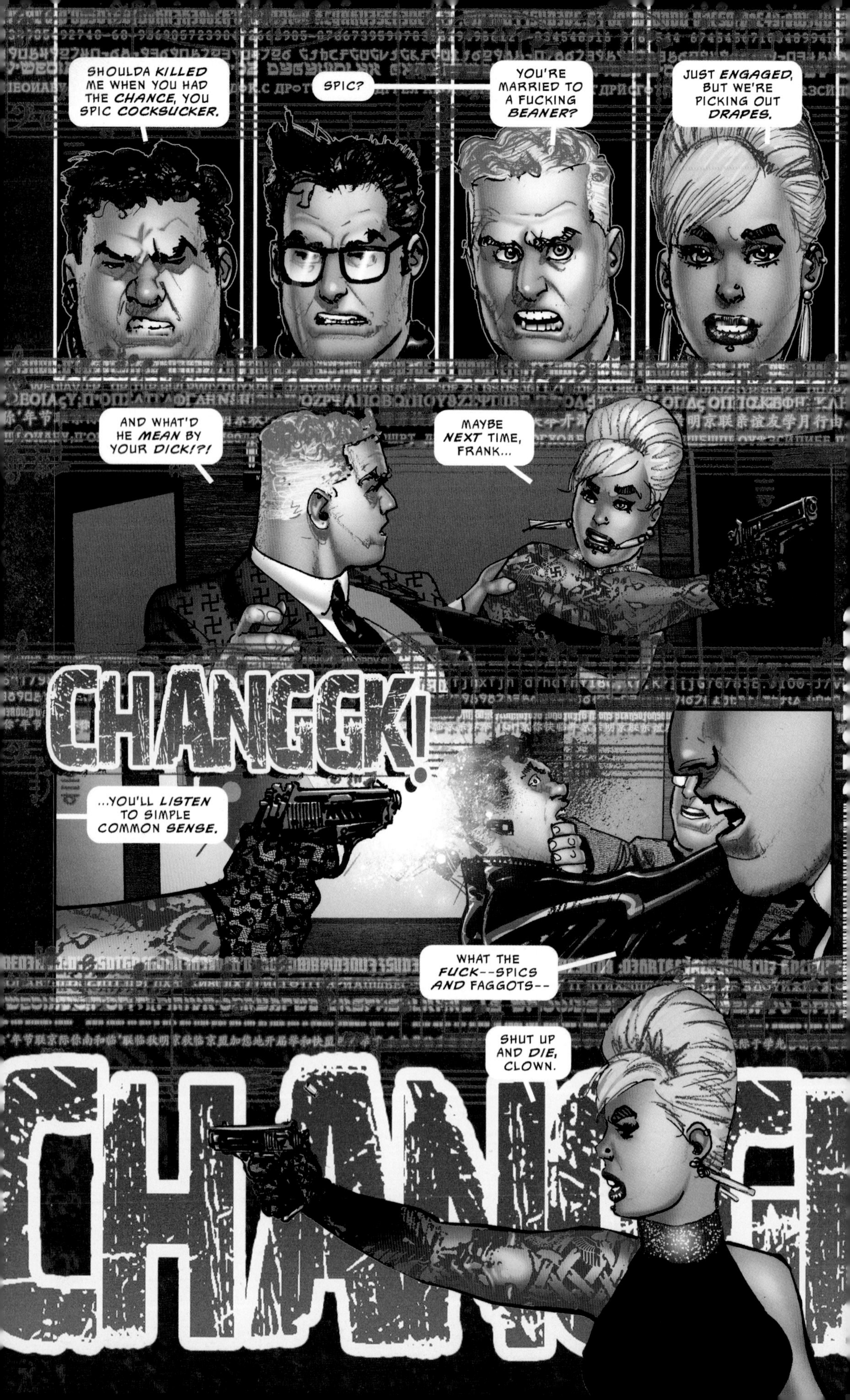
SHOULDA KILLED ME WHEN YOU HAD THE CHANCE, YOU SPIC COCKSUCKER.
SPIC?
YOU'RE MARRIED TO A FUCKING BEANER?
JUST ENGAGED, BUT WE'RE PICKING OUT DRAPES.
AND WHAT'D HE MEAN BY YOUR DICK!?!
MAYBE NEXT TIME, FRANK...
CHANGGK!
...YOU'LL LISTEN TO SIMPLE COMMON SENSE.
WHAT THE FUCK--SPICS AND FAGGOTS--
SHUT UP AND DIE, CLOWN.

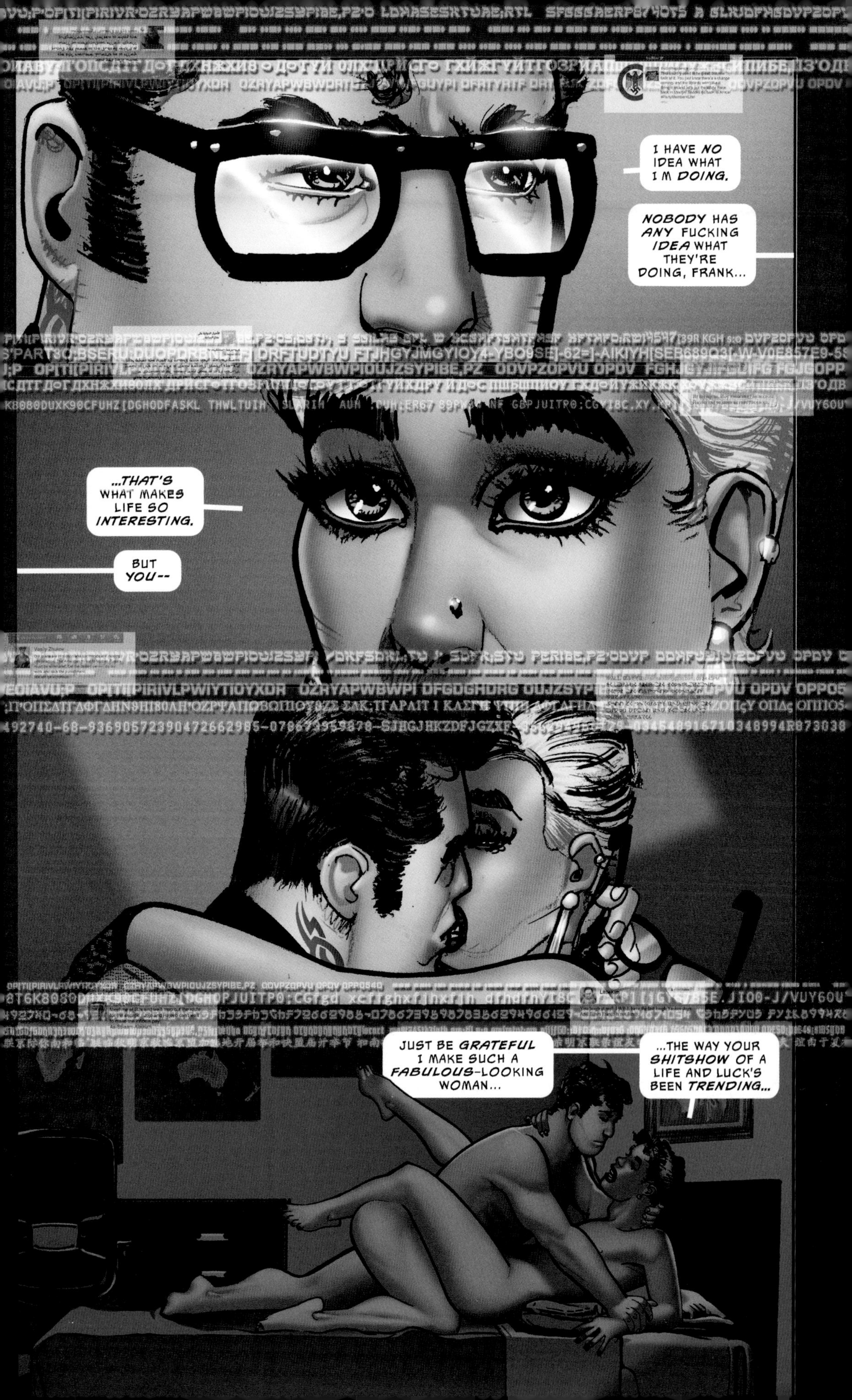
I HAVE NO IDEA WHAT I'M DOING.
NOBODY HAS ANY FUCKING IDEA WHAT THEY'RE DOING, FRANK...
...THAT'S WHAT MAKES LIFE SO INTERESTING.
BUT YOU--
JUST BE GRATEFUL I MAKE SUCH A FABULOUS-LOOKING WOMAN...
...THE WAY YOUR SHITSHOW OF A LIFE AND LUCK'S BEEN TRENDING...

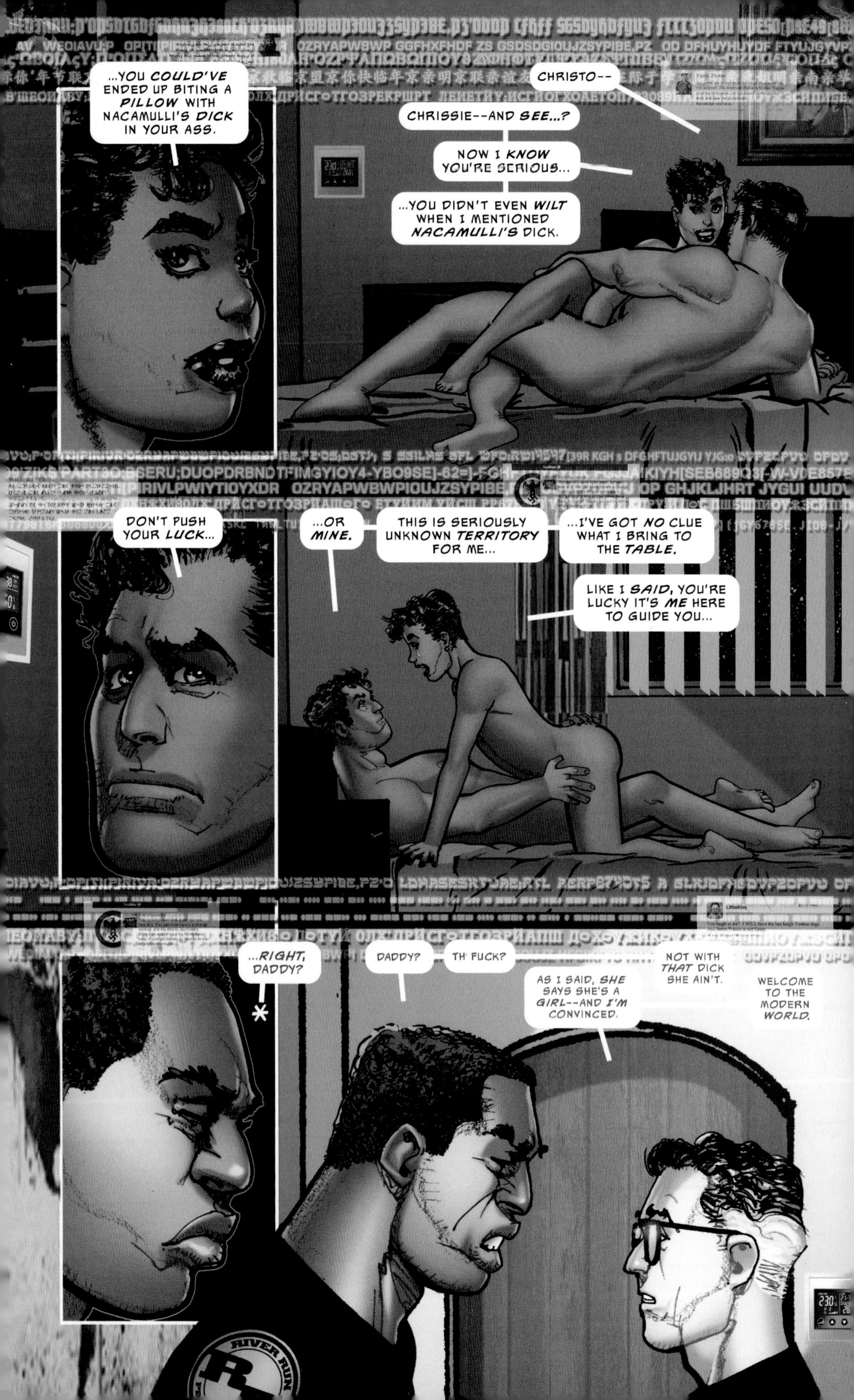
...YOU COULD'VE ENDED UP BITING A PILLOW WITH NACAMULLI'S DICK IN YOUR ASS.
CHRISTO--
CHRISSIE--AND SEE...?
NOW I KNOW YOU'RE SERIOUS...
...YOU DIDN'T EVEN WILT WHEN I MENTIONED NACAMULLI'S DICK.
DON'T PUSH YOUR LUCK...
...OR MINE.
THIS IS SERIOUSLY UNKNOWN TERRITORY FOR ME...
...I'VE GOT NO CLUE WHAT I BRING TO THE TABLE.
LIKE I SAID, YOU'RE LUCKY IT'S ME HERE TO GUIDE YOU...
...RIGHT, DADDY?
DADDY?
TH' FUCK?
AS I SAID, SHE SAYS SHE'S A GIRL--AND I'M CONVINCED.
NOT WITH THAT DICK SHE AIN'T.
WELCOME TO THE MODERN WORLD.
RIVER RUN

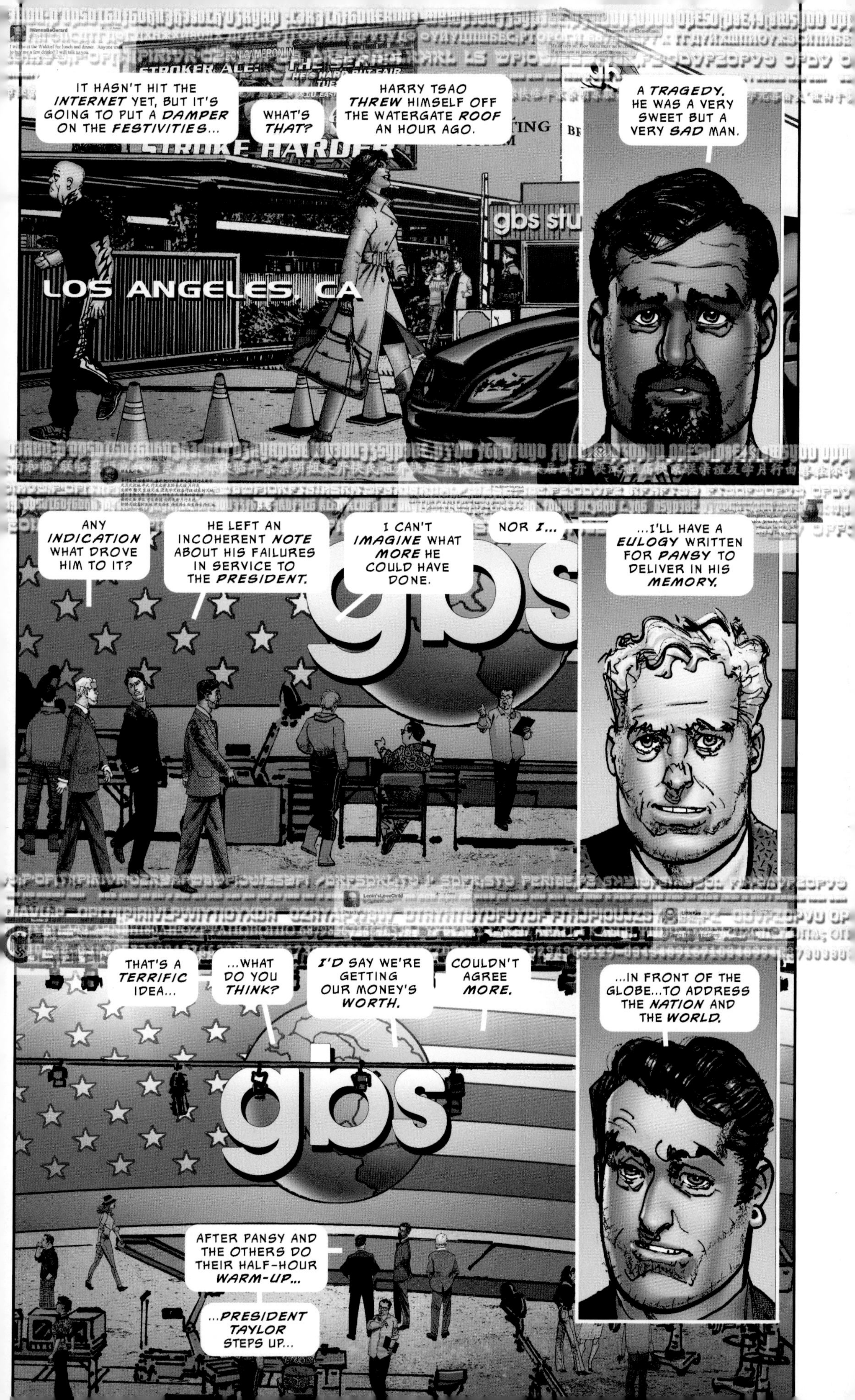
LOS ANGELES, CA
IT HASN'T HIT THE INTERNET YET, BUT IT'S GOING TO PUT A DAMPER ON THE FESTIVITIES...
WHAT'S THAT?
HARRY TSAO THREW HIMSELF OFF THE WATERGATE ROOF AN HOUR AGO.
A TRAGEDY. HE WAS A VERY SWEET BUT A VERY SAD MAN.
ANY INDICATION WHAT DROVE HIM TO IT?
HE LEFT AN INCOHERENT NOTE ABOUT HIS FAILURES IN SERVICE TO THE PRESIDENT.
I CAN'T IMAGINE WHAT MORE HE COULD HAVE DONE.
NOR I...
...I'LL HAVE A EULOGY WRITTEN FOR PANSY TO DELIVER IN HIS MEMORY.
THAT'S A TERRIFIC IDEA...
...WHAT DO YOU THINK?
I'D SAY WE'RE GETTING OUR MONEY'S WORTH.
COULDN'T AGREE MORE.
...IN FRONT OF THE GLOBE...TO ADDRESS THE NATION AND THE WORLD.
AFTER PANSY AND THE OTHERS DO THEIR HALF-HOUR WARM-UP...
...PRESIDENT TAYLOR STEPS UP...

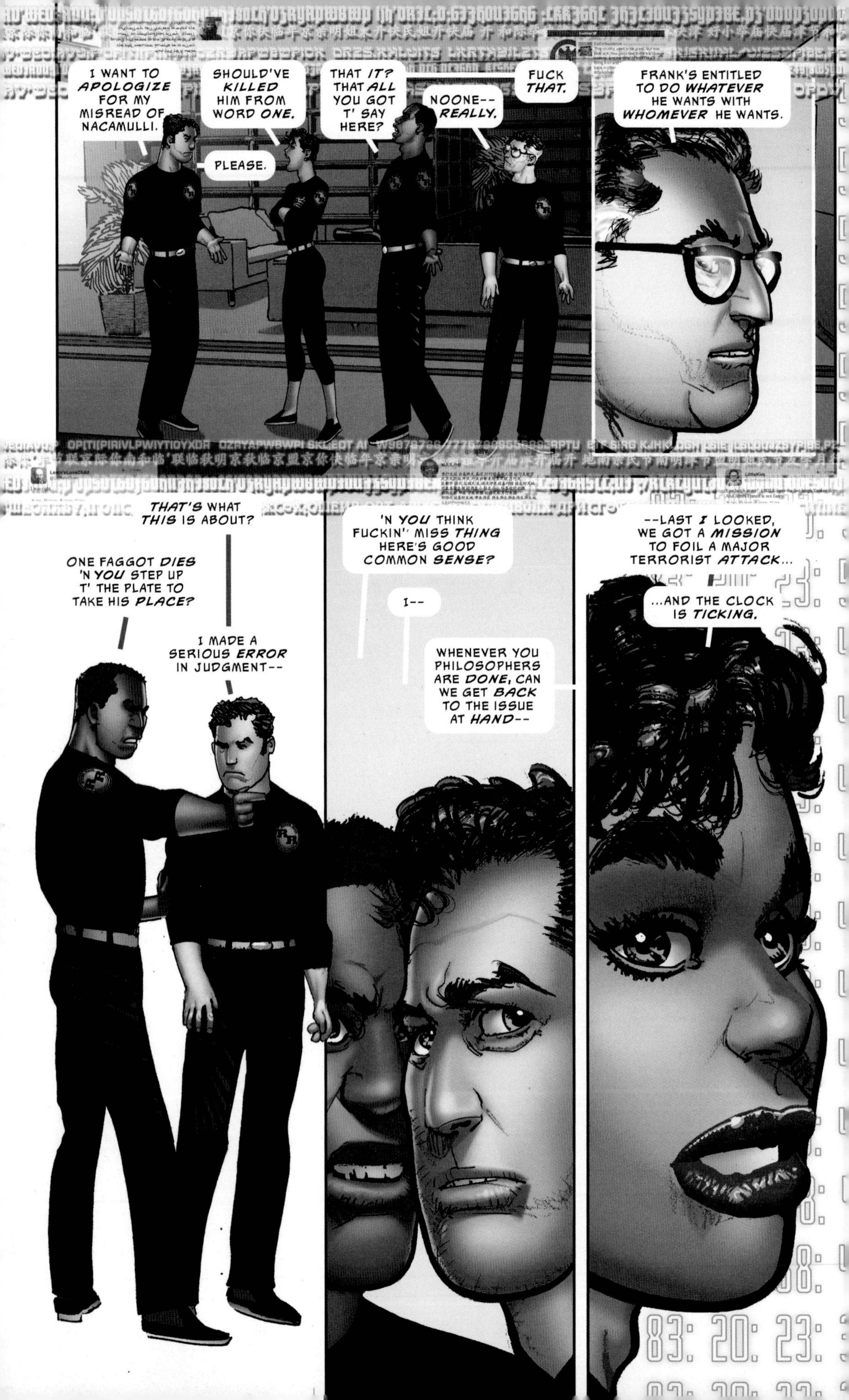
I WANT TO APOLOGIZE FOR MY MISREAD OF NACAMULLI.
SHOULD'VE KILLED HIM FROM WORD ONE.
PLEASE.
THAT IT? THAT ALL YOU GOT T' SAY HERE?
NOONE-- REALLY.
FUCK THAT.
FRANK'S ENTITLED TO DO WHATEVER HE WANTS WITH WHOMEVER HE WANTS.
THAT'S WHAT THIS IS ABOUT?
ONE FAGGOT DIES 'N YOU STEP UP T' THE PLATE TO TAKE HIS PLACE?
I MADE A SERIOUS ERROR IN JUDGMENT--
'N YOU THINK FUCKIN'' MISS THING HERE'S GOOD COMMON SENSE?
I--
WHENEVER YOU PHILOSOPHERS ARE DONE, CAN WE GET BACK TO THE ISSUE AT HAND--
--LAST I LOOKED, WE GOT A MISSION TO FOIL A MAJOR TERRORIST ATTACK...
...AND THE CLOCK IS TICKING.
83: 20: 23:

Part Six

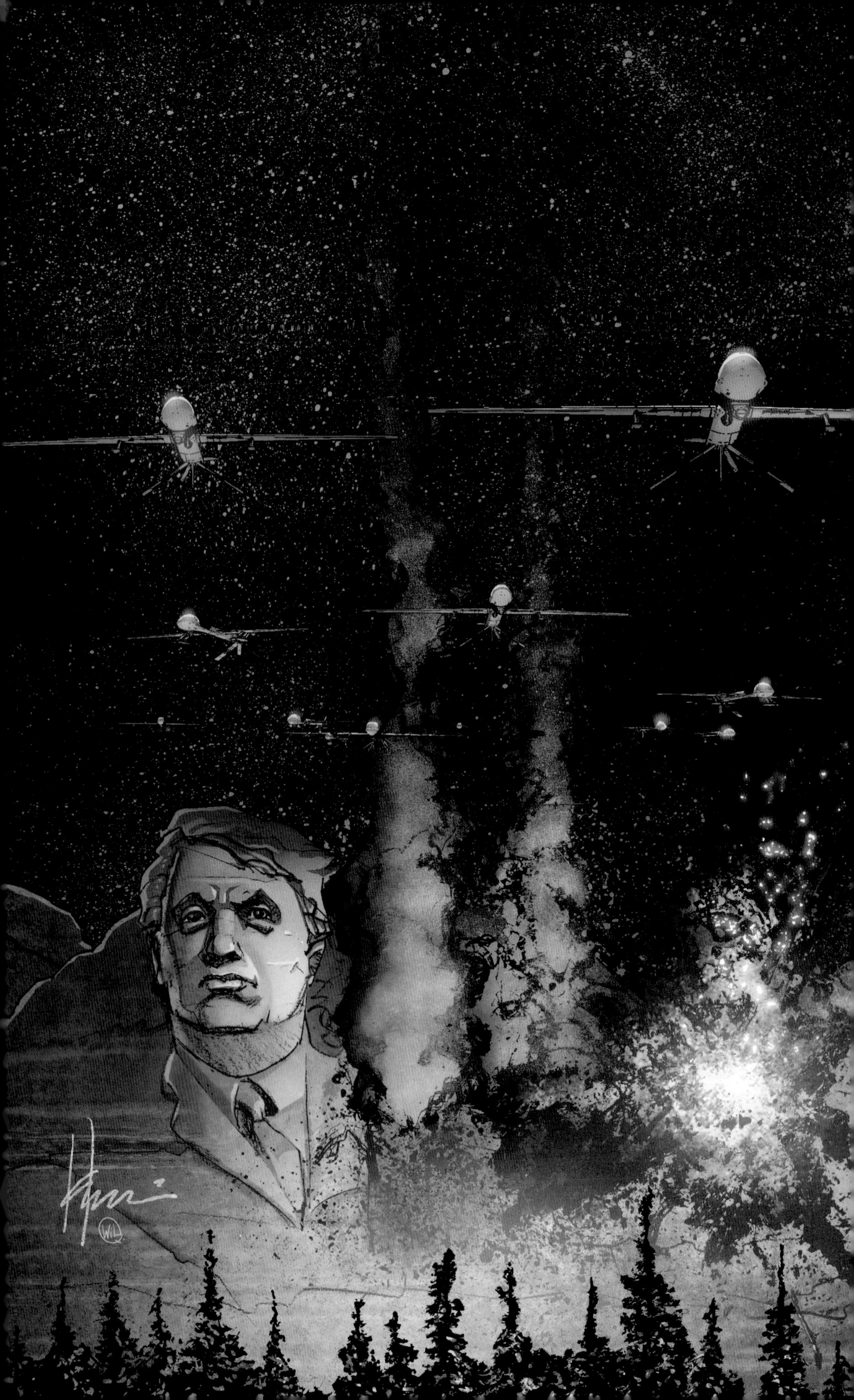

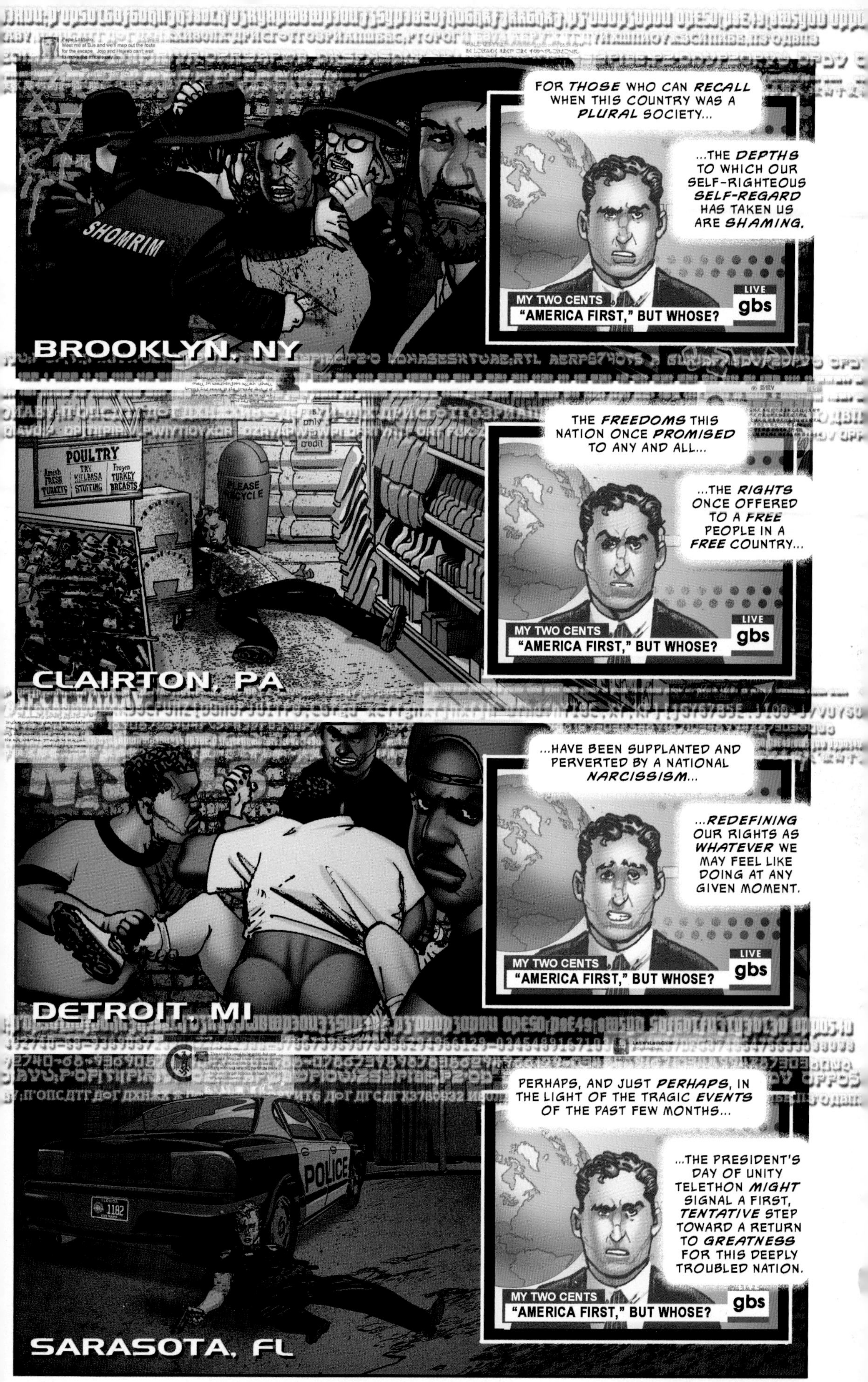
FOR THOSE WHO CAN RECALL WHEN THIS COUNTRY WAS A PLURAL SOCIETY...
...THE DEPTHS TO WHICH OUR SELF-RIGHTEOUS SELF-REGARD HAS TAKEN US ARE SHAMING.
SHOMRIM
MY TWO CENTS
"AMERICA FIRST," BUT WHOSE?
LIVE
gbs
BROOKLYN, NY
POULTRY
Amish FRESH TURKEYS
TRY KIELBASA STUFFING
Frozen TURKEY BREASTS
PLEASE RECYCLE
THE FREEDOMS THIS NATION ONCE PROMISED TO ANY AND ALL...
...THE RIGHTS ONCE OFFERED TO A FREE PEOPLE IN A FREE COUNTRY...
MY TWO CENTS
"AMERICA FIRST," BUT WHOSE?
LIVE
gbs
CLAIRTON, PA
...HAVE BEEN SUPPLANTED AND PERVERTED BY A NATIONAL NARCISSISM...
...REDEFINING OUR RIGHTS AS WHATEVER WE MAY FEEL LIKE DOING AT ANY GIVEN MOMENT.
MY TWO CENTS
"AMERICA FIRST," BUT WHOSE?
LIVE
gbs
DETROIT, MI
PERHAPS, AND JUST PERHAPS, IN THE LIGHT OF THE TRAGIC EVENTS OF THE PAST FEW MONTHS...
...THE PRESIDENT'S DAY OF UNITY TELETHON MIGHT SIGNAL A FIRST, TENTATIVE STEP TOWARD A RETURN TO GREATNESS FOR THIS DEEPLY TROUBLED NATION.
POLICE
1182
MY TWO CENTS
"AMERICA FIRST," BUT WHOSE?
gbs
SARASOTA, FL

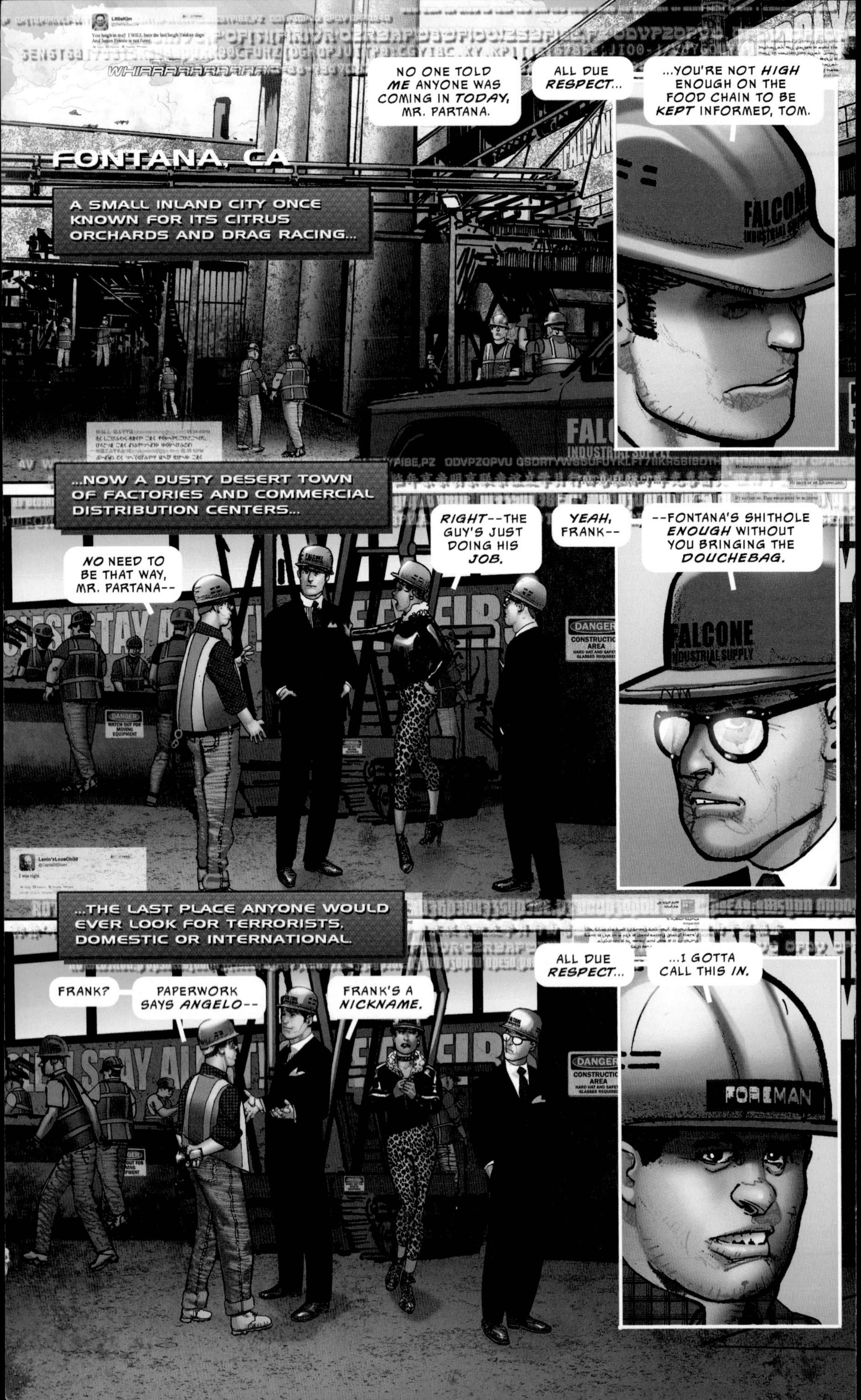
WHIRRRRRRRRRRR
FONTANA, CA
A SMALL INLAND CITY ONCE KNOWN FOR ITS CITRUS ORCHARDS AND DRAG RACING...
NO ONE TOLD *ME* ANYONE WAS COMING IN *TODAY*, MR. PARTANA.
ALL DUE *RESPECT*...
...YOU'RE NOT *HIGH* ENOUGH ON THE FOOD CHAIN TO BE *KEPT* INFORMED, TOM.
FALCONE INDUSTRIAL SUPPLY
...NOW A DUSTY DESERT TOWN OF FACTORIES AND COMMERCIAL DISTRIBUTION CENTERS...
NO NEED TO BE THAT WAY, MR. PARTANA--
RIGHT--THE GUY'S JUST DOING HIS *JOB*.
YEAH, FRANK--
--FONTANA'S SHITHOLE *ENOUGH* WITHOUT YOU BRINGING THE *DOUCHEBAG*.
DANGER
CONSTRUCTION AREA
HARD HAT AND SAFETY GLASSES REQUIRED
DANGER
WATCH OUT FOR MOVING EQUIPMENT
FALCONE INDUSTRIAL SUPPLY
...THE LAST PLACE ANYONE WOULD EVER LOOK FOR TERRORISTS, DOMESTIC OR INTERNATIONAL.
FRANK?
PAPERWORK SAYS *ANGELO*--
FRANK'S A *NICKNAME*.
ALL DUE *RESPECT*...
...I GOTTA CALL THIS *IN*.
FOREMAN

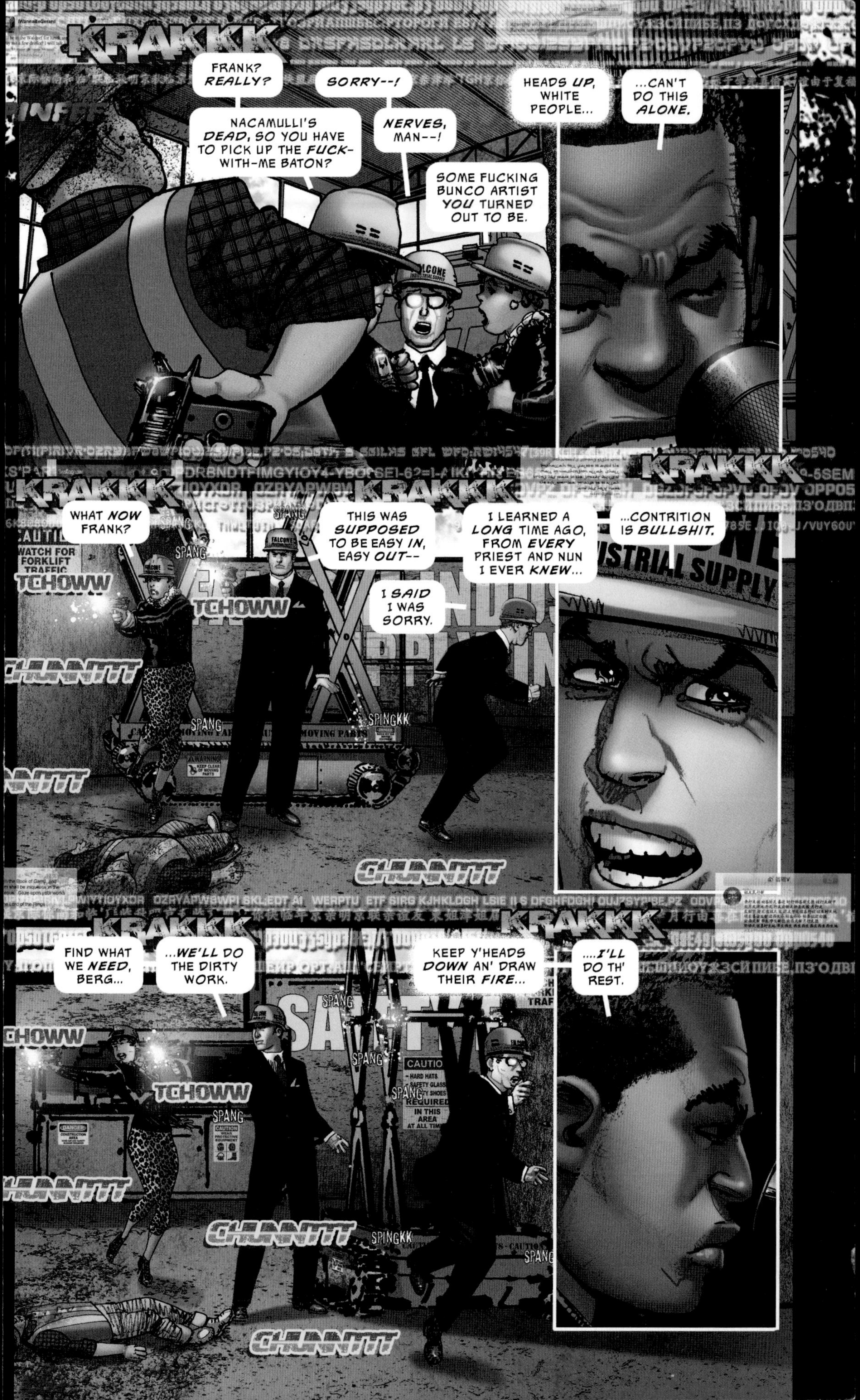
KRAKKK
FRANK? REALLY?
NACAMULLI'S DEAD, SO YOU HAVE TO PICK UP THE FUCK-WITH-ME BATON?
SORRY--!
NERVES, MAN--!
SOME FUCKING BUNCO ARTIST YOU TURNED OUT TO BE.
HEADS UP, WHITE PEOPLE...
...CAN'T DO THIS ALONE.
KRAKKK
KRAKKK
KRAKKK
WHAT NOW FRANK?
THIS WAS SUPPOSED TO BE EASY IN, EASY OUT--
I SAID I WAS SORRY.
I LEARNED A LONG TIME AGO, FROM EVERY PRIEST AND NUN I EVER KNEW...
...CONTRITION IS BULLSHIT.
TCHOWW
TCHOWW
SPANG
SPINGKK
CHUNNTTT
KRAKKK
KRAKKK
FIND WHAT WE NEED, BERG...
...WE'LL DO THE DIRTY WORK.
KEEP Y'HEADS DOWN AN' DRAW THEIR FIRE...
....I'LL DO TH' REST.
TCHOWW
TCHOWW
SPANG
SPINGKK
CHUNNTTT

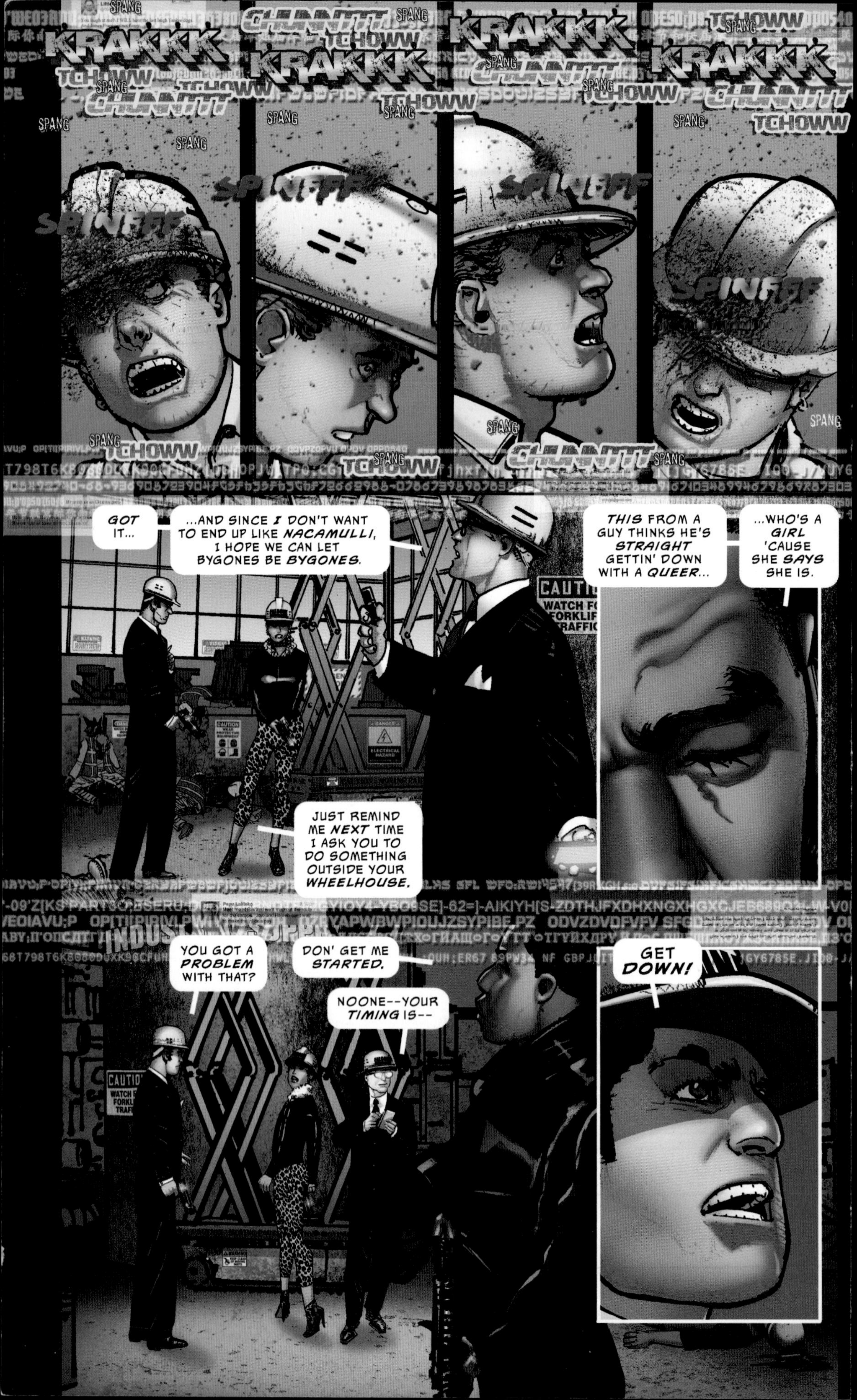
KRAKKK
CHUNNTTT
TCHOWW
SPANG
SPINFFF
GOT IT...
...AND SINCE I DON'T WANT TO END UP LIKE NACAMULLI, I HOPE WE CAN LET BYGONES BE BYGONES.
THIS FROM A GUY THINKS HE'S STRAIGHT GETTIN' DOWN WITH A QUEER...
...WHO'S A GIRL 'CAUSE SHE SAYS SHE IS.
CAUTION WATCH FOR FORKLIFT TRAFFIC
JUST REMIND ME NEXT TIME I ASK YOU TO DO SOMETHING OUTSIDE YOUR WHEELHOUSE.
YOU GOT A PROBLEM WITH THAT?
DON' GET ME STARTED.
NOONE--YOUR TIMING IS--
GET DOWN!

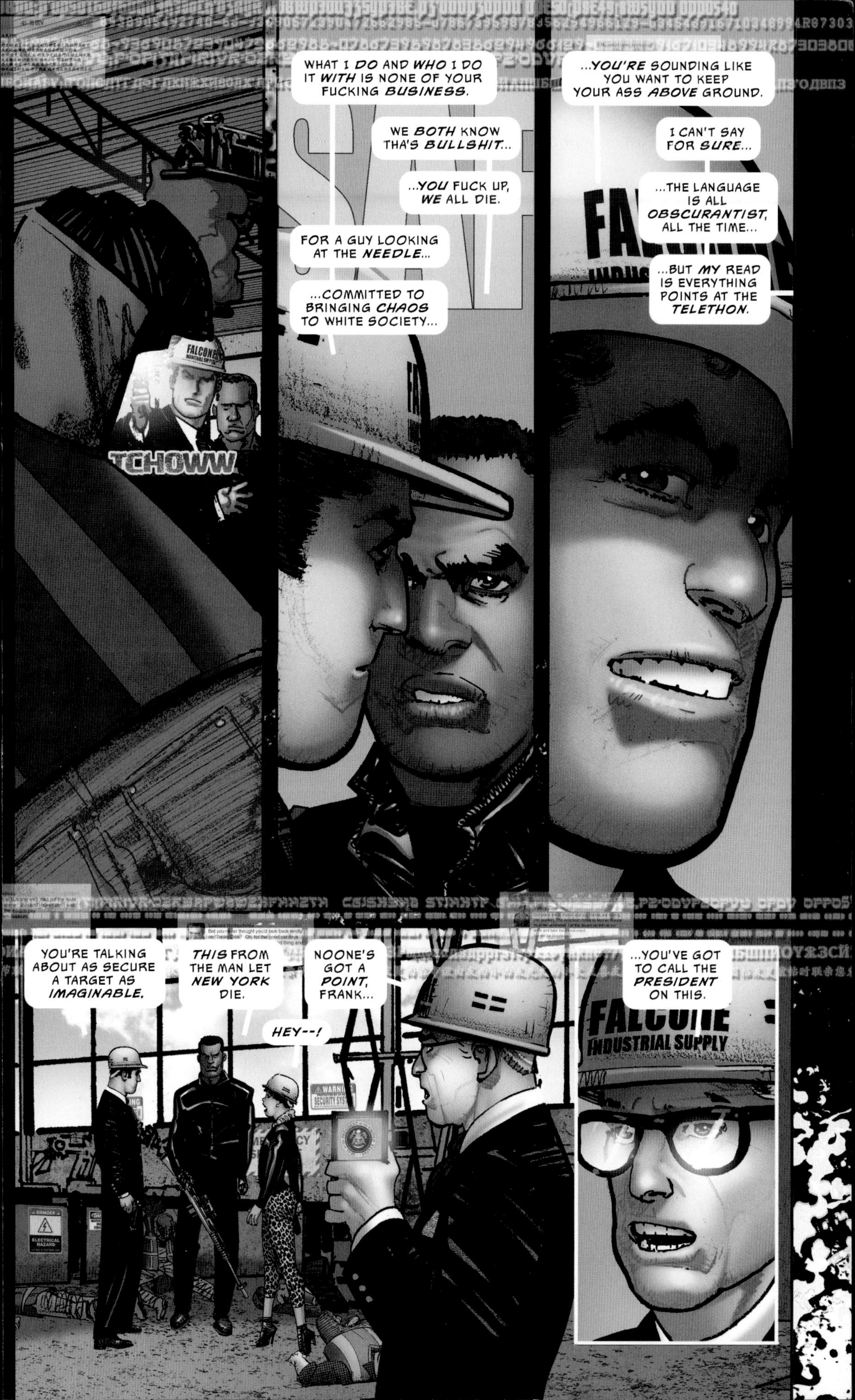
TCHOWW
WHAT I DO AND WHO I DO IT WITH IS NONE OF YOUR FUCKING BUSINESS.
WE BOTH KNOW THA'S BULLSHIT...
...YOU FUCK UP, WE ALL DIE.
FOR A GUY LOOKING AT THE NEEDLE...
...COMMITTED TO BRINGING CHAOS TO WHITE SOCIETY...
...YOU'RE SOUNDING LIKE YOU WANT TO KEEP YOUR ASS ABOVE GROUND.
I CAN'T SAY FOR SURE...
...THE LANGUAGE IS ALL OBSCURANTIST, ALL THE TIME...
...BUT MY READ IS EVERYTHING POINTS AT THE TELETHON.
YOU'RE TALKING ABOUT AS SECURE A TARGET AS IMAGINABLE.
THIS FROM THE MAN LET NEW YORK DIE.
NOONE'S GOT A POINT, FRANK...
HEY--!
...YOU'VE GOT TO CALL THE PRESIDENT ON THIS.
FALCONE INDUSTRIAL SUPPLY

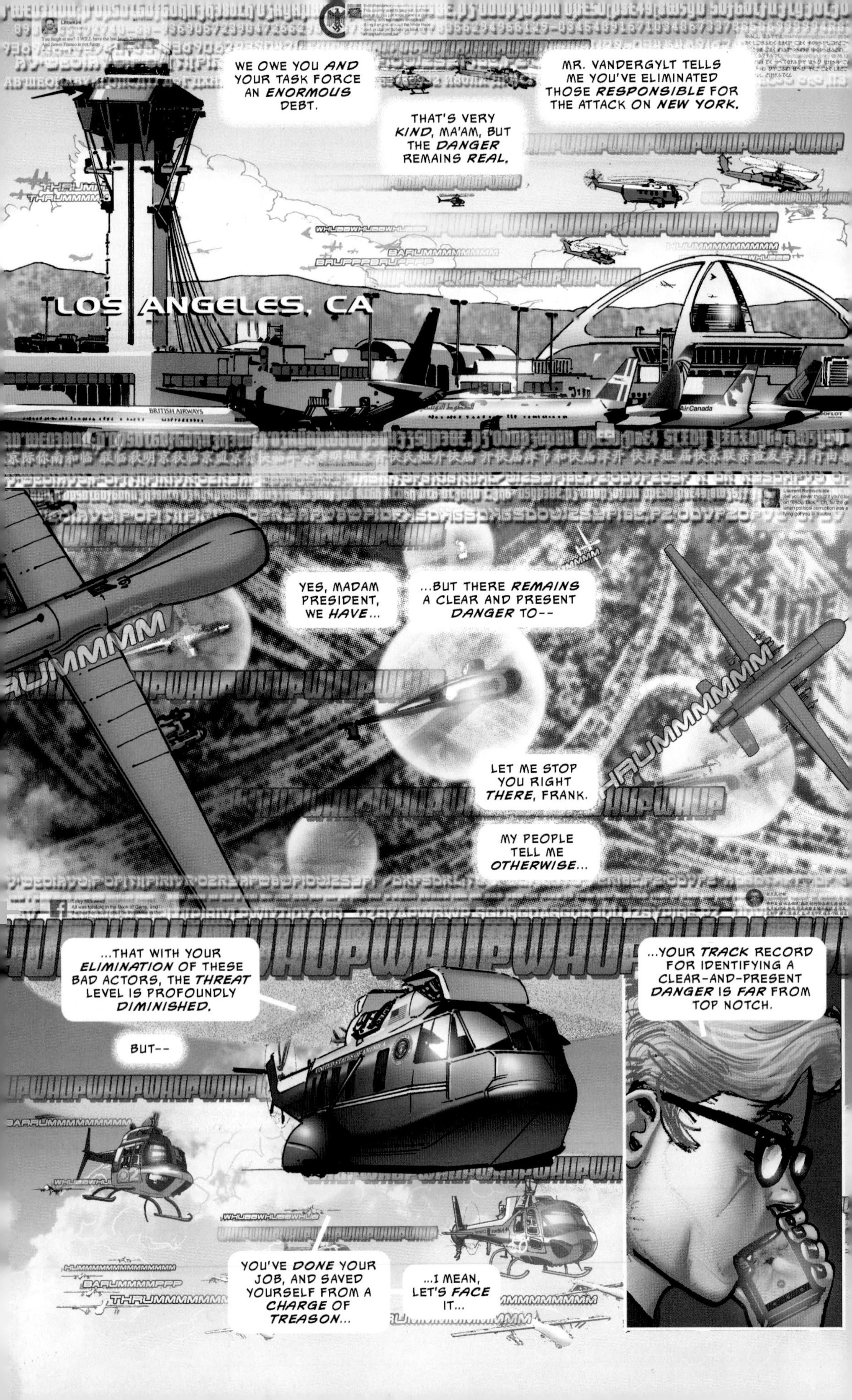
LOS ANGELES, CA
WE OWE YOU AND YOUR TASK FORCE AN ENORMOUS DEBT.
MR. VANDERGYLT TELLS ME YOU'VE ELIMINATED THOSE RESPONSIBLE FOR THE ATTACK ON NEW YORK.
THAT'S VERY KIND, MA'AM, BUT THE DANGER REMAINS REAL.
BRITISH AIRWAYS
Air Canada
YES, MADAM PRESIDENT, WE HAVE...
...BUT THERE REMAINS A CLEAR AND PRESENT DANGER TO--
LET ME STOP YOU RIGHT THERE, FRANK.
MY PEOPLE TELL ME OTHERWISE...
...THAT WITH YOUR ELIMINATION OF THESE BAD ACTORS, THE THREAT LEVEL IS PROFOUNDLY DIMINISHED.
BUT--
...YOUR TRACK RECORD FOR IDENTIFYING A CLEAR-AND-PRESENT DANGER IS FAR FROM TOP NOTCH.
YOU'VE DONE YOUR JOB, AND SAVED YOURSELF FROM A CHARGE OF TREASON...
...I MEAN, LET'S FACE IT...

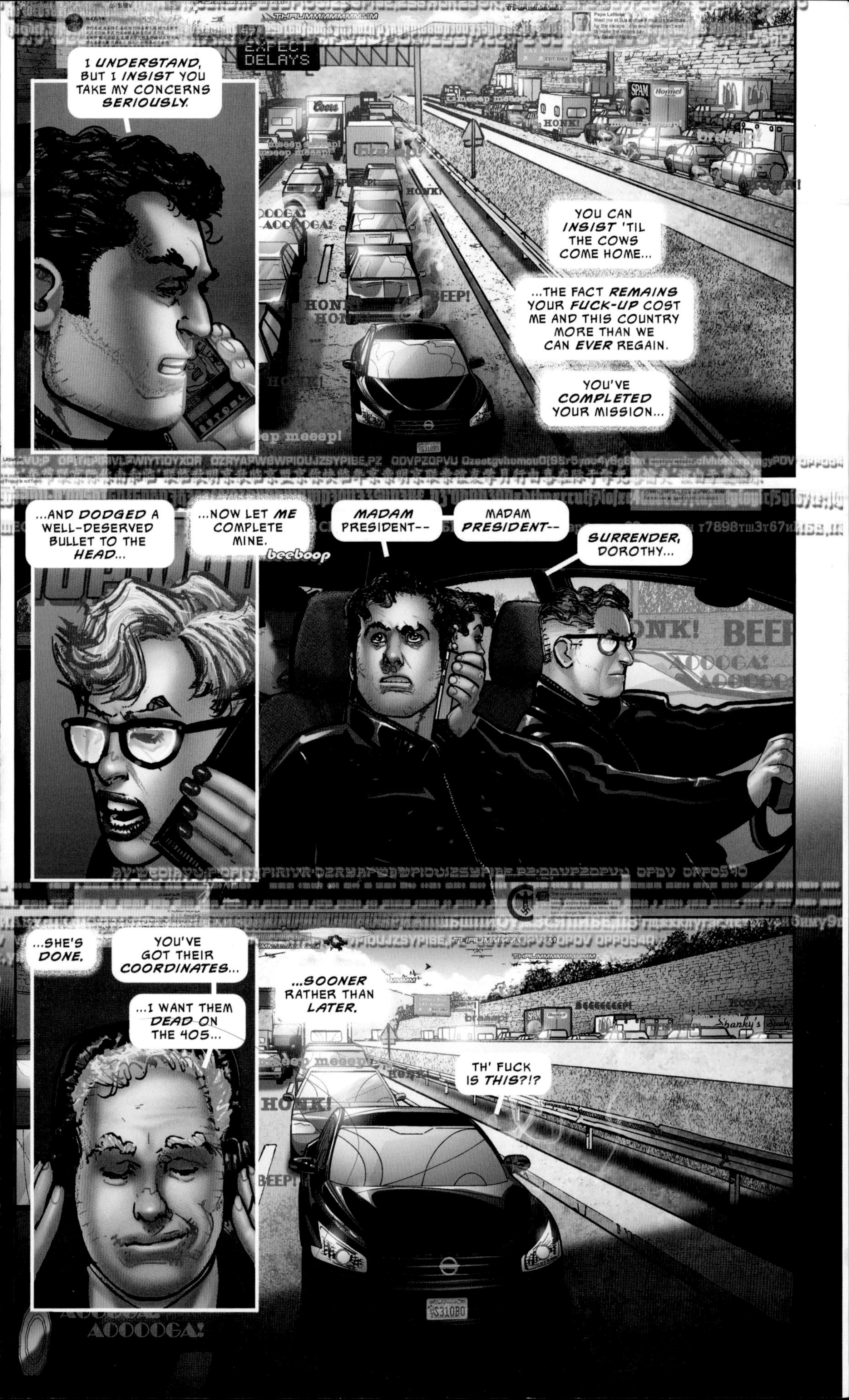
THRUMMMMMMMM
EXPECT DELAYS
I UNDERSTAND, BUT I INSIST YOU TAKE MY CONCERNS SERIOUSLY.
SPAM
HONK!
BEEP!
YOU CAN INSIST 'TIL THE COWS COME HOME...
...THE FACT REMAINS YOUR FUCK-UP COST ME AND THIS COUNTRY MORE THAN WE CAN EVER REGAIN.
YOU'VE COMPLETED YOUR MISSION...
...AND DODGED A WELL-DESERVED BULLET TO THE HEAD...
...NOW LET ME COMPLETE MINE.
beeboop
MADAM PRESIDENT--
MADAM PRESIDENT--
SURRENDER, DOROTHY...
...SHE'S DONE.
YOU'VE GOT THEIR COORDINATES...
...I WANT THEM DEAD ON THE 405...
...SOONER RATHER THAN LATER.
TH' FUCK IS THIS?!?
HONK!
BEEP!
AOOOOGA!

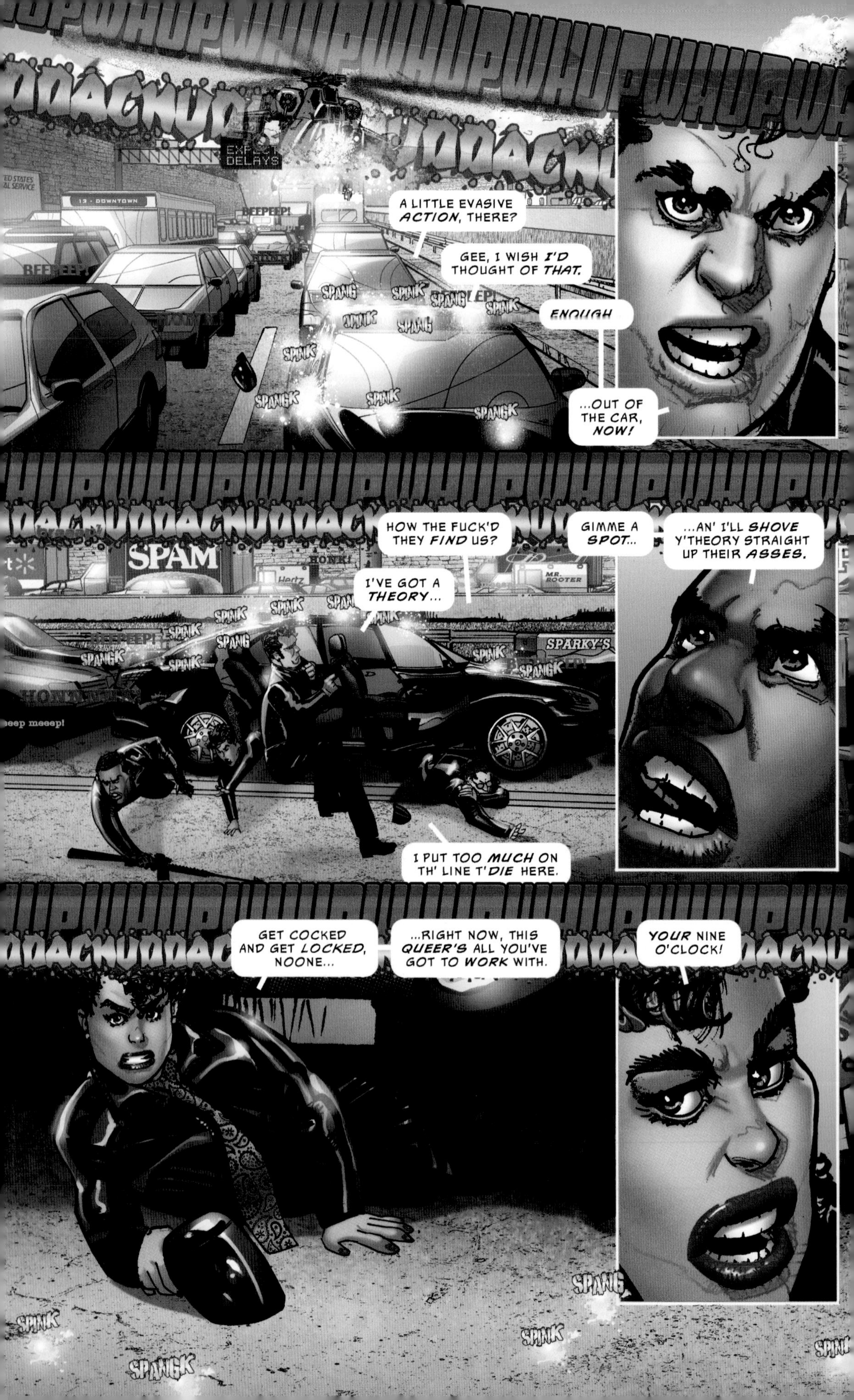
WHUPWHUPWHUPWHUPWHUPWH
DDACHUD
DDACHU
EXPECT DELAYS
13 - DOWNTOWN
BEEPEEP!
A LITTLE EVASIVE ACTION, THERE?
GEE, I WISH I'D THOUGHT OF THAT.
SPANG
SPINK
ENOUGH
...OUT OF THE CAR, NOW!
SPANGK
HOW THE FUCK'D THEY FIND US?
I'VE GOT A THEORY...
GIMME A SPOT...
...AN' I'LL SHOVE Y'THEORY STRAIGHT UP THEIR ASSES.
SPAM
HONK!
Hertz
MR. ROOTER
SPARKY'S
meep meeep!
I PUT TOO MUCH ON TH' LINE T'DIE HERE.
GET COCKED AND GET LOCKED, NOONE...
...RIGHT NOW, THIS QUEER'S ALL YOU'VE GOT TO WORK WITH.
YOUR NINE O'CLOCK!
SPANG
SPINK
SPANGK

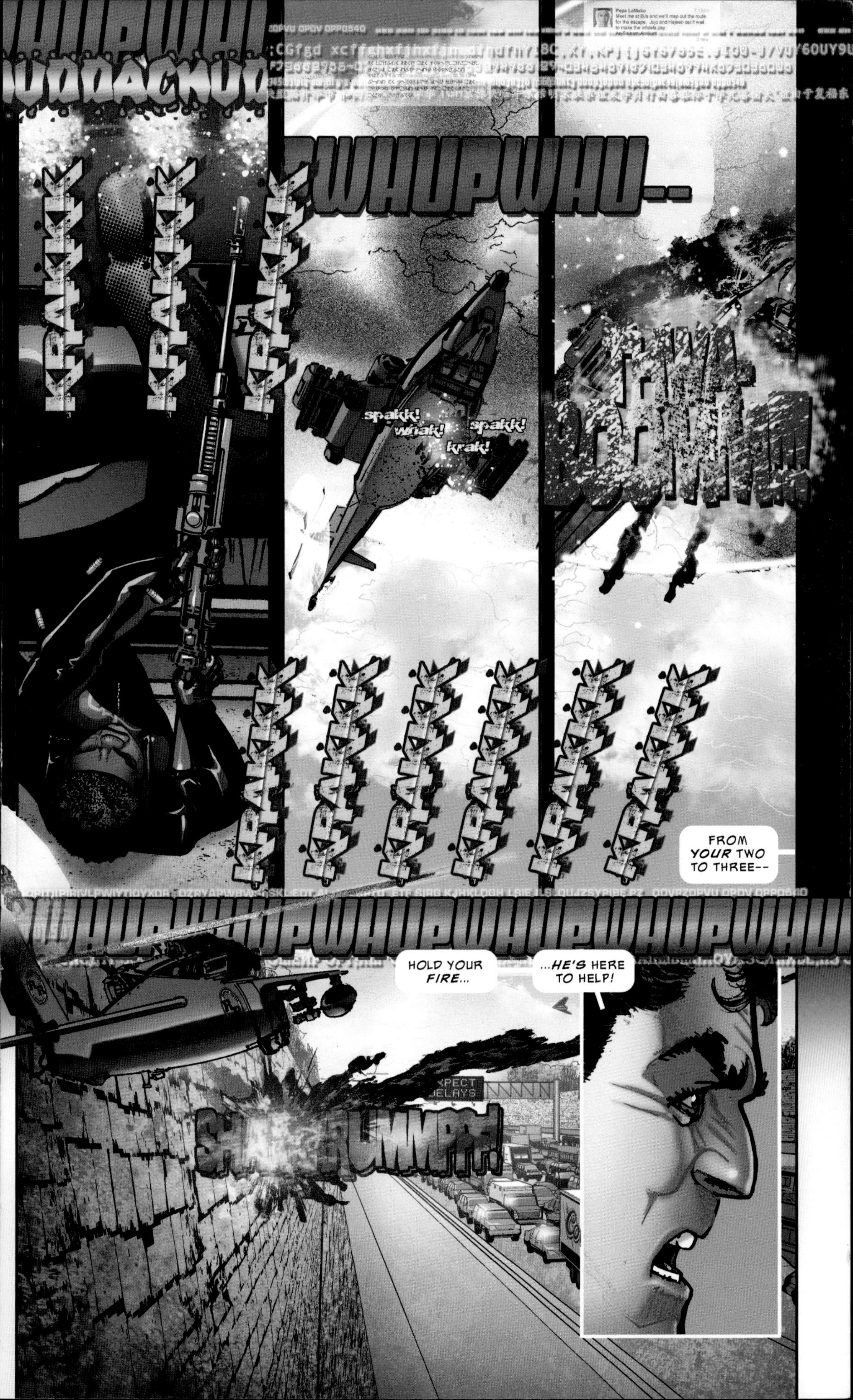
Pepe LaMoko
Meet me at BJs and we'll map out the route for the escape. Jojo and Hajeeb can't wait to make the infidels pay.
As-Salaam-Alaikum
KRAKK KRAKK KRAKK
WHUPWHU--
spakk! whak! spakk! krak!
KRAKK KRAKK KRAKK KRAKK KRAKK KRAKK
FROM YOUR TWO TO THREE--
HOLD YOUR FIRE...
...HE'S HERE TO HELP!

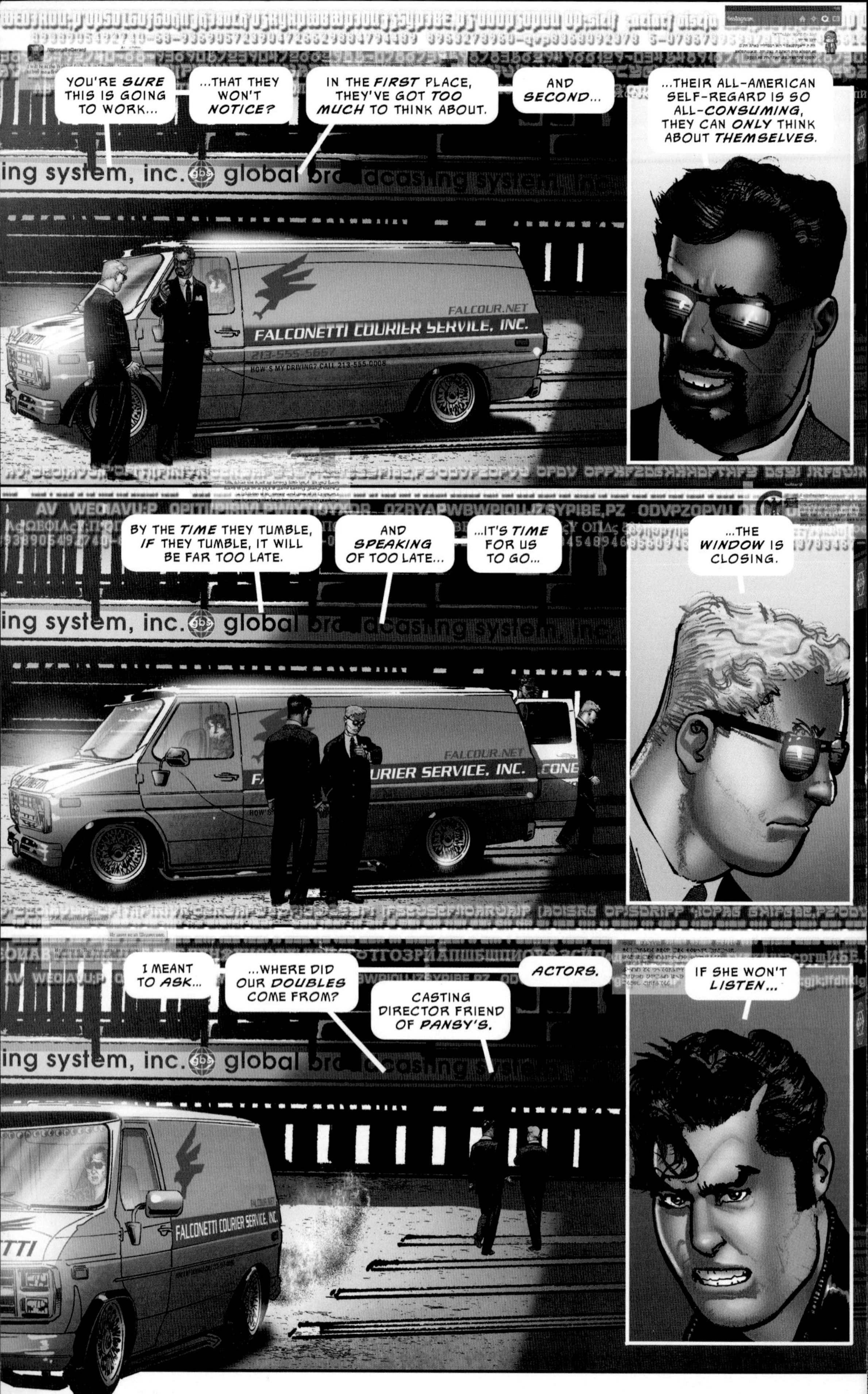
YOU'RE SURE THIS IS GOING TO WORK...
...THAT THEY WON'T NOTICE?
IN THE FIRST PLACE, THEY'VE GOT TOO MUCH TO THINK ABOUT.
AND SECOND...
...THEIR ALL-AMERICAN SELF-REGARD IS SO ALL-CONSUMING, THEY CAN ONLY THINK ABOUT THEMSELVES.
ing system, inc. gbs global broadcasting system, inc
FALCOUR.NET
FALCONETTI COURIER SERVICE, INC.
213-555-5657
HOW'S MY DRIVING? CALL 213-555-0008
BY THE TIME THEY TUMBLE, IF THEY TUMBLE, IT WILL BE FAR TOO LATE.
AND SPEAKING OF TOO LATE...
...IT'S TIME FOR US TO GO...
...THE WINDOW IS CLOSING.
I MEANT TO ASK...
...WHERE DID OUR DOUBLES COME FROM?
ACTORS.
CASTING DIRECTOR FRIEND OF PANSY'S.
IF SHE WON'T LISTEN...

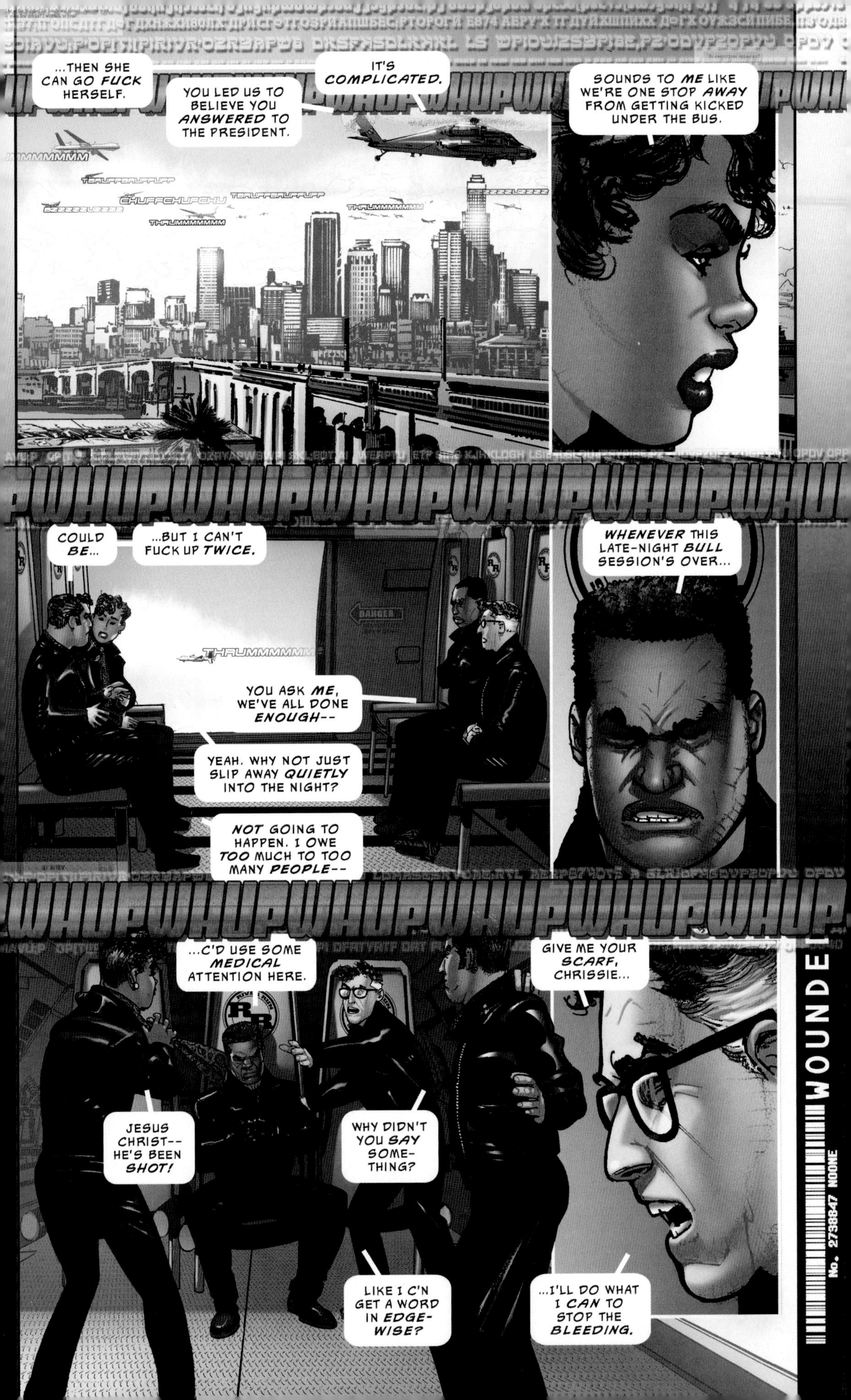

...THEN SHE CAN GO FUCK HERSELF.
YOU LED US TO BELIEVE YOU ANSWERED TO THE PRESIDENT.
IT'S COMPLICATED.
SOUNDS TO ME LIKE WE'RE ONE STOP AWAY FROM GETTING KICKED UNDER THE BUS.
THRUMMMMMMM
WHUPWHUPWHUPWHUPWHUP
COULD BE...
...BUT I CAN'T FUCK UP TWICE.
WHENEVER THIS LATE-NIGHT BULL SESSION'S OVER...
YOU ASK ME, WE'VE ALL DONE ENOUGH--
YEAH. WHY NOT JUST SLIP AWAY QUIETLY INTO THE NIGHT?
NOT GOING TO HAPPEN. I OWE TOO MUCH TO TOO MANY PEOPLE--
WHUPWHUPWHUPWHUPWHUP
...C'D USE SOME MEDICAL ATTENTION HERE.
GIVE ME YOUR SCARF, CHRISSIE...
JESUS CHRIST-- HE'S BEEN SHOT!
WHY DIDN'T YOU SAY SOME-THING?
LIKE I C'N GET A WORD IN EDGE-WISE?
...I'LL DO WHAT I CAN TO STOP THE BLEEDING.
WOUNDE
No. 2738847 NOONE

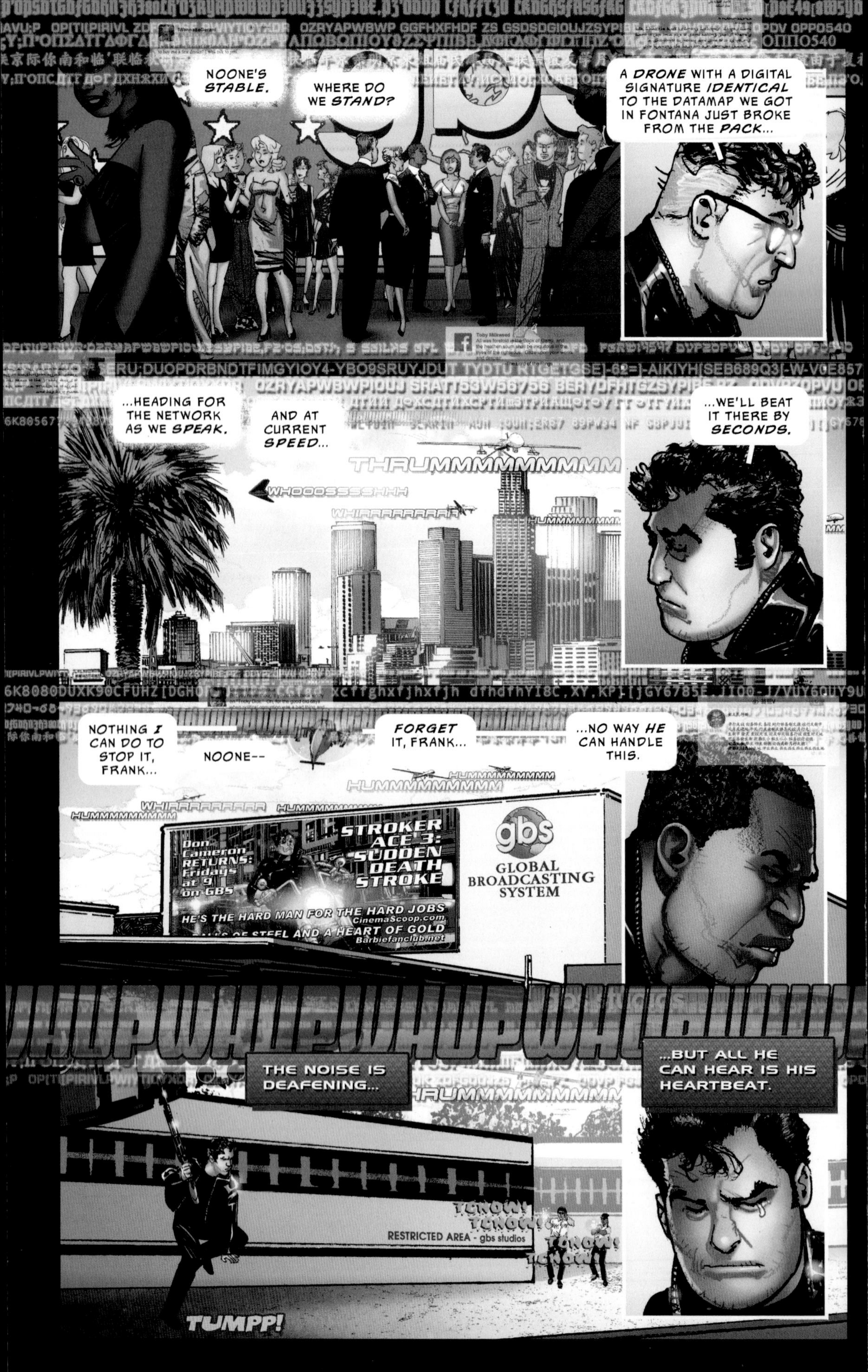
NOONE'S STABLE.
WHERE DO WE STAND?
A DRONE WITH A DIGITAL SIGNATURE IDENTICAL TO THE DATAMAP WE GOT IN FONTANA JUST BROKE FROM THE PACK...
...HEADING FOR THE NETWORK AS WE SPEAK.
AND AT CURRENT SPEED...
...WE'LL BEAT IT THERE BY SECONDS.
THRUMMMMMMMMMMM
WHOOOSSSSHHH
NOTHING I CAN DO TO STOP IT, FRANK...
NOONE--
FORGET IT, FRANK...
...NO WAY HE CAN HANDLE THIS.
STROKER ACE 3: SUDDEN DEATH STROKE
Don Cameron RETURNS: Fridays at 9 on GBS
HE'S THE HARD MAN FOR THE HARD JOBS
CinemaScoop.com
Barbiefanclub.net
gbs
GLOBAL BROADCASTING SYSTEM
THE NOISE IS DEAFENING...
...BUT ALL HE CAN HEAR IS HIS HEARTBEAT.
RESTRICTED AREA - gbs studios
TUMPP!

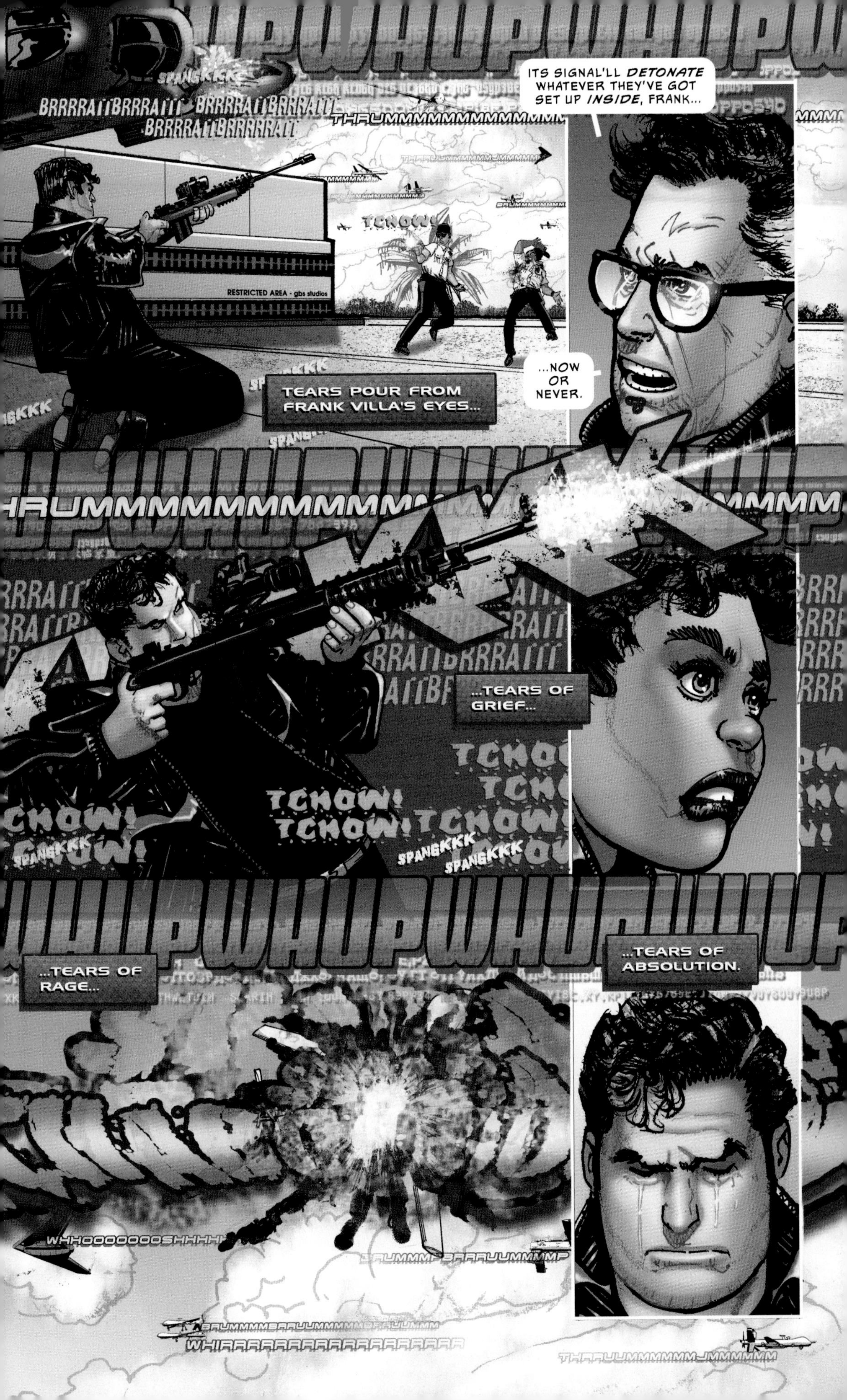
SPANGKKK
BRRRRATTBRRRATT BRRRRATTBRRRATT
BRRRRATTBRRRRRATT
THRUMMMMMMMMMMMMMM
ITS SIGNAL'LL *DETONATE* WHATEVER THEY'VE GOT SET UP *INSIDE*, FRANK...
TCHOW!
RESTRICTED AREA - gbs studios
...NOW OR NEVER.
TEARS POUR FROM FRANK VILLA'S EYES...
THRUMMMMMMMMMMMMMMMMMM
...TEARS OF GRIEF...
TCHOW! TCHOW! TCHOW!
SPANGKKK
SPANGKKK
...TEARS OF RAGE...
...TEARS OF ABSOLUTION.
WHHOOOOOOOOSHHHH
WHIRRRRRRRRRRRRRRRRRRR
THRRUUMMMMMMJMMMMMM

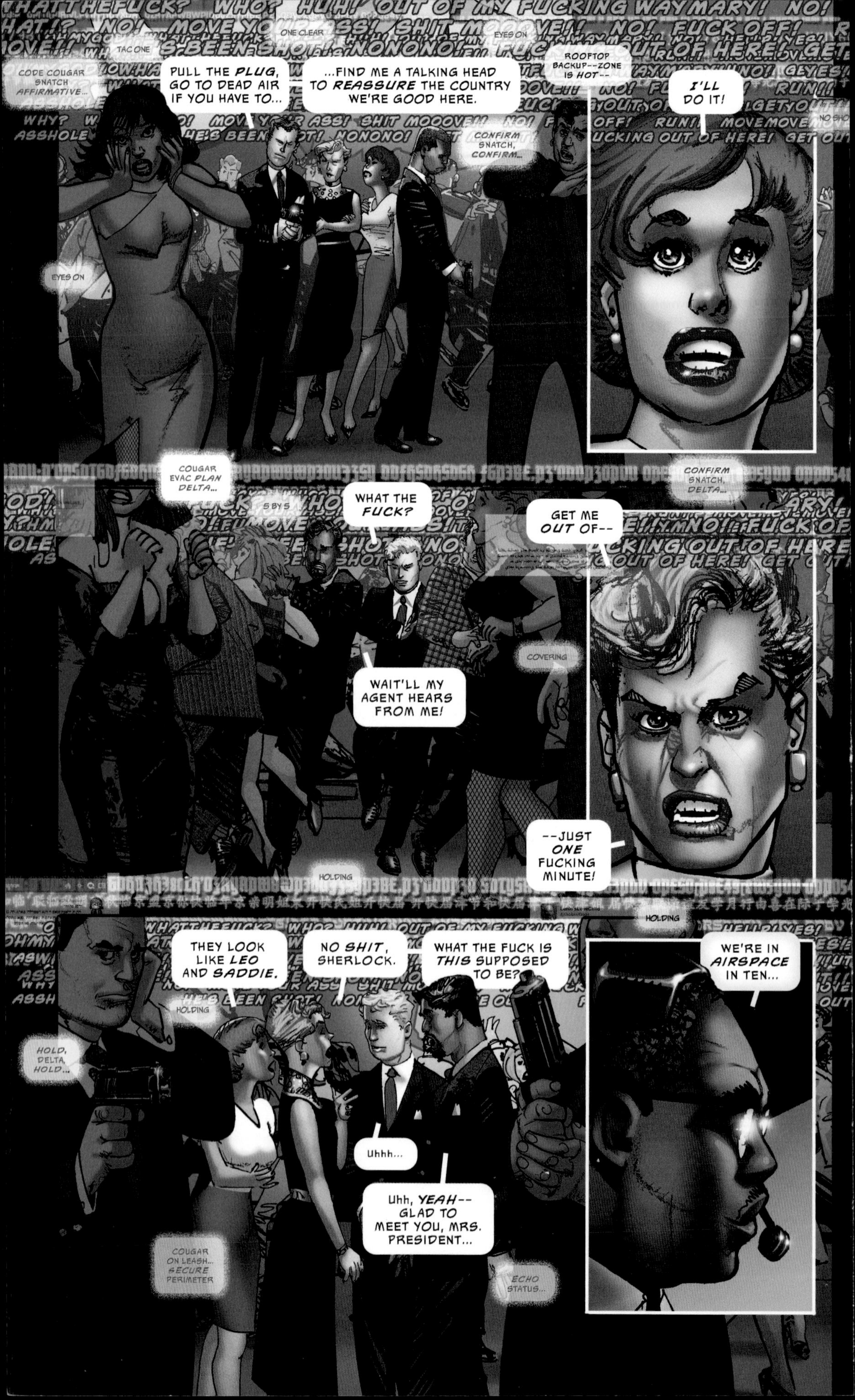
TAC ONE
ONE CLEAR
EYES ON
CODE COUGAR SNATCH AFFIRMATIVE...
PULL THE PLUG, GO TO DEAD AIR IF YOU HAVE TO...
...FIND ME A TALKING HEAD TO REASSURE THE COUNTRY WE'RE GOOD HERE.
ROOFTOP BACKUP--ZONE IS HOT--
I'LL DO IT!
CONFIRM SNATCH, CONFIRM...
EYES ON
COUGAR EVAC PLAN DELTA...
CONFIRM SNATCH, DELTA...
5 BY 5
WHAT THE FUCK?
GET ME OUT OF--
COVERING
WAIT'LL MY AGENT HEARS FROM ME!
--JUST ONE FUCKING MINUTE!
HOLDING
HOLDING
THEY LOOK LIKE LEO AND SADDIE.
NO SHIT, SHERLOCK.
WHAT THE FUCK IS THIS SUPPOSED TO BE?
WE'RE IN AIRSPACE IN TEN...
HOLDING
HOLD, DELTA, HOLD...
Uhhh...
Uhh, YEAH--GLAD TO MEET YOU, MRS. PRESIDENT...
COUGAR ON LEASH... SECURE PERIMETER
ECHO STATUS...

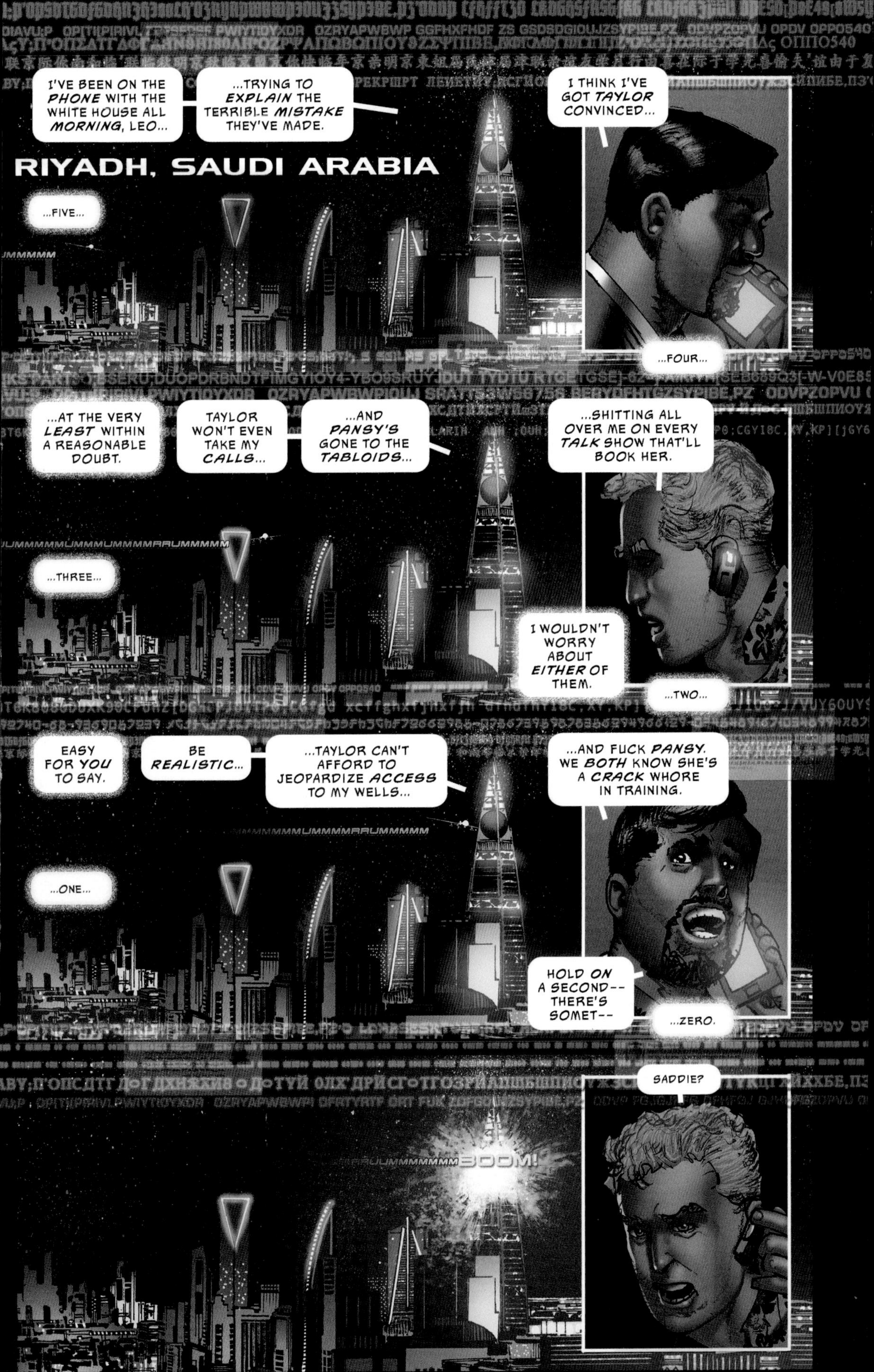
I'VE BEEN ON THE PHONE WITH THE WHITE HOUSE ALL MORNING, LEO...
...TRYING TO EXPLAIN THE TERRIBLE MISTAKE THEY'VE MADE.
I THINK I'VE GOT TAYLOR CONVINCED...
RIYADH, SAUDI ARABIA
...FIVE...
...FOUR...
...AT THE VERY LEAST WITHIN A REASONABLE DOUBT.
TAYLOR WON'T EVEN TAKE MY CALLS...
...AND PANSY'S GONE TO THE TABLOIDS...
...SHITTING ALL OVER ME ON EVERY TALK SHOW THAT'LL BOOK HER.
...THREE...
I WOULDN'T WORRY ABOUT EITHER OF THEM.
...TWO...
EASY FOR YOU TO SAY.
BE REALISTIC...
...TAYLOR CAN'T AFFORD TO JEOPARDIZE ACCESS TO MY WELLS...
...AND FUCK PANSY. WE BOTH KNOW SHE'S A CRACK WHORE IN TRAINING.
...ONE...
HOLD ON A SECOND-- THERE'S SOMET--
...ZERO.
SADDIE?
BOOM!

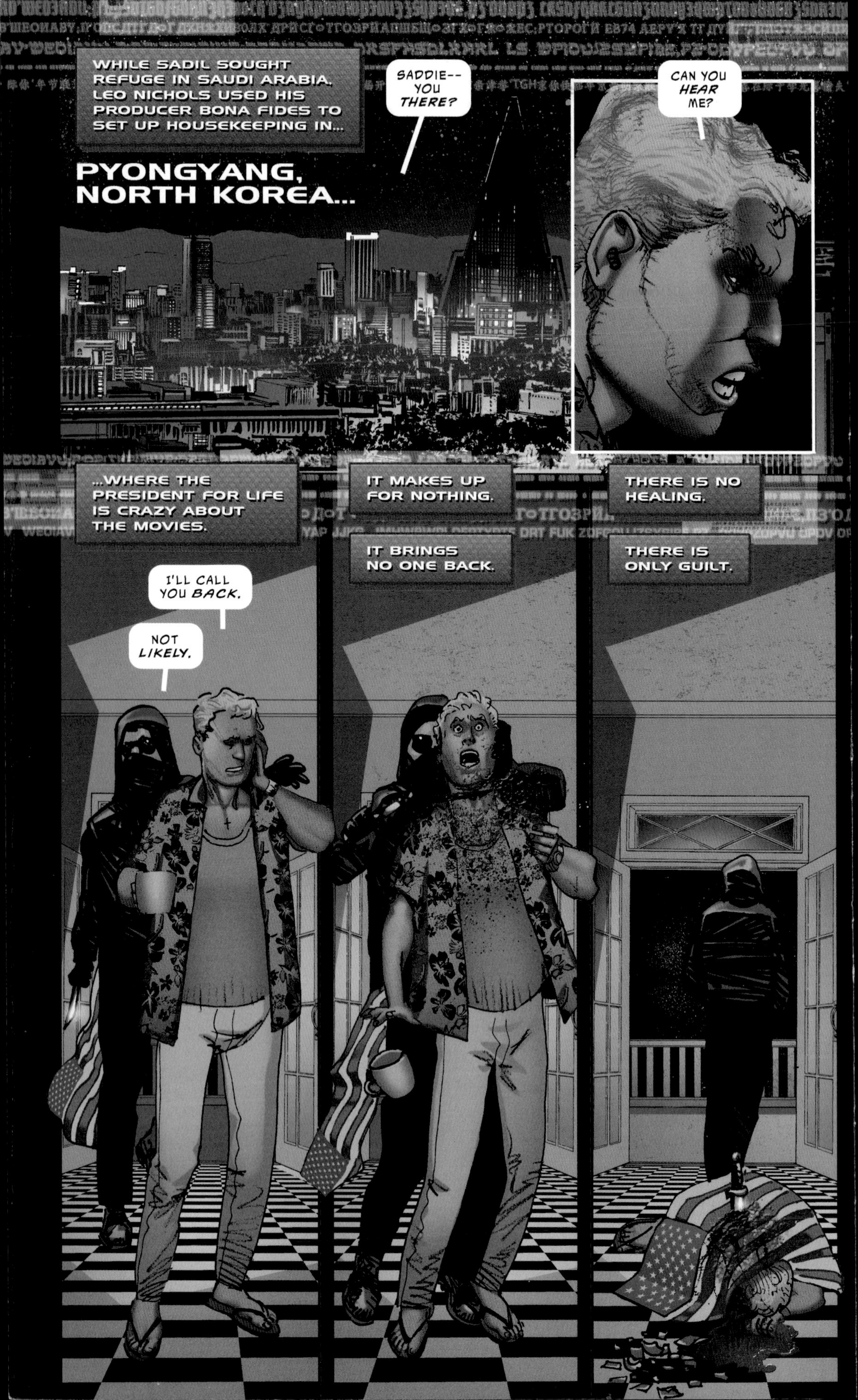
WHILE SADIL SOUGHT REFUGE IN SAUDI ARABIA, LEO NICHOLS USED HIS PRODUCER BONA FIDES TO SET UP HOUSEKEEPING IN...
PYONGYANG, NORTH KOREA...
SADDIE-- YOU THERE?
CAN YOU HEAR ME?
...WHERE THE PRESIDENT FOR LIFE IS CRAZY ABOUT THE MOVIES.
I'LL CALL YOU BACK.
NOT LIKELY.
IT MAKES UP FOR NOTHING.
IT BRINGS NO ONE BACK.
THERE IS NO HEALING.
THERE IS ONLY GUILT.

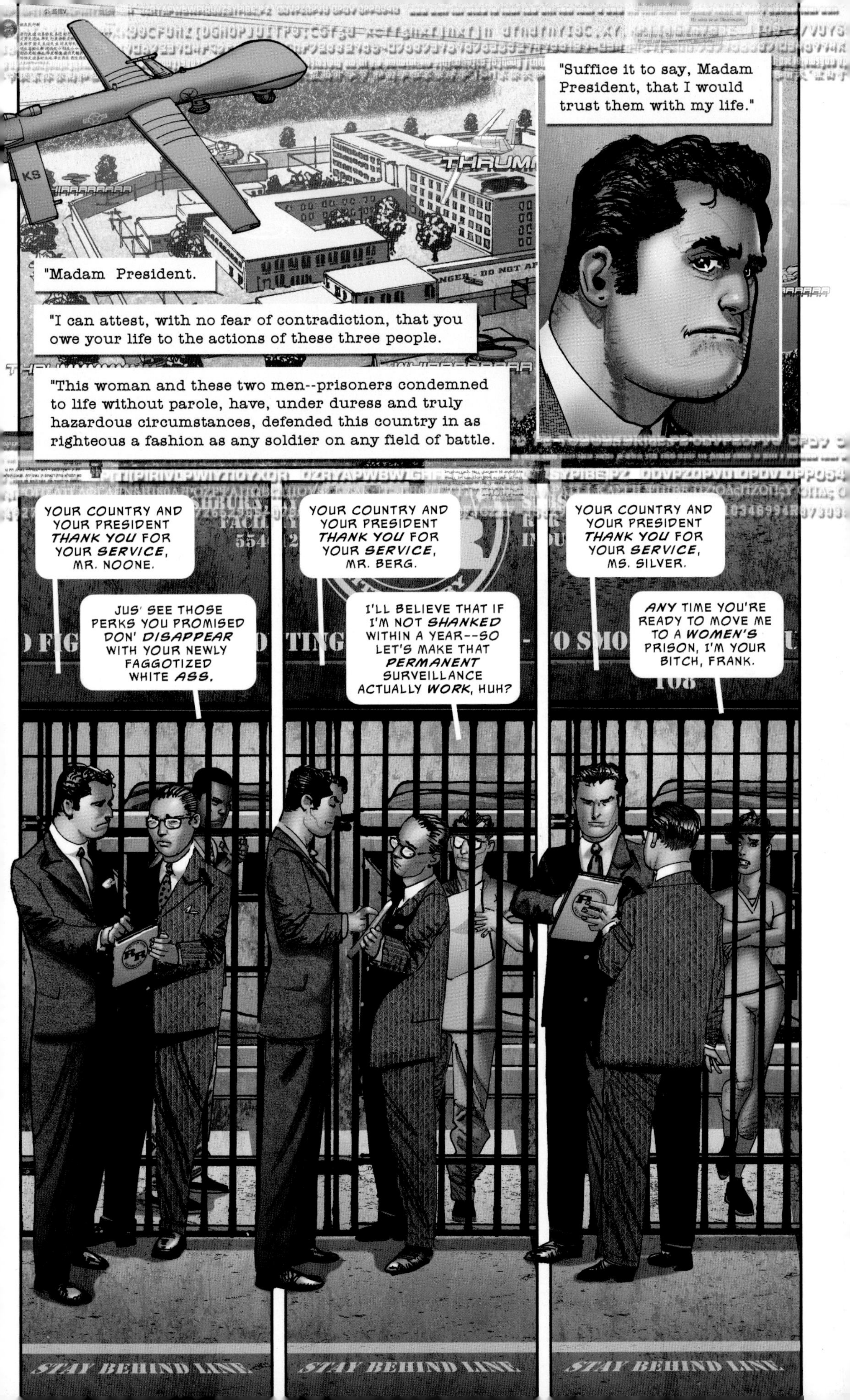

"Madam President.
"I can attest, with no fear of contradiction, that you owe your life to the actions of these three people.
"This woman and these two men--prisoners condemned to life without parole, have, under duress and truly hazardous circumstances, defended this country in as righteous a fashion as any soldier on any field of battle.
"Suffice it to say, Madam President, that I would trust them with my life."
YOUR COUNTRY AND YOUR PRESIDENT THANK YOU FOR YOUR SERVICE, MR. NOONE.
JUS' SEE THOSE PERKS YOU PROMISED DON' DISAPPEAR WITH YOUR NEWLY FAGGOTIZED WHITE ASS.
YOUR COUNTRY AND YOUR PRESIDENT THANK YOU FOR YOUR SERVICE, MR. BERG.
I'LL BELIEVE THAT IF I'M NOT SHANKED WITHIN A YEAR--SO LET'S MAKE THAT PERMANENT SURVEILLANCE ACTUALLY WORK, HUH?
YOUR COUNTRY AND YOUR PRESIDENT THANK YOU FOR YOUR SERVICE, MS. SILVER.
ANY TIME YOU'RE READY TO MOVE ME TO A WOMEN'S PRISON, I'M YOUR BITCH, FRANK.
STAY BEHIND LINE.
STAY BEHIND LINE.
STAY BEHIND LINE.

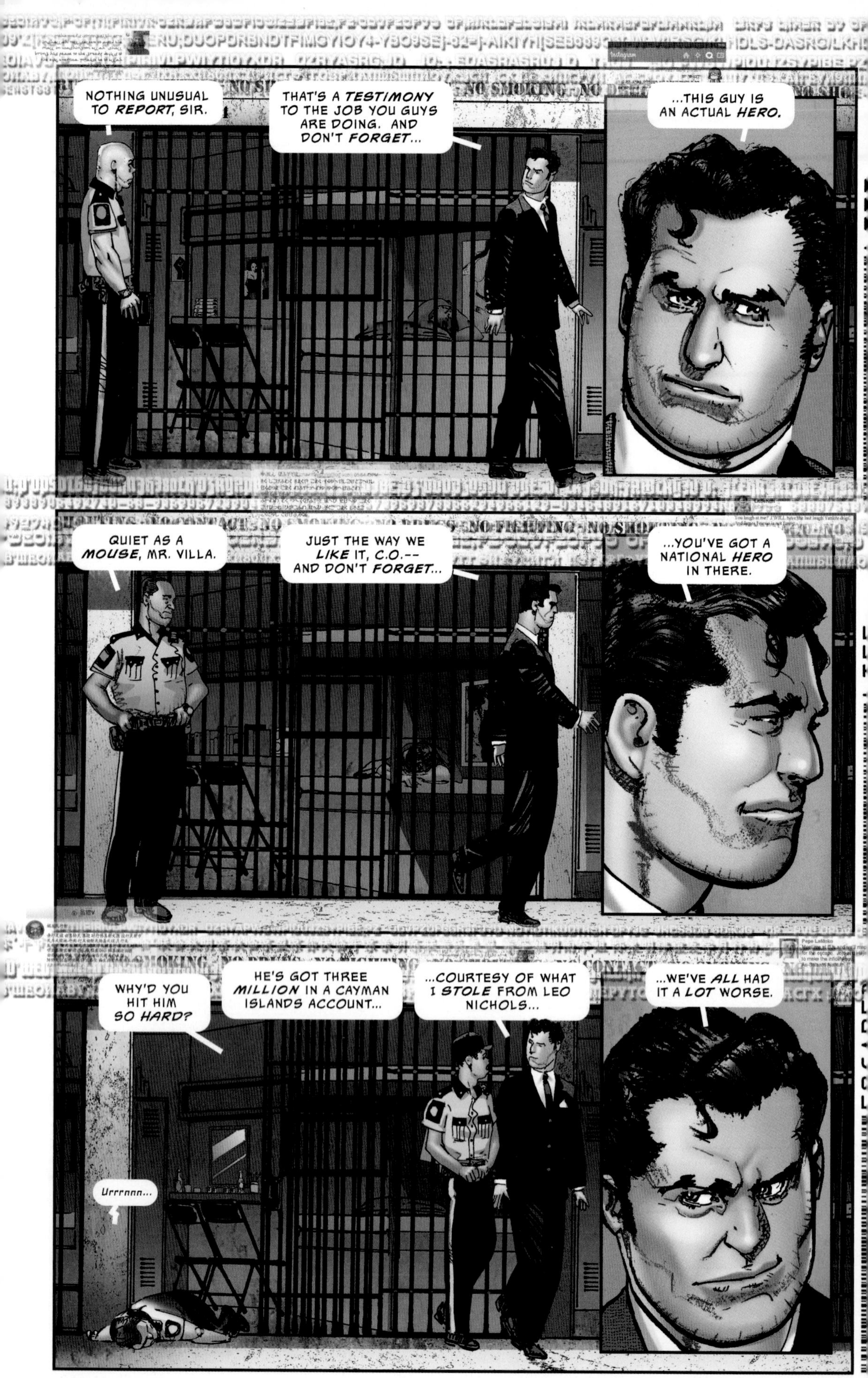

NOTHING UNUSUAL TO REPORT, SIR.
THAT'S A TESTIMONY TO THE JOB YOU GUYS ARE DOING. AND DON'T FORGET...
...THIS GUY IS AN ACTUAL HERO.
QUIET AS A MOUSE, MR. VILLA.
JUST THE WAY WE LIKE IT, C.O.-- AND DON'T FORGET...
...YOU'VE GOT A NATIONAL HERO IN THERE.
WHY'D YOU HIT HIM SO HARD?
HE'S GOT THREE MILLION IN A CAYMAN ISLANDS ACCOUNT...
...COURTESY OF WHAT I STOLE FROM LEO NICHOLS...
...WE'VE ALL HAD IT A LOT WORSE.
Urrrnnn...

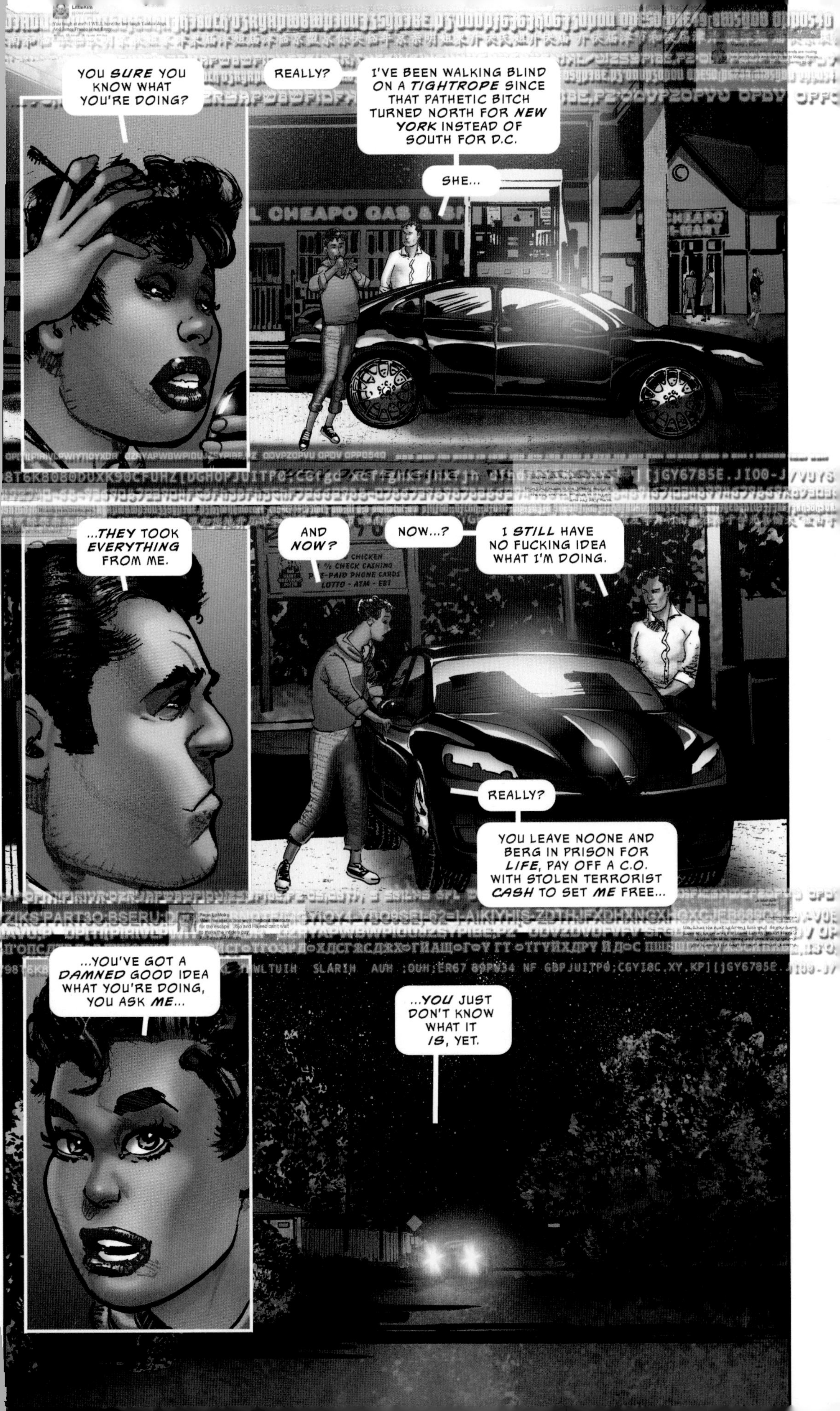
YOU *SURE* YOU KNOW WHAT YOU'RE DOING?
REALLY?
I'VE BEEN WALKING BLIND ON A *TIGHTROPE* SINCE THAT PATHETIC BITCH TURNED NORTH FOR *NEW YORK* INSTEAD OF SOUTH FOR D.C.
SHE...
...*THEY* TOOK *EVERYTHING* FROM ME.
AND *NOW?*
NOW...?
I *STILL* HAVE NO FUCKING IDEA WHAT I'M DOING.
REALLY?
YOU LEAVE NOONE AND BERG IN PRISON FOR *LIFE*, PAY OFF A C.O. WITH STOLEN TERRORIST *CASH* TO SET *ME* FREE...
...YOU'VE GOT A *DAMNED* GOOD IDEA WHAT YOU'RE DOING, YOU ASK *ME*...
...*YOU* JUST DON'T KNOW WHAT IT *IS*, YET.

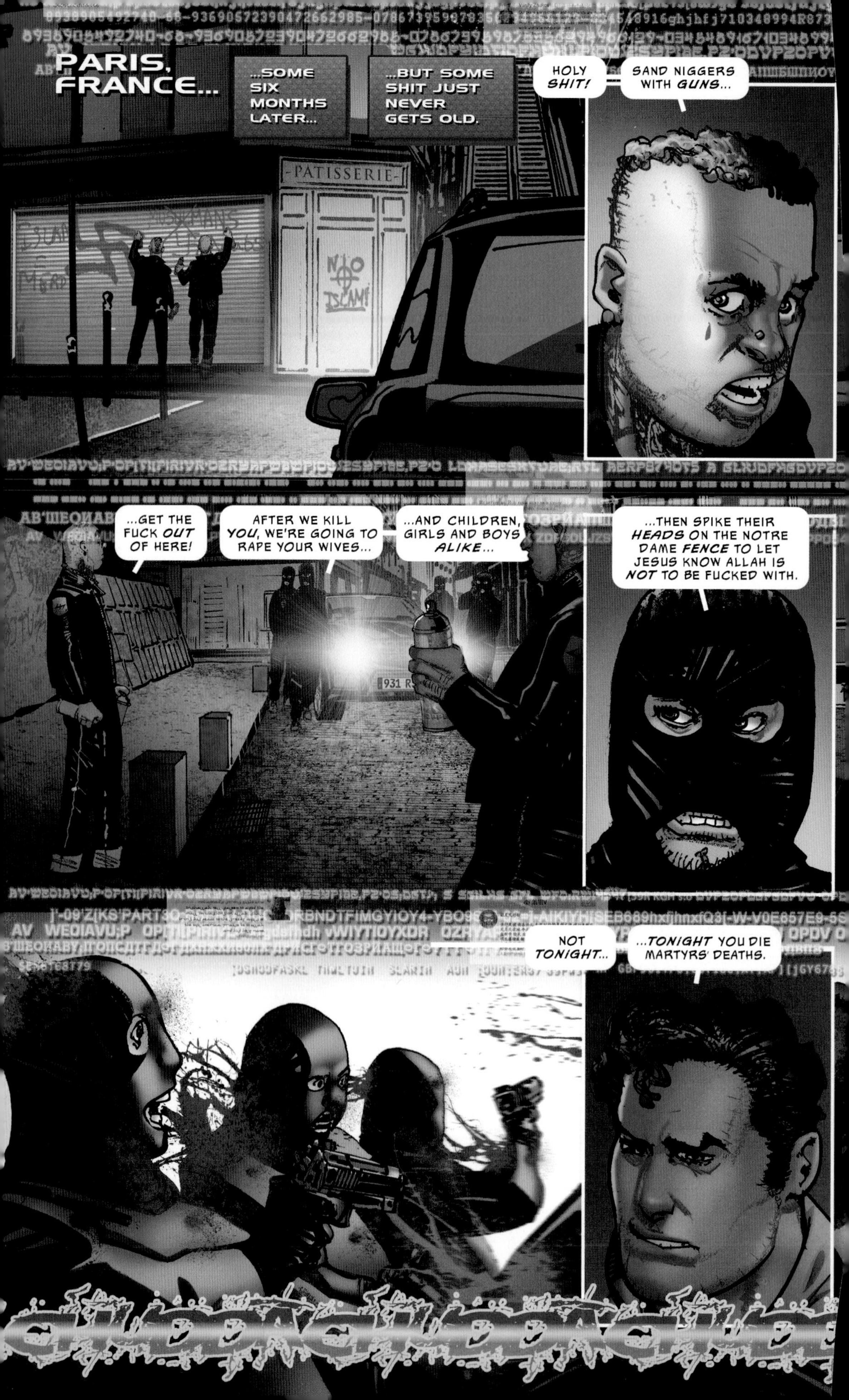
PARIS, FRANCE...
...SOME SIX MONTHS LATER...
...BUT SOME SHIT JUST NEVER GETS OLD.
PATISSERIE
HOLY SHIT!
SAND NIGGERS WITH GUNS...
...GET THE FUCK OUT OF HERE!
AFTER WE KILL YOU, WE'RE GOING TO RAPE YOUR WIVES...
...AND CHILDREN, GIRLS AND BOYS ALIKE...
...THEN SPIKE THEIR HEADS ON THE NOTRE DAME FENCE TO LET JESUS KNOW ALLAH IS NOT TO BE FUCKED WITH.
NOT TONIGHT...
...TONIGHT YOU DIE MARTYRS' DEATHS.

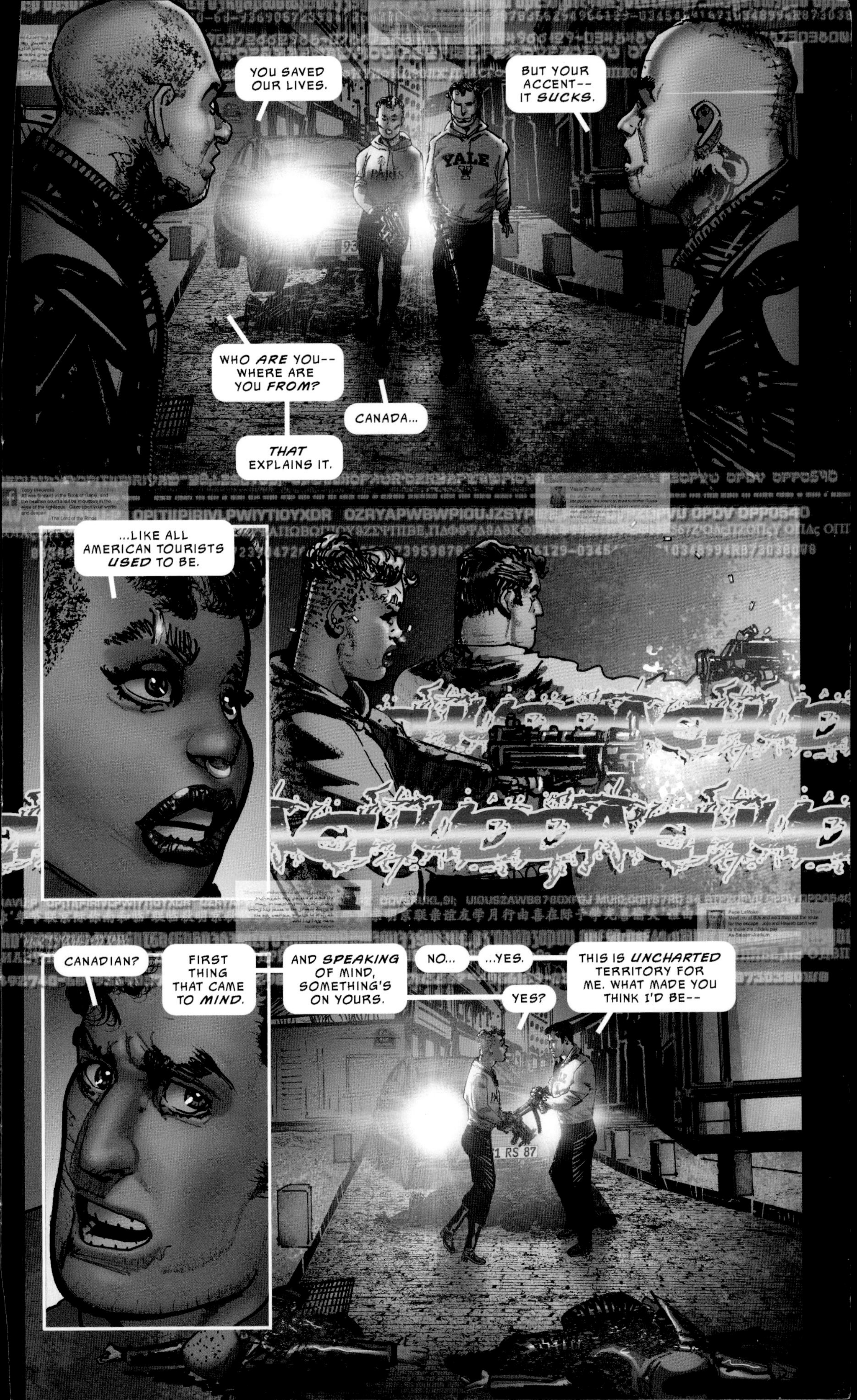
YOU SAVED OUR LIVES.
BUT YOUR ACCENT-- IT *SUCKS*.
WHO *ARE* YOU-- WHERE ARE YOU *FROM?*
CANADA...
THAT EXPLAINS IT.
...LIKE ALL AMERICAN TOURISTS *USED* TO BE.
CANADIAN?
FIRST THING THAT CAME TO *MIND*.
AND *SPEAKING* OF MIND, SOMETHING'S ON YOURS.
NO...
...YES.
YES?
THIS IS *UNCHARTED* TERRITORY FOR ME. WHAT MADE YOU THINK I'D BE--

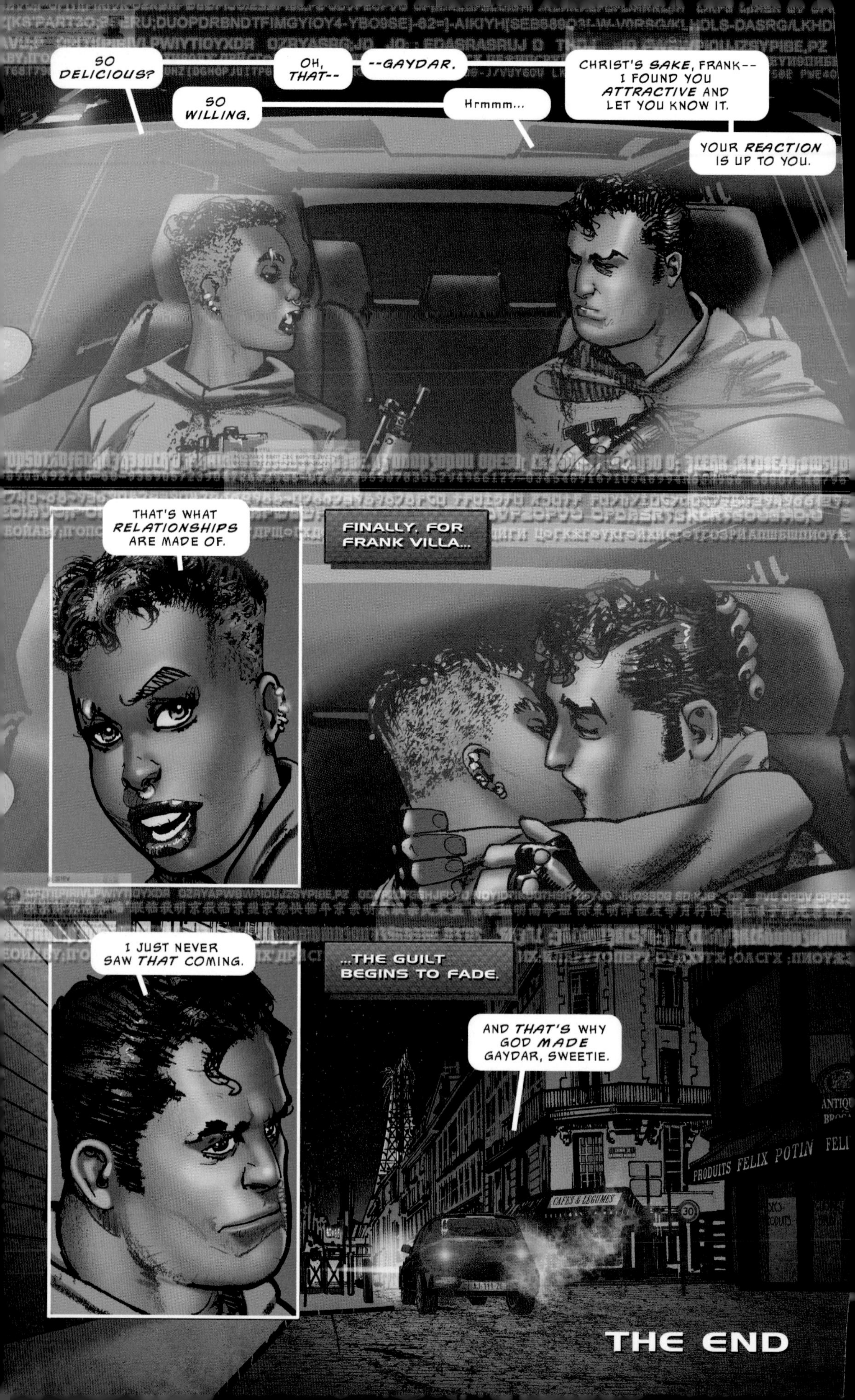

SO DELICIOUS?
OH, THAT--
SO WILLING.
Hrmmm...
--GAYDAR.
CHRIST'S SAKE, FRANK-- I FOUND YOU ATTRACTIVE AND LET YOU KNOW IT.
YOUR REACTION IS UP TO YOU.
THAT'S WHAT RELATIONSHIPS ARE MADE OF.
FINALLY, FOR FRANK VILLA...
I JUST NEVER SAW THAT COMING.
...THE GUILT BEGINS TO FADE.
AND THAT'S WHY GOD MADE GAYDAR, SWEETIE.
PRODUITS FELIX POTIN
CAFES & LEGUMES
THE END

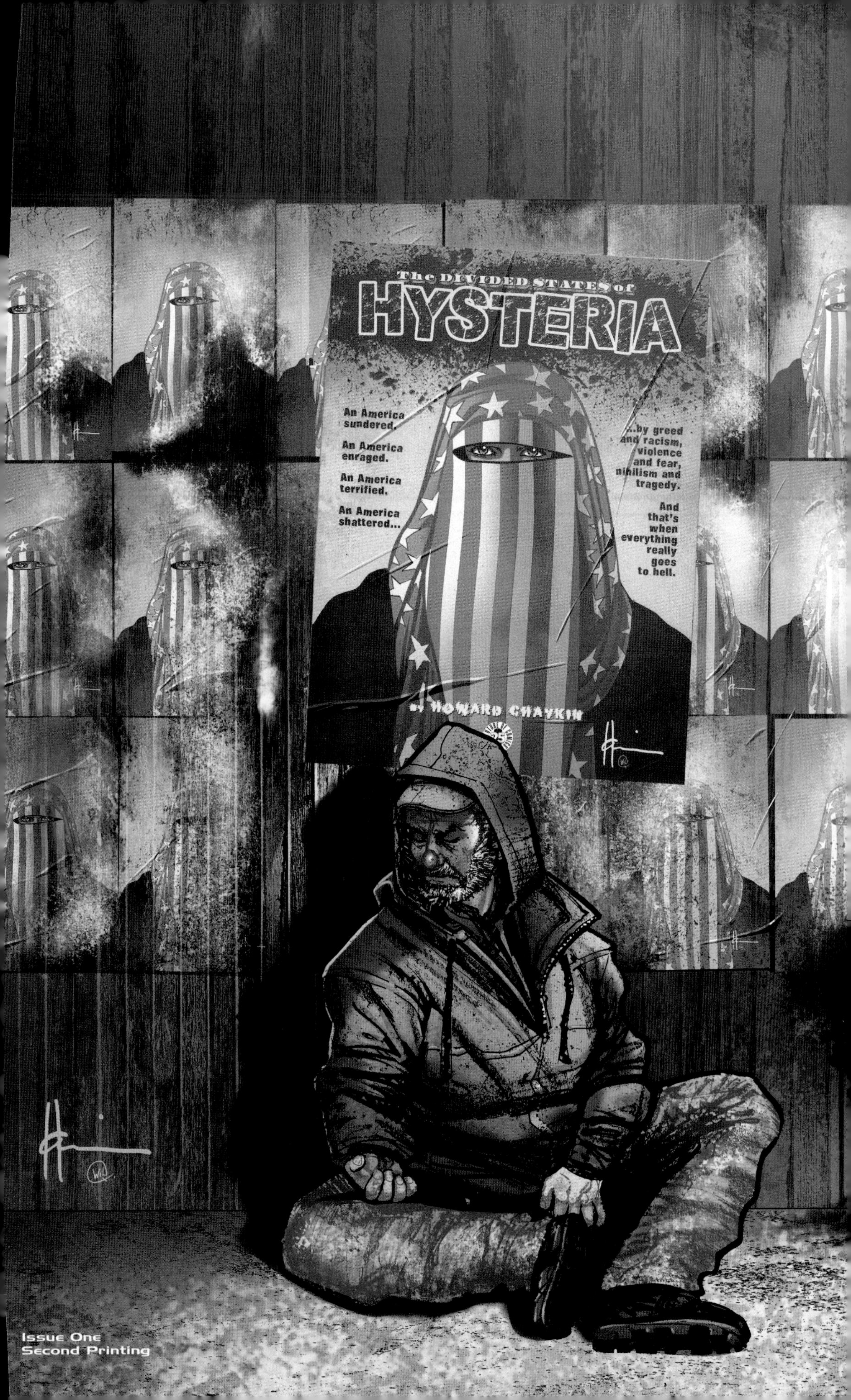
The DIVIDED STATES of
HYSTERIA
An America sundered.
An America enraged.
An America terrified.
An America shattered...
...by greed and racism, violence and fear, nihilism and tragedy.
And that's when everything really goes to hell.
by HOWARD CHAYKIN
Issue One
Second Printing

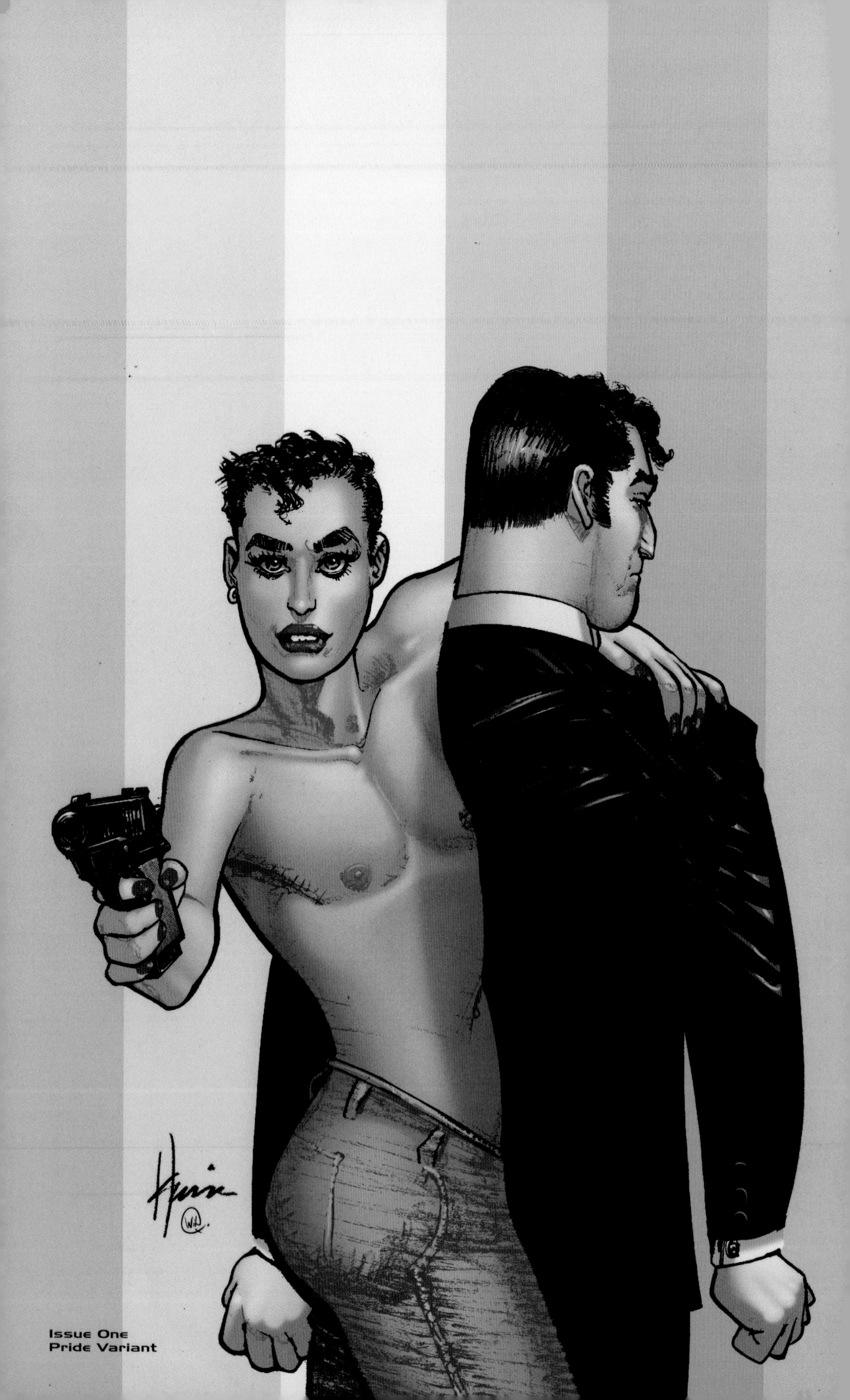

Issue One
Pride Variant

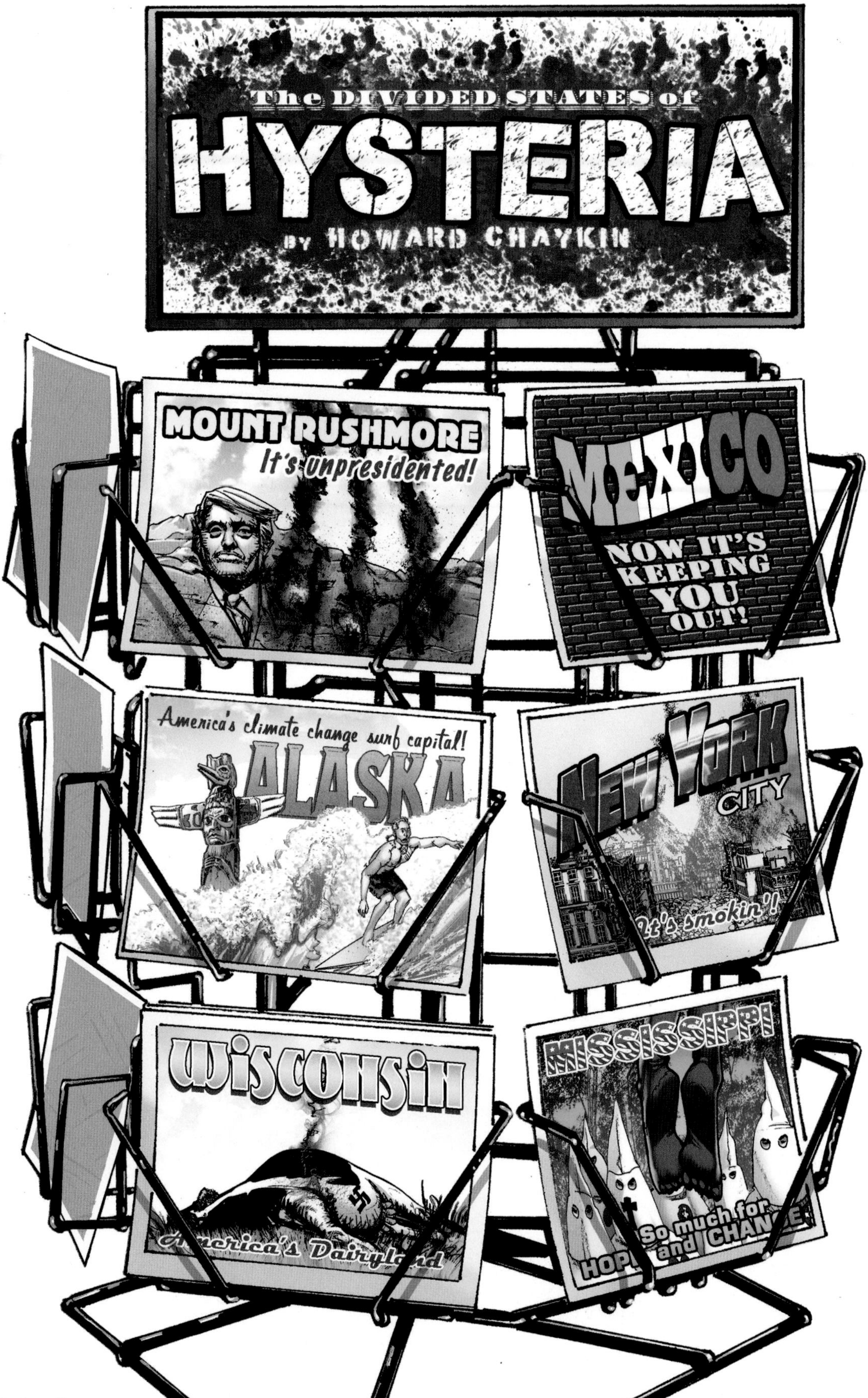
The DIVIDED STATES of
HYSTERIA
BY HOWARD CHAYKIN
MOUNT RUSHMORE
It's unpresidented!
MEXICO
NOW IT'S KEEPING YOU OUT!
America's climate change surf capital!
ALASKA
NEW YORK
CITY
It's smokin'!
WISCONSIN
America's Dairyland
MISSISSIPPI
So much for HOPE and CHANGE

Issue One
Blind Box
Variant

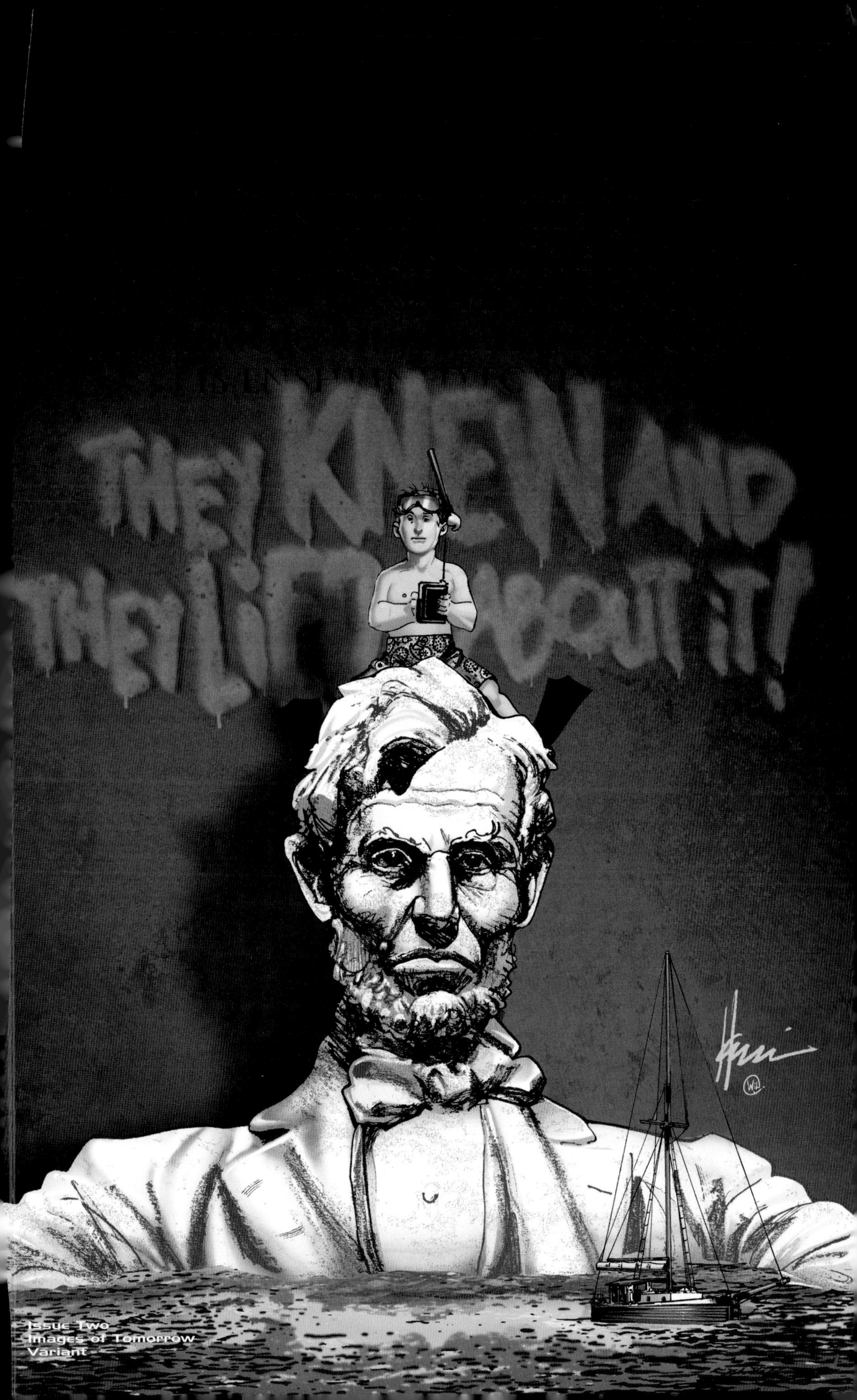
THEY KNEW AND
Issue Two
Images of Tomorrow
Variant

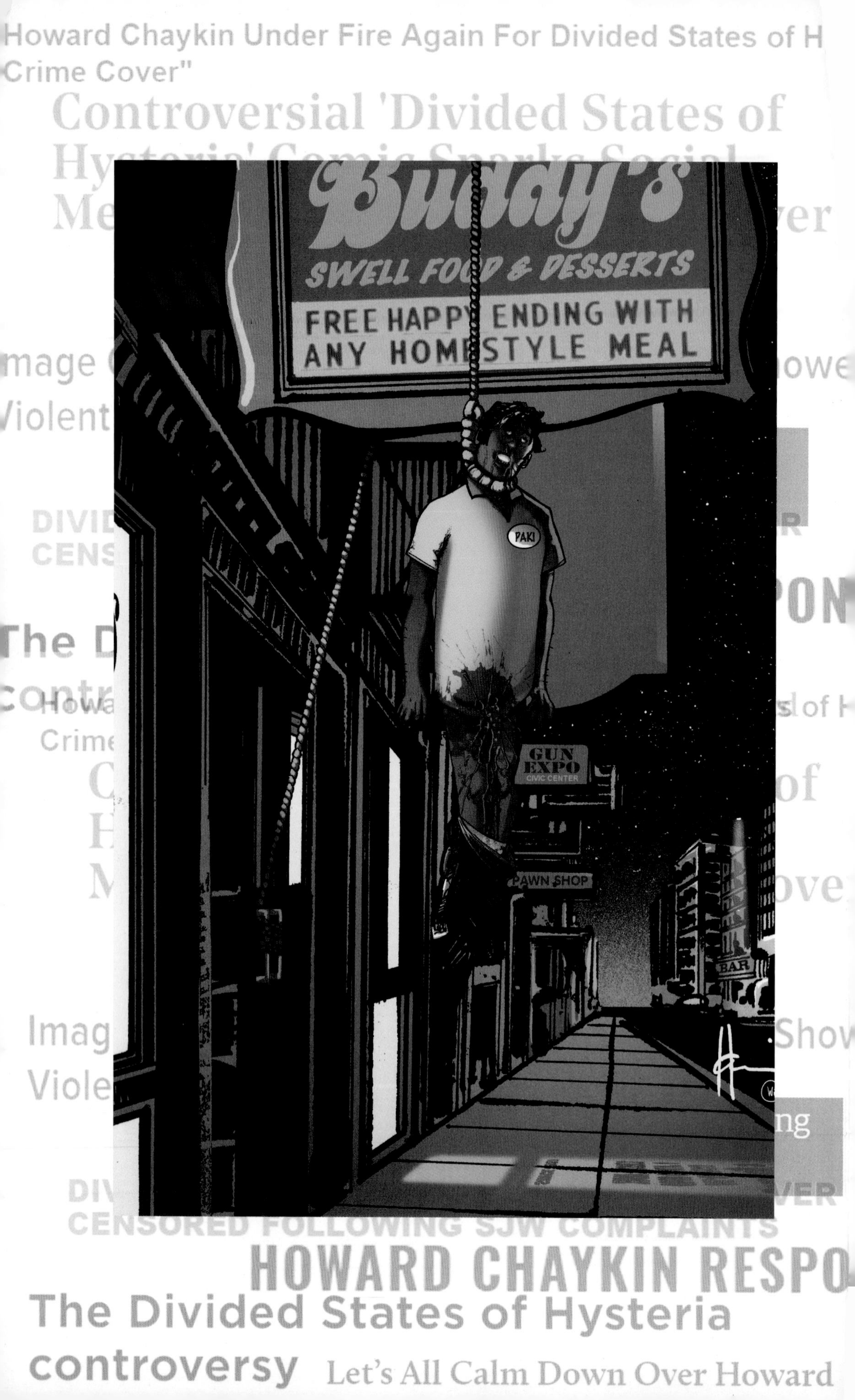

Howard Chaykin Under Fire Again For Divided States of H
Crime Cover"
Controversial 'Divided States of
Buddy's
SWELL FOOD & DESSERTS
FREE HAPPY ENDING WITH
ANY HOMESTYLE MEAL
PAKI
GUN
EXPO
CIVIC CENTER
PAWN SHOP
BAR
CENSORED FOLLOWING SJW COMPLAINTS
HOWARD CHAYKIN RESPO
The Divided States of Hysteria
controversy
Let's All Calm Down Over Howard

I'M JUST A SOUL WHOSE INTENTIONS ARE GOOD

[UNLESS YOU TELL ME THEY AREN'T]

I tend to work globally to locally. Textually, this means that I write every script for an entire arc of material before I begin to draw anything. This enables me to lay pipe, set up in exposition, buried or otherwise, in early issues that pays off logically in later episodes.

This global idea is applied to covers, as well. Once I completed the scripts for the first six-issue arc of The Divided States of Hysteria, and was into artwork, I delivered, as I recall, nine or ten cover concepts for the monthly comics to my editor.

After weeding this pile down to six covers, I went to work. Needless to say, one of those covers was a piece originally intended for issue number four that would instead become a flashpoint for people who felt qualified to dictate to me my own artistic intent. I did the artwork, and it was ready to go.

Or it was until this image, once made public through Pre-

views, sparked a slew of hostility from self-identified members of the progressive left.

Needless to say, but to be explicit, my intention was to create an image of horror, horror that is all too real and all too terrifying, as opposed to the vampire/werewolf/zombie stuff that is a tad too fantastical for my own frankly literal-minded sense of mortal terror.

Instead of seeing things this way, however, people with no actual interest in reading the book decided, for reasons which remain mystifying to me, that I was somehow promoting such an act of violence--that the depiction of the act was akin to the act itself.

A number of my fellow members of the creative community joined the holy crusade, canonizing for me the phrase, "I'm all for artistic freedom, but..."

I leave it to you to judge the irony here.

Within days of its unveil-

ing, the cover was withdrawn, a change to which I agreed in deference to the good people at IMAGE and the realities of the marketplace into which it was introduced. Still able as I was to tell the story I wanted to tell, it was an accommodation I was willing to make.

In a coda to all this, there was talk about doing a variant cover in support of Banned Book Week, September 24th to the 30th, 2017. And before the plug was pulled on this for reasons of no interest to anyone, I'd commissioned the esteemed Don Cameron to create the artwork for my Banned Book variant cover, seen on the back of this very page.

Once again, irony is for you to judge at your leisure and in good time.

Thanks for your kind attention,

Howard Victor Chaykin
--a prince.

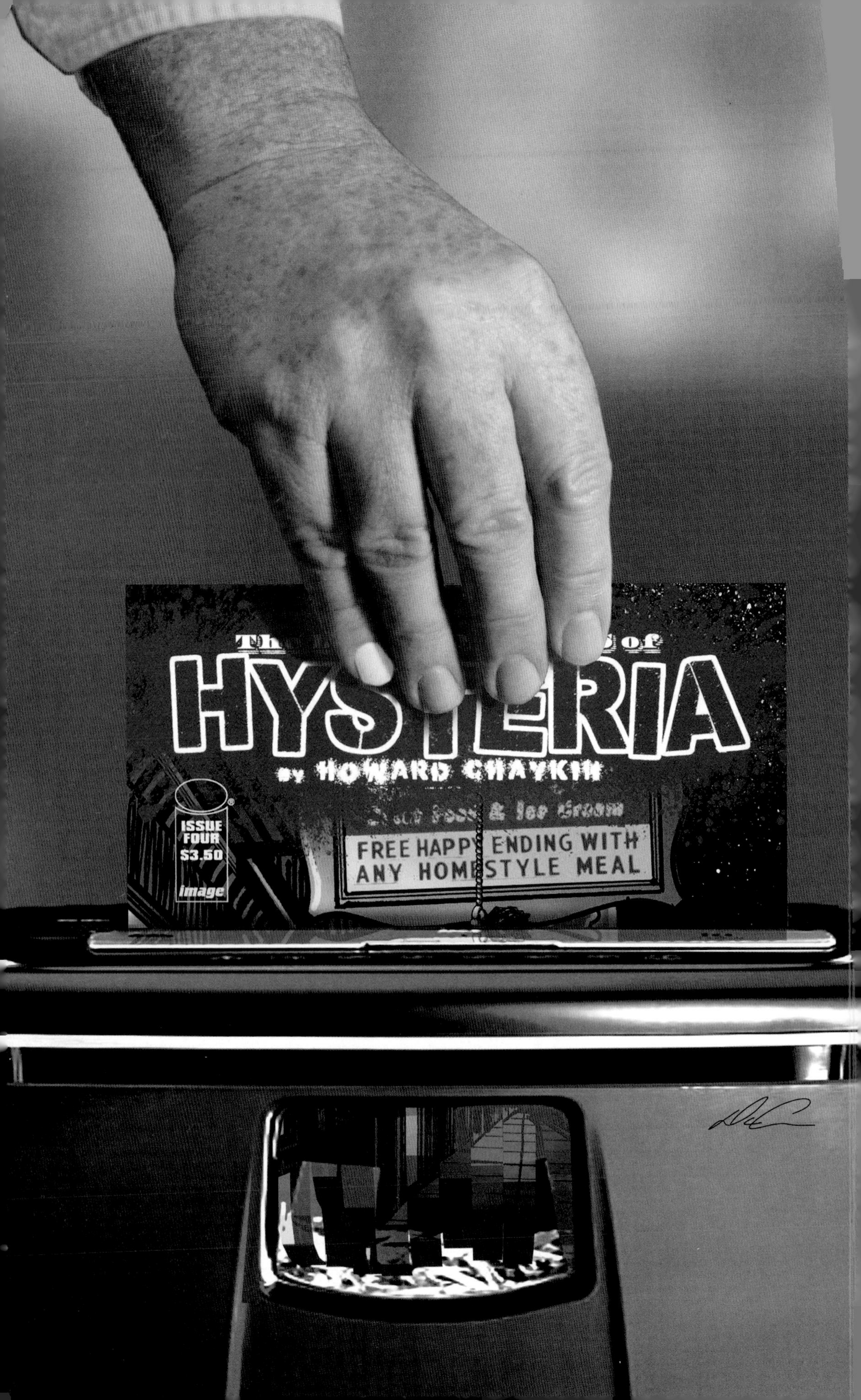

HYSTERIA
BY HOWARD CHAYKIN
ISSUE FOUR
$3.50
image
FREE HAPPY ENDING WITH
ANY HOMESTYLE MEAL

Just ONE panel...

KEN BRUZENAK is still alive and still working with Howard Chaykin. This is why.

In the beginning, there is the word.

Then, maybe a year or even more later, I get a phone call: "Chaykin here."

Howard likes words, and he trusts me to make them all fit somehow, but more importantly, to make them fit properly. No stomping all over the artwork or stabbing people with balloon tails. And everything I do has to work *with* the art, usually tucking behind figures, unless there is an important storytelling reason to overlap certain characters.

The sound effects and signage have to work with the design aesthetic of the material. *Divided States* is contemporary and modern in a Steven-Soderbergh-quasi-documentary fashion; global, sophisticated, fascist at times, and painstakingly realistic (by comic book standards). In the real world, there is signage and advertising everywhere you look, invisible in its pervasiveness, and my job is to simulate that omnipresence without completely burying the art in letterforms.

The choice to use round-corner rectangular balloons was to integrate into the more formal, appropriately "serious" story and art environment that just so happens to contain a lot of running

and shooting and blowing shit up. By contrast, when Howard and I worked on *Satellite Sam*, the 1950s setting and the black & white format called for more playful round balloon shapes that overwhelmed panel borders, bouncing strategically across then page. I don't use balloon outlines because they are unnecessary with modern printing, and I stick with simple geometric shapes because lumpy, jiggly, hand-drawn lines just don't cut it anymore. Even the word balloon's "tails" are simple straight lines, eschewing wild, loopy connectors and pointed spearheads for direct, linear informational directionals.

I use Photoshop to get the flexibility of effects I need -- and I exploit it for all it is worth. The computer does NOT make anything faster or better, and it does add a lot of extraneous chores to the process, but it is a reasonable trade-off. Illustrator makes pristine outlines for enlarging fonts 2000%, but comics are printed from 300-450 dpi rasterized Acrobat files, which destroys the argument for Illustrator and its clunky handling of color. Don't blame me for the eye-strain-inducing small size of the fonts, it's an industry standard, for the moment.

This is where it all starts -- a black-and-white bitmap and a script.

No balloon placements. No notes, and sometimes the art differs from the script description. The pictures are beautiful, but they don't always allow room sufficient for the text.

I hate covering the artwork. So does Howard. It's a puzzle to be solved. Geometric alignments reinforce his rectilinear compositional approach.

And it all has to work *with* the art. The words exist on a dimensional plane between the figures and the environmental background, and they have to fit, sometimes in multiple layers when there are several figures. Pulling the balloons inside the panel, rather than abutting the border, literally integrates them into the live art field.

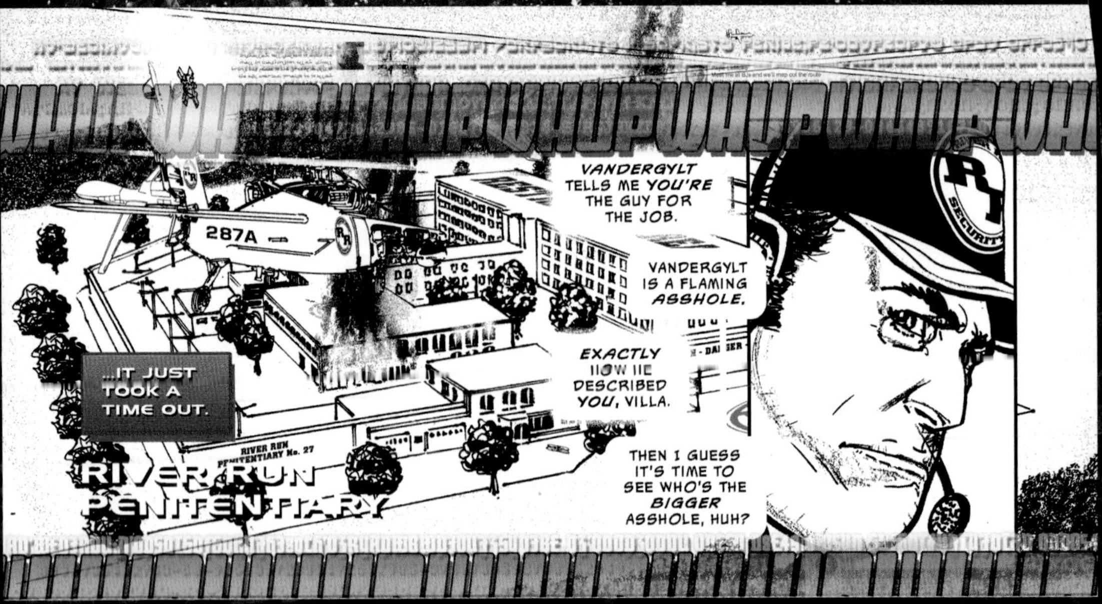
WHUPWHUPWHUPWHUPWHUPWHU
VANDERGYLT TELLS ME YOU'RE THE GUY FOR THE JOB.
VANDERGYLT IS A FLAMING ASSHOLE.
EXACTLY HOW HE DESCRIBED YOU, VILLA.
THEN I GUESS IT'S TIME TO SEE WHO'S THE BIGGER ASSHOLE, HUH?
...IT JUST TOOK A TIME OUT.
RIVER RUN PENITENTIARY
287A

So many ideas -- and a very limited space for them all.

Using the example of this single panel, we can see the WHUPWHUP of helicopters naturally has to come from the top of the panel, and must look mechanical, exotic and authoritarian. Signs have to strictly conform to the perspective of whatever building, car or surface they occupy. The typeset narrative captions provide parallel context that looks and reads like a musical bass-line through the page layout, visually bridging panels and directing the reader's attention. The balloons are aligned, and radio speech has a static fringe evoking electricity. Physical geography is established with a formatted headline, and there are about ten pieces of relevant signage, from the buildings to the helicopter.

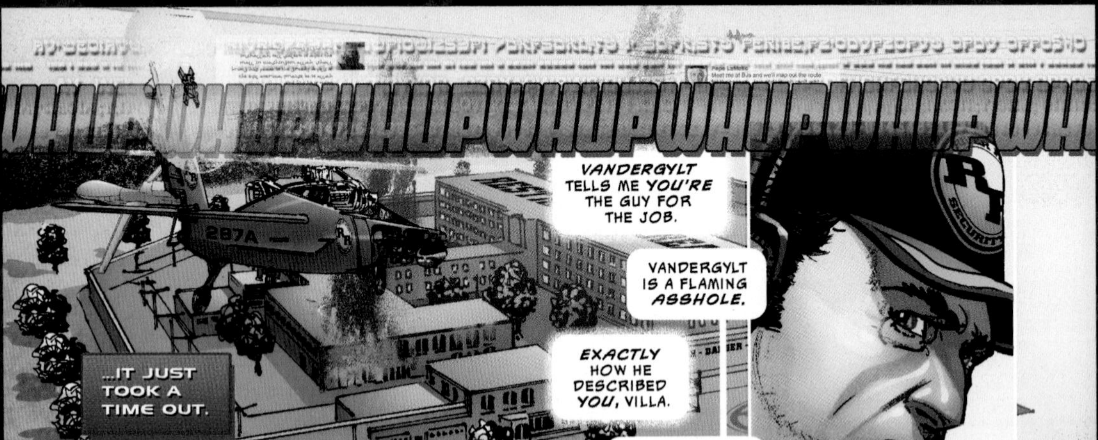
WHUPWHUPWHUPWHUPWHUPWHU
VANDERGYLT TELLS ME YOU'RE THE GUY FOR THE JOB.
VANDERGYLT IS A FLAMING ASSHOLE.
EXACTLY HOW HE DESCRIBED YOU, VILLA.
THEN I GUESS IT'S TIME TO SEE WHO'S THE BIGGER ASSHOLE, HUH?
...IT JUST TOOK A TIME OUT.
RIVER RUN PENITENTIARY
287A

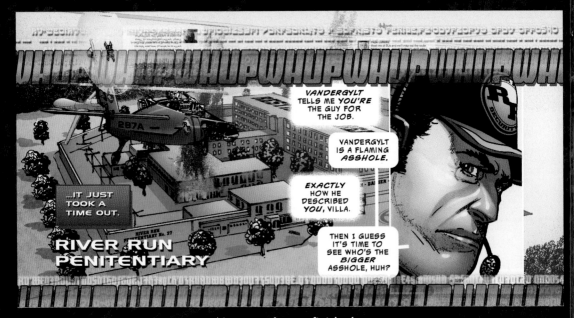

Not even close to finished yet.

Color forces a reevaluation of legibility, composition and tonal values. Sound effects are not solid, but transparently ethereal. Distance alters the value and legibility of colors, occasionally forcing a switch to reverse lettering.

There is pervasive radio and internet chatter throughout the book, unintelligible, yet recognizable as coded language. A wall of gibberish hovers over every panel, full of foreign alphabets and *faux* messages, vague and distant. On top of that is a second layer of text messaging from Facebook to Twitter to Moi Mir to Weibo, indicating the global reach of instant social networking and espionage.

And this is just ONE panel.

...and there's MORE!

Ramping up a new book often starts with a logo that defines the series' theme and ambience. The *Divided States* logo was necessarily formal but a little off-kilter, and went through a few iterations. The modern super-spy setting and pervasive telecommunications indicated a very literal type approach, with a hint of imbalance. I had also been trying for 35 years to convince someone a logo really *can* bleed off the sides of the cover in some fashion. I had a really effective application involving movement for *The Flash* 25 years ago, but...

The big Jackson Pollock splatter was a way to add multi-color effects and subtlety, and a kind of "post-modern" chaotic ambience. Anticipating and building in opportunities for color variations, negative image reversals and methods to silhouette the letterforms on any background were part of my process. The undefined shape lets me add or subtract volume and textures as needed to accommodate the artwork while maintaining

The UNITED STATES of
HYSTERIA

The UNITED STATES of
HYSTERIA
By HOWARD CHAYKIN

a signature stylistic technique. The splatter also provides a graphic link to various other motifs of the series, like bloody gunshot explosions, bullet wounds and text page formatting.

The herky-jerky "Hysteria" was obvious, and using a thick outline added flexibility and dimension to the color options. It also allowed for knockouts and show-through to the art underneath without resorting to comic book cliche drop shadows and forced perspective effects. The editor loved the topline font that blatantly reminds us of American money. Yes, at one point the title was *United*, but *Divided* felt more evocative of the overall concept. Howard's credit line scuttled about a bit looking for a non-symmetrical visual balance. The use of three different fonts flirts with violating multiple design principles, yet suits the themes of unprincipled greed, conceit and hysteria. Even the purple, magenta and black color in the initial proposal was keyed to coordinate with Jesus Aburtov's palette, layered to feel diseased and corrupt, with distinct edginess.

And then there's this other stuff.

RIVER RUN
RR
SECURITY
carribair
RUSCO PETROLEUM
W B SABI 2359523
DINGDINGDINGDING
CLANKCLANKCLANKCLANK
NAME : NACAMULLI, CESARE JOHN
NYSID : 7783452K
Arrest # : H834666237-C
Arrest : 12/27/2021
Charge : MURDER
Alias : Caesar, Little
478825 11-13-20
SILVER, CHRISTOPHER MICHAEL
SHERIFF, CLARK CO. LAS VEGAS, NEVADA
BOSTON POLICE
42649
PAUL EVAN BERG
12 23 21
CHICAGO POLICE DEPT.
04/23/2020 04:23PM
NOONE, HENRY JOHN
No. J 3740044036
I AM NOONE'S
AMERIKKKA

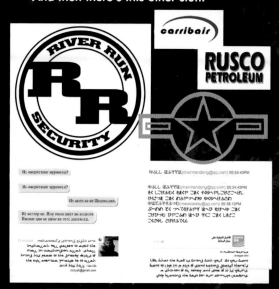

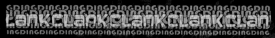

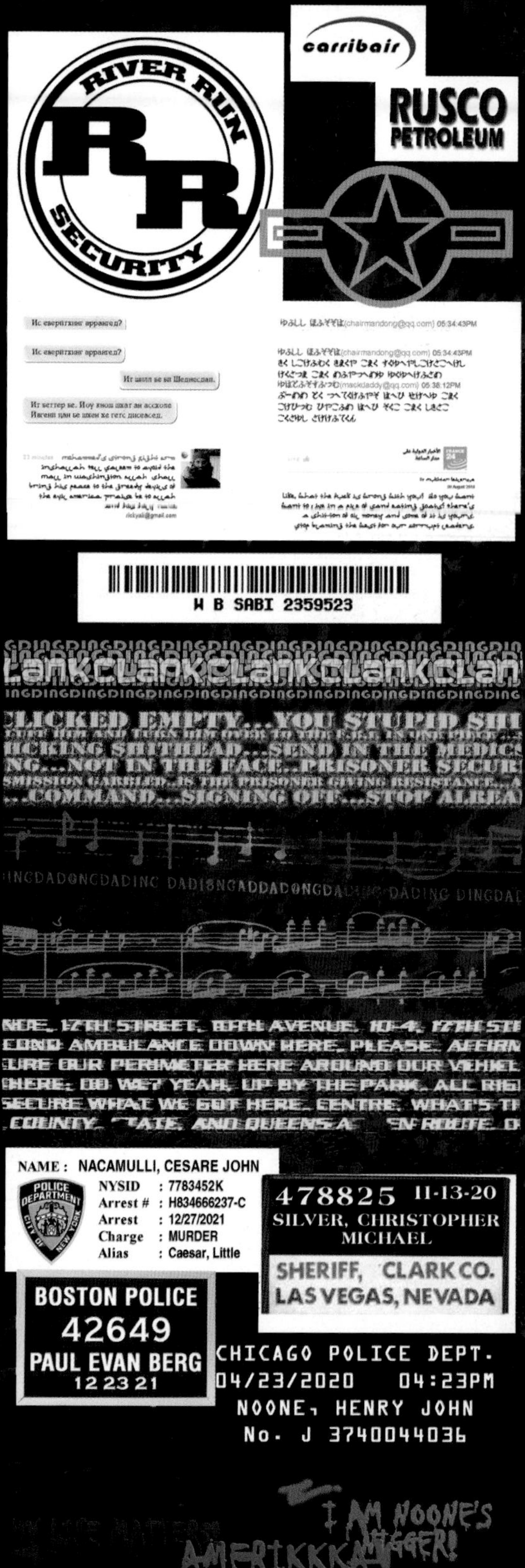

And that's just part of the first issue.

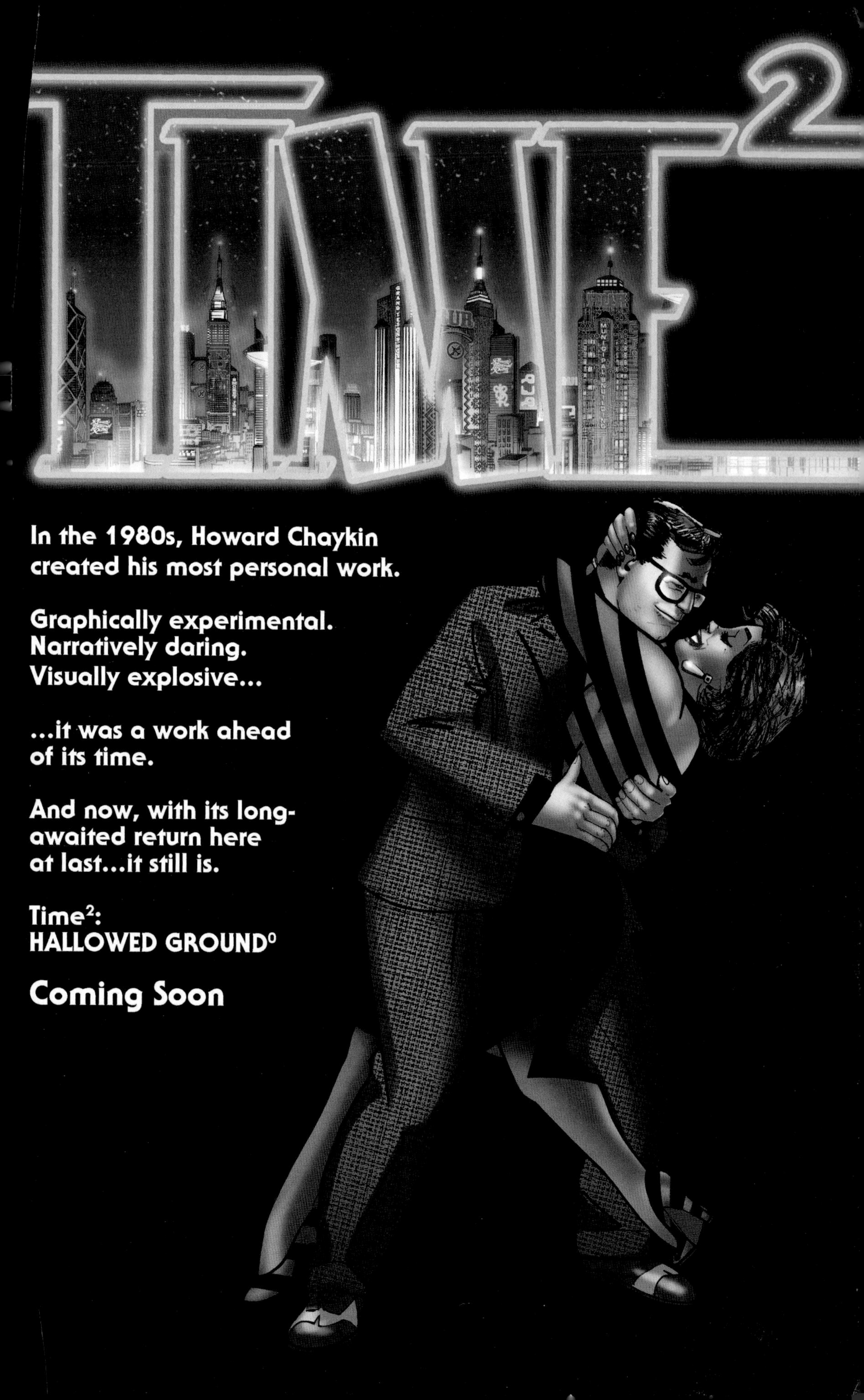
TIME^2
In the 1980s, Howard Chaykin created his most personal work.
Graphically experimental. Narratively daring. Visually explosive...
...it was a work ahead of its time.
And now, with its long-awaited return here at last...it still is.
Time^2: HALLOWED GROUND^0
Coming Soon

stboro Protests Marine Funeral

helf Just More 'Fresh Water' EPA Chief Says

New Sv

ICIDE BOMBERS 17

Killed   Pro-Life Supporter Kills

Pro-Choice Doctor

xican Wall No Es Bueno   PLO Rocke

Gettysburg 'P

ERRORISTS

Senators Avoid Town Hall Co

tock Market Soars as Jobs I

OAL MINES CLOSING

Member' of Congress Texted

to Opponent's Wife   1% Ove

ealth Bill Stalls: Sick People

GBT betrayed   Financial Collapse In

SIS SNIP

Discount Handguns, Pistols & Revolve

Zika in Every Sta

nner Claims Opponent Helped Russians Hack E

加西喜新生 快生友文西迎 生由明谊友